Sixty English Literary Ballads

英国バラッド詩60撰

山中光義／中島久代／宮原牧子
鎌田明子／David Taylor［編著］

九州大学出版会

"STOP! STOP! JOHN GILPIN!—HERE'S THE HOUSE!"

From George Barnett Smith, ed., *Illustrated British Ballads, Old and New,* London, 1881.

まえがき

I. イギリスに「バラッド詩」('literary ballad')と呼べる新しいタイプの詩が生まれたのは 18 世紀に入ってからである。もともと文字を持たない民衆によってうたい継がれてきた口承物語歌「バラッド」が蒐集・印刷されるようになって，民族の遺産としてのバラッドの存在に，そして，その想像力あふれる物語の世界に，多くの詩人たちが注目するようになり，以来，今日まで独特のバラッド模倣詩を数多く生み出してきた。

ロマン派詩人 William Wordsworth によって高い評価を受けた Thomas Percy 編纂の *Reliques of Ancient English Poetry*（1765）がバラッド詩流行の大きな契機となったことは否定できない。しかし，それに遡る半世紀の間に，次の 3 編の重要なアンソロジーがすでに編集・出版されていた。

1. James Watson, ed., *Choice Collection of Comic and Serious Scots Poems*, 1706; 2nd ed. 1709; 3rd ed. 1711.
   これにはいわゆる純粋な 'folk ballad' は含まれておらず，すべてが 'broadside ballad' であるが，スコットランド方言による詩に対する関心を高めた点で，その貢献は高く評価される。
2. Ambrose Phillips, attrib., *A Collection of Old Ballads*, 1st and 2nd eds., 1723; 3rd ed. 1725.
   これは初の本格的な 'folk ballad' のコレクションで，159 篇中 23 篇が Percy の *Reliques* に再録された。
3. Allan Ramsay, ed., *The Tea-Table Miscellany*, 1723; 2nd ed. 1726?; 3rd ed. 1727?; 4th ed. 1737.
   これには純粋な 'folk ballad' 以外に，編者 Ramsay 自身の作品を含めて，本書にも採用した William Hamilton の "The Braes of Yarrow" その他のバラッド詩が収録されている。

実は，Percy の *Reliques* 初版 176 篇中には，Hamilton その他 12 名の詩人のバラッド詩が収録されている。すなわち，*Reliques* そのものが，純粋な口承バラッド，ブ

ロードサイド・バラッド，そしてバラッド詩の三者を含めたバラッド集なのである。（以下，純粋な口承バラッドとブロードサイド・バラッドを一括して「伝承バラッド」と呼ぶ。）

以後，19世紀に入ってバラッド蒐集熱は一段と高まり，以下に示すものはその代表的なコレクションであるが，その内の何編かを除いていずれも伝承バラッドとバラッド詩の両方を含んでいるというのが実態である。

1. Sir Walter Scott, ed., *Minstrelsy of the Scottish Border*, 3 vols., 1802–03.
   第3部は 'Imitations of the Ancient Ballad' としてまとめられ，Scott 自身を含む9名の詩人のバラッド詩19篇が収められている。
2. Robert Jamieson, ed., *Popular Ballads and Songs, from Tradition, Manuscripts, and Scarce Editions*, 1806.
3. William Motherwell, ed., *Minstrelsy Ancient and Modern*, 1827.
4. Peter Buchan, ed., *Ancient Ballads and Songs of the North of Scotland*, 1828.
5. Robert Chambers, ed., *The Scottish Ballads*, 1829.
   80篇中12篇が Elizabeth Wardlaw の "Hardyknute" や Hamilton の "The Braes of Yarrow" を含むバラッド詩である。
6. Charles Gavan Duffy, ed., *The Ballad Poetry of Ireland*, 1845; reaching its 39th edition by 1866.
   85篇中69篇が Clarence Mangan, Samuel Ferguson, Thomas Davis その他の詩人たちによるバラッド詩である。
7. Francis James Child, ed., *The English and Scottish Ballads*, 8 vols., 1857–58.
8. William Edmondstoune Aytoun, ed., *The Ballads of Scotland*, 2 vols., 1858.
9. William Allingham, ed., *The Ballad Book*, 1864; *Songs, Ballads and Stories*, 1877.
10. F. J. Furnivall, and J. W. Hales, eds., *Bishop Percy's Folio Manuscript: Ballads and Romances*, 3 vols., 1867–68. F. J. Furnivall, ed., *Bishop Percy's Folio Manuscript: Loose and Humorous Songs*, 1868.
11. George Barnett Smith, ed., *Illustrated British Ballads, Old and New*, 2 vols., 1881.
    87名の詩人による117篇のバラッド詩を含む。
12. John O'Leary, et. al. eds., *Poems and Ballads of Young Ireland*, 1888.
    W. B. Yeats や Katharine Tynan ら11名の詩人による27篇のバラッド詩を含む。

上記のものを含む過去のバラッド・コレクションからバラッド詩をすべて排除し

て可能な限り純粋な伝承バラッドのみを集大成したのが Francis James Child 編纂の *The English and Scottish Popular Ballads*（1882–98）である。以後 Child 版を補足する形で 20 世紀に入ってもバラッドの蒐集は続けられたが，今日一般的に伝承バラッドに言及する場合，Child 編纂の 305 篇をキャノンとして利用するのが習わしである。

II.「バラッドとは何か」という問いに答えて，20 世紀初頭の優れたバラッド学者 W. P. Ker は次のように言った。

> In spite of Socrates and his logic we may venture to say "A ballad is *The Milldams of Binnorie* and *Sir Patrick Spens* and *The Douglas Tragedy* and *Lord Randal* and *Child Maurice*, and things of that sort." [W. P. Ker, *Form and Style in Poetry* (1928; London, 1966) 3]

すなわち，この問いを検討するに当たって，我々は一応，依拠すべきキャノンとしての Child 版を持っているのである。

一方，「バラッド詩とは何か」——これに答えて Malcolm Laws はまず，次のように述べる。

> [Literary ballads] are the product and possession not of the common people of village or city but of sophisticated poets writing for literate audiences. They are printed poems rather than songs, and they have no traditional life. Despite great variations among individual examples, the literary ballads as a class are conscious and deliberate imitations of folk and broadside ballads. [G. Malcolm Laws, Jr., *The British Literary Ballad: A Study in Poetic Imitation* (Carbondale, 1972) xi]

Laws は更に続けて，そして結局 Ker に倣って，次のように言う。

> In the field of balladry, definition by example has often been found more enlightening than abstract verbalizing. Thus one may begin by identifying as literary ballads such frequently anthologized poems as the following: Wordsworth's "Lucy Gray," Scott's "The Eve of St. John," Southey's "The Battle of Blenheim," Tennyson's "The Charge of the Light Brigade," Rossetti's "Sister Helen," Housman's "Is My Team Ploughing?" Hardy's "Ah, Are You Digging on My Grave?" and Yeats's "The Ballad of Father Gilligan." (Laws 1)

Laws が挙げたものはいずれもポピュラーなバラッド詩のアンソロジー・ピースであるが，実は，伝承バラッドにおける Child 版に対応しうるようなバラッド詩の包括的なアンソロジーを今日まで我々は持っていないというのが実情である。上に紹介した 19 世紀の George Barnett Smith による 117 篇が最大のもので，20

世紀に入っては Anne Henry Ehrenpreis の *The Literary Ballad* (1966) における 28 名の詩人による 41 篇が唯一最大のアンソロジーである。日本においては，原一郎編 *Poems and Ballads*（研究社出版，1969; 改訂 1976）における 15 篇，藪下卓郎・山中光義編 *Traditional and Literary Ballads*（大阪教育図書，1980）における 19 篇，中島久代・宮原牧子・山中光義編『英国物語詩 14 撰』（松柏社，1998）における 11 篇がある。いずれも過去 3 世紀にわたるバラッド詩を通観するには少な過ぎると言わざるをえない。

III. 依拠すべきアンソロジーが極端に少ないことがバラッド詩研究の障害になっていることは否めない。換言すれば，「バラッド詩とは何か」を判断する上での基本的材料としてのテキストそのものを，我々はまとまった形で持っていないのである。詩人が伝承バラッドの何を模倣したと指摘できるか。模倣から出発しながら，自立した作品として優れたものになっていればいるほど，ある意味で模倣の痕跡を明瞭な形では留めていない場合も多く，バラッド詩の見極めの難しさは正に模倣からの逸脱の点に発生すると言うこともできるのである。一様の定義づけは不可能であるという前提の上で，目安としてバラッド詩の構成要素を次の 5 つの点に整理した捉え方を提示しておきたい。

 1. 直接的模倣
　明らかな元歌がある場合で，これがもっとも判りやすいケースである。例えば，"Fair Margaret and Sweet William" (Child 74B) を元歌とした David Mallet の "Margaret's Ghost" (1723) や Thomas Tickell の "Lucy and Colin" (1725)，"Gentle Herdsman, Tell to Me" (*Reliques*, vol. 2, bk. 1, XIV) を元歌とした Oliver Goldsmith の "The Hermit; or, Edwin and Angelina" (c. 1761)，"The Farmer's Curst Wife" (Child 278 A) を元歌とした Robert Burns の "The Carle of Kellyburn Braes" (1794)，"The Twa Sisters" (Child 10C) を元歌とした Alfred Tennyson の "The Sisters" (1832) などである。

 2. 技法(形式)的模倣
　物語歌としての伝承バラッドにはいくつかの物語技法の特徴がある。形式としての 'ballad stanza' と呼ばれるものは，弱強四歩格 ('iambic tetrameter') 二行対句で 'refrain' が挿入される場合とされない場合，弱強四歩格と三歩格 ('trimeter') が交互し，*a b c b* と押韻する場合がある。変形として，四歩格のみで，*a b a b* ないし *a b c b* と押韻する場合もある。詩人が 'ballad stanza' を採用している場合は，基本的に伝承バラッドを意識していると捉えてよいであろ

う。その他，コンヴェンショナルなバラッドの物語技法としては，'repetition' あるいは 'refrain' の利用，'contrast' あるいは 'parallelism' を用いる表現法，'dialogue'，'abrupt opening'，'mystic number' の活用などがある。例えば，Percy の "The Friar of Orders Gray" (1765)，Samuel Taylor Coleridge の "The Rime of the Ancient Mariner" (1798)，Charles Kingsley の "The Three Fishers" (1851)，Dante Gabriel Rossetti の "Sister Helen" (?1851)，A. C. Swinburne の "The King's Daughter" (1866) などである。

3. 題材の模倣

戦い，恋愛悲劇，呪い，亡霊，妖精，変身 ('metamorphosis') など，伝承バラッドが取り扱ってきた様々な題材やモチーフを利用する。例えば，Lady Elizabeth Wardlaw の "Hardyknute" (1719)，M. G. Lewis の "Alonzo the Brave and Fair Imogine" (1796)，Wordsworth の "The Thorn" (1798)，Percy Bysshe Shelley の "Sister Rosa: a Ballad" (1811)，Scott の "Alice Brand" (1810)，John Keats の "La Belle Dame sans Merci" (1819) などである。

4. 様式化の模倣

詩人たちはとりわけ伝承バラッド独特の様式化された物語技法に惹かれたようである。登場人物の感情の抑制と非個性化 ('impersonalization')，物語の断片化 ('fragmentation') などを意図的に模倣した。例えば，William Blake の "William Bond" (c. 1803)，William Morris の "Two Red Roses across the Moon" (1858)，Walter de la Mare の "The Silver Penny" (1902)，William Butler Yeats の "Crazy Jane and the Bishop" (1929)，William Plomer の "The Widow's Plot: or, She Got What Was Coming to Her" (1940) などである。

5. バラッド的精神風土 (Ethos) の模倣

口承バラッドの持つ自己劇化，遊戯性，無常観（風化意識），アイロニーとユーモア，パロディ，ブロードサイド・バラッドの持つ感傷性，教訓性，時事性（現代性）などを取り込む。例えば，Robert Southey の "The Battle of Blenheim" (1798)，Thomas Hood の "Faithless Sally Brown" (1822)，William Makepeace Thackeray の "Little Billee" (1849)，A. E. Housman の "Is My Team Ploughing?" (1896)，Thomas Hardy の "Ah, Are You Digging on My Grave?" (1913)，W. H. Auden の "Miss Gee" (1937) などである。

もちろん，上記5つの要素が重複して個々の作品を成立させているわけで，最終

的にバラッド詩の味は，様々なバラッド的要素を個々の詩人がどのように味付けしてみせるかに懸かってくるのである。

IV. 我々5名の編著者は，今回，詩人59名の作品60篇に解説と語註を付したアンソロジーを編纂した。将来的には3世紀にわたる網羅的なアンソロジーを編纂すべく，すでにその作業に取りかかっているところであるが，取りあえず時代別に15篇ずつを選んで配列し，これによって一応の「バラッド詩とは何か」に答える材料は提供しえたのではないかと期待している。

　本書の分担は下記の通りである。
　　山　中: まえがき，作品 1–15 の解説と語註(18世紀)
　　Taylor: Introduction，語註の監修
　　鎌　田: 作品 16–30 の解説と語註(ロマン派)
　　宮　原: 作品 31–45 の解説と語註(ヴィクトリア朝)
　　中　島: 作品 46–60 の解説と語註(19・20世紀)

5名は相互に点検を重ねたが，誤りの箇所については読者のご教示を請う次第である。

V. 本書の刊行は，日本学術振興会平成14年度科学研究費補助金(研究成果公開促進費)の交付を受けて実現した。ここに深く謝意を表するものである。また，出版を快諾いただいた九州大学出版会藤木雅幸編集長，ならびに編集の労をとっていただいた二場由起美さんに，心からのお礼を申し上げたい。

2002年6月

編著者

Introduction

The sixty pieces collected in this volume offer a convenient yet full introduction to one of the most remarkable and enduring of artistic forms: the literary ballad — a sophisticated narrative poem derived from the traditional ancient 'folk' ballads of the British Isles. It is worth remembering at the outset the long and inspirational traditions of folk-song created by the peoples of England, Scotland, Ireland and Wales and how the appeal of the literary ballad of the kind collected here, along with its subject matter and use of Celtic dialects for poetic English, has its origins in the various languages, myths, legends and countless old songs of the four nations of the region. These rich heritages of verse storytelling are reflected in the different countries where the narratives of the ballads take place, this collection's recognition of the usual tendency to situate the poems in the English literary context notwithstanding.

Historically, scholars have had no difficulty in appreciating the ballad's more distant forebears, assimilating the form as further testimony of English literary achievement, and recognizing a number of ballads by the great poets as major works of art. Defining the literary ballad, however, has been a more complex business. Where the most famous among the pieces have received the standard attentions of literary critical debate, while incidentally being recognized as part of the ballad tradition, a great number of literary ballads have suffered neglect due to the lesser or at least more ambiguous status designated to balladry overall. This has long been the case, irrespective of the qualities evident in a piece by a major poet or virtual unknown. It is the aim of this collection to redress this situation, to some extent, by compiling a comprehensive selection of works, with masterpieces assembled for comparison along with more controversially distinctive but still valuable elements of the literary tradition, and in its emphasis on literary balladry alone, this anthology becomes the most inclusive of its kind to date. It is hoped that the edition's trajectory from the early eighteenth century through to the major poets of the middle of the twentieth indicates the extent of the ballad's interest for poets throughout modern English literary history. As analysts of the ballad have long recognized, any number of major poets tried their hand at writing several if not many ballads, reawakening and sustaining interest in this most lasting of poetic practices. And it is the belief — that poets did not stoop occasionally to what has been perceived as an undoubtedly pleasurable though intrinsically inferior style, but rather that as 'balladeers' they wrote, however successfully, intent on maintaining the significance of the distant poetic tradition lying behind the 'literary' — that this volume holds as its chief justification.

*

To a large degree, the issues involved in closely defining a literary ballad, which have so vexed scholars, can help the reader to an immediate appreciation of the form. Despite the controversies over the internal dynamics of these extraordinary imitations of the ancient song tradition (inferior *because* imitations?), it is in the very range of stylized techniques, elements of extreme subject matter, location and characterization that a recognizably literary universe emerges. The highly accessible versification such as the pleasing, almost invariably regular stress patterns of the stanzas, so easily satirized but enjoyed, propel diverse narratives through the centuries, and ultimately cohere as a unified set of actions and themes describing fundamental human experiences. A complete reading of the sixty ballads will provide insights into the development of this intriguing manner of writing — from the achieved but wilful artifice of the Anglo-Scots dialect in "Hardyknute", successful in its mischievous intention to deceive early eighteenth century readers as an authentic ancient relic, to terse, modern colloquialisms; from tales of heroic acts of swordsmanship to the diagnosis of cancer. The above journey, from Lady Elizabeth Wardlaw to W. H. Auden, spans a great array of characters and settings, costume and scene changes, but in the midst of an agreeable wealth of contrasting periods and details, the specific continuities of a developing literary genre can be discerned.

"Hardyknute" stands emblematically at the beginning of the collection, as one of the first great ballad imitations and representative of literary balladry as a whole. Indeed, multiple readings of this tale of the legendary defence of Scotland, one of the lengthier pieces here, make ideal preparation for the works that follow. The medieval castle and battlefield, the swashbuckling, near-superhuman old hero, the absolute, fairy tale virtue and beauty of his wife and daughter, and the wounded, saturnine young knight, all described in the wry archaisms of Wardlaw's verse, accumulate as a typical ballad world: romantic, distant and yet highly recognizable, the details of folk traditions being almost subconsciously familiar to all readers. Hardyknute's victory against the invading Norsemen is revoked by his anguished return to the inexplicable darkness and desertion of his castle, and likely abduction of his daughter by the mysterious young knight. If the ballad were to end at stanza 39 in triumphalist mood, Wardlaw's anachronistic mention of the later commemorative monument aside, it could stand unproblematically as a successful imitation of a traditional war ballad. However, the warrior's emotional turmoil as his fortunes change, and the open-ended, obscure conclusion to the story are among the first instances of psychological and narrative complexities entering the ballad genre, and it is in the drama of the literary balladeer from the eighteenth century onwards, engaging with the attractions of the old verses while appropriating them inevitably for more modern concerns, that these sixty and countless other ballad imitations retain their interest.

*

The works of the three centuries included here have not necessarily been chosen as representative or prime examples of the literary ballad. Established, and much discussed imitations such as Coleridge's "The Rime of the Ancient Mariner" or Dante Gabriel Rossetti's "The Blessed Damozel" have been omitted on the grounds of their great familiarity, but to widen perspectives on their involvement in ballad imitation, some less anthologized pieces by the famous poets are given. Similarly, neglected names or works, most of whom were well-known in the late eighteenth and nineteenth centuries when the ballad enjoyed its great popularity in revival, are given their place in the hope of demonstrating the breadth of the imitative tradition and its characteristics, as in the cases of the parodic ballads by Thomas Hood or Henry Duff Traill, or the tragic romances of William Robert Spencer.

With its rhythmical momentum and, perhaps most attractively of all, in its commitment to succinct, accessible narrative, the literary ballad grants the reader a uniquely concise access to the vagaries of character emotion and psychological response. In a crucial set of departures from traditional ballad techniques, most notably in the shift away from the impersonality and 'distance' of the original narratives, the literary ballads seem to interact organically as a whole, self-consciously sharing their plot-lines, character types, moral perspectives, dress codes, colours, sounds and arrestingly finite elements of vocabulary as if in both formal communion and genial defiance of the tradition to which they aspire and from which they must inevitably be excluded, and thus exclude themselves. Strikingly, the poems, though they may be centuries apart in conception, are more alike than they are unlike, and irrespective of the particular periods for the English language, which might claim works for their local aspects of style or subject matter, a series of mutual themes and details can be easily recognized as governing the ballads in their entirety, suggesting each piece as an individually nuanced facet of a single extended narrative.

*

The ballad world is not the happiest of places. Nor is it for the fainthearted, for the reader, no longer able to participate in the doubtless cheery group rituals of the sung refrains, which once kept the darker elements of the stories at bay, is repeatedly confronted with allegorical yarns intended to unsettle or terrify. And, of course, entertain, for the almost hypnotic scansion and swift advances of plot and character rarely fail in drawing us delightedly on towards the untimely demise of a noble hero, innocent heroine, inconstant beauty or debased villain. In fact we are almost constantly reminded of the timeless human predilection for accounts of disaster, replete with 'the gory details', as long as we are not at any personal risk ourselves, the word 'gory' actually appearing in several of the following ballads to leave us in no doubt as to the horror of a scene. Courage, strength, sincerity or just simple good intentions are not virtues enough for a man to overcome the more powerful agencies set against him in the worlds depicted here. The confusion and regret, which finally detract from the great warrior's otherwise heroic life in "Hardyknute", are developed and surpassed in the subsequent ballads. Hardyknute's deep remorse at his decisions is echoed by Prince Llewelyn in Spencer's "Beth Gêlert", where another great man is humbled by an irrevocable error of judgment. Political heroes are remembered solely to make their way to the gallows on more than one occasion, a pattern culminating in the image of one of mankind's principal guides approaching death in A. E. Housman's Christian allegory, "The Carpenter's Son". The likelihoods of drowning or oblivion in sea-battle reiterate the hazards of the sailor's profession with the 'mournful spectres' of Richard Glover's "Admiral Hosier's Ghost" emerging to warn the victorious English fleet against celebrating without thought for the less fortunate crews of maritime wars past. The three thousand ghosts' relatively benign return can be prescribed to an ultimate lack of intimacy between all involved. Inconstant lovers, however, can expect much worse such as the visitation in "Margaret's Ghost", where the avenging spirit of the abandoned maiden arrives recognizably in her mortal shape, a corporeal revenant, 'from her midnight grave' to accuse and upbraid her 'faithless swain'. The same post-mortem discontent is planned in Thomas Tickell's "Lucy and Colin", as the jilted fiancée disrupts her former lover's wedding, by having her corpse carried to the village celebration in a macabre pact with her friends.

Love proves almost always to be a perilous business. Where men regularly undergo an early death to atone for their weakness and infidelity, they may also be witnessed as mourned beloveds, haplessly murdered for their unwise choice of bride. Even in the handful of ballads where lovers are harmonious, the predominant tones are intensely melancholic, as in Coleridge's "Love", or of exhaustion and relief such as felt by the parents-to-be in D. G. Rossetti's "Stratton Water". The joyful, fantasy reunions of "The Hermit" and "The Friar of Orders Gray" take place in the wake of the most arduous tests for the human heart, and despite our gratitude for the presence of Robbie Burns's "A Red, Red Rose", at hand to provide romantic consolation, we might skeptically wonder at the traditional extremity of the lover's vows, and dwell on how frequently they are reported to have been broken elsewhere. There is, indeed, something 'ominous, ominous' about the utopian courtship and engagement recorded in the fixed, beaming smile of John Betjeman's "A Subaltern's Love-song".

Possibilities for a man's suffering continue in Tennyson's "The Lord of Burleigh", where deception ruins and ends a potentially happy marriage. The paternal state is also thwarted, with fatherhood's joys grimly absent from James Hogg's "Sir David Graeme" or Thomas Hardy's "A Sunday Morning Tragedy", where girl children are lost respectively to the desperate measures of angry pursuit and a recklessly administered contraceptive remedy. Byron's depiction of fratricide and murder, and Oscar's subsequent revenge visitation 'in the midst of general mirth', drawing freely on Shakespeare's returning Banquo, is at its most poignant as a dramatization of a father's insurmountable sense of loss. If a man is not further assailed by mythological figures from folk lore or damned by seductresses or religious retribution, there is always the comic ballad ready to persecute its inmates. Luckless John Gilpin's best intentions to please his wife on their long-postponed wedding anniversary holiday go predictably awry as his 'frighted steed' bolts anywhere but to the appointed party rooms, instead sending him on 'like an arrow' through the turnpike gates of various towns. Lewis Carroll extends the black comic setting of the old British toll roads in his jubilant tour de force in which an elder brother, having skewered his sibling as fishing bait, amuses himself with merciless puns, indifferent to the younger boy's fears and to the will of 'desolate Fate':

> I stick to my perch and your perch sticks to you,
>   We are really extremely alike;

> I've a turn-pike up here, and I very much fear
> You may soon have a turn with a pike.

Despite being pursued as much by linguistic play as hungry freshwater predators 'the lad . . . so tender and young' resides within the conventions of helpless ensnarement that habitually beset the ballad victim. Essential to the comic force inherent in so many of the ballads in their arch histrionics and spectacular problematizing of the human condition is a clear metaphorical reach towards the human mind and the depth of its anxieties over mortality and the possibility of eternal love. The insistent, plaintive tones of the literary ballad interlocutors hint at an increasingly atheistic and self-questioning age far removed from the bleak stoicism of the earlier relics.

The ballads from the twentieth century included here are no less reliant on, indeed emphasise the figures of the earlier literary tradition, as in Robert Graves's sombre inversion of Carroll's lethal tableau, where a vision brings realization of emotional confinement and loss: 'Already it was too late: the bait swallowed, / The hook fast.' Similarly, Vernon Watkins's inspired narrator, in his parabolic search for sensual and intellectual knowledge, is left to curse the folly of self-delusion and gain the lonely understanding that he has been his own life's principal obstacle. However, in traditional manner, there is time to rail against the traps set by the mythic female in the reasoning towards a man's downfall: 'O let me be, you women!'

It is, of course, the ballad tradition that conceived one of the greatest of femmes fatales, 'La Belle Dame Sans Merci', and Shelley's monk in "Sister Rosa" might well be in sympathy with the note of tragic despair in Watkins's outburst. Nevertheless, the briefest of encounters with the ballads ought to reveal that the range of hazardous situations invented for womanhood to endure or succumb to equals if not exceeds the predicaments directed against men — one method of classifying the narratives is to group them according to the fate of their women characters. Perhaps historical accuracy provides the most troubling role in the anxious or grieving wife awaiting the return or death of her husband from sea or warfare. Unjust political conflicts also claim husbands and sweethearts leaving woman to grieve, as they must when their innocent lovers are murdered. Women may suffer for the sin of self-love as in Charles Kingsley's "Ballad of Earl Haldan's Daughter", where vanity is rewarded with isolation.

But it is in the routine but enticing subject of infidelity that the balladeer allows his imagination free rein to embellish the painful reality of lost love. Transformed into a 'grimly ghost', the betrayed Margaret must stand at the foot of disloyal William's bed to list her complaints of an early death for love before returning to her newfound sister 'the hungry worm'. The same fate belongs to Thomas Tickell's Lucy, who shares Margaret's 'winding sheet' in place of wedding apparel, while William Julius Mickle in turn aligns Lucy's sufferings with those of his insulted countess of "Cumnor Hall" by closely revisiting Tickell's theatrical omens:

> Three times, all in the dead of night,
>   A bell was heard to ring;
> And at her window, shrieking thrice,
>   The raven flap'd his wing.
> "Lucy and Colin"

> The death-belle thrice was hearde to ring,
>   An aërial voyce was hearde to call,
> And thrice the raven flapp'd its wyng
>   Arounde the tow'rs of Cumnor Hall.
> "Cumnor Hall"

At least spurned women are granted ghostly opportunities of revenge, but it is the faithless female, who is most at the mercy of the grotesque comic energies of the Gothic horror-ballad, with its infamous repertoire of missing and unexpected suitors, decaying bodies, medieval paraphernalia and predictable but potent lighting and sound effects. Dead and half forgotten, as decomposing corpse, skeleton or ghoul, the lover returns to exact his horrifying recompense. Unable to trust in heavenly guidance, Walter Scott's Helen blasphemously despairs, only to be reunited with the 'mould'ring flesh' of her mounted Crusader betrothed and find herself, like John Gilpin, transported helplessly by a 'thundering steed'. Her punishments — a necrophiliac embrace, *danse macabre*, and likely damnation — are triumphantly amplified in M. G. Lewis's Imogine, whose hellish wedding celebrations with her 'skeleton-knight' are ordained to continue four times annually. The horror-ballad, for all its exuberant melodrama, offers the spectacle of poets knowingly participating in a style in which they, like their anti-heroines, get carried away. As if his own ghastly but great contribution is not enough to declare zestful exploitation, Lewis provides us with a stanza by stanza self-parody, "Giles Jollup the Grave, and Brown Sally Green", worth comparing with "Alonzo the Brave and Fair Imogine" for its understanding of the great distinction in tonal effect — from irony to bathos — achieved in its brazen vocabulary shifts, while the conventional metrics remain intact. To turn from Lewis's versifications to the poetry of William Blake might usually describe the movement back from the ridiculous to the sublime. Nonetheless, the temptations of the horror-ballad's resources can also claim the relish and expertise with which Blake engages with its clearly defined machinery, its penchant for necrophilia included, to predate Oscar Wilde by over a century in rejuvenating Salomé's transgressive impulses. Elenor, though guiltless of betrayal, is forced to suffer the facts of her lover's murder from his own decapitated head, and join her harassed sisters from other ballads in death and purgatorial penance:

> She sat with dead cold limbs, stiffen'd to stone;
> She took the gory head up in her arms;
> She kiss'd the pale lips; she had no tears to shed;
> She hugg'd it to her breast, and groan'd her last.

Well away from the 'grinning skulls, and corruptible death', which Blake proffers as the stock-in-trade of the Gothic balladeer's 'fancy' as much as that of the tormented heroine, love's contingencies still pursue womanhood into the grave, albeit in ballads ranging widely in lyric tone and emotional register. Swinburne's Pre-Raphaelite masterpiece "The King's Daughter" establishes an exquisite series of lyrical and visual effects, particularly in its refrains, prior to confirming the son's incestuous will and his sister's concluding dismal awareness of her death and damnation. In "Auld Robin Gray", notably by a woman poet, the distinct treatment of a young girl's infidelity in misfortune, ending in a kind of death-in-life, results in one of the most successful and touching of the eighteenth century imitations. Thomas Campbell's Highland romance sets the human will in contest and inevitable tragic defeat against the forces of fate and wild nature, with 'the scowl of heaven' presiding over the drowning of Lord Ullin's daughter and the ineffectual, wholly male community, who are 'left lamenting'. The violence of the natural world compounds the anxieties of jealousy felt by Robert Browning's narrator, who, with the arrival of Porphyria, the delicate object of his affections, finds murder the means to calm his 'heart fit to break', and treat us to a further instance of romantic union between the living and the dead. Dispatched in the hope that 'she felt no pain', Porphyria's 'smiling rosy little head' finds complete analogy in Jennifer's last moments, 'relaxed, still smiling', as William Plomer recovers the theme of strangulation and testifies to the ballad's flexibility of re-invention: his sinister version of twentieth century pastoral reconfiguring the untamed beauties of the old ballads' background terrains prior to tragic event.

Lest the reader sense a strain of morbid misogyny driving not a few of the imaginations collected here — the archetypal damsel might be a little too available for her distress — there are the works that are forthright in suggesting the need for more just scenarios for their women characters than circumstance has allowed. Wordsworth's uncharitable farmer summarily receives the providential curse of a perpetually cold body through the prayers of the poverty stricken Goody Blake, while W. B. Yeats's Moll Magee and Robert Buchanan's 'wan Woman', both 'weary', must remain itinerant in their social rejection, having given birth, but lacking a father's help.

Thomas Hardy's sympathies clearly lie with his beleagured heroine as do George Meredith's with his in their accounts of unwanted pregnancy and the shame of premarital love, both implying choice of the ballad's narrative strengths to raise social issues. Sympathy clearly sways against William Allingham's King Henry VIII in his delight at news of Anne Boleyn's execution and flight to the more fortunate 'beautiful Jane Seymour', the word 'glee' being attached to him as it is to male miscreants throughout these poems. Both W. H. Auden's Miss Gee and John Davidson's nun are allowed to escape respectively into explorations of erotic fantasy and reality, with Auden's great modern work combining the savage comic aggression characteristically meted out on the balladic body with an overriding will for compassion as reflexive of its own war struck period as it is of tradition.

Miss Gee's parlous condition, coldly scrutinized by medicine and the intelligentsia, is anticipated in one of the literary tradition's most explicit parodies as Thomas Hood exultantly exposes the absurdities of the ongoing assault on the body, his ghostly Mary in a typical heroine's lament, detailing the various locations of her dismembered form, and warning her lover of the futility, in her case, of conventional graveside regret:

> Don't go to weep upon my grave,
> And think that there I be;
>
> They haven't left an atom there
> Of my anatomie.

Approaching the ballads for the first time, one might profitably start with the parodies and satires, which, despite their varying degrees of antagonism towards the form, contain their own acid anatomies of elements to be found throughout. Between them, Hood, and Henry Duff Traill, in his more caustic analysis, openly mocking D. G. Rossetti's "Sister Helen", accurately pick up on many of the formal, thematic and verbal tropes active across the entire range of works. Hood is right to conclude his dissection of the body with the heart, the most frequently referenced part of all, though the human eye observing the taxing events of these imaginations and their effects upon our mortal 'clay' follows closely as a presence.

Traill felicitously has his little male interlocutor antagonize his balladeer elder sister with pertinent questions. Though she may lack the golden tresses adorning the majority of female victims, she is suitably clad in green, the predominant hue of the ballad's restricted palette of colours, while also possessing a 'face so yellowy white', also correct, as a 'ghastly', 'wan', 'pale face' regularly marks the 'fear' of participants, male or female. Hood's catalogue of major body parts spares us the customary blanched cheeks, though it does remember the theatrical weeping that so often in these lines accompanies human grief. Either parodist might also have considered the essential sonic effects — the 'loude and dysmalle dynnne' (Chatterton) of the 'shrilly sounding, / Hideous yells and shrieks' (Glover) — which accompany the characters' tribulations throughout, though the more cheerful notes in the ancient melodies of the pibroch and the harp are also likely to be heard. Like so many before her, Hood's Mary returns to address her lover from the afterlife, but in Traill it is the style itself that has been 'Done-to-death', the elder brother's sonnet monologue advising against pursuing the ballad style any longer.

Happily, Traill was premature in his judgement, and countless poets after him, as we see, were to disagree and return to the welcoming possibilities for traditional subjects, rhythms and refrains to continue a style in fascination and affection, perhaps even out of need. Both Hood and Traill are in touch with the ballad's potential for ridicule in its performance rituals and routine obsession with death, but miss the vital opposite pole in the form's central duality of Thanatos and Eros. The countless uses of 'love' and its variants jostle undauntedly against those of 'death', probably in ultimate excess, triumphing in human passion, and standing as permanent tribute to the ancient love songs that prefigure the long literary heritage which is the true context of these ballads, and in which they merit reappraisal.

*

Most commentary on the literary ballad states the essential commonplace that these works risk the paradox of their creation: emerging with their own uniqueness out of a poet's desire to imitate, they have neither the authenticity of the ancient models nor the freedoms of sophisticated, subjective verse, but stand in hybrid relation to both, the one dimension inevitably in conflict with the other, and resulting in voices wavering between the sentimental and the sepulchral. Nevertheless, in the longevity of the poet's love affair with the ballad and his apparent freedom from anxiety of influence lies an argument for renewed attention. If nothing else, lacking melodies and the original folk community to perform them, these ballads might be familiar to us in their alternative literary anxiety, that of audience, as they offer the peculiarly modern scenario of poems singing fondly to one another.

David Taylor

目　次

まえがき　　　　　　　　　　　　　　　　　　　　　　　　　　　i
Introduction　by David Taylor　　　　　　　　　　　　　　　vii

1	*Hardyknute*　by Lady Elizabeth Wardlaw	1
2	*Sweet William's Farewell to Black-Ey'd Susan*　by John Gay	11
3	*The Braes of Yarrow*　by William Hamilton	12
4	*Margaret's Ghost*　by David Mallet	16
5	*Lucy and Colin*　by Thomas Tickell	19
6	*Admiral Hosier's Ghost*　by Richard Glover	21
7	*Jemmy Dawson*　by William Shenstone	24
8	*The Hermit; or, Edwin and Angelina*　by Oliver Goldsmith	26
9	*The Friar of Orders Gray*　by Thomas Percy	32
10	*Auld Robin Gray*　by Lady Anne Lindsay	36
11	*Bristowe Tragedie: or the Dethe of Syr Charles Bawdin*　by Thomas Chatterton	37
12	*The Braes of Yarrow*　by John Logan	49
13	*The Diverting History of John Gilpin*　by William Cowper	50
14	*Cumnor Hall*　by William Julius Mickle	58
15	*A Red, Red Rose*　by Robert Burns	62
16	*Fair Elenor*　by William Blake	62
17	*William and Helen*　by Sir Walter Scott	65
18	*Alonzo the Brave and Fair Imogine*　by M. G. Lewis	74
19	*Giles Jollup the Grave, and Brown Sally Green*　by M. G. Lewis	77
20	*Goody Blake, and Harry Gill*　by William Wordsworth	80
21	*Bishop Bruno*　by Robert Southey	83
22	*Love*　by Samuel Taylor Coleridge	85
23	*Beth Gêlert; or, The Grave of the Greyhound*　by William Robert Spencer	89
24	*The Elfin-King*　by John Leyden	92
25	*Oscar of Alva*　by George Gordon Byron	98

26	*Sir David Graeme* by James Hogg	108
27	*Lord Ullin's Daughter* by Thomas Campbell	113
28	*Sister Rosa: a Ballad* by Percy Bysshe Shelley	115
29	*La Belle Dame sans Merci* by John Keats	118
30	*Mary's Ghost* by Thomas Hood	120
31	*Porphyria's Lover* by Robert Browning	122
32	*The Lord of Burleigh* by Alfred Tennyson	124
33	*The Execution of Montrose* by William Edmondstoune Aytoun	126
34	*The Knight and the Lady* by William Makepeace Thackeray	133
35	*The Two Brothers* by Lewis Carroll	135
36	*Ballad of Earl Haldan's Daughter* by Charles Kingsley	140
37	*The Ballad of Keith of Ravelston* by Sydney Thompson Dobell	141
38	*Love from the North* by Christina Georgina Rossetti	143
39	*The Sailing of the Sword* by William Morris	144
40	*Margaret's Bridal Eve* by George Meredith	146
41	*The King's Daughter* by A. C. Swinburne	152
42	*Stratton Water* by Dante Gabriel Rossetti	154
43	*King Henry's Hunt* by William Allingham	159
44	*After Dilettante Concetti* by Henry Duff Traill	162
45	*The Ballad of the Wayfarer* by Robert W. Buchanan	164
46	*The Bridge of Death* by Andrew Lang	166
47	*The Ballad of Moll Magee* by William Butler Yeats	167
48	*The Last Rhyme of True Thomas* by Rudyard Kipling	169
49	*A Ballad of a Nun* by John Davidson	174
50	*The Carpenter's Son* by A. E. Housman	179
51	*Screaming Tarn* by Robert Bridges	180
52	*The Yarn of the Loch Achray* by John Masefield	184
53	*A Sunday Morning Tragedy* by Thomas Hardy	186
54	*The Ghost* by Walter de la Mare	190
55	*The Murder on the Downs* by William Plomer	191
56	*The Enchanted Knight* by Edwin Muir	193
57	*Miss Gee* by W. H. Auden	194
58	*A Subaltern's Love-song* by John Betjeman	197
59	*The Foreboding* by Robert Graves	199
60	*Ballad of the Three Coins* by Vernon Watkins	199

解説と語註　205

List of Texts　275

Acknowledgements	279
Index of Titles	281
Index of First Lines	283
Index of Authors	285

1 Hardyknute

Lady Elizabeth Wardlaw (1677–1727)

I.
Stately stept he east the wa',
    And stately stept he west,
Full seventy years he now had seen,
    Wi' scarce seven years of rest.
He liv'd when Britons breach of faith
    Wrought Scotland mickle wae:
And ay his sword tauld to their cost,
    He was their deadlye fae.

II.
High on a hill his castle stood,
    With ha's and tow'rs a height,
And goodly chambers fair to se,
    Where he lodged mony a knight.
His dame sae peerless anes and fair,
    For chast and beauty deem'd,
Nae marrow had in all the land,
    Save ELENOR the queen.

III.
Full thirteen sons to him she bare,
    All men of valour stout;
In bloody fight with sword in hand
    Nine lost their lives bot doubt:
Four yet remain, lang may they live
    To stand by liege and land;
High was their fame, high was their might,
    And high was their command.

IV.
Great love they bare to FAIRLY fair,
    Their sister saft and dear,
Her girdle shaw'd her middle gimp,
    And gowden glist her hair.
What waefu' wae her beauty bred!
    Waefu' to young and auld,

Waefu' I trow to kyth and kin,
    As story ever tauld.

V.

The king of Norse in summer tyde,
    Puff'd up with pow'r and might,
Landed in fair Scotland the isle
    With mony a hardy knight.
The tydings to our good Scots king
    Came, as he sat at dine,
With noble chiefs in brave aray,
    Drinking the blood-red wine.

VI.

'To horse, to horse, my royal liege,
    Your faes stand on the strand,
Full twenty thousand glittering spears
    The king of Norse commands.'
'Bring me my steed Mage dapple gray,'
    Our good king rose and cry'd,
A trustier beast in a' the land
    A Scots king nevir try'd.

VII.

'Go, little page, tell Hardyknute,
    That lives on hill sae hie,
To draw his sword, the dread of faes,
    And haste and follow me.'
The little page flew swift as dart
    Flung by his master's arm,
'Come down, come down, lord Hardyknute,
    And rid your king frae harm.'

VIII.

Then red, red grew his dark-brown cheeks,
    Sae did his dark-brown brow;
His looks grew keen, as they were wont
    In dangers great to do;
He's ta'en a horn as green as glass,
    And gi'en five sounds sae shill,
That trees in green wood shook thereat,
    Sae loud rang ilka hill.

IX.

His sons in manly sport and glee,
    Had past that summer's morn,
When low down in a grassy dale,
    They heard their father's horn.
'That horn,' quo' they, 'ne'er sounds in peace,
    We've other sport to bide.'
And soon they hy'd them up the hill,
    And soon were at his side.

X.

'Late, late yestreen I ween'd in peace
    To end my lengthened life,
My age might well excuse my arm
    Frae manly feats of strife;
But now that Norse do's proudly boast
    Fair Scotland to inthrall,
It's ne'er be said of Hardyknute,
    He fear'd to fight or fall.

XI.

Robin of Rothsay, bend thy bow,
    Thy arrows shoot sae leel,
That mony a comely countenance
    They've turnd to deadly pale.
Brade Thomas, take you but your lance,
    You need nae weapons mair,
If you fight wi't as you did anes
    'Gainst Westmoreland's fierce heir.

XII.

And Malcolm, light of foot as stag
    That runs in forest wild,
Get me my thousands three of men
    Well bred to sword and shield:
Bring me my horse and harnisine
    My blade of mettal clear.
If faes but ken'd the hand it bare,
    They soon had fled for fear.

XIII.

Farewell my dame sae peerless good,

(And took her by the hand),
Fairer to me in age you seem,
  Than maids for beauty fam'd.
My youngest son shall here remain
  To guard these stately towers,
And shut the silver bolt that keeps
  Sae fast your painted bowers.'

XIV.

And first she wet her comely cheiks,
  And then her boddice green,
Her silken cords of twirtle twist,
  Well plett with silver sheen;
And apron set with mony a dice
  Of needle-wark sae rare,
Wove by nae hand, as ye may guess,
  Save that of Fairly fair.

XV.

And he has ridden o'er muir and moss,
  O'er hills and mony a glen,
When he came to a wounded knight
  Making a heavy mane;
'Here maun I lye, here maun I dye,
  By treacherie's false guiles;
Witless I was that e'er ga faith
  To wicked woman's smiles.'

XVI.

'Sir knight, gin you were in my bower,
  To lean on silken seat,
My lady's kindly care you'd prove,
  Who ne'er knew deadly hate:
Herself wou'd watch you a' the day,
  Her maids a dead of night;
And Fairly fair your heart wou'd chear,
  As she stands in your sight.

XVII.

Arise young knight, and mount your stead,
  Full lowns the shynand day:
Choose frae my menzie whom ye please

To lead you on the way.'
With smileless look, and visage wan
   The wounded knight reply'd,
'Kind chieftain, your intent pursue,
   For here I maun abyde.

XVIII.

To me nae after day nor night
   Can e'er be sweet or fair,
But soon beneath some draping tree,
   Cauld death shall end my care.'
With him nae pleading might prevail;
   Brave Hardyknute to gain
With fairest words, and reason strong,
   Strave courteously in vain.

XIX.

Syne he has gane far hynd out o'er
   Lord Chattan's land sae wide;
That lord a worthy wight was ay,
   When faes his courage sey'd:
Of Pictish race by mother's side,
   When Picts rul'd Caledon,
Lord Chattan claim'd the princely maid,
   When he sav'd Pictish crown.

XX.

Now with his fierce and stalwart train,
   He reach'd a rising hight,
Quhair braid encampit on the dale,
   Norss menzie lay in sicht.
'Yonder, my valiant sons and feirs,
   Our raging revers wait
On the unconquert Scottish sward
   To try with us their fate.

XXI.

Make orisons to him that sav'd
   Our sauls upon the rude;
Syne bravely shaw your veins are fill'd
   With Caledonian blude.'
Then furth he drew his trusty glave,

While thousands all around
Drawn frae their sheaths glanc'd in the sun;
And loud the bougles sound.

XXII.

To joyn his king adoun the hill
    In hast his merch he made,   170
While, playand pibrochs, minstralls meit
    Afore him stately strade.
'Thrice welcome, valiant stoup of weir,
    Thy nations shield and pride;
Thy king nae reason has to fear   175
    When thou art by his side.'

XXIII.

When bows were bent and darts were thrawn;
    For thrang scarce cou'd they flee;
The darts clove arrows as they met,
    The arrows dart the tree.   180
Lang did they rage and fight fu' fierce,
    With little skaith to mon,
But bloody, bloody was the field,
    Ere that lang day was done.

XXIV.

The king of Scots, that sindle brook'd   185
    The war that look'd like play,
Drew his braid sword, and brake his bow,
    Sin bows seem'd but delay.
Quoth noble Rothsay, 'Mine I'll keep,
    I wat it's bled a score.'   190
'Haste up my merry men,' cry'd the king,
    As he rode on before.

XXV.

The king of Norse he sought to find,
    With him to mense the faught,
But on his forehead there did light   195
    A sharp unsonsie shaft;
As he his hand put up to feel
    The wound, an arrow keen,
O waefu' chance! there pinn'd his hand

In midst between his een.

XXVI.
'Revenge, revenge,' cry'd Rothsay's heir,
   'Your mail-coat sha' na bide
The strength and sharpness of my dart:'
   Then sent it through his side.
Another arrow well he mark'd,
   It pierc'd his neck in twa,
His hands then quat the silver reins,
   He low as earth did fa'.

XXVII.
'Sair bleids my liege, sair, sair he bleeds!'
   Again wi' might he drew
And gesture dread his sturdy bow,
   Fast the braid arrow flew:
Wae to the knight he ettled at;
   Lament now, queen Elgreed;
High dames, too, wail your darling's fall,
   His youth and comely meed.

XXVIII.
'Take aff, take aff his costly jupe
   (Of gold well was it twin'd,
Knit like the fowler's net, through quhilk,
   His steelly harness shin'd)
Take, Norse, that gift frae me, and bid
   Him venge the blood it bears;
Say, if he face my bended bow,
   He sure nae weapon fears.'

XXIX.
Proud Norse with giant body tall,
   Braid shoulders and arms strong,
Cry'd, 'Where is Hardyknute sae fam'd,
   And fear'd at Britain's throne:
Tho' Britons tremble at his name,
   I soon shall make him wail,
That e'er my sword was made sae sharp,
   Sae saft his coat of mail.'

XXX.

That brag his stout heart cou'd na bide,
   It lent him youthfu' micht:
'I'm Hardyknute; this day,' he cry'd,   235
   'To Scotland's king I heght
To lay thee low, as horses hoof;
   My word I mean to keep.'
Syne with the first stroke e'er he strake,
   He garr'd his body bleed.   240

XXXI.

Norss' een like gray gosehawk's stair'd wyld,
   He sigh'd wi' shame and spite;
'Disgrac'd is now my far-fam'd arm
   That left thee power to strike:'
Then ga' his head a blow sae fell,   245
   It made him doun to stoup,
As laigh as he to ladies us'd
   In courtly guise to lout.

XXXII.

Fu' soon he rais'd his bent body,
   His bow he marvell'd sair,   250
Sin blows till then on him but darr'd
   As touch of Fairly fair:
Norse marvell'd too as sair as he
   To see his stately look;
Sae soon as e'er he strake a fae,   255
   Sae soon his life he took.

XXXIII.

Where like a fire to heather set,
   Bauld Thomas did advance,
Ane sturdy fae with look enrag'd
   Up toward him did prance;   260
He spurr'd his steid through thickest ranks
   The hardy youth to quell,
Wha stood unmov'd at his approach
   His fury to repell.

XXXIV.

'That short brown shaft sae meanly trimm'd,   265

Looks like poor Scotlands gear,
But dreadfull seems the rusty point!'
And loud he leugh in jear.
'Oft Britons blood has dimm'd its shine;
This point cut short their vaunt:' 270
Syne pierc'd the boasters bearded cheek;
Nae time he took to taunt.

XXXV.

Short while he in his saddle swang,
His stirrup was nae stay,
Sae feeble hang his unbent knee 275
Sure taiken he was fey:
Swith on the harden't clay he fell,
Right far was heard the thud:
But Thomas look't nae as he lay
All waltering in his blud: 280

XXXVI.

With careless gesture, mind unmov't,
On rode he north the plain;
His seem in throng of fiercest strife,
When winner ay the same:
Nor yet his heart dames dimplet cheek 285
Could mease soft love to bruik,
Till vengefu' Ann return'd his scorn,
Then languid grew his luik.

XXXVII.

In thraws of death, with walowit cheik
All panting on the plain, 290
The fainting corps of warriours lay,
Ne're to arise again;
Ne're to return to native land,
Nae mair with blithsome sounds
To boast the glories of the day, 295
And shaw their shining wounds.

XXXVIII.

On Norways coast the widowit dame
May wash the rocks with tears,
May lang luik ow'r the shipless seas

    Befor her mate appears.
Cease, Emma, cease to hope in vain;
    Thy lord lyes in the clay;
The valiant Scots nae revers thole
    To carry life away.

XXXIX.

Here on a lee, where stands a cross
    Set up for monument,
Thousands fu' fierce that summer's day
    Fill'd keen war's black intent.
Let Scots, while Scots, praise Hardyknute,
    Let Norse the name ay dread,
Ay how he faught, aft how he spar'd,
    Shall latest ages read.

XL.

Now loud and chill blew th' westlin wind,
    Sair beat the heavy shower,
Mirk grew the night ere Hardyknute
    Wan near his stately tower.
His tow'r that us'd wi' torches blaze
    To shine sae far at night,
Seem'd now as black as mourning weed,
    Nae marvel sair he sigh'd.

XLI.

'There's nae light in my lady's bower,
    There's nae light in my ha';
Nae blink shines round my Fairly fair,
    Nor ward stands on my wa',
'What bodes it? Robert, Thomas, say;' —
    Nae answer fitts their dread.
'Stand back, my sons, I'le be your guide;'
    But by they past with speed.

XLII.

'As fast I've sped owre Scotland's faes,' —
    There ceas'd his brag of weir,
Sair sham'd to mind ought but his dame,
    And maiden Fairly fair.
Black fear he felt, but what to fear

He wist nae yet; wi' dread
Sair shook his body, sair his limbs, 335
And a' the warrior fled.

1719

2 *Sweet William's Farewell to Black-Ey'd Susan*

John Gay (1685–1732)

All in the *Downs* the fleet was moor'd,
   The streamers waving in the wind,
When black-ey'd *Susan* came aboard.
   Oh! where shall I my true love find!
Tell me, ye jovial sailors, tell me true, 5
If my sweet *William* sails among the crew.

William, who high upon the yard,
   Rock'd with the billow to and fro,
Soon as her well-known voice he heard,
   He sigh'd, and cast his eyes below: 10
The cord slides swiftly through his glowing hands
And, (quick as lightning,) on the deck he stands.

So the sweet lark, high-pois'd in air,
   Shuts close his pinions to his breast,
(If, chance, his mate's shrill call he hear) 15
   And drops at once into her nest.
The noblest Captain in the *British* fleet,
Might envy *William*'s lip those kisses sweet.

O *Susan, Susan*, lovely dear,
   My vows shall ever true remain; 20
Let me kiss off that falling tear,
   We only part to meet again.
Change, as ye list, ye winds; my heart shall be
The faithful compass that still points to thee.

Believe not what the landmen say, 25
    Who tempt with doubts thy constant mind:
They'll tell thee, sailors, when away,
    In ev'ry port a mistress find.
Yes, yes, believe them when they tell thee so,
For thou art present wheresoe'er I go. 30

If to far *India*'s coast we sail,
    Thy eyes are seen in di'monds bright,
Thy breath is *Africk*'s spicy gale,
    Thy skin is ivory, so white.
Thus ev'ry beauteous object that I view, 35
Wakes in my soul some charm of lovely *Sue*.

Though battel call me from thy arms,
    Let not my pretty *Susan* mourn;
Though cannons roar, yet safe from harms,
    William shall to his Dear return. 40
Love turns aside the balls that round me fly,
Lest precious tears should drop from *Susan*'s eye.

The boatswain gave the dreadful word,
    The sails their swelling bosom spread,
No longer must she stay aboard: 45
    They kiss'd, she sigh'd, he hung his head.
Her less'ning boat, unwilling rows to land:
Adieu, she cries! and wav'd her lilly hand.

1720

3   *The Braes of Yarrow*

William Hamilton (1704–54)

A. Busk ye, busk ye, my bonny bonny bride,
    Busk ye, busk ye, my winsome marrow,
  Busk ye, busk ye, my bonny bonny bride,

And think nae mair on the Braes of Yarrow.

B.   Where gat ye that bonny bonny bride?
       Where gat ye that winsome marrow?
A.   I gat her where I dare na weil be seen,
       Puing the birks on the Braes of Yarrow.

    Weep not, weep not, my bonny bonny bride,
       Weep not, weep not, my winsome marrow;
    Nor let thy heart lament to leive
       Puing the birks on the Braes of Yarrow.

B.   Why does she weep, thy bonny bonny bride?
       Why does she weep thy winsome marrow?
    And why dare ye nae mair weil be seen
       Puing the birks on the Braes of Yarrow?

A.   Lang maun she weep, lang maun she, maun she weep,
       Lang maun she weep with dule and sorrow;
    And lang maun I nae mair weil be seen
       Puing the birks on the Braes of Yarrow.

    For she has tint her luver, luver dear,
       Her luver dear, the cause of sorrow;
    And I hae slain the comliest swain
       That eir pu'd birks on the Braes of Yarrow.

    Why rins thy stream, O Yarrow, Yarrow, reid?
       Why on thy braes heard the voice of sorrow?
    And why yon melancholious weids
       Hung on the bonny birks of Yarrow?

    What's yonder floats on the rueful rueful flude?
       What's yonder floats?   O dule and sorrow!
    O 'tis he the comely swain I slew
       Upon the duleful Braes of Yarrow.

    Wash, O wash his wounds, his wounds in tears,
       His wounds in tears with dule and sorrow;
    And wrap his limbs in mourning weids,
       And lay him on the Braes of Yarrow.

> Then build, then build, ye sisters, sisters sad,
>   Ye sisters sad, his tomb with sorrow;
> And weep around in waeful wise
>   His hapless fate on the Braes of Yarrow.
>
> Curse ye, curse ye, his useless, useless shield,
>   My arm that wrought the deed of sorrow,
> The fatal spear that pierc'd his breast,
>   His comely breast on the Braes of Yarrow.
>
> Did I not warn thee, not to, not to luve?
>   And warn from fight? but to my sorrow
> Too rashly bauld a stronger arm
>   Thou mett'st, and fell'st on the Braes of Yarrow.
>
> Sweet smells the birk, green grows, green grows the grass,
>   Yellow on Yarrow's bank the gowan,
> Fair hangs the apple frae the rock,
>   Sweet the wave of Yarrow flowan.
>
> Flows Yarrow sweet? as sweet, as sweet flows Tweed,
>   As green its grass, its gowan as yellow,
> As sweet smells on its braes the birk,
>   The apple frae its rock as mellow.
>
> Fair was thy luve, fair fair indeed thy luve,
>   In flow'ry bands thou didst him fetter;
> Tho' he was fair, and well beluv'd again
>   Than me he never luv'd thee better.
>
> Busk ye, then, busk, my bonny bonny bride,
>   Busk ye, busk ye, my winsome marrow,
> Busk ye, and luve me on the banks of Tweed,
>   And think nae mair on the Braes of Yarrow.
>
> C. How can I busk a bonny bonny bride,
>   How can I busk a winsome marrow,
>   How luve him upon the banks of Tweed,
>   That slew my luve on the Braes of Yarrow?
>
>   O Yarrow fields, may never never rain,
>   Nor dew thy tender blossoms cover,

The Braes of Yarrow

For there was basely slain my luve,
    My luve, as he had not been a lover.

The boy put on his robes, his robes of green,
    His purple vest, 'twas my awn sewing:
Ah! wretched me! I little, little kenn'd
    He was in these to meet his ruin.

The boy took out his milk-white, milk-white steed,
    Unheedful of my dule and sorrow:
But ere the toofall of the night
    He lay a corps on the Braes of Yarrow.

Much I rejoyc'd that waeful waeful day;
    I sang, my voice the woods returning:
But lang ere night the spear was flown,
    That slew my luve, and left me mourning.

What can my barbarous barbarous father do,
    But with his cruel rage pursue me?
My luver's blood is on thy spear,
    How canst thou, barbarous man, then wooe me?

My happy sisters may be, may be proud
    With cruel, and ungentle scoffin',
May bid me seek on Yarrow's Braes
    My luver nailed in his coffin.

My brother Douglas may upbraid, upbraid,
    And strive with threatning words to muve me:
My luver's blood is on thy spear,
    How canst thou ever bid me luve thee?

Yes, yes, prepare the bed, the bed of luve,
    With bridal sheets my body cover,
Unbar, ye bridal maids, the door,
    Let in the expected husband lover.

But who the expected husband husband is?
    His hands, methinks, are bath'd in slaughter:
Ah me! what ghastly spectre's yon
    Comes in his pale shroud, bleeding after?

Pale as he is, here lay him, lay him down, 105
   O lay his cold head on my pillow;
Take aff, take aff these bridal weids,
   And crown my careful head with willow.

Pale tho' thou art, yet best, yet best beluv'd,
   O could my warmth to life restore thee! 110
Yet lye all night between my breists,
   No youth lay ever there before thee.

Pale, pale indeed, O luvely luvely youth,
   Forgive, forgive so foul a slaughter,
And lye all night between my breists, 115
   No youth shall ever lye there after.

A. Return, return, O mournful, mournful bride,
   Return and dry thy useless sorrow:
Thy luver heeds none of thy sighs,
   He lyes a corps in the Braes of Yarrow. 120

1723

4 Margaret's Ghost

David Mallet (?1705–65)

'Twas at the silent solemn hour,
   When night and morning meet;
In glided Margaret's grimly ghost,
   And stood at William's feet.

Her face was like an April morn, 5
   Clad in a wintry cloud:
And clay-cold was her lily hand,
   That held her sable shrowd.

So shall the fairest face appear,

When youth and years are flown:
Such is the robe that kings must wear,
    When death has reft their crown.

Her bloom was like the springing flower,
    That sips the silver dew;
The rose was budded in her cheek,
    Just opening to the view.

But love had, like the canker worm,
    Consum'd her early prime:
The rose grew pale, and left her cheek;
    She dy'd before her time.

'Awake!' she cry'd, 'thy true love calls,
    Come from her midnight grave;
Now let thy pity hear the maid,
    Thy love refus'd to save.

This is the dark and dreary hour,
    When injur'd ghosts complain;
Now yawning graves give up their dead,
    To haunt the faithless swain.

Bethink thee, William, of thy fault,
    Thy pledge, and broken oath:
And give me back my maiden vow,
    And give me back my troth.

Why did you promise love to me,
    And not that promise keep?
Why did you swear mine eyes were bright,
    Yet leave those eyes to weep?

How could you say my face was fair,
    And yet that face forsake?
How could you win my virgin heart,
    Yet leave that heart to break?

Why did you say my lip was sweet,
    And made the scarlet pale?
And why did I, young witless maid,

Believe the flattering tale?

That face, alas! no more is fair;
   These lips no longer red:
Dark are my eyes, now clos'd in death,
   And every charm is fled.

The hungry worm my sister is;
   This winding-sheet I wear:
And cold and weary lasts our night,
   Till that last morn appear.

But hark! the cock has warn'd me hence!
   A long and last adieu!
Come see, false man, how low she lies,
   Who dy'd for love of you.'

The lark sung loud; the morning smil'd,
   With beams of rosy red:
Pale William shook in ev'ry limb,
   And raving left his bed.

He hyed him to the fatal place,
   Where Margaret's body lay;
And stretch'd him on the grass-green turf,
   That wrapt her breathless clay.

And thrice he call'd on Margaret's name,
   And thrice he wept full sore:
Then laid his cheek to her cold grave,
   And word spake never more.

1723

5 Lucy and Colin

Thomas Tickell (1685–1740)

Of Leinster, fam'd for maidens fair,
    Bright Lucy was the grace;
Nor ere did Liffy's limpid stream
    Reflect so fair a face.

Till luckless love, and pining care
    Impair'd her rosy hue,
Her coral lip, and damask cheek,
    And eyes of glossy blue.

Oh! have you seen a lily pale,
    When beating rains descend?
So droop'd the slow-consuming maid;
    Her life now near its end.

By Lucy warn'd, of flattering swains,
    Take heed, ye easy fair:
Of vengeance due to broken vows,
    Ye perjured swains, beware.

Three times, all in the dead of night,
    A bell was heard to ring;
And at her window, shrieking thrice,
    The raven flap'd his wing.

Too well the love-lorn maiden knew
    That solemn boding sound;
And thus, in dying words, bespoke
    The virgins weeping round.

'I hear a voice, you cannot hear,
    Which says, I must not stay:
I see a hand, you cannot see,
    Which beckons me away.

By a false heart, and broken vows,
    In early youth I die.

Am I to blame because his bride
   Is thrice as rich as I?

Ah Colin! give not her thy vows;
   Vows due to me alone:
Nor thou, fond maid, receive his kiss,
   Nor think him all thy own.

To-morrow in the church to wed,
   Impatient, both prepare;
But know, fond maid, and know, false man,
   That Lucy will be there.

Then bear my corse; ye comrades, bear,
   The bridegroom blithe to meet;
He in his wedding-trim so gay,
   I in my winding-sheet.'

She spoke, she dy'd; — her corse was borne,
   The bridegroom blithe to meet;
He in his wedding trim so gay,
   She in her winding-sheet.

Then what were perjur'd Colin's thoughts?
   How were those nuptials kept?
The bride-men flock'd round Lucy dead,
   And all the village wept.

Confusion, shame, remorse, despair
   At once his bosom swell:
The damps of death bedew'd his brow,
   He shook, he groan'd, he fell.

From the vain bride (ah bride no more!)
   The varying crimson fled,
When, stretch'd before her rival's corse,
   She saw her husband dead.

Then to his Lucy's new-made grave,
   Convey'd by trembling swains,
One mould with her, beneath one sod,
   For ever now remains.

Oft at their grave the constant hind 65
   And plighted maid are seen;
With garlands gay, and true-love knots
   They deck the sacred green.

But, swain forsworn, whoe'er thou art,
   This hallow'd spot forbear; 70
Remember Colin's dreadful fate,
   And fear to meet him there.

1725

6   *Admiral Hosier's Ghost*

Richard Glover (1712–85)

As near Porto-Bello lying
   On the gently swelling flood,
At midnight with streamers flying
   Our triumphant navy rode;

There while Vernon sate all-glorious 5
   From the Spaniards' late defeat:
And his crews, with shouts victorious,
   Drank success to England's fleet:

On a sudden shrilly sounding,
   Hideous yells and shrieks were heard; 10
Then each heart with fear confounding,
   A sad troop of ghosts appear'd,
All in dreary hammocks shrouded,
   Which for winding-sheets they wore,
And with looks by sorrow clouded 15
   Frowning on that hostile shore.

On them gleam'd the moon's wan lustre,
   When the shade of Hosier brave

His pale bands was seen to muster
    Rising from their watry grave. 20
O'er the glimmering wave he hy'd him,
    Where the Burford rear'd her sail,
With three thousand ghosts beside him,
    And in groans did Vernon hail.

'Heed, oh! heed our fatal story, 25
    I am Hosier's injur'd ghost,
You, who now have purchas'd glory,
    At this place where I was lost!
Tho' in Porto-Bello's ruin
    You now triumph free from fears, 30
When you think on our undoing,
    You will mix your joy with tears.

See these mournful spectres sweeping
    Ghastly o'er this hated wave,
Whose wan cheeks are stain'd with weeping; 35
    These were English captains brave.
Mark those numbers pale and horrid,
    Those were once my sailors bold:
Lo! each hangs his drooping forehead,
    While his dismal tale is told. 40

I, by twenty sail attended,
    Did this Spanish town affright;
Nothing then its wealth defended
    But my orders not to fight.
Oh! that in this rolling ocean 45
    I had cast them with disdain,
And obey'd my heart's warm motion
    To have quell'd the pride of Spain!

For resistance I could fear none,
    But with twenty ships had done 50
What thou, brave and happy Vernon,
    Hast atchiev'd with six alone.
Then the Bastimentos never
    Had our foul dishonour seen,
Nor the sea the sad receiver 55
    Of this gallant train had been.

Thus, like thee, proud Spain dismaying,
    And her galleons leading home,
Though condemn'd for disobeying,
    I had met a traitor's doom,
To have fallen, my country crying,
    He has play'd an English part!
Had been better far than dying
    Of a griev'd and broken heart.

Unrepining at thy glory,
    Thy successful arms we hail;
But remember our sad story,
    And let Hosier's wrongs prevail.
Sent in this foul clime to languish,
    Think what thousands fell in vain,
Wasted with disease and anguish,
    Not in glorious battle slain.

Hence, with all my train attending
    From their oozy tombs below,
Thro' the hoary foam ascending,
    Here I feed my constant woe:
Here the Bastimentos viewing,
    We recal our shameful doom,
And our plaintive cries renewing,
    Wander thro' the midnight gloom.

O'er these waves for ever mourning
    Shall we roam depriv'd of rest,
If to Britain's shores returning
    You neglect my just request;
After this proud foe subduing,
    When your patriot friends you see,
Think on vengeance for my ruin,
    And for England sham'd in me.'

1739

7   *Jemmy Dawson*

William Shenstone (1714–63)

1. Come listen to my mournful tale,
   Ye tender hearts and lovers dear!
   Nor will you scorn to heave a sigh,
   Nor need you blush to shed a tear.

2. And thou dear Kitty! peerless maid!
   Do thou a pensive ear incline;
   For thou canst weep at every woe,
   And pity every plaint — but mine.

3. Young Dawson was a gallant boy,
   A brighter never trod the plain;
   And well he loved one charming maid,
   And dearly was he loved again.

4. One tender maid, she loved him dear;
   Of gentle blood the damsel came;
   And faultless was her beauteous form,
   And spotless was her virgin fame.

5. But curse on party's hateful strife,
   That led the favour'd youth astray;
   The day the rebel clans appear'd —
   O had he never seen that day!

6. Their colours and their sash he wore,
   And in the fatal dress was found;
   And now he must that death endure
   Which gives the brave the keenest wound.

7. How pale was then his true love's cheek,
   When Jemmy's sentence reach'd her ear!
   For never yet did Alpine snows
   So pale, or yet so chill appear.

8. With faltering voice she, weeping, said,
   "O Dawson! monarch of my heart!

Think not thy death shall end our loves,
For thou and I will never part.

9   "Yet might sweet mercy find a place,
And bring relief to Jemmy's woes,
O George! without a prayer for thee,
My orisons should never close.

10   "The gracious prince that gave him life,
Would crown a never-dying flame;
And every tender babe I bore
Should learn to lisp the giver's name.

11   "But though he should be dragg'd in scorn
To yonder ignominious tree;
He shall not want one constant friend
To share the cruel Fates' decree."

12   Oh! then her mourning coach was call'd;
The sledge moved slowly on before;
Though borne in a triumphal car,
She had not loved her favourite more.

13   She follow'd him, prepared to view
The terrible behests of law;
And the last scene of Jemmy's woes,
With calm and steadfast eye she saw.

14   Distorted was that blooming face,
Which she had fondly loved so long;
And stifled was that tuneful breath,
Which in her praise had sweetly sung:

15   And sever'd was that beauteous neck,
Round which her arms had fondly closed;
And mangled was that beauteous breast,
On which her lovesick head reposed:

16   And ravish'd was that constant heart,
She did to every heart prefer;
For though it could its king forget,
'Twas true and loyal still to her.

17 Amid those unrelenting flames   65
    She bore this constant heart to see;
    But when 'twas moulder'd into dust,
    "Yet, yet," she cried, "I follow thee.

18 "My death, my death alone can show
    The pure, the lasting love I bore: 70
    Accept, O Heaven! of woes like ours,
    And let us, let us weep no more."

19 The dismal scene was o'er and past,
    The lover's mournful hearse retired;
    The maid drew back her languid head,   75
    And, sighing forth his name, expired.

20 Though justice ever must prevail,
    The tear my Kitty sheds is due;
    For seldom shall she hear a tale
    So sad, so tender, yet so true.   80

1746

8 *The Hermit; or, Edwin and Angelina*

Oliver Goldsmith (1728–74)

I.
"Turn, gentle Hermit of the dale,
   And guide my lonely way,
To where yon taper cheers the vale
   With hospitable ray.

II.
"For here forlorn and lost I tread,   5
   With fainting steps and slow;
Where wilds, immeasurably spread,
   Seem length'ning as I go."

III.

"Forbear, my son," the Hermit cries,
    "To tempt the dang'rous gloom;
For yonder faithless phantom flies
    To lure thee to thy doom.

IV.

"Here to the houseless child of want
    My door is open still;
And though my portion is but scant,
    I give it with good will.

V.

"Then turn to-night, and freely share
    Whate'er my cell bestows;
My rushy couch and frugal fare,
    My blessing and repose.

VI.

"No flocks that range the valley free
    To slaughter I condemn;
Taught by that Power that pities me,
    I learn to pity them:

VII.

"But from the mountain's grassy side
    A guiltless feast I bring;
A scrip with herbs and fruits supplied,
    And water from the spring.

VIII.

"Then, pilgrim, turn, thy cares forego;
    All earth-born cares are wrong;
Man wants but little here below,
    Nor wants that little long."

IX.

Soft as the dew from Heaven descends,
    His gentle accents fell:
The modest stranger lowly bends,
    And follows to the cell.

X.

Far in a wilderness obscure
   The lonely mansion lay,
A refuge to the neighb'ring poor
   And strangers led astray.   40

XI.

No stores beneath its humble thatch
   Required a master's care;
The wicket, op'ning with a latch,
   Receiv'd the harmless pair.

XII.

And now, when busy crowds retire   45
   To take their ev'ning rest,
The Hermit trimm'd his little fire,
   And cheer'd his pensive guest:

XIII.

And spread his vegetable store,
   And gayly press'd, and smil'd;   50
And skill'd in legendary lore,
   The ling'ring hours beguil'd.

XIV.

Around in sympathetic mirth
   Its tricks the kitten tries,
The cricket chirrups in the hearth,   55
   The crackling faggot flies.

XV.

But nothing could a charm impart
   To sooth the stranger's woe;
For grief was heavy at his heart,
   And tears began to flow.   60

XVI.

His rising cares the Hermit spied,
   With answ'ring care opprest:
"And whence, unhappy youth," he cried,
   "The sorrows of thy breast?

XVII.

"From better habitations spurn'd,
    Reluctant dost thou rove?
Or grieve for friendship unreturn'd,
    Or unregarded love?

XVIII.

"Alas! the joys that fortune brings
    Are trifling, and decay;
And those who prize the paltry things,
    More trifling still than they.

XIX.

"And what is friendship but a name,
    A charm that lulls to sleep;
A shade that follows wealth or fame,
    But leaves the wretch to weep?

XX.

"And love is still an emptier sound,
    The modern fair-one's jest;
On earth unseen, or only found
    To warm the turtle's nest.

XXI.

"For shame, fond youth, thy sorrows hush,
    And spurn the sex," he said:
But while he spoke, a rising blush
    His love-lorn guest betray'd.

XXII.

Surpris'd he sees new beauties rise,
    Swift mantling to the view;
Like colours o'er the morning skies,
    As bright, as transient too.

XXIII.

The bashful look, the rising breast,
    Alternate spread alarms:
The lovely stranger stands confest
    A maid in all her charms.

XXIV.

"And ah! forgive a stranger rude,
   A wretch forlorn," she cried;
"Whose feet unhallow'd thus intrude
   Where Heaven and you reside.

XXV.

"But let a maid thy pity share,
   Whom love has taught to stray;
Who seeks for rest, but finds despair
   Companion of her way.

XXVI.

"My father liv'd beside the Tyne,
   A wealthy lord was he;
And all his wealth was mark'd as mine,
   He had but only me.

XXVII.

"To win me from his tender arms,
   Unnumber'd suitors came;
Who prais'd me for imputed charms,
   And felt, or feign'd a flame.

XXVIII.

"Each hour a mercenary crowd
   With richest proffers strove;
Among the rest young Edwin bow'd,
   But never talk'd of love.

XXIX.

"In humble, simplest habit clad,
   No wealth nor power had he;
Wisdom and worth were all he had,
   But these were all to me.

XXX.

"And when, beside me in the dale,
   He carol'd lays of love,
His breath lent fragrance to the gale,
   And music to the grove.

XXXI.

"The blossom opening to the day,
    The dews of Heaven refin'd,
Could nought of purity display
    To emulate his mind.

XXXII.

"The dew, the blossom on the tree,
    With charms inconstant shine;
Their charms were his, but wo to me,
    Their constancy was mine.

XXXIII.

"For still I tried each fickle art,
    Importunate and vain;
And while his passion touch'd my heart,
    I triumph'd in his pain.

XXXIV.

"Till quite dejected with my scorn,
    He left me to my pride;
And sought a solitude forlorn,
    In secret, where he died.

XXXV.

"But mine the sorrow, mine the fault,
    And well my life shall pay;
I'll seek the solitude he sought,
    And stretch me where he lay.

XXXVI.

"And there forlorn, despairing, hid,
    I'll lay me down and die;
'Twas so for me that Edwin did,
    And so for him will I."

XXXVII.

"Forbid it, Heaven!" the Hermit cried,
    And clasp'd her to his breast:
The wond'ring fair one turn'd to chide —
    'Twas Edwin's self that prest.

XXXVIII.
"Turn, Angelina, ever dear!
   My charmer, turn to see 150
Thy own, thy long-lost Edwin here,
   Restor'd to love and thee.

XXXIX.
"Thus let me hold thee to my heart,
   And every care resign:
And shall we never, never part, 155
   My life — my all that's mine?

XL.
No, never from this hour to part,
   We'll live and love so true;
The sigh that rends thy constant heart,
   Shall break thy Edwin's too." 160

c. 1761

9   The Friar of Orders Gray

Thomas Percy (1729–1811)

It was a friar of orders gray
   Walkt forth to tell his beades;
And he met with a lady faire
   Clad in a pilgrime's weedes.

'Now Christ thee save, thou reverend friar, 5
   I pray thee tell to me,
If ever at yon holy shrine
   My true love thou didst see.'

'And how should I know your true love
   From many another one?' 10
'O, by his cockle hat, and staff,

And by his sandal shoone.

But chiefly by his face and mien,
    That were so fair to view;
His flaxen locks that sweetly curl'd,
    And eyne of lovely blue.'

'O, lady, he is dead and gone!
    Lady, he's dead and gone!
And at his head a green grass turfe,
    And at his heels a stone.

Within these holy cloysters long
    He languisht, and he dyed,
Lamenting of a ladyes love,
    And 'playning of her pride.

Here bore him barefac'd on his bier
    Six proper youths and tall,
And many a tear bedew'd his grave
    Within yon kirk-yard wall.'

'And art thou dead, thou gentle youth!
    And art thou dead and gone!
And didst thou dye for love of me!
    Break, cruel heart of stone!'

'O, weep not, lady, weep not soe;
    Some ghostly comfort seek:
Let not vain sorrow rive thy heart,
    Ne teares bedew thy cheek.'

'O, do not, do not, holy friar,
    My sorrow now reprove;
For I have lost the sweetest youth,
    That e'er wan ladyes love.

And nowe, alas! for thy sad losse,
    I'll evermore weep and sigh;
For thee I only wisht to live,
    For thee I wish to dye.'

'Weep no more, lady, weep no more,
   Thy sorrowe is in vaine:
For violets pluckt the sweetest showers
   Will ne'er make grow againe.

Our joys as winged dreams doe flye,
   Why then should sorrow last?
Since grief but aggravates thy losse,
   Grieve not for what is past.'

'O, say not soe, thou holy friar;
   I pray thee, say not soe:
For since my true-love dyed for mee,
   'Tis meet my tears should flow.

And will he ne'er come again?
   Will he ne'er come again?
Ah! no, he is dead and laid in his grave,
   For ever to remain.

His cheek was redder than the rose;
   The comliest youth was he!
But he is dead and laid in his grave:
   Alas, and woe is me!'

'Sigh no more, lady, sigh no more,
   Men were deceivers ever:
One foot on sea and one on land,
   To one thing constant never.

Hadst thou been fond, he had been false,
   And left thee sad and heavy;
For young men ever were fickle found,
   Since summer trees were leafy.'

'Now say not so, thou holy friar,
   I pray thee say not soe;
My love he had the truest heart:
   O, he was ever true!

And art thou dead, thou much-lov'd youth,
   And didst thou dye for mee?

Then farewell home; for ever-more
    A pilgrim I will bee.

But first upon my true-love's grave
    My weary limbs I'll lay,
And thrice I'll kiss the green-grass turf,
    That wraps his breathless clay.'

'Yet stay, fair lady; rest awhile
    Beneath this cloyster wall:
See through the hawthorn blows the cold wind,
    And drizzly rain doth fall.'

'O, stay me not, thou holy friar;
    O stay me not, I pray;
No drizzly rain that falls on me,
    Can wash my fault away.'

'Yet stay, fair lady, turn again,
    And dry those pearly tears;
For see, beneath this gown of gray
    Thy owne true-love appears.

Here forc'd by grief, and hopeless love,
    These holy weeds I sought;
And here amid these lonely walls
    To end my days I thought.

But haply, for my year of grace
    Is not yet past away,
Might I still hope to win thy love,
    No longer would I stay.'

'Now farewell grief, and welcome joy
    Once more unto my heart;
For since I have found thee, lovely youth,
    We never more will part.'

1765

10 Auld Robin Gray

Lady Anne Lindsay (1750–1825)

When the sheep are in the fauld, when the cows come hame,
When a' the weary world to quiet rest are gane,
The woes of my heart fa' in showers frae my ee,
Unken'd by my gudeman, who soundly sleeps by me.

Young Jamie loo'd me weel, and sought me for his bride;   5
But saving ae crown-piece, he'd naething else beside.
To make the crown a pound, my Jamie gaed to sea;
And the crown and the pound, oh! they were baith for me!

Before he had been gane a twelvemonth and a day,
My father brak his arm, our cow was stown away;   10
My mither she fell sick — my Jamie was at sea —
And auld Robin Gray, oh! he came a-courting me.

My father cou'dna work, my mother cou'dna spin;
I toil'd day and night, but their bread I cou'dna win;
And Rob maintain'd them baith, and, wi' tears in his ee,   15
Said, 'Jenny, oh! for their sakes, will you marry me?'

My heart it said na, and I look'd for Jamie back;
But hard blew the winds, and his ship was a wrack:
His ship it was a wrack!   Why didna Jenny dee?
Or, wherefore am I spared to cry out, Woe is me!   20

My father argued sair — my mother didna speak,
But she look'd in my face till my heart was like to break:
They gied him my hand, but my heart was in the sea;
And so auld Robin Gray, he was gudeman to me.

I hadna been his wife, a week but only four,   25
When mournfu' as I sat on the stane at my door,
I saw my Jamie's ghaist — I cou'dna think it he,
Till he said, 'I'm come hame, my love, to marry thee!'

O sair, sair did we greet, and mickle say of a';
Ae kiss we took, nae mair — I bad him gang awa.   30

I wish that I were dead, but I'm no like to dee;
For O, I am but young to cry out, Woe is me!

I gang like a ghaist, and I carena much to spin;
I darena think o' Jamie, for that wad be a sin.
But I will do my best a gude wife aye to be, 35
For auld Robin Gray, oh! he is sae kind to me.

1771

11 Bristowe Tragedie: or the Dethe of Syr Charles Bawdin

Thomas Chatterton (1752–70)

The featherd songster chaunticleer
   Han wounde hys bugle horne,
And tolde the earlie villager
   The commynge of the morne:

Kynge EDWARDE sawe the ruddie streakes 5
   Of lyghte eclypse the greie;
And herde the raven's crokynge throte
   Proclayme the fated daie.

"Thou'rt ryght," quod hee, "for, by the Godde
   "That syttes enthron'd on hyghe! 10
"CHARLES BAWDIN, and hys fellowes twaine,
   "To-daie shall surelie die."

Thenne wythe a jugge of nappy ale
   Hys Knyghtes dydd onne hymm waite;
"Goe tell the traytour, thatt to-daie 15
   "Hee leaves thys mortall state."

Syr CANTERLONE thenne bendedd lowe,
   Wythe harte brymm-fulle of woe;

Hee journey'd to the castle-gate,
   And to Syr CHARLES dydd goe. 20

Butt whenne hee came, hys children twaine,
   And eke hys lovynge wyfe,
Wythe brinie tears dydd wett the floore,
   For goode Syr CHARLESES lyfe.

"O goode Syr CHARLES!" sayd CANTERLONE, 25
   "Badde tydyngs I doe brynge."
"Speke boldlie, manne," sayd brave Syr CHARLES,
   "Whatte says thie traytor kynge?"

"I greeve to telle, before yonne sonne
   "Does fromme the welkinn flye, 30
"Hee hath uponne hys honour sworne,
   "Thatt thou shalt surelie die."

"Wee all must die," quod brave Syr CHARLES;
   "Of thatte I'm not affearde;
"Whatte bootes to lyve a little space? 35
   "Thanke JESU, I'm prepar'd:

"Butt telle thye kynge, for myne hee's not,
   "I'de sooner die to-daie
"Thanne lyve hys slave, as manie are,
   "Tho' I shoulde lyve for aie." 40

Thenne CANTERLONE hee dydd goe out,
   To telle the maior straite
To gett all thynges ynne reddyness
   For goode Syr CHARLESES fate.

Thenne Maisterr CANYNGE saughte the kynge, 45
   And felle down onne hys knee;
"I'm come," quod hee, "unto your grace
   "To move your clemencye."

Thenne quod the kynge, "Youre tale speke out,
   "You have been much oure friende; 50
"Whatever youre request may bee,
   "Wee wylle to ytte attende."

"My nobile leige! alle my request
   "Ys for a nobile knyghte,
"Who, tho' may hap hee has donne wronge,   55
   "He thoghte ytte stylle was ryghte:

"Hee has a spouse and children twaine,
   "Alle rewyn'd are for aie;
"Yff thatt you are resolv'd to lett
   "CHARLES BAWDIN die to-daie."   60

"Speke nott of such a traytour vile,"
   The kynge ynne furie sayde;
"Before the evening starre doth sheene,
   "BAWDIN shall loose hys hedde:

"Justice does loudlie for hym calle,   65
   "And hee shalle have hys meede:
"Speke, Maister CANYNGE!   Whatte thynge else
   "Att present doe you neede?"

"My nobile leige!" goode CANYNGE sayde,
   "Leave justice to our Godde,   70
"And laye the yronne rule asyde;
   "Be thyne the olyve rodde.

"Was Godde to serche our hertes and reines,
   "The best were synners grete;
"CHRIST's vycarr only knowes ne synne,   75
   "Ynne alle thys mortall state.

"Lett mercie rule thyne infante reigne,
   "'Twylle faste thye crowne fulle sure;
"From race to race thy familie
   "Alle sov'reigns shall endure: 80

"But yff wythe bloode and slaughter thou
   "Beginne thy infante reigne,
"Thy crowne uponne thy childrennes brows
   "Wylle never long remayne."

"CANYNGE, awaie! thys traytour vile   85
   "Has scorn'd my power and mee;

"Howe canst thou thenne for such a manne
"Intreate my clemencye?"

"My nobile leige! the trulie brave
"Wylle val'rous actions prize, 90
"Respect a brave and nobile mynde,
"Altho' ynne enemies."

"Canynge, awaie! By Godde ynne Heav'n
"Thatt dydd mee beinge gyve,
"I wylle nott taste a bitt of breade 95
"Whilst thys Syr Charles dothe lyve.

"By Marie, and alle Seinctes ynne Heav'n,
"Thys sunne shall be hys laste."
Thenne Canynge dropt a brinie teare,
And from the presence paste. 100

Wyth herte brymm-fulle of gnawynge grief,
Hee to Syr Charles dydd goe,
And satt hymm downe uponne a stoole,
And teares beganne to flowe.

"Wee all must die," quod brave Syr Charles; 105
"Whatte bootes ytte howe or whenne;
"Dethe ys the sure, the certaine fate
"Of all wee mortall menne.

"Saye why, my friend, thie honest soul
"Runns overr att thyne eye; 110
"Is ytte for my most welcome doome
"Thatt thou dost child-lyke crye?"

Quod godlie Canynge, "I doe weepe,
"Thatt thou so soone must dye,
"And leave thy sonnes and helpless wyfe; 115
"'Tys thys thatt wettes myne eye."

"Thenne drie the tears thatt out thyne eye
"From godlie fountaines sprynge;
"Dethe I despise, and alle the power
"Of Edwarde, traytor kynge. 120

"Whan throgh the tyrant's welcom means
  "I shall resigne my lyfe,
"The Godde I serve wylle soone provyde
  "For bothe mye sonnes and wyfe.

"Before I sawe the lyghtsome sunne,   125
  "Thys was appointed mee;
"Shall mortal manne repyne or grudge
  "Whatt Godde ordeynes to bee?

"Howe oft ynne battaile have I stoode,
  "Whan thousands dy'd arounde;   130
"Whan smokynge streemes of crimson bloode
  "Imbrew'd the fatten'd grounde:

"How dydd I knowe thatt ev'ry darte,
  "Thatt cutte the airie waie,
"Myghte nott fynde passage toe my harte,   135
  "And close myne eyes for aie?

"And shall I nowe, forr feere of dethe,
  "Looke wanne and bee dysmayde?
"Ne! fromm my herte flie childyshe feere,
  "Bee alle the manne display'd.   140

"Ah, goddelyke HENRIE! Godde forefende,
  "And guarde thee and thye sonne,
"Yff 'tis hys wylle; but yff 'tis nott,
  "Why thenne hys wylle bee donne.

"My honest friende, my faulte has beene   145
  "To serve Godde and mye prynce;
"And thatt I no tyme-server am,
  "My dethe wylle soone convynce.

"Ynne Londonne citye was I borne,
  "Of parents of grete note;   150
"My fadre dydd a nobile armes
  "Emblazon onne hys cote:

"I make ne doubte butt hee ys gone
  "Where soone I hope to goe;

"Where wee for ever shall bee blest,   155
    "From oute the reech of woe:

"Hee taughte mee justice and the laws
    "Wyth pitie to unite;
"And eke hee taughte mee howe to knowe
    "The wronge cause fromm the ryghte: 160

"Hee taughte mee wythe a prudent hande
    "To feede the hungrie poore,
"Ne lett mye sarvants dryve awaie
    "The hungrie fromme my doore:

"And none can saye, butt alle mye lyfe   165
    "I have hys wordyes kept;
"And summ'd the actyonns of the daie
    "Eche nyghte before I slept.

"I have a spouse, goe aske of her,
    "Yff I defyl'd her bedde?   170
"I have a kynge, and none can laie
    "Blacke treason onne my hedde.

"Ynne Lent, and onne the holie eve,
    "Fromm fleshe I dydd refrayne;
"Whie should I thenne appeare dismay'd   175
    "To leave thys worlde of payne?

"Ne! hapless Henrie!   I rejoyce,
    "I shalle ne see thye dethe;
"Moste willynglie ynne thye just cause
    "Doe I resign my brethe.   180

"Oh, fickle people! rewyn'd londe!
    "Thou wylt kenne peace ne moe;
"Whyle Richard's sonnes exalt themselves,
    "Thye brookes wythe bloude wylle flowe.

"Saie, were ye tyr'd of godlie peace,   185
    "And godlie Henrie's reigne,
"Thatt you dydd choppe youre easie daies
    "For those of bloude and peyne?

"Whatte tho' I onne a sledde bee drawne,
    "And mangled by a hynde,
"I doe defye the traytor's pow'r,
    "Hee can ne harm my mynde;

"Whatte tho', uphoisted onne a pole,
    "Mye lymbes shall rotte ynne ayre,
"And ne ryche monument of brasse
    "CHARLES BAWDIN'S name shall bear;

"Yett ynne the holie booke above,
    "Whyche tyme can't eate awaie,
"There wythe the sarvants of the Lorde
    "Mye name shall lyve for aie.

"Thenne welcome dethe! for lyfe eterne
    "I leave thys mortall lyfe:
"Farewell, vayne worlde, and alle that's deare,
    "Mye sonnes and lovynge wyfe!

"Nowe dethe as welcome to mee comes,
    "As e'er the moneth of Maie;
"Nor woulde I even wyshe to lyve,
    "Wyth my dere wyfe to staie."

Quod CANYNGE, "'Tys a goodlie thynge
    "To bee prepar'd to die;
"And from thys world of peyne and grefe
    "To Godde ynne Heav'n to flie."

And nowe the bell beganne to tolle,
    And claryonnes to sounde;
Syr CHARLES hee herde the horses feete
    A prauncyng onne the grounde:

And just before the officers,
    His lovynge wyfe came ynne,
Weepynge unfeigned teeres of woe,
    Wythe loude and dysmalle dynne.

"Sweet FLORENCE! nowe I praie forbere,
    "Ynne quiet lett mee die;

"Praie Godde, thatt ev'ry Christian soule
    "Maye looke onne dethe as I.

"Sweet FLORENCE! why these brinie teeres?   225
    "Theye washe my soule awaie,
"And almost make mee wyshe for lyfe,
    "Wyth thee, sweete dame, to staie.

"'Tys butt a journie I shalle goe
    "Untoe the lande of blysse;   230
"Nowe, as a proofe of husbande's love,
    "Receive thys holie kysse."

Thenne FLORENCE, fault'ring ynne her saie,
    Tremblynge these wordyes spoke,
"Ah, cruele EDWARDE! bloudie kynge!   235
    "My herte ys welle nyghe broke:

"Ah, sweete Syr CHARLES! why wylt thou goe,
    "Wythoute thye lovynge wyfe?
"The cruelle axe thatt cuttes thye necke,
    "Ytte eke shall ende mye lyfe."   240

And nowe the officers came ynne
    To brynge Syr CHARLES awaie,
Whoe turnedd toe his lovynge wyfe,
    And thus toe her dydd saie:

"I goe to lyfe, and nott to dethe;   245
    "Truste thou ynne Godde above,
"And teache thye sonnes to feare the Lorde,
    "And ynne theyre hertes hym love:

"Teache them to runne the nobile race
    "Thatt I theyre fader runne: 250
"FLORENCE! shou'd dethe thee take — adieu!
    "Yee officers, leade onne."

Thenne FLORENCE rav'd as anie madde,
    And dydd her tresses tere;
"Oh! staie, mye husbande! lorde! and lyfe!" —   255
    Syr CHARLES thenne dropt a teare.

'Tyll tyredd oute wythe ravynge loud,
    Shee fellen onne the flore;
Syr CHARLES exerted alle hys myghte,
    And march'd fromm oute the dore. 260

Uponne a sledde hee mounted thenne,
    Wythe lookes fulle brave and swete;
Lookes, thatt enshone ne moe concern
    Thanne anie ynne the strete.

Before hym went the council-menne, 265
    Ynne scarlett robes and golde,
And tassils spanglynge ynne the sunne,
    Muche glorious to beholde:

The Freers of Seincte AUGUSTYNE next
    Appeared to the syghte, 270
Alle cladd ynne homelie russett weedes,
    Of godlie monkysh plyghte:

Ynne diffraunt partes a godlie psaume
    Moste sweetlie theye dydd chaunt;
Behynde theyre backes syx mynstrelles came, 275
    Who tun'd the strunge bataunt.

Thenne fyve-and-twentye archers came;
    Echone the bowe dydd bende,
From rescue of kynge HENRIES friends
    Syr CHARLES forr to defend. 280

Bolde as a lyon came Syr CHARLES,
    Drawne onne a clothe-layde sledde,
Bye two blacke stedes ynne trappynges white,
    Wyth plumes uponne theyre hedde:

Behynde hym fyve-and-twentye moe 285
    Of archers stronge and stoute,
Wyth bended bowe echone ynne hande,
    Marched ynne goodlie route:

Seincte JAMESES Freers marched next,
    Echone hys parte dyd chaunt; 290

Behynde theyre backs syx mynstrelles came,
   Who tun'd the strunge bataunt:

Thenne came the maior and eldermenne,
   Ynne clothe of scarlett deck't;
And theyre attendyng menne echone, 295
   Lyke Easterne princes trickt:

And after them, a multitude
   Of citizenns dydd thronge;
The wyndowes were alle fulle of heddes,
   As hee dydd passe alonge. 300

And whenne hee came to the hyghe crosse,
   Syr CHARLES dydd turne and saie,
"O Thou, thatt savest manne fromme synne,
   "Washe mye soule clean thys daie!"

Att the grete mynsterr wyndowe sat 305
   The kynge ynne myckle state,
To see CHARLES BAWDIN goe alonge
   To hys most welcom fate.

Soone as the sledde drewe nyghe enowe,
   Thatt EDWARDE hee myghte heare, 310
The brave Syr CHARLES hee dydd stande uppe,
   And thus hys wordes declare:

"Thou seest mee, EDWARDE! traytour vile!
   "Expos'd to infamie;
"Butt bee assur'd, disloyall manne! 315
   "I'm greaterr nowe thanne thee.

"Bye foule proceedyngs, murdre, bloude,
   "Thou wearest nowe a crowne;
"And hast appoynted mee to dye,
   "By power nott thyne owne. 320

"Thou thynkest I shall dye to-daie;
   "I have beene dede 'till nowe,
"And soone shall lyve to weare a crowne
   "For aie uponne my browe:

"Whylst thou, perhapps, for som few yeares, 325
    "Shalt rule thys fickle lande,
"To lett them knowe howe wyde the rule
    "'Twixt kynge and tyrant hande:

"Thye pow'r unjust, thou traytour slave!
    "Shall falle onne thye owne hedde"— 330
Fromm out of hearyng of the kynge
    Departed thenne the sledde.

Kynge Edwarde's soule rush'd to hys face,
    Hee turn'd hys hedde awaie,
And to hys broder Gloucester 335
    Hee thus dydd speke and saie:

"To hym that soe-much-dreaded dethe
    "Ne ghastlie terrors brynge,
"Beholde the manne! hee spake the truthe,
    "Hee's greater thanne a kynge!" 340

"Soe lett hym die!"   Duke Richard sayde;
    "And maye echone oure foes
"Bende downe theyre neckes to bloudie axe,
    "And feede the carryon crowes."

And nowe the horses gentlie drewe 345
    Syr Charles uppe the hyghe hylle;
The axe dydd glysterr ynne the sunne,
    Hys pretious bloude to spylle.

Syrr Charles dydd uppe the scaffold goe,
    As uppe a gilded carre 350
Of victorye, bye val'rous chiefs
    Gayn'd ynne the bloudie warre:

And to the people hee dydd saie,
    "Beholde you see mee dye,
"For servynge loyally mye kynge, 355
    "Mye kynge most rightfullie.

"As longe as Edwarde rules thys lande,
    "Ne quiet you wylle knowe;

"Youre sonnes and husbandes shalle bee slayne,
   "And brookes wythe bloude shalle flowe. 360

"You leave youre goode and lawfulle kynge,
   "Whenne ynne adversitye;
"Lyke mee, untoe the true cause stycke,
   "And for the true cause dye."

Thenne hee, wyth preestes, uponne hys knees, 365
   A pray'r to Godde dydd make,
Beseechynge hym unto hymselfe
   Hys partynge soule to take.

Thenne, kneelynge downe, hee layd hys hedde
   Most seemlie onne the blocke; 370
Whyche fromme hys bodie fayre at once
   The able heddes-manne stroke:

And oute the bloude beganne to flowe,
   And rounde the scaffolde twyne;
And teares, enow to washe't awaie, 375
   Dydd flowe fromme each mann's eyne.

The bloudie axe hys bodie fayre
   Ynnto foure parties cutte;
And ev'rye parte, and eke hys hedde,
   Uponne a pole was putte. 380

One parte dydd rotte onne Kynwulph-hylle,
   One onne the mynster-tower,
And one from off the castle-gate
   The crowen dydd devoure:

The other onne Seyncte Powle's goode gate, 385
   A dreery spectacle;
Hys hedde was plac'd onne the hyghe crosse,
   Ynne hyghe-streete most nobile.

Thus was the ende of BAWDIN's fate:
   Godde prosper longe oure kynge, 390
And grante hee maye, wyth BAWDIN's soule,
   Ynne heav'n Godd's mercie synge!

1768

12   The Braes of Yarrow

John Logan (1748–88)

'Thy braes were bonny, Yarrow stream!
　'When first on them I met my lover;
'Thy braes how dreary, Yarrow stream!
　'When now thy waves his body cover!
'For ever now, O Yarrow stream!　　　　　　　　　5
　'Thou art to me a stream of sorrow;
'For never on thy banks shall I
　'Behold my love, the flower of Yarrow.

'He promised me a milk-white steed,
　'To bear me to his father's bowers;　　　　　　10
'He promised me a little page,
　'To 'squire me to his father's towers;
'He promised me a wedding-ring, —
　'The wedding-day was fix'd to-morrow; —
'Now he is wedded to his grave,　　　　　　　　15
　'Alas, his watery grave, in Yarrow!

'Sweet were his words when last we met;
　'My passion I as freely told him!
'Clasp'd in his arms, I little thought
　'That I should never more behold him!　　　　20
'Scarce was he gone, I saw his ghost;
　'It vanish'd with a shriek of sorrow;
'Thrice did the water-wraith ascend,
　'And gave a doleful groan thro' Yarrow.

'His mother from the window look'd,　　　　　　25
　'With all the longing of a mother;
'His little sister weeping walk'd
　'The green-wood path to meet her brother:
'They sought him east, they sought him west,
　'They sought him all the forest thorough;　　　30
'They only saw the cloud of night,
　'They only heard the roar of Yarrow!

'No longer from thy window look,

'Thou hast no son, thou tender mother!
'No longer walk, thou lovely maid!
    'Alas, thou hast no more a brother!
'No longer seek him east or west,
    'And search no more the forest thorough;
'For, wandering in the night so dark,
    'He fell a lifeless corse in Yarrow.

'The tear shall never leave my cheek,
    'No other youth shall be my marrow;
'I'll seek thy body in the stream,
    'And then with thee I'll sleep in Yarrow.'
The tear did never leave her cheek,
    No other youth became her marrow;
She found his body in the stream,
    And now with him she sleeps in Yarrow.

1781

13 The Diverting History of John Gilpin,

Showing how he went farther than he intended,
and came safe home again.

William Cowper (1731–1800)

John Gilpin was a citizen
    Of credit and renown,
A train-band captain eke was he
    Of famous London town.

John Gilpin's spouse said to her dear —
    Though wedded we have been
These twice ten tedious years, yet we
    No holiday have seen.

To-morrow is our wedding-day,
    And we will then repair

The Diverting History of John Gilpin

   Unto the Bell at Edmonton
      All in a chaise and pair.

My sister, and my sister's child,
    Myself, and children three,
Will fill the chaise; so you must ride
    On horseback after we.

He soon replied — I do admire
    Of womankind but one,
And you are she, my dearest dear,
    Therefore it shall be done.

I am a linen-draper bold,
    As all the world doth know,
And my good friend the calender
    Will lend his horse to go.

Quoth Mrs. Gilpin — That's well said;
    And, for that wine is dear,
We will be furnish'd with our own,
    Which is both bright and clear.

John Gilpin kiss'd his loving wife;
    O'erjoy'd was he to find
That, though on pleasure she was bent,
    She had a frugal mind.

The morning came, the chaise was brought,
    But yet was not allow'd
To drive up to the door, lest all
    Should say that she was proud.

So three doors off the chaise was stay'd,
    Where they did all get in;
Six precious souls, and all agog
    To dash through thick and thin!

Smack went the whip, round went the wheels,
    Were never folk so glad,
The stones did rattle underneath,
    As if Cheapside were mad.

John Gilpin at his horse's side
    Seiz'd fast the flowing mane,
And up he got, in haste to ride,
    But soon came down again;

For saddle-tree scarce reach'd had he,
    His journey to begin,
When, turning round his head, he saw
    Three customers come in.

So down he came; for loss of time,
    Although it griev'd him sore,
Yet loss of pence, full well he knew,
    Would trouble him much more.

'Twas long before the customers
    Were suited to their mind,
When Betty screaming came down stairs —
    "The wine is left behind!"

Good lack! quoth he — yet bring it me,
    My leathern belt likewise,
In which I bear my trusty sword
    When I do exercise.

Now mistress Gilpin (careful soul!)
    Had two stone bottles found,
To hold the liquor that she lov'd,
    And keep it safe and sound.

Each bottle had a curling ear,
    Through which the belt he drew,
And hung a bottle on each side,
    To make his balance true.

Then, over all, that he might be
    Equipp'd from top to toe,
His long red cloak, well brush'd and neat,
    He manfully did throw.

Now see him mounted once again
    Upon his nimble steed,

Full slowly pacing o'er the stones,
    With caution and good heed!

But, finding soon a smoother road
    Beneath his well-shod feet,
The snorting beast began to trot,
    Which gall'd him in his seat.

So, Fair and softly, John he cried,
    But John he cried in vain;
That trot became a gallop soon,
    In spite of curb and rein.

So stooping down, as needs he must
    Who cannot sit upright,
He grasp'd the mane with both his hands,
    And eke with all his might.

His horse, who never in that sort
    Had handled been before,
What thing upon his back had got
    Did wonder more and more.

Away went Gilpin, neck or nought;
    Away went hat and wig! —
He little dreamt, when he set out,
    Of running such a rig!

The wind did blow, the cloak did fly,
    Like streamer long and gay,
Till, loop and button failing both,
    At last it flew away.

Then might all people well discern
    The bottles he had slung;
A bottle swinging at each side,
    As hath been said or sung.

The dogs did bark, the children scream'd,
    Up flew the windows all;
And ev'ry soul cried out — Well done!
    As loud as he could bawl.

Away went Gilpin — who but he?
    His fame soon spread around —
He carries weight! he rides a race!
    'Tis for a thousand pound!

And still, as fast as he drew near,
    'Twas wonderful to view
How in a trice the turnpike-men
    Their gates wide open threw.

And now, as he went bowing down
    His reeking head full low,
The bottles twain behind his back
    Were shatter'd at a blow.

Down ran the wine into the road,
    Most piteous to be seen,
Which made his horse's flanks to smoke
    As they had basted been.

But still he seem'd to carry weight,
    With leathern girdle brac'd;
For all might see the bottle-necks
    Still dangling at his waist.

Thus all through merry Islington
    These gambols he did play,
And till he came unto the Wash
    Of Edmonton so gay.

And there he threw the wash about
    On both sides of the way,
Just like unto a trundling mop,
    Or a wild goose at play.

At Edmonton his loving wife
    From the balcony spied
Her tender husband, wond'ring much
    To see how he did ride.

Stop, stop, John Gilpin! — Here's the house —
    They all at once did cry;

The dinner waits, and we are tir'd:
    Said Gilpin — So am I!

But yet his horse was not a whit
    Inclin'd to tarry there;   150
For why? — his owner had a house
    Full ten miles off, at Ware.

So like an arrow swift he flew,
    Shot by an archer strong;
So did he fly — which brings me to   155
    The middle of my song.

Away went Gilpin, out of breath,
    And sore against his will,
Till at his friend the calender's
    His horse at last stood still.   160

The calender, amaz'd to see
    His neighbour in such trim,
Laid down his pipe, flew to the gate,
    And thus accosted him: —

What news? what news? your tidings tell;   165
    Tell me you must and shall —
Say why bare-headed you are come,
    Or why you come at all?

Now Gilpin had a pleasant wit,
    And lov'd a timely joke;   170
And thus unto the calender
    In merry guise he spoke: —

I came because your horse would come;
    And, if I well forebode,
My hat and wig will soon be here —   175
    They are upon the road.

The calender, right glad to find
    His friend in merry pin,
Return'd him not a single word,
    But to the house went in;   180

Whence straight he came with hat and wig;
    A wig that flow'd behind,
A hat not much the worse for wear,
    Each comely in its kind.

He held them up, and, in his turn,
    Thus show'd his ready wit —
My head is twice as big as your's,
    They therefore needs must fit.

But let me scrape the dirt away
    That hangs upon your face;
And stop and eat, for well you may
    Be in a hungry case.

Said John — It is my wedding-day,
    And all the world would stare,
If wife should dine at Edmonton
    And I should dine at Ware!

So, turning to his horse, he said —
    I am in haste to dine;
'Twas for your pleasure you came here,
    You shall go back for mine.

Ah, luckless speech, and bootless boast!
    For which he paid full dear;
For, while he spake, a braying ass
    Did sing most loud and clear;

Whereat his horse did snort, as he
    Had heard a lion roar,
And gallop'd off with all his might,
    As he had done before.

Away went Gilpin, and away
    Went Gilpin's hat and wig!
He lost them sooner than at first —
    For why? — they were too big!

Now, mistress Gilpin, when she saw
    Her husband posting down

Into the country far away,
    She pull'd out half a crown;

And thus unto the youth she said
    That drove them to the Bell —
This shall be yours when you bring back
    My husband safe and well.

The youth did ride, and soon did meet
    John coming back amain;
Whom in a trice he tried to stop,
    By catching at his rein;

But, not performing what he meant,
    And gladly would have done,
The frighted steed he frighted more,
    And made him faster run.

Away went Gilpin, and away
    Went post-boy at his heels! —
The post-boy's horse right glad to miss
    The lumb'ring of the wheels.

Six gentlemen upon the road,
    Thus seeing Gilpin fly,
With post-boy scamp'ring in the rear,
    They rais'd the hue and cry:

Stop thief! stop thief! — a highwayman!
    Not one of them was mute;
And all and each that pass'd that way
    Did join in the pursuit.

And now the turnpike gates again
    Flew open in short space;
The toll-men thinking, as before,
    That Gilpin rode a race.

And so he did — and won it too! —
    For he got first to town;
Nor stopp'd till where he had got up
    He did again get down.

Now let us sing — Long live the king,
   And Gilpin long live he; 250
And, when he next doth ride abroad,
   May I be there to see!

1782

14   Cumnor Hall

William Julius Mickle (1735–88)

The dews of summer nighte did falle,
   The moone (sweete regente of the skye)
Silver'd the walles of Cumnor Halle,
   And manye an oake that grewe therebye.

Nowe noughte was hearde beneath the skies, 5
   (The soundes of busye lyfe were stille,)
Save an unhappie ladie's sighes,
   That issued from that lonelye pile.

"Leicester," shee cried "is thys thy love
   "That thou so oft has sworne to mee, 10
"To leave mee in thys lonelye grove,
   "Immurr'd in shameful privitie?

"No more thou com'st with lover's speede,
   "Thy once-beloved bryde to see;
"But bee shee alive, or bee shee deade, 15
   "I feare (sterne earle's) the same to thee.

"Not so the usage I receiv'd,
   "When happye in my father's halle;
"No faithlesse husbande then me griev'd,
   "No chilling feares did mee appall. 20

"I rose up with the chearful morne,

"No lark more blith, no flow'r more gaye;
"And, like the birde that hauntes the thorne,
    "So merrylie sung the live-long daye.

"If that my beautye is but smalle,
    "Among court ladies all despis'd;
"Why didst thou rend it from that halle,
    "Where (scorneful earle) it well was priz'de?

"And when you first to mee made suite,
    "How fayre I was you oft woulde saye!
"And, proude of conquest — pluck'd the fruite,
    "Then lefte the blossom to decaye.

"Yes, nowe neglected and despis'd,
    "The rose is pale — the lilly's deade —
"But hee that once their charmes so priz'd,
    "Is sure the cause those charmes are fledde.

"For knowe, when sick'ning griefe doth preye
    "And tender love's repay'd with scorne,
"The sweetest beautye will decaye —
    "What flow'ret can endure the storme?

"At court I'm tolde is beauty's throne,
    "Where everye lady's passing rare;
"That eastern flow'rs, that shame the sun,
    "Are not so glowing, not soe fayre.

"Then, earle, why didst thou leave the bedds
    "Where roses and where lillys vie,
"To seek a primrose, whose pale shades
    "Must sicken — when those gaudes are bye?

"'Mong rural beauties I was one,
    "Among the fields wild flow'rs are faire;
"Some countrye swayne might mee have won,
    "And thoughte my beautie passing rare.

"But, Leicester, (or I much am wronge)
    "Or tis not beautye lures thy vowes;
"Rather ambition's gilded crowne

"Makes thee forget thy humble spouse.

"Then, Leicester, why, again I pleade,
    "(The injur'd surelye may repyne,)
"Why didst thou wed a countrye mayde,
    "When some fayre princesse might be thyne?   60

"Why didst thou praise my humble charmes,
    "And, oh! then leave them to decaye?
"Why didst thou win me to thy armes,
    "Then leave me to mourne the live-long daye?

"The village maidens of the plaine   65
    "Salute me lowly as they goe;
"Envious they marke my silken trayne,
    "Nor thinke a countesse can have woe.

"The simple nymphs! they little knowe,
    "How farre more happy's their estate —   70
"— To smile for joye — than sigh for woe —
    "— To be contente — than to be greate.

"Howe farre lesse bleste am I than them?
    "Dailye to pyne and waste with care!
"Like the poore plante, that from its stem   75
    "Divided — feeles the chilling ayre.

"Nor (cruel earl!) can I enjoye
    "The humble charmes of solitude;
"Your minions proude my peace destroye,
    "By sullen frownes or pratings rude.   80

"Laste nyghte, as sad I chanc'd to straye,
    "The village deathe-bell smote my eare;
"They wink'd asyde, and seem'd to saye,
    "Countesse, prepare — thy end is neare.

"And nowe, while happye peasantes sleepe,   85
    "Here I set lonelye and forlorne;
"No one to soothe mee as I weepe,
    "Save phylomel on yonder thorne.

"My spirits flag — my hopes decaye —
   "Still that dreade deathe-bell smites my eare;
"And many a boding seems to saye,
   "Countess, prepare — thy end is neare."

Thus sore and sad that ladie griev'd,
   In Cumnor Halle so lone and dreare;
And manye a heartefelte sighe shee heav'd,
   And let falle manye a bitter teare.

And ere the dawne of daye appear'd,
   In Cumnor Hall so lone and dreare,
Full manye a piercing screame was hearde,
   And manye a crye of mortal feare.

The death-belle thrice was hearde to ring,
   An aërial voyce was hearde to call,
And thrice the raven flapp'd its wyng
   Arounde the tow'rs of Cumnor Hall.

The mastiffe howl'd at village doore,
   The oaks were shatter'd on the greene;
Woe was the houre — for never more
   That haplesse countesse e'er was seene.

And in that manor now no more
   Is chearful feaste and sprightly balle;
For ever since that drearye houre
   Have spirits haunted Cumnor Hall.

The village maides, with fearful glance,
   Avoid the antient mossgrowne walle;
Nor ever leade the merrye dance,
   Among the groves of Cumnor Halle.

Full manye a travellor oft hath sigh'd,
   And pensive wepte the countess' falle,
As wand'ring onwards they've espied
   The haunted tow'rs of Cumnor Halle.

1784

15 A Red, Red Rose

Robert Burns (1759–96)

O my luve's like a red, red rose,
    That's newly sprung in June:
O my luve's like the melodie,
    That's sweetly played in tune.
As fair art thou, my bonnie lass,   5
    So deep in luve am I:
And I will luve thee still, my dear,
    Till a' the seas gang dry.

Till a' the seas gang dry, my dear,
    And the rocks melt wi' the sun;   10
I will luve thee still, my dear,
    While the sands o' life shall run.
And fare thee weel, my only luve!
    And fare thee weel awhile!
And I will come again, my luve,   15
    Though it were ten thousand mile.

1794

16 Fair Elenor

William Blake (1757–1827)

The bell struck one, and shook the silent tower;
The graves give up their dead: fair Elenor
Walk'd by the castle gate, and lookèd in.
A hollow groan ran thro' the dreary vaults.

She shriek'd aloud, and sunk upon the steps,   5
On the cold stone her pale cheeks.   Sickly smells
Of death issue as from a sepulchre,

And all is silent but the sighing vaults.

Chill Death withdraws his hand, and she revives;
Amaz'd, she finds herself upon her feet,
And, like a ghost, thro' narrow passages
Walking, feeling the cold walls with her hands.

Fancy returns, and now she thinks of bones
And grinning skulls, and corruptible death
Wrapp'd in his shroud; and now fancies she hears
Deep sighs, and sees pale sickly ghosts gliding.

At length, no fancy but reality
Distracts her.   A rushing sound, and the feet
Of one that fled, approaches. — Ellen stood
Like a dumb statue, froze to stone with fear.

The wretch approaches, crying: 'The deed is done;
Take this, and send it by whom thou wilt send;
It is my life — send it to Elenor: —
He's dead, and howling after me for blood!

'Take this,' he cried; and thrust into her arms
A wet napkin, wrapp'd about; then rush'd
Past, howling: she receiv'd into her arms
Pale death, and follow'd on the wings of fear.

They pass'd swift thro' the outer gate; the wretch,
Howling, leap'd o'er the wall into the moat,
Stifling in mud.   Fair Ellen pass'd the bridge,
And heard a gloomy voice cry 'Is it done?'

As the deer wounded, Ellen flew over
The pathless plain; as the arrows that fly
By night, destruction flies, and strikes in darkness.
She fled from fear, till at her house arriv'd.

Her maids await her; on her bed she falls,
That bed of joy, where erst her lord hath press'd:
'Ah, woman's fear!' she cried; 'ah, cursèd duke!
Ah, my dear lord! ah, wretched Elenor!

'My lord was like a flower upon the brows
Of lusty May!   Ah, life as frail as flower!
O ghastly death! withdraw thy cruel hand,
Seek'st thou that flow'r to deck thy horrid temples?

'My lord was like a star in the highest heav'n   45
Drawn down to earth by spells and wickedness;
My lord was like the opening eyes of day
When western winds creep softly o'er the flowers;

'But he is darken'd; like the summer's noon
Clouded; fall'n like the stately tree, cut down;   50
The breath of heaven dwelt among his leaves.
O Elenor, weak woman, fill'd with woe!'

Thus having spoke, she raisèd up her head,
And saw the bloody napkin by her side,
Which in her arms she brought; and now, tenfold   55
More terrifièd, saw it unfold itself.

Her eyes were fix'd; the bloody cloth unfolds,
Disclosing to her sight the murder'd head
Of her dear lord, all ghastly pale, clotted
With gory blood; it groan'd, and thus it spake: 60

'O Elenor, I am thy husband's head,
Who, sleeping on the stones of yonder tower,
Was 'reft of life by the accursèd duke!
A hirèd villain turn'd my sleep to death!

'O Elenor, beware the cursèd duke;   65
O give not him thy hand, now I am dead;
He seeks thy love; who, coward, in the night,
Hirèd a villain to bereave my life.'

She sat with dead cold limbs, stiffen'd to stone;
She took the gory head up in her arms;   70
She kiss'd the pale lips; she had no tears to shed;
She hugg'd it to her breast, and groan'd her last.

1783

17   William and Helen

Sir Walter Scott (1771–1832)

I.
From heavy dreams fair Helen rose,
   And eyed the dawning red:
"Alas, my love, thou tarriest long!
   O art thou false or dead?" —

II.
With gallant Fred'rick's princely power   5
   He sought the bold Crusade;
But not a word from Judah's wars
   Told Helen how he sped.

III.
With Paynim and with Saracen
   At length a truce was made,   10
And every knight return'd to dry
   The tears his love had shed.

IV.
Our gallant host was homeward bound
   With many a song of joy;
Green waved the laurel in each plume,   15
   The badge of victory.

V.
And old and young, and sire and son,
   To meet them crowd the way,
With shouts, and mirth, and melody,
   The debt of love to pay.   20

VI.
Full many a maid her true-love met,
   And sobb'd in his embrace,
And flutt'ring joy in tears and smiles
   Array'd full many a face.

VII.

Nor joy nor smile for Helen sad;
    She sought the host in vain;
For none could tell her William's fate,
    If faithless, or if slain.

VIII.

The martial band is past and gone;
    She rends her raven hair,
And in distraction's bitter mood
    She weeps with wild despair.

IX.

"O rise, my child," her mother said,
    "Nor sorrow thus in vain;
A perjured lover's fleeting heart
    No tears recall again." —

X.

"O mother, what is gone, is gone,
    What's lost for ever lorn:
Death, death alone can comfort me;
    O had I ne'er been born!

XI.

"O break, my heart, — O break at once!
    Drink my life-blood, Despair!
No joy remains on earth for me,
    For me in heaven no share." —

XII.

"O enter not in judgment, Lord!"
    The pious mother prays;
"Impute not guilt to thy frail child!
    She knows not what she says.

XIII.

"O say thy pater noster, child!
    O turn to God and grace!
His will, that turn'd thy bliss to bale,
    Can change thy bale to bliss." —

XIV.

"O mother, mother, what is bliss?
    O mother, what is bale?
My William's love was heaven on earth, 55
    Without it earth is hell.

XV.

"Why should I pray to ruthless Heaven,
    Since my loved William's slain?
I only pray'd for William's sake,
    And all my prayers were vain." — 60

XVI.

"O take the sacrament, my child,
    And check these tears that flow;
By resignation's humble prayer,
    O hallow'd be thy woe!" —

XVII.

"No sacrament can quench this fire, 65
    Or slake this scorching pain;
No sacrament can bid the dead
    Arise and live again.

XVIII.

"O break, my heart, — O break at once!
    Be thou my god, Despair! 70
Heaven's heaviest blow has fallen on me,
    And vain each fruitless prayer." —

XIX.

"O enter not in judgment, Lord,
    With thy frail child of clay!
She knows not what her tongue has spoke; 75
    Impute it not, I pray!

XX.

"Forbear, my child, this desperate woe,
    And turn to God and grace;
Well can devotion's heavenly glow
    Convert thy bale to bliss." — 80

XXI.

"O mother, mother, what is bliss?
    O mother, what is bale?
Without my William what were heaven,
    Or with him what were hell?" —

XXII.

Wild she arraigns the eternal doom,
    Upbraids each sacred power,
Till, spent, she sought her silent room,
    All in the lonely tower.

XXIII.

She beat her breast, she wrung her hands,
    Till sun and day were o'er,
And through the glimmering lattice shone
    The twinkling of the star.

XXIV.

Then, crash! the heavy drawbridge fell
    That o'er the moat was hung;
And, clatter! clatter! on its boards
    The hoof of courser rung.

XXV.

The clank of echoing steel was heard
    As off the rider bounded;
And slowly on the winding stair
    A heavy footstep sounded.

XXVI.

And hark! and hark! a knock — Tap! tap!
    A rustling stifled noise; —
Door-latch and tinkling staples ring; —
    At length a whispering voice.

XXVII.

Awake, awake, arise, my love!
    How, Helen, dost thou fare?
Wak'st thou, or sleep'st? laugh'st thou, or weep'st?
    Hast thought on me, my fair?" —

XXVIII.

"My love! my love! — so late by night! —
    I waked, I wept for thee:
Much have I borne since dawn of morn;
    Where, William, couldst thou be?" —

XXIX.

"We saddle late — from Hungary
    I rode since darkness fell;
And to its bourne we both return
    Before the matin-bell." —

XXX.

"O rest this night within my arms,
    And warm thee in their fold!
Chill howls through hawthorn bush the wind: —
    My love is deadly cold." —

XXXI.

"Let the wind howl through hawthorn bush!
    This night we must away;
The steed is wight, the spur is bright;
    I cannot stay till day.

XXXII.

"Busk, busk, and boune!   Thou mount'st behind
    Upon my black barb steed:
O'er stock and stile, a hundred miles,
    We haste to bridal bed." —

XXXIII.

"To-night — to-night a hundred miles! —
    O dearest William, stay!
The bell strikes twelve — dark, dismal hour!
    O wait, my love, till day!" —

XXXIV.

"Look here, look here — the moon shines clear —
    Full fast I ween we ride;
Mount and away! for ere the day
    We reach our bridal bed.

XXXV.

"The black barb snorts, the bridle rings;
   Haste, busk, and boune, and seat thee!
The feast is made, the chamber spread,
   The bridal guests await thee." —   140

XXXVI.

Strong love prevail'd: She busks, she bounes,
   She mounts the barb behind,
And round her darling William's waist
   Her lily arms she twined.

XXXVII.

And, hurry! hurry! off they rode,   145
   As fast as fast might be;
Spurn'd from the courser's thundering heels
   The flashing pebbles flee.

XXXVIII.

And on the right, and on the left,
   Ere they could snatch a view,   150
Fast, fast each mountain, mead, and plain,
   And cot, and castle, flew.

XXXIX.

"Sit fast — dost fear? — The moon shines clear —
   Fleet goes my barb — keep hold!
Fear'st thou?" — "O no!" she faintly said;   155
   "But why so stern and cold?"

XL.

"What yonder rings? what yonder sings?
   Why shrieks the owlet grey?" —
"'Tis death-bells' clang, 'tis funeral song,
   The body to the clay.   160

XLI.

"With song and clang, at morrow's dawn,
   Ye may inter the dead:
To-night I ride, with my young bride,
   To deck our bridal bed.

XLII.
"Come with thy choir, thou coffin'd guest, 165
  To swell our nuptial song!
Come, priest, to bless our marriage feast!
  Come all, come all along!" —

XLIII.
Ceased clang and song; down sunk the bier;
  The shrouded corpse arose: 170
And, hurry! hurry! all the train
  The thundering steed pursues.

XLIV.
And, forward! forward! on they go;
  High snorts the straining steed;
Thick pants the rider's labouring breath, 175
  As headlong on they speed.

XLV.
"O William, why this savage haste?
  And where thy bridal bed?" —
"'Tis distant far, low, damp, and chill,
  And narrow, trustless maid." — 180

XLVI.
"No room for me?" — "Enough for both; —
  Speed, speed, my barb, thy course!" —
O'er thundering bridge, through boiling surge,
  He drove the furious horse.

XLVII.
Tramp! tramp! along the land they rode, 185
  Splash! splash! along the sea;
The scourge is wight, the spur is bright,
  The flashing pebbles flee.

XLVIII.
Fled past on right and left how fast
  Each forest, grove, and bower! 190
On right and left fled past how fast
  Each city, town, and tower!

XLIX.

"Dost fear? dost fear? The moon shines clear,
    Dost fear to ride with me? —
Hurrah! hurrah! the dead can ride!" —
    "O William, let them be! —

L.

"See there, see there! What yonder swings
    And creaks 'mid whistling rain?" —
"Gibbet and steel, th' accursed wheel;
    A murderer in his chain. —

LI.

"Hollo! thou felon, follow here:
    To bridal bed we ride;
And thou shalt prance a fetter dance
    Before me and my bride." —

LII.

And, hurry! hurry! clash, clash, clash!
    The wasted form descends;
And fleet as wind through hazel bush
    The wild career attends.

LIII.

Tramp! tramp! along the land they rode,
    Splash! splash! along the sea;
The scourge is red, the spur drops blood,
    The flashing pebbles flee.

LIV.

How fled what moonshine faintly show'd!
    How fled what darkness hid!
How fled the earth beneath their feet,
    The heaven above their head!

LV.

"Dost fear? dost fear? The moon shines clear,
    And well the dead can ride;
Does faithful Helen fear for them?" —
    "O leave in peace the dead!" —

LVI.
"Barb! Barb! methinks I hear the cock;
    The sand will soon be run:
Barb! Barb! I smell the morning air;
    The race is wellnigh done." —

LVII.
Tramp! tramp! along the land they rode,   225
    Splash! splash! along the sea;
The scourge is red, the spur drops blood,
    The flashing pebbles flee.

LVIII.
"Hurrah! hurrah! well ride the dead;
    The bride, the bride is come;   230
And soon we reach the bridal bed,
    For, Helen, here's my home." —

LIX.
Reluctant on its rusty hinge
    Revolved an iron door,
And by the pale moon's setting beam   235
    Were seen a church and tower.

LX.
With many a shriek and cry whiz round
    The birds of midnight, scared;
And rustling like autumnal leaves
    Unhallow'd ghosts were heard.   240

LXI.
O'er many a tomb and tombstone pale
    He spurr'd the fiery horse,
Till sudden at an open grave
    He check'd the wondrous course.

LXII.
The falling gauntlet quits the rein,   245
    Down drops the casque of steel,
The cuirass leaves his shrinking side,
    The spur his gory heel.

LXIII.

The eyes desert the naked skull,
    The mould'ring flesh the bone,
Till Helen's lily arms entwine
    A ghastly skeleton.

LXIV.

The furious barb snorts fire and foam,
    And, with a fearful bound,
Dissolves at once in empty air,
    And leaves her on the ground.

LXV.

Half seen by fits, by fits half heard,
    Pale spectres flit along,
Wheel round the maid in dismal dance,
    And howl the funeral song;

LXVI.

"E'en when the heart's with anguish cleft,
    Revere the doom of Heaven,
Her soul is from her body reft;
    Her spirit be forgiven!"

1796

18   Alonzo the Brave and Fair Imogine

M. G. Lewis (1775–1818)

A warrior so bold and a virgin so bright
    Conversed, as they sat on the green;
They gazed on each other with tender delight:
Alonzo the Brave was the name of the knight,
    The maid's was the Fair Imogine.

—— "And, oh!" said the youth, "since to-morrow I go

"To fight in a far-distant land,
"Your tears for my absence soon leaving to flow,
"Some other will court you, and you will bestow
    "On a wealthier suitor your hand." ——

—— "Oh! hush these suspicions," Fair Imogine said,
    "Offensive to love and to me!
"For, if you be living, or if you be dead,
"I swear by the Virgin, that none in your stead
    "Shall husband of Imogine be.

"And if e'er for another my heart should decide,
    "Forgetting Alonzo the Brave,
"God grant, that, to punish my falsehood and pride,
"Your ghost at the marriage may sit by my side,
"May tax me with perjury, claim me as bride,
    "And bear me away to the grave!" ——

To Palestine hasten'd the hero so bold;
    His love she lamented him sore:
But scarce had a twelvemonth elapsed, when behold,
A Baron all cover'd with jewels and gold
    Arrived at Fair Imogine's door.

His treasure, his presents, his spacious domain,
    Soon made her untrue to her vows:
He dazzled her eyes; he bewilder'd her brain;
He caught her affections so light and so vain,
    And carried her home as his spouse.

And now had the marriage been bless'd by the priest;
    The revelry now was begun:
The tables they groan'd with the weight of the feast;
Nor yet had the laughter and merriment ceased,
    When the bell of the castle toll'd — "one!"

Then first with amazement Fair Imogine found
    That a stranger was placed by her side:
His air was terrific; he utter'd no sound;
He spoke not, he moved not, he look'd not around,
    But earnestly gazed on the bride.

His vizor was closed, and gigantic his height;
    His armour was sable to view:
All pleasure and laughter were hush'd at his sight;
The dogs, as they eyed him, drew back in affright;
    The lights in the chamber burnt blue!

His presence all bosoms appear'd to dismay;
    The guests sat in silence and fear:
At length spoke the bride, while she trembled: — "I pray,
"Sir Knight, that your helmet aside you would lay,
    "And deign to partake of our cheer." ——

The lady is silent: the stranger complies,
    His vizor he slowly unclosed:
Oh! then what a sight met Fair Imogine's eyes!
What words can express her dismay and surprise,
    When a skeleton's head was exposed!

All present then utter'd a terrified shout;
    All turn'd with disgust from the scene.
The worms they crept in, and the worms they crept out,
And sported his eyes and his temples about,
    While the spectre address'd Imogine:

"Behold me, thou false one! behold me!" he cried;
    "Remember Alonzo the Brave!
"God grants, that, to punish thy falsehood and pride,
"My ghost at thy marriage should sit by thy side,
"Should tax thee with perjury, claim thee as bride,
    "And bear thee away to the grave!"

Thus saying, his arms round the lady he wound,
    While loudly she shriek'd in dismay;
Then sank with his prey through the wide-yawning ground:
Nor ever again was Fair Imogine found,
    Or the spectre who bore her away.

Not long lived the Baron: and none since that time
    To inhabit the castle presume;
For chronicles tell, that, by order sublime,
There Imogine suffers the pain of her crime,
    And mourns her deplorable doom.

At midnight four times in each year does her sprite,
    When mortals in slumber are bound,
Array'd in her bridal apparel of white,   80
Appear in the hall with the skeleton-knight,
    And shriek as he whirls her around.

While they drink out of skulls newly torn from the grave,
    Dancing round them pale spectres are seen:
Their liquor is blood, and this horrible stave   85
They howl: — "To the health of Alonzo the Brave,
    "And his consort, the False Imogine!"

1796

19   *Giles Jollup the Grave, and Brown Sally Green*

M. G. Lewis (1775–1818)

A Doctor so prim and a sempstress so tight
    Hob-a-nobb'd in some right marasquin;
They suck'd up the cordial with truest delight:
Giles Jollup the Grave *was just five feet in height,*
    And four feet the brown Sally Green.   5

—— "And as," said Giles Jollup, "to-morrow I go
    "*To physic a feverish land,*
"At some sixpenny hop, or perhaps the Mayor's show,
"You'll tumble in love with some smart city beau,
    "And with him share your shop in the Strand." ——   10

— "Lord! how can you think so?" brown Sally Green said;
    "You must know mighty little of me;
"For if you be living, or if you be dead,
"I swear, 'pon my honour, that none in your stead
    "Shall husband of Sally Green be.   15

"And if e'er for another my heart should decide,

"False to you and the faith which I gave,
"God grant that, at dinner too amply supplied,
"Over-eating may give me a pain in my side;
"May your ghost then bring rhubarb to physic the bride,
    "And send her well-dosed to the grave!" ——

Away went poor Giles, to what place is not told:
    Sally wept, till she blew her nose sore!
But scarce had a twelvemonth elapsed, when behold!
A brewer, quite stylish, his gig that way roll'd,
    And stopp'd it at Sally Green's door.

His wealth, his pot-belly, and whisky of cane,
    Soon made her untrue to her vows;
The steam of strong beer now bewildering her brain,
He caught her while tipsy! denials were vain,
    So he carried her home as his spouse.

And now the roast beef had been bless'd by the priest,
    To cram now the guests had begun:
Tooth and nail like a wolf fell the bride on the feast;
Nor yet had the clash of her knife and fork ceased,
    When a bell — ('twas a dustman's) — toll'd — "one!"

Then first with amazement Brown Sally Green found
    That a stranger was stuck by her side:
His cravat and his ruffles with snuff were embrown'd;
He ate not, he drank not, but, turning him round,
    Sent some pudding away to be fried! ! !

His wig was turn'd forwards, and short was his height;
    His apron was dirty to view:
The women (oh! wondrous) were hush'd at his sight:
The cats, as they eyed him, drew back (well they might),
    For his body was pea-green and blue!

Now, as all wish'd to speak, but none knew what to say,
    They look'd mighty foolish and queer:
At length spoke the bride, while she trembled — "I pray,
"Dear sir, your peruke that aside you would lay,
    "And partake of some strong or small beer!" ——

The sempstress is silent; the stranger complies,
   And his wig from his phiz deigns to pull.
Adzooks! what a squall Sally gave through surprize!
Like a pig that is stuck how she open'd her eyes,
   When she recognized Jollup's bare skull!

Each miss then exclaim'd, while she turn'd up her snout,
   —— "Sir, your head isn't fit to be seen!" —
The pot-boys ran in, and the pot-boys ran out,
And couldn't conceive what the noise was about,
   While the Doctor address'd Sally Green:

—— "Behold me, thou jilt-flirt! behold me!" he cried;
   "You've broken the faith which you gave!
"God grants, that, to punish your falsehood and pride,
"Over-eating should give you a pain in your side:
"Come, swallow this rhubarb! I'll physic the bride,
   "And send her well-dosed to the grave!" ——

Thus saying, the physic her throat he forced down,
   In spite of whate'er she could say;
Then bore to his chariot the damsel so brown;
Nor ever again was she seen in that town,
   Or the Doctor who whisk'd her away.

Not long liv'd the Brewer: and none since that time
   To make use of the brewhouse presume;
For 'tis firmly believed, that, by order sublime,
There Sally Green suffers the pain of her crime,
   And bawls to get out of the room.

At midnight four times in each year does her sprite
   With shrieks make the chamber resound:
— "I won't take the rhubarb!" she squalls in affright,
While, a cup in his left hand, a draught in his right,
   Giles Jollup pursues her around!

With wigs so well powder'd, their fees while they crave,
   Dancing round them twelve doctors are seen:
They drink chicken-broth, while this horrible stave
Is twang'd through each nose — "To Giles Jollup the Grave,
   "And his patient, the sick Sally Green!" ——

1801

20   Goody Blake, and Harry Gill

William Wordsworth (1770–1850)

Oh! what's the matter? what's the matter?
What is't that ails young Harry Gill?
That evermore his teeth they chatter,
Chatter, chatter, chatter still.
Of waistcoats Harry has no lack, 5
Good duffle grey, and flannel fine;
He has a blanket on his back,
And coats enough to smother nine.

In March, December, and in July,
'Tis all the same with Harry Gill; 10
The neighbours tell, and tell you truly,
His teeth they chatter, chatter still.
At night, at morning, and at noon,
'Tis all the same with Harry Gill;
Beneath the sun, beneath the moon, 15
His teeth they chatter, chatter still.

Young Harry was a lusty drover,
And who so stout of limb as he?
His cheeks were red as ruddy clover,
His voice was like the voice of three. 20
Auld Goody Blake was old and poor,
Ill fed she was, and thinly clad;
And any man who pass'd her door,
Might see how poor a hut she had.

All day she spun in her poor dwelling, 25
And then her three hours' work at night!
Alas! 'twas hardly worth the telling,
It would not pay for candle-light.
— This woman dwelt in Dorsetshire,
Her hut was on a cold hill-side, 30
And in that country coals are dear,
For they come far by wind and tide.

By the same fire to boil their pottage,

Two poor old dames, as I have known,
Will often live in one small cottage,
But she, poor woman, dwelt alone.
'Twas well enough when summer came,
The long, warm, lightsome summer-day,
Then at her door the *canty* dame
Would sit, as any linnet gay.

But when the ice our streams did fetter,
Oh! then how her old bones would shake!
You would have said, if you had met her,
'Twas a hard time for Goody Blake.
Her evenings then were dull and dead;
Sad case it was, as you may think,
For very cold to go to bed,
And then for cold not sleep a wink.

Oh joy for her! when e'er in winter
The winds at night had made a rout,
And scatter'd many a lusty splinter,
And many a rotten bough about.
Yet never had she, well or sick,
As every man who knew her says,
A pile before-hand, wood or stick,
Enough to warm her for three days.

Now, when the frost was past enduring,
And made her poor old bones to ache,
Could any thing be more alluring,
Than an old hedge to Goody Blake?
And now and then, it must be said,
When her old bones were cold and chill,
She left her fire, or left her bed,
To seek the hedge of Harry Gill.

Now Harry he had long suspected
This trespass of old Goody Blake,
And vow'd that she should be detected,
And he on her would vengeance take.
And oft from his warm fire he'd go,
And to the fields his road would take,
And there, at night, in frost and snow,

He watch'd to seize old Goody Blake.

And once, behind a rick of barley,
Thus looking out did Harry stand;
The moon was full and shining clearly,
And crisp with frost the stubble-land.
— He hears a noise — he's all awake —
Again? — on tip-toe down the hill
He softly creeps — 'Tis Goody Blake,
She's at the hedge of Harry Gill.

Right glad was he when he beheld her:
Stick after stick did Goody pull,
He stood behind a bush of elder,
Till she had filled her apron full.
When with her load she turned about,
The bye-road back again to take,
He started forward with a shout,
And sprang upon poor Goody Blake.

And fiercely by the arm he took her,
And by the arm he held her fast,
And fiercely by the arm he shook her,
And cried, "I've caught you then at last!"
Then Goody, who had nothing said,
Her bundle from her lap let fall;
And kneeling on the sticks, she pray'd
To God that is the judge of all.

She pray'd, her wither'd hand uprearing,
While Harry held her by the arm —
"God! who art never out of hearing,
"O may he never more be warm!"
The cold, cold moon above her head,
Thus on her knees did Goody pray,
Young Harry heard what she had said,
And icy-cold he turned away.

He went complaining all the morrow
That he was cold and very chill:
His face was gloom, his heart was sorrow,
Alas! that day for Harry Gill!

That day he wore a riding-coat,
But not a whit the warmer he:
Another was on Thursday brought,
And ere the Sabbath he had three.

'Twas all in vain, a useless matter,
And blankets were about him pinn'd;
Yet still his jaws and teeth they clatter,
Like a loose casement in the wind.
And Harry's flesh it fell away;
And all who see him say 'tis plain,
That, live as long as live he may,
He never will be warm again.

No word to any man he utters,
A-bed or up, to young or old;
But ever to himself he mutters,
"Poor Harry Gill is very cold."
A-bed or up, by night or day;
His teeth they chatter, chatter still.
Now think, ye farmers all, I pray,
Of Goody Blake and Harry Gill.

1798

21 Bishop Bruno

Robert Southey (1774–1843)

Bishop Bruno awoke in the dead midnight,
And he heard his heart beat loud with affright:
He dreamt he had rung the Palace bell,
And the sound it gave was his passing knell.

Bishop Bruno smiled at his fears so vain,
He turned to sleep and he dreamt again;
He rang at the palace gate once more,

And Death was the Porter that open'd the door.

He started up at the fearful dream,
And he heard at his window the screech-owl scream;   10
Bishop Bruno slept no more that night, . .
Oh! glad was he when he saw the day-light!

Now he goes forth in proud array,
For he with the Emperor dines to-day;
There was not a Baron in Germany   15
That went with a nobler train than he.

Before and behind his soldiers ride,
The people throng'd to see their pride;
They bow'd the head, and the knee they bent,
But nobody blest him as he went.   20

So he went on stately and proud,
When he heard a voice that cried aloud,
"Ho! ho!   Bishop Bruno! you travel with glee, . .
But I would have you know, you travel to me!"

Behind and before and on either side,   25
He look'd, but nobody he espied;
And the Bishop at that grew cold with fear,
For he heard the words distinct and clear.

And when he rang at the Palace bell,
He almost expected to hear his knell;   30
And when the Porter turn'd the key,
He almost expected Death to see.

But soon the Bishop recover'd his glee,
For the Emperor welcomed him royally;
And now the tables were spread, and there   35
Were choicest wines and dainty fare.

And now the Bishop had blest the meat,
When a voice was heard as he sat in his seat, . .
"With the Emperor now you are dining with glee,
But know, Bishop Bruno! you sup with me!"   40

The Bishop then grew pale with affright,
And suddenly lost his appetite;
All the wine and dainty cheer
Could not comfort his heart that was sick with fear.

But by little and little recovered he,   45
For the wine went flowing merrily,
Till at length he forgot his former dread,
And his cheeks again grew rosy red.

When he sat down to the royal fare
Bishop Bruno was the saddest man there;   50
But when the masquers enter'd the hall,
He was the merriest man of all.

Then from amid the masquers' crowd
There went a voice hollow and loud, . .
"You have past the day, Bishop Bruno, in glee;   55
But you must pass the night with me!"

His cheek grows pale, and his eye-balls glare,
And stiff round his tonsure bristled his hair;
With that there came one from the masquers' band,
And took the Bishop by the hand.   60

The bony hand suspended his breath,
His marrow grew cold at the touch of Death;
On saints in vain he attempted to call,
Bishop Bruno fell dead in the palace hall.

1798

22   Love

Samuel Taylor Coleridge (1772–1834)

All thoughts, all passions, all delights,

Whatever stirs this mortal frame,
All are but ministers of Love,
   And feed his sacred flame.

Oft in my waking dreams do I
Live o'er again that happy hour,
When midway on the mount I lay,
   Beside the ruined tower.

The moonshine, stealing o'er the scene
Had blended with the lights of eve;
And she was there, my hope, my joy,
   My own dear Genevieve!

She leant against the armèd man,
The statue of the armèd knight;
She stood and listened to my lay,
   Amid the lingering light.

Few sorrows hath she of her own,
My hope! my joy! my Genevieve!
She loves me best, whene'er I sing
   The songs that make her grieve.

I played a soft and doleful air,
I sang an old and moving story —
An old rude song, that suited well
   That ruin wild and hoary.

She listened with a flitting blush,
With downcast eyes and modest grace;
For well she knew, I could not choose
   But gaze upon her face.

I told her of the Knight that wore
Upon his shield a burning brand;
And that for ten long years he wooed
   The Lady of the Land.

I told her how he pined: and ah!
The deep, the low, the pleading tone
With which I sang another's love,

Interpreted my own.

She listened with a flitting blush,
With downcast eyes, and modest grace;
And she forgave me, that I gazed
    Too fondly on her face!

But when I told the cruel scorn
That crazed that bold and lovely Knight,
And that he crossed the mountain-woods,
    Nor rested day nor night;

That sometimes from the savage den,
And sometimes from the darksome shade,
And sometimes starting up at once
    In green and sunny glade, —

There came and looked him in the face
An angel beautiful and bright;
And that he knew it was a Fiend,
    This miserable Knight!

And that unknowing what he did,
He leaped amid a murderous band,
And saved from outrage worse than death
    The Lady of the Land!

And how she wept, and clasped his knees;
And how she tended him in vain —
And ever strove to expiate
    The scorn that crazed his brain; —

And that she nursed him in a cave;
And how his madness went away,
When on the yellow forest-leaves
    A dying man he lay; —

His dying words — but when I reached
That tenderest strain of all the ditty,
My faultering voice and pausing harp
    Disturbed her soul with pity!

All impulses of soul and sense
Had thrilled my guileless Genevieve; 70
The music and the doleful tale,
   The rich and balmy eve;

And hopes, and fears that kindle hope,
An undistinguishable throng,
And gentle wishes long subdued, 75
   Subdued and cherished long!

She wept with pity and delight,
She blushed with love, and virgin-shame;
And like the murmur of a dream,
   I heard her breathe my name. 80

Her bosom heaved — she stepped aside,
As conscious of my look she stepped —
Then suddenly, with timorous eye
   She fled to me and wept.

She half enclosed me with her arms, 85
She pressed me with a meek embrace;
And bending back her head, looked up,
   And gazed upon my face.

'Twas partly love, and partly fear,
And partly 'twas a bashful art, 90
That I might rather feel, than see,
   The swelling of her heart.

I calmed her fears, and she was calm,
And told her love with virgin pride;
And so I won my Genevieve, 95
   My bright and beauteous Bride.

1799

23 Beth Gêlert; or, The Grave of the Greyhound

William Robert Spencer (1769–1834)

The spearmen heard the bugle sound,
And cheerly smiled the morn;
And many a brach, and many a hound,
Obeyed Llewelyn's horn.

And still he blew a louder blast, 5
And gave a lustier cheer:
'Come, Gêlert, come, wer't never last
Llewelyn's horn to hear.

'Oh where does faithful Gêlert roam,
The flower of all his race; 10
So true, so brave, a lamb at home,
A lion in the chase?'

'Twas only at Llewelyn's board
The faithful Gêlert fed;
He watched, he served, he cheered his lord, 15
And sentinelled his bed.

In sooth he was a peerless hound,
The gift of royal John;
But now no Gêlert could be found,
And all the chase rode on. 20

And now, as o'er the rocks and dells
The gallant chidings rise,
All Snowdon's craggy chaos yells
The many-mingled cries.

That day Llewelyn little loved 25
The chase of hart and hare;
And scant and small the booty proved,
For Gêlert was not there.

Unpleased Llewelyn homeward hied,
When near the portal seat 30

His truant Gêlert he espied,
Bounding his lord to greet.

But when he gained his castle door
Aghast the chieftain stood;
The hound all o'er was smeared with gore,
His lips, his fangs, ran blood.

Llewelyn gazed with fierce surprise;
Unused such looks to meet,
His favourite checked his joyful guise,
And crouched, and licked his feet.

Onward in haste Llewelyn passed,
And on went Gêlert too;
And still, where'er his eyes he cast,
Fresh blood-gouts shocked his view.

O'erturned his infant's bed he found,
With blood-stained covert rent;
And all around the walls and ground
With recent blood besprent.

He called his child — no voice replied —
He searched with terror wild;
Blood, blood he found on every side,
But nowhere found his child.

'Hell hound! my child's by thee devoured,'
The frantic father cried;
And to the hilt his vengeful sword
He plunged in Gêlert's side.

His suppliant looks, as prone he fell,
No pity could impart;
But still his Gêlert's dying yell
Passed heavy o'er his heart.

Aroused by Gêlert's dying yell,
Some slumberer wakened nigh:
What words the parent's joy could tell
To hear his infant's cry!

Concealed beneath a tumbled heap
His hurried search had missed,
All glowing from his rosy sleep,
The cherub boy he kissed.

Nor scathe had he, nor harm, nor dread,
But, the same couch beneath,
Lay a gaunt wolf, all torn and dead,
Tremendous still in death.

Ah, what was then Llewelyn's pain!
For now the truth was clear;
His gallant hound the wolf had slain,
To save Llewelyn's heir.

Vain, vain was all Llewelyn's woe:
'Best of thy kind, adieu!
The frantic blow, which laid thee low,
This heart shall ever rue.'

And now a gallant tomb they raise,
With costly sculpture decked;
And marbles storied with his praise
Poor Gêlert's bones protect.

There never could the spearman pass,
Or forester, unmoved;
There, oft the tear-besprinkled grass
Llewelyn's sorrow proved.

And there he hung his horn and spear,
And there, as evening fell,
In fancy's ear he oft would hear
Poor Gêlert's dying yell.

And till great Snowdon's rocks grow old,
And cease the storm to brave,
The consecrated spot shall hold
The name of 'Gêlert's grave'.

1800

24　The Elfin-King

John Leyden (1775–1811)

— "O swift, and swifter far he speeds
　　"Than earthly steed can run;
"But I hear not the feet of his courser fleet,
　　"As he glides o'er the moorland dun." —

Lone was the strath where he crossed their path,　　5
　　And wide did the heath extend,
The Knight in Green on that moor is seen
　　At every seven years' end.

And swift is the speed of his coal-black steed,
　　As the leaf before the gale,　　10
But never yet have that courser's feet
　　Been heard on hill or dale.

But woe to the wight who meets the Green Knight,
　　Except on his faulchion arm
Spell-proof he bear, like the brave St. Clair,　　15
　　The holy Trefoil's charm;

For then shall fly his gifted eye,
　　Delusions false and dim;
And each unbless'd shade shall stand pourtray'd
　　In ghostly form and limb.　　20

O swift, and swifter far he speeds
　　Than earthly steed can run;
— "He skims the blue air," said the brave St. Clair,
　　"Instead of the heath so dun.

"His locks are bright as the streamer's light,　　25
　　"His cheeks like the rose's hue;
"The Elfin-King, like the merlin's wing
　　"Are his pinions of glossy blue." —

— "No Elfin-King, with azure wing,
　　"On the dark brown moor I see;　　30

"But a courser keen, and a Knight in Green,
    "And full fair I ween is he.

"Nor Elfin-King, nor azure wing,
    "Nor ringlets sparkling bright;" —
Sir Geoffry cried, and forward hied   35
    To join the stranger Knight.

He knew not the path of the lonely strath,
    Where the Elfin-King went his round;
Or he never had gone with the Green Knight on,
    Nor trode the charmed ground.   40

How swift they flew! no eye could view
    Their track on heath or hill;
Yet swift across both moor and moss
    St. Clair did follow still.

And soon was seen a circle green,   45
    Where a shadowy wassel crew
Amid the ring did dance and sing,
    In weeds of watchet blue.

And the windlestrae, so limber and gray,
    Did shiver beneath the tread   50
Of the coursers' feet, as they rushed to meet
    The morrice of the dead.

— "Come here, come here, with thy green feere,
    "Before the bread be stale;
"To roundel dance with speed advance,   55
    "And taste our wassel ale." —

Then up to the Knight came a grizzly wight,
    And sounded in his ear,
— "Sir Knight, eschew this goblin crew,
    "Nor taste their ghostly cheer." —   60

The tabors rung, the lilts were sung,
    And the Knight the dance did lead;
But the maidens fair seem'd round him to stare,
    With eyes like the glassy bead.

The glance of their eye, so cold and so dry,
    Did almost his heart appal;
Their motion is swift, but their limbs they lift
    Like stony statues all.

Again to the Knight came the grizzly wight,
    When the roundel dance was o'er;
— "Sir Knight, eschew this goblin crew,
    "Or rue for evermore." —

But forward press'd the dauntless guest
    To the tables of ezlar red,
And there was seen the Knight in Green,
    To grace the fair board head.

And before that Knight was a goblet bright
    Of emerald smooth and green,
The fretted brim was studded full trim
    With mountain rubies sheen.

Sir Geoffry the Bold of the cup laid hold,
    With heath-ale mantling o'er;
And he saw as he drank that the ale never shrank,
    But mantled as before.

Then Sir Geoffry grew pale as he quaffed the ale,
    And cold as the corpse of clay;
And with horny beak the ravens did shriek,
    And flutter'd o'er their prey.

But soon throughout the revel rout
    A strange commotion ran,
For beyond the round, they heard the sound
    Of the steps of an uncharm'd man.

And soon to St. Clair the grim wight did repair,
    From the midst of the wassel crew;
— "Sir Knight, beware of the revellers there,
    "Nor do as they bid thee do." —

— "What woeful wight art thou," said the Knight,
    "To haunt this wassel fray?" —

The Elfin-King

— "I was once," quoth he, "a mortal, like thee,
    "Though now I'm an Elfin gray.

"And the Knight so Bold as the corpse lies cold,
    "Who trode the green sward ring;
"He must wander along with that restless throng,
    "For aye, with the Elfin-King.

"With the restless crew, in weeds so blue,
    "The hapless Knight must wend;
"Nor ever be seen on haunted green
    "Till the weary seven years end.

"Fair is the mien of the Knight in Green,
    "And bright his sparkling hair;
"'Tis hard to believe how malice can live
    "In the breast of aught so fair.

"And light and fair are the fields of air,
    "Where he wanders to and fro;
"Still doom'd to fleet from the regions of heat,
    "To the realms of endless snow.

"When high over head fall the streamers red,
    "He views the blessed afar;
"And in stern despair darts through the air
    "To earth, like a falling star.

"With his shadowy crew, in weeds so blue,
    "That Knight for aye must run;
"Except thou succeed in a perilous deed,
    "Unseen by the holy sun.

"Who ventures the deed, and fails to succeed,
    "Perforce must join the crew:" —
— "Then brief, declare," said the brave St. Clair,
    "A deed that a Knight may do." —

"Mid the sleet and the rain thou must here remain,
    "By the haunted green sward ring,
"Till the dance wax slow, and the song faint and low,
    "Which the crew unearthly sing.

"Then right at the time of the matin chime,
   "Thou must tread the unhallow'd ground,
"And with mystic pace the circles trace 135
   "That enclose it nine times round.

"And next must thou pass the rank green grass
   "To the tables of ezlar red;
"And the goblet clear away must thou bear,
   "Nor behind thee turn thy head. 140

"And ever anon as thou tread'st upon
   "The sward of the green charm'd ring,
"Be no word express'd in that space unbless'd
   "That 'longeth of holy thing.

"For the charm'd ground is all unsound, 145
   "And the lake spreads wide below,
"And the Water-Fiend there, with the Fiend of Air,
   "Is leagued for mortals' woe." —

Mid the sleet and the rain did St. Clair remain
   Till the evening star did rise; 150
And the rout so gay did dwindle away
   To the elritch dwarfy size.

When the moon beams pale fell through the white hail,
   With a wan and a watery ray,
Sad notes of woe seem'd round him to grow, 155
   The dirge of the Elfins gray.

And right at the time of the matin chime
   His mystic pace began,
And murmurs deep around him did creep,
   Like the moans of a murder'd man. 160

The matin bell was tolling farewell,
   When he reach'd the central ring,
And there he beheld, to ice congeal'd,
   That crew, with the Elfin-King.

For ay, at the knell of the matin bell, 165
   When the black monks wend to pray,

The spirits unbless'd have a glimpse of rest
  Before the dawn of day.

The sigh of the trees, and the rush of the breeze,
  Then pause on the lonely hill;   170
And the frost of the dead clings round their head,
  And they slumber cold and still.

The Knight took up the emerald cup,
  And the ravens hoarse did scream,
And the shuddering Elfins half rose up,   175
  And murmur'd in their dream:

They inwardly mourn'd, and the thin blood return'd
  To every icy limb;
And each frozen eye, so cold and so dry,
  'Gan roll with lustre dim.   180

Then brave St. Clair did turn him there,
  To retrace the mystic track,
He heard the sigh of his lady fair,
  Who sobbed behind his back.

He started quick, and his heart beat thick,   185
  And he listen'd in wild amaze;
But the parting bell on his ear it fell,
  And he did not turn to gaze.

With panting breast, as he forward press'd,
  He trode on a mangled head;   190
And the skull did scream, and the voice did seem
  The voice of his mother dead.

He shuddering trode: — On the great name of God
  He thought, — but he nought did say;
And the green sward did shrink, as about to sink,   195
  And loud laugh'd the Elfins gray.

And loud did resound, o'er the unbless'd ground,
  The wings of the blue Elf-King;
And the ghostly crew to reach him flew,
  But he cross'd the charmed ring[.]   200

The morning was gray, and dying away
    Was the sound of the matin bell;
And far to the west the Fays that ne'er rest,
    Fled where the moon-beams fell.

And Sir Geoffry the Bold, on the unhallow'd mold,   205
    Arose from the green witch-grass;
And he felt his limbs like a dead man's cold,
    And he wist not where he was.

And that cup so rare, which the brave St. Clair
    Did bear from the ghostly crew,   210
Was suddenly changed, from the emerald fair,
    To the ragged whinstone blue;
And instead of the ale that mantled there,
    Was the murky midnight dew.

1801

25   *Oscar of Alva*

George Gordon Byron (1788–1824)

How sweetly shines through azure skies,
    The lamp of heaven on Lora's shore;
Where Alva's hoary turrets rise,
    And hear the din of arms no more.

But often has yon rolling moon   5
    On Alva's casques of silver play'd;
And view'd, at midnight's silent noon,
    Her chiefs in gleaming mail array'd:

And on the crimson'd rocks beneath,
    Which scowl o'er ocean's sullen flow   10
Pale in the scatter'd ranks of death,
    She saw the gasping warrior low;

While many an eye which ne'er again
    Could mark the rising orb of day,
Turn'd feebly from the gory plain,
    Beheld in death her fading ray.

Once to those eyes the lamp of Love,
    They blest her dear propitious light;
But now she glimmer'd from above,
    A sad, funereal torch of night.

Faded is Alva's noble race,
    And gray her towers are seen afar;
No more her heroes urge the chase,
    Or roll the crimson tide of war.

But who was last of Alva's clan?
    Why grows the moss on Alva's stone?
Her towers resound no steps of man,
    They echo to the gale alone.

And when that gale is fierce and high,
    A sound is heard in yonder hall;
It rises hoarsely through the sky,
    And vibrates o'er the mouldering wall.

Yes, when the eddying tempest sighs,
    It shakes the shield of Oscar brave;
But there no more his banners rise,
    No more his plumes of sable wave.

Fair shone the sun on Oscar's birth,
    When Angus hail'd his eldest born;
The vassals round their chieftain's hearth
    Crowd to applaud the happy morn.

They feast upon the mountain deer,
    The pibroch raised its piercing note:
To gladden more their highland cheer,
    The strains in martial numbers float:

And they who heard the war-notes wild
    Hoped that one day the pibroch's strain

Should play before the hero's child
   While he should lead the tartan train.

Another year is quickly past,
   And Angus hails another son;   50
His natal day is like the last,
   Nor soon the jocund feast was done.

Taught by their sire to bend the bow,
   On Alva's dusky hills of wind,
The boys in childhood chased the roe,   55
   And left their hounds in speed behind.

But ere their years of youth are o'er,
   They mingle in the ranks of war;
They lightly wheel the bright claymore,
   And send the whistling arrow far.   60

Dark was the flow of Oscar's hair,
   Wildly it stream'd along the gale;
But Allan's locks were bright and fair,
   And pensive seem'd his cheek, and pale.

But Oscar own'd a hero's soul,   65
   His dark eye shone through beams of truth;
Allan had early learn'd control,
   And smooth his words had been from youth.

Both, both were brave: the Saxon spear
   Was shiver'd oft beneath their steel;   70
And Oscar's bosom scorn'd to fear,
   But Oscar's bosom knew to feel;

While Allan's soul belied his form,
   Unworthy with such charms to dwell:
Keen as the lightning of the storm,   75
   On foes his deadly vengeance fell.

From high Southannon's distant tower
   Arrived a young and noble dame;
With Kenneth's lands to form her dower,
   Glenalvon's blue-eyed daughter came;   80

And Oscar claim'd the beauteous bride,
   And Angus on his Oscar smiled:
It soothed the father's feudal pride
   Thus to obtain Glenalvon's child.

Hark to the pibroch's pleasing note!
   Hark to the swelling nuptial song!
In joyous strains the voices float,
   And still the choral peal prolong.

See how the heroes' blood-red plumes
   Assembled wave in Alva's hall;
Each youth his varied plaid assumes,
   Attending on their chieftain's call.

It is not war their aid demands,
   The pibroch plays the song of peace;
To Oscar's nuptials throng the bands,
   Nor yet the sounds of pleasure cease.

But where is Oscar? sure 't is late:
   Is this a bridegroom's ardent flame?
While thronging guests and ladies wait,
   Nor Oscar nor his brother came.

At length young Allan join'd the bride:
   "Why comes not Oscar," Angus said:
"Is he not here?" the youth replied;
   "With me he roved not o'er the glade:

"Perchance, forgetful of the day,
   'Tis his to chase the bounding roe;
Or ocean's waves prolong his stay;
   Yet Oscar's bark is seldom slow."

"Oh, no!" the anguish'd sire rejoin'd,
   "Nor chase nor wave my boy delay;
Would he to Mora seem unkind?
   Would aught to her impede his way?

"Oh, search, ye chiefs! oh, search around!
   Allan, with these through Alva fly;

Till Oscar, till my son is found,
    Haste, haste, nor dare attempt reply."

All is confusion — through the vale
    The name of Oscar hoarsely rings,
It rises on the murmuring gale,
    Till night expands her dusky wings;

It breaks the stillness of the night,
    But echoes through her shades in vain,
It sounds through morning's misty light,
    But Oscar comes not o'er the plain.

Three days, three sleepless nights, the Chief
    For Oscar search'd each mountain cave;
Then hope is lost; in boundless grief,
    His locks in gray-torn ringlets wave.

"Oscar! my son! — thou God of Heav'n
    Restore the prop of sinking age!
Or if that hope no more is given,
    Yield his assassin to my rage.

"Yes, on some desert rocky shore
    My Oscar's whiten'd bones must lie;
Then grant, thou God! I ask no more,
    With him his frantic sire may die!

"Yet he may live, — away, despair!
    Be calm, my soul! he yet may live;
T' arraign my fate, my voice forbear!
    O God! my impious prayer forgive.

"What, if he live for me no more,
    I sink forgotten in the dust,
The hope of Alva's age is o'er;
    Alas! can pangs like these be just?"

Thus did the hapless parent mourn,
    Till Time, which soothes severest woe,
Had bade serenity return,
    And made the tear-drop cease to flow.

For still some latent hope survived
    That Oscar might once more appear;
His hope now droop'd and now revived,
    Till Time had told a tedious year.

Days roll'd along, the orb of light
    Again had run his destined race;
No Oscar bless'd his father's sight,
    And sorrow left a fainter trace.

For youthful Allan still remain'd,
    And now his father's only joy:
And Mora's heart was quickly gain'd,
    For beauty crown'd the fair-hair'd boy.

She thought that Oscar low was laid,
    And Allan's face was wondrous fair;
If Oscar lived, some other maid
    Had claim'd his faithless bosom's care.

And Angus said, if one year more
    In fruitless hope was pass'd away,
His fondest scruples should be o'er,
    And he would name their nuptial day.

Slow roll'd the moons, but blest at last
    Arrived the dearly destined morn;
The year of anxious trembling past,
    What smiles the lovers' cheeks adorn!

Hark to the pibroch's pleasing note!
    Hark to the swelling nuptial song!
In joyous strains the voices float,
    And still the choral peal prolong.

Again the clan, in festive crowd,
    Throng through the gate of Alva's hall;
The sounds of mirth re-echo loud,
    And all their former joy recall.

But who is he, whose darken'd brow
    Glooms in the midst of general mirth?

Before his eyes' far fiercer glow
    The blue flames curdle o'er the hearth.

Dark is the robe which wraps his form, 185
    And tall his plume of gory red;
His voice is like the rising storm,
    But light and trackless is his tread.

'T is noon of night, the pledge goes round,
    The bridegroom's health is deeply quaff'd; 190
With shouts the vaulted roofs resound,
    And all combine to hail the draught.

Sudden the stranger-chief arose,
    And all the clamorous crowd are hush'd;
And Angus' cheek with wonder glows, 195
    And Mora's tender bosom blush'd.

"Old man!" he cried, "this pledge is done;
    Thou saw'st 't was duly drank by me:
It hail'd the nuptials of thy son:
    Now will I claim a pledge from thee. 200

"While all around is mirth and joy,
    To bless thy Allan's happy lot,
Say, had'st thou ne'er another boy?
    Say, why should Oscar be forgot?"

"Alas!" the hapless sire replied, 205
    The big tear starting as he spoke,
"When Oscar left my hall, or died,
    This aged heart was almost broke.

"Thrice has the earth revolved her course
    Since Oscar's form has bless'd my sight; 210
And Allan is my last resource,
    Since martial Oscar's death or flight."

"'T is well," replied the stranger stern,
    And fiercely flash'd his rolling eye:
"Thy Oscar's fate I fain would learn; 215
    Perhaps the hero did not die.

"Perchance, if those whom most he loved
 Would call, thy Oscar might return;
Perchance the chief has only roved;
 For him thy beltane yet may burn.   220

"Fill high the bowl the table round,
 We will not claim the pledge by stealth;
With wine let every cup be crown'd;
 Pledge me departed Oscar's health."

"With all my soul," old Angus said,   225
 And fill'd his goblet to the brim;
"Here's to my boy! alive or dead,
 I ne'er shall find a son like him."

"Bravely, old man, this health has sped;
 But why does Allan trembling stand?   230
Come, drink remembrance of the dead,
 And raise thy cup with firmer hand."

The crimson glow of Allan's face
 Was turn'd at once to ghastly hue;
The drops of death each other chase   235
 Adown in agonizing dew.

Thrice did he raise the goblet high,
 And thrice his lips refused to taste;
For thrice he caught the stranger's eye
 On his with deadly fury placed.   240

"And is it thus a brother hails
 A brother's fond remembrance here?
If thus affection's strength prevails,
 What might we not expect from fear?"

Roused by the sneer, he raised the bowl,   245
 "Would Oscar now could share our mirth!"
Internal fear appall'd his soul;
 He said, and dash'd the cup to earth.

"'T is he!   I hear my murderer's voice!"
 Loud shrieks a darkly gleaming form,   250

"A murderer's voice!" the roof replies,
    And deeply swells the bursting storm.

The tapers wink, the chieftains shrink,
    The stranger's gone, — amidst the crew
A form was seen in tartan green,   255
    And tall the shade terrific grew.

His waist was bound with a broad belt round,
    His plume of sable stream'd on high;
But his breast was bare, with the red wounds there,
    And fix'd was the glare of his glassy eye.   260

And thrice he smiled, with his eye so wild,
    On Angus bending low the knee;
And thrice he frown'd on a chief on the ground,
    Whom shivering crowds with horror see.

The bolts loud roll, from pole to pole,   265
    The thunders through the welkin ring,
And the gleaming form, through the mist of the storm,
    Was borne on high by the whirlwind's wing.

Cold was the feast, the revel ceased,
    Who lies upon the stony floor?   270
Oblivion press'd old Angus' breast,
    At length his life-pulse throbs once more.

"Away, away! let the leech essay
    To pour the light on Allan's eyes:"
His sand is done, — his race is run;   275
    Oh! never more shall Allan rise!

But Oscar's breast is cold as clay,
    His locks are lifted by the gale:
And Allan's barbed arrow lay
    With him in dark Glentanar's vale.   280

And whence the dreadful stranger came,
    Or who, no mortal wight can tell;
But no one doubts the form of flame,
    For Alva's sons knew Oscar well.

Ambition nerved young Allan's hand, 285
　　Exulting demons wing'd his dart;
While Envy waved her burning brand,
　　And pour'd her venom round his heart.

Swift is the shaft from Allan's bow;
　　Whose streaming life-blood stains his side? 290
Dark Oscar's sable crest is low,
　　The dart has drunk his vital tide.

And Mora's eye could Allan move,
　　She bade his wounded pride rebel;
Alas! that eyes which beam'd with love 295
　　Should urge the soul to deeds of hell.

Lo! seest thou not a lonely tomb
　　Which rises o'er a warrior dead?
It glimmers through the twilight gloom;
　　Oh! that is Allan's nuptial bed. 300

Far, distant far, the noble grave
　　Which held his clan's great ashes stood;
And o'er his corse no banners wave,
　　For they were stain'd with kindred blood.

What minstrel gray, what hoary bard, 305
　　Shall Allan's deeds on harp-strings raise?
The song is glory's chief reward,
　　But who can strike a murderer's praise?

Unstrung, untouch'd, the harp must stand,
　　No minstrel dare the theme awake; 310
Guilt would benumb his palsied hand,
　　His harp in shuddering chords would break.

No lyre of fame, no hallow'd verse,
　　Shall sound his glories high in air:
A dying father's bitter curse, 315
　　A brother's death-groan echoes there.

1806

26 Sir David Graeme

James Hogg (1770–1835)

The dow flew east, the dow flew west,
    The dow flew far ayont the fell;
An' sair at e'en she seemed distrest,
    But what perplex'd her could not tell.

But aye she coo'd wi' mournfu' croon,
    An' ruffled a' her feathers fair;
An' lookit sad as she war boun'
    To leave the land for evermair.

The lady wept, an' some did blame, —
    She didna blame the bonnie dow,
But sair she blamed Sir David Graeme,
    Because the knight had broke his vow.

For he had sworn by the starns sae bright,
    An' by their bed on the dewy green,
To meet her there on St. Lambert's night,
    Whatever dangers lay between;

To risk his fortune an' his life
    In bearing her frae her father's towers,
To gie her a' the lands o' Dryfe,
    An' the Enzie-holm wi' its bonnie bowers.

The day arrived, the evening came,
    The lady looked wi' wistful ee;
But, O, alas! her noble Graeme
    Frae e'en to morn she didna see.

An' she has sat her down an' grat;
    The warld to her like a desert seemed;
An' she wyted this an' she wyted that,
    But o' the real cause never dreamed.

The sun had drunk frae Keilder fell
    His beverage o' the morning dew;

Sir David Graeme

The deer had crouched her in the dell,
    The heather oped its bells o' blue;

The lambs were skipping on the brae,
    The laverock hiche attour them sung,
An' aye she hailed the jocund day,
    Till the wee, wee tabors o' heaven rung.

The lady to her window hied,
    And it opened owre the banks o' Tyne;
"An', O, alak!" she said, an' sighed,
    "Sure ilka breast is blythe but mine!

"Where hae ye been, my bonnie dow,
    That I hae fed wi' the bread an' wine?
As roving a' the country through,
    O, saw ye this fause knight o' mine?"

The dow sat down on the window tree,
    An' she carried a lock o' yellow hair;
Then she perched upon that lady's knee,
    An' carefully she placed it there.

"What can this mean? This lock's the same
    That aince was mine. Whate'er betide,
This lock I gae to Sir David Graeme,
    The flower of a' the Border side.

"He might hae sent it by squire or page,
    An' no letten the wily dow steal't awa;
'Tis a matter for the lore and the counsels of age,
    But the thing I canna read at a'."

The dow flew east, the dow flew west,
    The dow she flew far ayont the fell,
An' back she came wi' panting breast,
    Ere the ringing o' the castle bell.

She lighted ahiche on the holly-tap,
    An' she cried, "cur-dow," an' fluttered her wing;
Then flew into that lady's lap,
    An' there she placed a diamond ring.

"What can this mean? This ring is the same 65
   That aince was mine. Whate'er betide,
This ring I gae to Sir David Graeme,
   The flower of a' the Border side.

"He sends me back the love-tokens true!
   Was ever poor maiden perplexed like me? 70
'Twould seem he's reclaimed his faith an' his vow,
   But all is fauldit in mystery."

An' she has sat her down an' grat,
   The world to her a desert seemed;
An' she wyted this an' she wyted that, 75
   But o' the real cause never dreamed.

When, lo! Sir David's trusty hound,
   Wi' humpling back, an' a waefu' ee,
Came cringing in an' lookit around,
   But his look was hopeless as could be. 80

He laid his head on that lady's knee,
   An' he lookit as somebody he would name,
An' there was a language in his howe ee,
   That was stronger than a tongue could frame.

She fed him wi' the milk an' the bread, 85
   An' ilka good thing that he wad hae;
He lickit her hand, he coured his head,
   Then slowly, slowly he slunkered away.

But she has eyed her fause knight's hound,
   An' a' to see where he wad gae: 90
He whined, an' he howled, an' lookit around,
   Then slowly, slowly he trudged away.

Then she's casten aff her coal black shoon,
   An' her bonnie silken hose, sae glancin' an' sheen;
She kiltit her wilye coat an' broidered gown, 95
   An' away she has linkit over the green.

She followed the hound owre muirs an' rocks,
   Through mony a dell an' dowie glen,

Sir David Graeme

Till frae her brow an' bonnie goud locks,
    The dewe dreepit down like the drops o' rain.

An' aye she said, "My love may be hid,
    An' darena come to the castle to me;
But him I will find and dearly I'll chide,
    For lack o' stout heart an' courtesye.

"But ae kind press to his manly breast,
    An' ae kind kiss in the moorland glen,
Will weel atone for a' that is past; —
    O wae to the paukie snares o' men!"

An' aye she eyed the gray sloth hound,
    As he windit owre Deadwater fell,
Till he came to the den wi' the moss inbound,
    An' O, but it kythed a lonesome dell!

An' he waggit his tail, an' he fawned about,
    Then he coured him down sae wearilye;
"Ah! yon's my love, I hae found him out,
    He's lying waiting in the dell for me.

"To meet a knight near the fall of night
    Alone in this untrodden wild,
It scarcely becomes a lady bright,
    But I'll vow that the hound my steps beguiled."

Alack! whatever a maiden may say,
    True has't been said, an' aften been sung,
The ee her heart's love will betray,
    An' the secret will sirple frae her tongue.

"What ails my love, that he looks nae roun',
    A lady's stately step to view?
Ah me! I hae neither stockings nor shoon,
    An' my feet are sae white wi' the moorland dew.

"Sae sound as he sleeps in his hunting gear,
    To waken him great pity would be;
Deaf is the man that caresna to hear,
    And blind is he wha wantsna to see."

Sae saftly she treads the wee green swaird,
    Wi' the lichens an' the ling a' fringed around
"My een are darkened wi' some wul-weird,
    What ails my love, he sleeps sae sound?"

She gae ae look, she needit but ane,
    For it left nae sweet uncertaintye;
She saw a wound through his shoulder bane,
    An' in his brave breast two or three.

There wasna sic een on the Border green,
    As the piercing een o' Sir David Graeme;
She glisked wi' her ee where these een should be,
    But the raven had been there afore she came.

There's a cloud that fa's darker than the night,
    An' darkly on that lady it came:
There's a sleep as deep as the sleep outright, —
    'Tis without a feeling or a name;

'Tis a dull an' a dreamless lethargye,
    For the spirit strays owre vale an' hill,
An' the bosom is left a vacancy,
    An' when it comes back it is darker still.

O shepherd lift that comely corpse,
    Well may you see no wound is there;
There's a faint rose 'mid the bright dew drops,
    An' they have not wet her glossy hair.

There's a lady has lived in Hoswood tower,
    'Tis seven years past on St. Lambert's day,
An' aye when comes the vesper hour
    These words an' no more can she say:

"They slew my love on the wild Swaird green,
    As he was on his way to me;
An' the ravens picked his bonnie blue een,
    An' the tongue that was formed for courtesye.

"My brothers they slew my comely knight,
    An' his grave is red blood to the brim:

I thought to have slept out the lang, lang night,
   But they've wakened me, and wakened not him!"

1807

27   Lord Ullin's Daughter

Thomas Campbell (1777–1844)

A chieftain to the Highlands bound
   Cries 'Boatman, do not tarry!
And I'll give thee a silver pound
   To row us o'er the ferry.'

'Now who be ye would cross Lochgyle,   5
   This dark and stormy water?'
'O, I'm the chief of Ulva's isle,
   And this Lord Ullin's daughter.

'And fast before her father's men
   Three days we've fled together,   10
For, should he find us in the glen,
   My blood would stain the heather.

'His horsemen hard behind us ride;
   Should they our steps discover,
Then who will cheer my bonny bride   15
   When they have slain her lover?'

Outspoke the hardy Highland wight,
   'I'll go, my chief!   I'm ready;
It is not for your silver bright,
   But for your winsome lady.   20

'And, by my word! the bonny bird
   In danger shall not tarry;
So, though the waves are raging white

I'll row you o'er the ferry.'

By this the storm grew loud apace,
    The water-wraith was shrieking;
And in the scowl of heaven each face
    Grew dark as they were speaking.

But still, as wilder blew the wind,
    And as the night grew drearer,
Adown the glen rode armèd men —
    Their trampling sounded nearer.

'O haste thee, haste!' the lady cries,
    'Though tempests round us gather;
I'll meet the raging of the skies,
    But not an angry father.'

The boat has left a stormy land,
    A stormy sea before her, —
When, oh! too strong for human hand,
    The tempest gathered o'er her.

And still they rowed amidst the roar
    Of waters fast prevailing:
Lord Ullin reached that fatal shore, —
    His wrath was changed to wailing.

For sore dismayed, through storm and shade,
    His child he did discover:
One lovely hand she stretched for aid,
    And one was round her lover.

'Come back! come back!' he cried in grief
    Across the stormy water:
'And I'll forgive your Highland chief,
    My daughter! oh my daughter!'

'Twas vain: the loud waves lashed the shore,
    Return or aid preventing;
The waters wild went o'er his child,
    And he was left lamenting.

1809

28 Sister Rosa: a Ballad

Percy Bysshe Shelley (1792–1822)

I
The death-bell beats! —
The mountain repeats
The echoing sound of the knell;
    And the dark Monk now
    Wraps the cowl round his brow,
As he sits in his lonely cell.

II
    And the cold hand of death
    Chills his shuddering breath,
As he lists to the fearful lay
    Which the ghosts of the sky,
    As they sweep wildly by,
Sing to departed day.
    And they sing of the hour
    When the stern fates had power
To resolve Rosa's form to its clay.

III
    But that hour is past;
    And that hour was the last
Of peace to the dark Monk's brain.
    Bitter tears, from his eyes, gushed silent and fast;
And he strove to suppress them in vain.

IV
Then his fair cross of gold he dashed on the floor,
When the death-knell struck on his ear. —
    'Delight is in store
    For her evermore;
But for me is fate, horror, and fear.'

V
    Then his eyes wildly rolled,
    When the death-bell tolled,
And he raged in terrific woe.

    And he stamped on the ground, —
    But when ceased the sound,
Tears again began to flow.

VI

    And the ice of despair
    Chilled the wild throb of care,
And he sate in mute agony still;
    Till the night-stars shone through the cloudless air,
And the pale moonbeam slept on the hill.

VII

    Then he knelt in his cell: —
    And the horrors of hell
Were delights to his agonized pain,
    And he prayed to God to dissolve the spell,
Which else must for ever remain.

VIII

And in fervent pray'r he knelt on the ground,
    Till the abbey bell struck One:
His feverish blood ran chill at the sound:
    A voice hollow and horrible murmured around —
    'The term of thy penance is done!'

IX

    Grew dark the night;
    The moonbeam bright
Waxed faint on the mountain high;
    And, from the black hill,
    Went a voice cold and still, —
'Monk! thou art free to die.'

X

    Then he rose on his feet,
    And his heart loud did beat,
And his limbs they were palsied with dread;
    Whilst the grave's clammy dew
    O'er his pale forehead grew;
And he shuddered to sleep with the dead.

XI

And the wild midnight storm
  Raved around his tall form,
As he sought the chapel's gloom:
  And the sunk grass did sigh
  To the wind, bleak and high,
As he searched for the new-made tomb.

XII

And forms, dark and high,
  Seemed around him to fly,
And mingle their yells with the blast:
  And on the dark wall
  Half-seen shadows did fall,
As enhorrored he onward passed.

XIII

And the storm-fiends wild rave
  O'er the new-made grave,
And dread shadows linger around.
  The Monk called on God his soul to save,
And, in horror, sank on the ground.

XIV

Then despair nerved his arm
  To dispel the charm,
And he burst Rosa's coffin asunder.
  And the fierce storm did swell
  More terrific and fell,
And louder pealed the thunder.

XV

And laughed, in joy, the fiendish throng,
  Mixed with ghosts of the mouldering dead:
And their grisly wings, as they floated along,
  Whistled in murmurs dread.

XVI

And her skeleton form the dead Nun reared
  Which dripped with the chill dew of hell.
In her half-eaten eyeballs two pale flames appeared,
And triumphant their gleam on the dark Monk glared,

As he stood within the cell. 90

XVII

And her lank hand lay on his shuddering brain;
   But each power was nerved by fear. —
'I never, henceforth, may breathe again;
Death now ends mine anguished pain. —
   The grave yawns, — we meet there.' 95

XVIII

And her skeleton lungs did utter the sound,
   So deadly, so lone, and so fell,
That in long vibrations shuddered the ground;
And as the stern notes floated around,
   A deep groan was answered from hell. 100

1811

29 *La Belle Dame sans Merci*

John Keats (1795–1821)

I.

Ah, what can ail thee, wretched wight,
   Alone and palely loitering;
The sedge is wither'd from the lake,
   And no birds sing.

II.

Ah, what can ail thee, wretched wight, 5
   So haggard and so woe-begone?
The squirrel's granary is full,
   And the harvest's done.

III.

I see a lily on thy brow,
   With anguish moist and fever dew; 10

And on thy cheek a fading rose
   Fast withereth too.

IV.
I met a lady in the meads
   Full beautiful, a faery's child;
Her hair was long, her foot was light,
   And her eyes were wild.

V.
I set her on my pacing steed,
   And nothing else saw all day long;
For sideways would she lean, and sing
   A faery's song.

VI.
I made a garland for her head,
   And bracelets too, and fragrant zone;
She look'd at me as she did love,
   And made sweet moan.

VII.
She found me roots of relish sweet,
   And honey wild, and manna dew;
And sure in language strange she said,
   I love thee true.

VIII.
She took me to her elfin grot,
   And there she gaz'd and sighed deep,
And there I shut her wild sad eyes —
   So kiss'd to sleep.

IX.
And there we slumber'd on the moss,
   And there I dream'd, ah woe betide,
The latest dream I ever dream'd
   On the cold hill side.

X.
I saw pale kings, and princes too,
   Pale warriors, death-pale were they all;

Who cry'd — "La belle Dame sans merci
   Hath thee in thrall!" 40

XI.
I saw their starv'd lips in the gloam
   With horrid warning gaped wide,
And I awoke, and found me here
   On the cold hill side.

XII.
And this is why I sojourn here 45
   Alone and palely loitering,
Though the sedge is wither'd from the lake,
   And no birds sing.

1819

30   Mary's Ghost

Thomas Hood (1799–1845)

'Twas in the middle of the night,
   To sleep young William tried,
When Mary's ghost came stealing in,
   And stood at his bed-side.

O William dear!   O William dear! 5
   My rest eternal ceases;
Alas! my everlasting peace
   Is broken into pieces.

I thought the last of all my cares
   Would end with my last minute; 10
But tho' I went to my long home,
   I didn't stay long in it.

The body-snatchers they have come,

And made a snatch at me;
It's very hard them kind of men
    Won't let a body be!

You thought that I was buried deep,
    Quite decent like and chary,
But from her grave in Mary-bone
    They've come and boned your Mary.

The arm that used to take your arm
    Is took to Dr. Vyse;
And both my legs are gone to walk
    The hospital at Guy's.

I vow'd that you should have my hand,
    But fate gives us denial;
You'll find it there, at Doctor Bell's,
    In spirits and a phial.

As for my feet, the little feet
    You used to call so pretty,
There's one, I know, in Bedford Row,
    The t'other in the city.

I can't tell where my head is gone,
    But Doctor Carpue can:
As for my trunk, it's all pack'd up
    To go by Pickford's van.

I wish you'd go to Mr. P.
    And save me such a ride!
I don't half like the outside place,
    They've took for my inside.

The cock it crows — I must be gone!
    My William, we must part!
But I'll be yours in death, altho'
    Sir Astley has my heart.

Don't go to weep upon my grave,
    And think that there I be;
They haven't left an atom there

Of my anatomie.

1827

31 Porphyria's Lover

Robert Browning (1812–89)

The rain set early in to-night,
    The sullen wind was soon awake,
It tore the elm-tops down for spite,
    And did its worst to vex the lake:
I listened with heart fit to break. 5
When glided in Porphyria; straight
    She shut the cold out and the storm,
And kneeled and made the cheerless grate
    Blaze up, and all the cottage warm;
Which done, she rose, and from her form 10
Withdrew the dripping cloak and shawl,
    And laid her soiled gloves by, untied
Her hat and let the damp hair fall,
    And, last, she sat down by my side
    And called me. When no voice replied, 15
She put my arm about her waist,
    And made her smooth white shoulder bare,
And all her yellow hair displaced,
    And, stooping, made my cheek lie there,
    And spread, o'er all, her yellow hair, 20
Murmuring how she loved me — she
    Too weak, for all her heart's endeavour,
To set its struggling passion free
    From pride, and vainer ties dissever,
    And give herself to me for ever. 25
But passion sometimes would prevail,
    Nor could to-night's gay feast restrain
A sudden thought of one so pale
    For love of her, and all in vain:

So, she was come through wind and rain.
Be sure I looked up at her eyes
   Happy and proud; at last I knew
Porphyria worshipped me; surprise
   Made my heart swell, and still it grew
   While I debated what to do.
That moment she was mine, mine, fair,
   Perfectly pure and good: I found
A thing to do, and all her hair
   In one long yellow string I wound
   Three times her little throat around,
And strangled her. No pain felt she;
   I am quite sure she felt no pain.
As a shut bud that holds a bee,
   I warily oped her lids: again
   Laughed the blue eyes without a stain.
And I untightened next the tress
   About her neck; her cheek once more
Blushed bright beneath my burning kiss:
   I propped her head up as before,
   Only, this time my shoulder bore
Her head, which droops upon it still:
   The smiling rosy little head,
So glad it has its utmost will,
   That all it scorned at once is fled,
   And I, its love, am gained instead!
Porphyria's love: she guessed not how
   Her darling one wish would be heard.
And thus we sit together now,
   And all night long we have not stirred,
   And yet God has not said a word!

1836

32 The Lord of Burleigh

Alfred Tennyson (1809–92)

In her ear he whispers gaily,
   'If my heart by signs can tell,
Maiden, I have watch'd thee daily,
   And I think thou lov'st me well.'
She replies, in accents fainter, 5
   'There is none I love like thee.'
He is but a landscape-painter,
   And a village maiden she.
He to lips, that fondly falter,
   Presses his without reproof: 10
Leads her to the village altar,
   And they leave her father's roof.
'I can make no marriage present:
   Little can I give my wife.
Love will make our cottage pleasant, 15
   And I love thee more than life.'
They by parks and lodges going
   See the lordly castles stand:
Summer woods, about them blowing,
   Made a murmur in the land. 20
From deep thought himself he rouses,
   Says to her that loves him well,
'Let us see these handsome houses
   Where the wealthy nobles dwell.'
So she goes by him attended, 25
   Hears him lovingly converse,
Sees whatever fair and splendid
   Lay betwixt his home and hers;
Parks with oak and chestnut shady,
   Parks and order'd gardens great, 30
Ancient homes of lord and lady,
   Built for pleasure and for state.
All he shows her makes him dearer:
   Evermore she seems to gaze
On that cottage growing nearer, 35
   Where they twain will spend their days.
O but she will love him truly!

He shall have a cheerful home;
She will order all things duly,
   When beneath his roof they come.   40
Thus her heart rejoices greatly,
   Till a gateway she discerns
With armorial bearings stately,
   And beneath the gate she turns;
Sees a mansion more majestic   45
   Than all those she saw before:
Many a gallant gay domestic
   Bows before him at the door.
And they speak in gentle murmur,
   When they answer to his call,   50
While he treads with footstep firmer,
   Leading on from hall to hall.
And, while now she wonders blindly,
   Nor the meaning can divine,
Proudly turns he round and kindly,   55
   'All of this is mine and thine.'
Here he lives in state and bounty,
   Lord of Burleigh, fair and free,
Not a lord in all the county
   Is so great a lord as he.   60
All at once the colour flushes
   Her sweet face from brow to chin:
As it were with shame she blushes,
   And her spirit changed within.
Then her countenance all over   65
   Pale again as death did prove:
But he clasp'd her like a lover,
   And he cheer'd her soul with love.
So she strove against her weakness,
   Tho' at times her spirit sank: 70
Shaped her heart with woman's meekness
   To all duties of her rank:
And a gentle consort made he,
   And her gentle mind was such
That she grew a noble lady,   75
   And the people loved her much.
But a trouble weigh'd upon her,
   And perplex'd her, night and morn,
With the burthen of an honour

     Unto which she was not born.
Faint she grew, and ever fainter,
     And she murmur'd, 'Oh, that he
Were once more that landscape-painter,
     Which did win my heart from me!'
So she droop'd and droop'd before him,
     Fading slowly from his side:
Three fair children first she bore him,
     Then before her time she died.
Weeping, weeping late and early,
     Walking up and pacing down,
Deeply mourn'd the Lord of Burleigh,
     Burleigh-house by Stamford-town.
And he came to look upon her,
     And he look'd at her and said,
'Bring the dress and put it on her,
     That she wore when she was wed.'
Then her people, softly treading,
     Bore to earth her body, drest
In the dress that she was wed in,
     That her spirit might have rest.

1833–34

33 The Execution of Montrose

William Edmondstoune Aytoun (1813–65)

I.

Come hither, Evan Cameron!
     Come, stand beside my knee —
I hear the river roaring down
     Towards the wintry sea.
There's shouting on the mountain-side
     There's war within the blast —
Old faces look upon me,
     Old forms go trooping past:

I hear the pibroch wailing
    Amidst the din of fight,
And my dim spirit wakes again
    Upon the verge of night.

II.

'Twas I that led the Highland host
    Through wild Lochaber's snows,
What time the plaided clans came down
    To battle with Montrose.
I've told thee how the Southrons fell
    Beneath the broad claymore,
And how we smote the Campbell clan
    By Inverlochy's shore.
I've told thee how we swept Dundee,
    And tamed the Lindsays' pride;
But never have I told thee yet
    How the great Marquis died.

III.

A traitor sold him to his foes;
    O deed of deathless shame!
I charge thee, boy, if e'er thou meet
    With one of Assynt's name —
Be it upon the mountain's side,
    Or yet within the glen,
Stand he in martial gear alone,
    Or backed by armèd men —
Face him, as thou wouldst face the man
    Who wronged thy sire's renown;
Remember of what blood thou art,
    And strike the caitiff down!

IV.

They brought him to the Watergate,
    Hard bound with hempen span,
As though they held a lion there,
    And not a fenceless man.
They set him high upon a cart —
    The hangman rode below —
They drew his hands behind his back,
    And bared his noble brow.

Then, as a hound is slipped from leash,
    They cheered the common throng,
And blew the note with yell and shout,
    And bade him pass along.

V.

It would have made a brave man's heart
    Grow sad and sick that day,
To watch the keen malignant eyes
    Bent down on that array.
There stood the Whig west-country lords,
    In balcony and bow;
There sat their gaunt and withered dames,
    And their daughters all a-row.
And every open window
    Was full as full might be
With black-robed Covenanting carles,
    That goodly sport to see!

VI.

But when he came, though pale and wan,
    He looked so great and high,
So noble was his manly front,
    So calm his steadfast eye; —
The rabble rout forbore to shout,
    And each man held his breath,
For well they knew the hero's soul
    Was face to face with death.
And then a mournful shudder
    Through all the people crept,
And some that came to scoff at him
    Now turned aside and wept.

VII.

But onwards — always onwards,
    In silence and in gloom,
The dreary pageant laboured,
    Till it reached the house of doom.
Then first a woman's voice was heard
    In jeer and laughter loud,
And an angry cry and a hiss arose
    From the heart of the tossing crowd:

Then as the Græme looked upwards,
  He saw the ugly smile
Of him who sold his king for gold —
  The master-fiend Argyle!

VIII.
The Marquis gazed a moment,
  And nothing did he say,
But the cheek of Argyle grew ghastly pale,
  And he turned his eyes away.
The painted harlot by his side,
  She shook through every limb,
For a roar like thunder swept the street,
  And hands were clenched at him;
And a Saxon soldier cried aloud,
  "Back, coward, from thy place!
For seven long years thou hast not dared
  To look him in the face."

IX.
Had I been there with sword in hand,
  And fifty Camerons by,
That day through high Dunedin's streets
  Had pealed the slogan-cry.
Not all their troops of trampling horse,
  Nor might of mailèd men —
Not all the rebels in the south
  Had borne us backwards then!
Once more his foot on Highland heath
  Had trod as free as air,
Or I, and all who bore my name,
  Been laid around him there!

X.
It might not be. They placed him next
  Within the solemn hall,
Where once the Scottish kings were throned
  Amidst their nobles all.
But there was dust of vulgar feet
  On that polluted floor,
And perjured traitors filled the place
  Where good men sate before.

With savage glee came Warristoun
　　To read the murderous doom;
And then uprose the great Montrose
　　In the middle of the room.

XI.

"Now, by my faith as belted knight,
　　And by the name I bear,
And by the bright Saint Andrew's cross
　　That waves above us there —
Yea, by a greater, mightier oath —
　　And oh, that such should be! —
By that dark stream of royal blood
　　That lies 'twixt you and me —
I have not sought in battle-field
　　A wreath of such renown,
Nor dared I hope on my dying day
　　To win the martyr's crown!

XII.

"There is a chamber far away
　　Where sleep the good and brave,
But a better place ye have named for me
　　Than by my father's grave.
For truth and right, 'gainst treason's might,
　　This hand hath always striven,
And ye raise it up for a witness still
　　In the eye of earth and heaven.
Then nail my head on yonder tower —
　　Give every town a limb —
And God who made shall gather them:
　　I go from you to Him!"

XIII.

The morning dawned full darkly,
　　The rain came flashing down,
And the jagged streak of the levin-bolt
　　Lit up the gloomy town:
The thunder crashed across the heaven,
　　The fatal hour was come;
Yet aye broke in with muffled beat,
　　The 'larm of the drum.

There was madness on the earth below
    And anger in the sky,
And young and old, and rich and poor,   155
    Came forth to see him die.

XIV.
Ah, God! that ghastly gibbet!
    How dismal 'tis to see
The great tall spectral skeleton,
    The ladder and the tree!   160
Hark! hark! it is the clash of arms —
    The bells begin to toll —
"He is coming! he is coming!
    God's mercy on his soul!"
One last long peal of thunder —   165
    The clouds are cleared away,
And the glorious sun once more looks down
    Amidst the dazzling day.

XV.
"He is coming! he is coming!"
    Like a bridegroom from his room,   170
Came the hero from his prison
    To the scaffold and the doom.
There was glory on his forehead,
    There was lustre in his eye,
And he never walked to battle   175
    More proudly than to die:
There was colour in his visage,
    Though the cheeks of all were wan,
And they marvelled as they saw him pass,
    That great and goodly man!   180

XVI.
He mounted up the scaffold,
    And he turned him to the crowd;
But they dared not trust the people,
    So he might not speak aloud.
But he looked upon the heavens,   185
    And they were clear and blue,
And in the liquid ether
    The eye of God shone through!

    Yet a black and murky battlement
        Lay resting on the hill,   190
    As though the thunder slept within —
        All else was calm and still.

XVII.

    The grim Geneva ministers
        With anxious scowl drew near,
    As you have seen the ravens flock   195
        Around the dying deer.
    He would not deign them word nor sign,
        But alone he bent the knee;
    And veiled his face for Christ's dear grace
        Beneath the gallows-tree.   200
    Then radiant and serene he rose,
        And cast his cloak away:
    For he had ta'en his latest look
        Of earth and sun and day.

XVIII.

    A beam of light fell o'er him,   205
        Like a glory round the shriven,
    And he climbed the lofty ladder
        As it were the path to heaven.
    Then came a flash from out the cloud,
        And a stunning thunder-roll;   210
    And no man dared to look aloft,
        For fear was on every soul.
    There was another heavy sound,
        A hush and then a groan;
    And darkness swept across the sky —   215
        The work of death was done!

1844

34 The Knight and the Lady

William Makepeace Thackeray (1811–63)

There's in the Vest a city pleasant
  To vich King Bladud gev his name,
And in that city there's a Crescent
  Vere dwelt a noble knight of fame.

Although that galliant knight is oldish,   5
  Although Sir John as grey grey air,
Hage has not made his busum coldish
  His Art still beats tewodds the Fair!

'Twas two years sins, this knight so splendid,
  Peraps fateagued with Bath's routines,   10
To Paris towne his phootsteps bended
  In sutch of gayer folks and seans.

His and was free, his means was easy,
  A nobler, finer gent than he
Ne'er drove about the Shons-Eleesy,   15
  Or paced the Roo de Rivolee.

A brougham and pair Sir John prowided,
  In which abroad he loved to ride;
But ar! he most of all enjyed it,
  When some one helse was sittin' inside!   20

That "some one helse" a lovely dame was,
  Dear ladies, you will heasy tell —
Countess Grabrowski her sweet name was,
  A noble title, ard to spell.

This faymus Countess ad a daughter   25
  Of lovely form and tender art;
A nobleman in marridge sought her,
  By name the Baron of Saint Bart.

Their pashn touched the noble Sir John,
  It was so pewer and profound;   30

Lady Grabrowski he did urge on
    With Hyming's wreeth their loves to crownd.

"O, come to Bath, to Lansdowne Crescent,"
    Says kind Sir John, "and live with me;
The living there's uncommon pleasant —   35
    I'm sure you'll find the hair agree.

"O, come to Bath, my fair Grabrowski,
    And bring your charming girl," sezee;
"The Barring here shall have the ouse-key,
    Vith breakfast, dinner, lunch, and tea.   40

"And when they've passed an appy winter,
    Their opes and loves no more we'll bar;
The marridge-vow they'll enter inter,
    And I at church will be their Par."

To Bath they went to Lansdowne Crescent,   45
    Where good Sir John he did provide
No end of teas and balls incessant,
    And hosses both to drive and ride.

He was so Ospitably busy,
    When Miss was late, he'd make so bold   50
Upstairs to call out, "Missy, Missy,
    Come down, the coffy's getting cold!"

But O! 'tis sadd to think such bounties
    Should meet with such return as this;
O Barring of Saint Bart, O Countess   55
    Grabrowski, and O cruel Miss!

He married you at Bath's fair Habby,
    Saint Bart he treated like a son —
And wasn't it uncommon shabby
    To do what you have went and done!   60

My trembling And amost refewses
    To write the charge which Sir John swore,
Of which the Countess he ecuses,
    Her daughter and her son-in-lore.

My Mews quite blushes as she sings of
    The fatle charge which now I quote:
He says Miss took his two best rings off,
    And pawned 'em for a tenpun note.

"Is this the child of honest parince,
    To make away with folks' best things?
Is this, pray, like the wives of Barrins,
    To go and prig a gentleman's rings?"

Thus thought Sir John, by anger wrought on,
    And to rewenge his injured cause,
He brought them hup to Mr. Broughton,
    Last Vensday veek as ever waws.

If guiltless, how she have been slandered!
    If guilty, wengeance will not fail:
Meanwhile the lady is remanded
    And gev three hundred pouns in bail.

1848

35   The Two Brothers

Lewis Carroll (1832–98)

There were two brothers at Twyford school,
    And when they had left the place,
It was, "Will ye learn Greek and Latin?
    Or will ye run me a race?
Or will ye go up to yonder bridge,
    And there we will angle for dace?"

"I'm too stupid for Greek and for Latin,
    I'm too lazy by half for a race,
So I'll even go up to yonder bridge,
    And there we will angle for dace."

He has fitted together two joints of his rod,
    And to them he has added another,
And then a great hook he took from his book,
    And ran it right into his brother.

Oh much is the noise that is made among boys
    When playfully pelting a pig,
But a far greater pother was made by his brother
    When flung from the top of the brigg.

The fish hurried up by the dozens,
    All ready and eager to bite,
For the lad that he flung was so tender and young,
    It quite gave them an appetite.

Said he, "Thus shall he wallop about
    And the fish take him quite at their ease,
For me to annoy it was ever his joy,
    Now I'll teach him the meaning of 'Tees'!"

The wind to his ear brought a voice,
    "My brother, you didn't had ought ter!
And what have I done that you think it such fun
    To indulge in the pleasure of slaughter?

"A good nibble or bite is my chiefest delight,
    When I'm merely expected to *see*,
But a bite from a fish is not quite what I wish,
    When I get it performed upon *me*;
And just now here's a swarm of dace at my arm,
    And a perch has got hold of my knee.

"For water my thirst was not great at the first,
    And of fish I have quite sufficien ——"
"Oh fear not!" he cried, "for whatever betide,
    We are both in the selfsame condition!

"I am sure that our state's very nearly alike
    (Not considering the question of slaughter),
For I have my perch on the top of the bridge,
    And you have your perch in the water.

"I stick to my perch and your perch sticks to you, 45
    We are really extremely alike;
I've a turn-pike up here, and I very much fear
    You may soon have a turn with a pike."

"Oh, grant but one wish! If I'm took by a fish
    (For your bait is your brother, good man!) 50
Pull him up if you like, but I hope you will strike
    As gently as ever you can."

"If the fish be a trout, I'm afraid there's no doubt
    I must strike him like lightning that's greased;
If the fish be a pike, I'll engage not to strike, 55
    Till I've waited ten minutes at least."

"But in those ten minutes to desolate Fate
    Your brother a victim may fall!"
"I'll reduce it to five, so *perhaps* you'll survive,
    But the chance is exceedingly small." 60

"Oh hard is your heart for to act such a part;
    Is it iron, or granite, or steel?"
"Why, I really can't say — it is many a day
    Since my heart was accustomed to feel.

"'Twas my heart-cherished wish for to slay many fish 65
    Each day did my malice grow worse,
For my heart didn't soften with doing it so often
    But rather, I should say, the reverse."

"Oh would I were back at Twyford school,
    Learning lessons in fear of the birch!" 70
"Nay, brother!" he cried, "for whatever betide,
    You are better off here with your perch!

"I am sure you'll allow you are happier now,
    With nothing to do but to play;
And this single line here, it is perfectly clear, 75
    Is much better than thirty a day!

"And as to the rod hanging over your head,
    And apparently ready to fall,

That, you know, was the case, when you lived in that place,
    So it need not be reckoned at all.

"Do you see that old trout with a turn-up-nose snout?
    (Just to speak on a pleasanter theme),
Observe, my dear brother, our love for each other —
    He's the one I like best in the stream.

"To-morrow I mean to invite him to dine
    (We shall all of us think it a treat);
If the day should be fine, I'll just *drop him a line*,
    And we'll settle what time we're to meet.

"He hasn't been into society yet,
    And his manners are not of the best,
So I think it quite fair that it should be *my* care,
    To see that he's properly dressed."

Many words brought the wind of "cruel" and "kind",
    And that "man suffers more than the brute":
Each several word with patience he heard,
    And answered with wisdom to boot.

"What? prettier swimming in the stream,
    Than lying all snugly and flat?
Do but look at that dish filled with glittering fish,
    Has Nature a picture like that?

"What? a higher delight to be drawn from the sight
    Of fish full of life and of glee?
What a noodle you are! 'tis delightfuller far
    To kill them than let them go free!

"I know there are people who prate by the hour
    Of the beauty of earth, sky, and ocean;
Of the birds as they fly, of the fish darting by,
    Rejoicing in Life and in Motion.

"As to any delight to be got from the sight,
    It is all very well for a flat,
But *I* think it all gammon, for hooking a salmon
    Is better than twenty of that!

"They say that a man of a right-thinking mind
    Will *love* the dumb creatures he sees —
What's the use of his mind, if he's never inclined
    To pull a fish out of the Tees?

"Take my friends and my home — as an outcast I'll roam:
    Take the money I have in the Bank;
It is just what I wish, but deprive me of *fish*,
    And my life would indeed be a blank!"

Forth from the house his sister came,
    Her brothers for to see,
But when she saw that sight of awe,
    The tear stood in her e'e.

"Oh what bait's that upon your hook,
    My brother, tell to me?"
"It is but the fantailed pigeon,
    He would not sing for me."

"Whoe'er would expect a pigeon to sing,
    A simpleton he must be!
But a pigeon-cote is a different thing
    To the coat that there I see!"

"Oh what bait's that upon your hook,
    Dear brother, tell to me?"
"It is my younger brother," he cried,
    "Oh woe and dole is me!

"I's mighty wicked, that I is!
    Or how could such things be?
Farewell, farewell, sweet sister,
    I'm going o'er the sea."

"And when will you come back again,
    My brother, tell to me?"
"When chub is good for human food,
    And that will never be!"

She turned herself right round about,
    And her heart brake into three,

Said, "One of the two will be wet through and through,
And t'other'll be late for his tea!"

1853

36 Ballad of Earl Haldan's Daughter

Charles Kingsley (1819–75)

It was Earl Haldan's daughter,
   She looked across the sea;
She looked across the water;
   And long and loud laughed she:
'The locks of six princesses   5
   Must be my marriage fee,
So hey bonny boat, and ho bonny boat!
   Who comes a wooing me?'

It was Earl Haldan's daughter,
   She walked along the sand;   10
When she was aware of a knight so fair,
   Came sailing to the land.
His sails were all of velvet,
   His mast of beaten gold,
And 'Hey bonny boat, and ho bonny boat!   15
   Who saileth here so bold?'

'The locks of five princesses
   I won beyond the sea;
I clipt their golden tresses,
   To fringe a cloak for thee.   20
One handful yet is wanting,
   But one of all the tale;
So hey bonny boat, and ho bonny boat!
   Furl up thy velvet sail!'

He leapt into the water,   25

That rover young and bold;
He gript Earl Haldan's daughter,
He clipt her locks of gold:
'Go weep, go weep, proud maiden,
    The tale is full to-day.
Now hey bonny boat, and ho bonny boat!
    Sail Westward ho! away!'

1854

37   The Ballad of Keith of Ravelston

Sydney Thompson Dobell (1824–74)

The murmur of the mourning ghost
    That keeps the shadowy kine,
'O, Keith of Ravelston,
    The sorrows of thy line!'

Ravelston, Ravelston,
    The merry path that leads
Down the golden morning hill,
    And thro' the silver meads;

Ravelston, Ravelston,
    The stile beneath the tree,
The maid that kept her mother's kine,
    The song that sang she!

She sang her song, she kept her kine,
    She sat beneath the thorn,
When Andrew Keith of Ravelston
    Rode thro' the Monday morn.

His henchmen sing, his hawk-bells ring,
    His belted jewels shine;
O, Keith of Ravelston,

          The sorrows of thy line!

Year after year, where Andrew came,
    Comes evening down the glade,
And still there sits a moonshine ghost
    Where sat the sunshine maid.

Her misty hair is faint and fair,
    She keeps the shadowy kine;
O, Keith of Ravelston,
    The sorrows of thy line!

I lay my hand upon the stile,
    The stile is lone and cold,
The burnie that goes babbling by
    Says naught that can be told.

Yet, stranger! here, from year to year,
    She keeps her shadowy kine;
O, Keith of Ravelston,
    The sorrows of thy line!

Step out three steps, where Andrew stood —
    Why blanch thy cheeks for fear?
The ancient stile is not alone,
    'Tis not the burn I hear!

She makes her immemorial moan,
    She keeps her shadowy kine;
O, Keith of Ravelston,
    The sorrows of thy line!

1856

38 *Love from the North*

Christina Georgina Rossetti (1830–94)

I had a love in soft south land,
    Beloved through April far in May;
He waited on my lightest breath,
    And never dared to say me nay.

He saddened if my cheer was sad,   5
    But gay he grew if I was gay;
We never differed on a hair,
    My yes his yes, my nay his nay.

The wedding hour was come, the aisles
    Were flushed with sun and flowers that day;   10
I pacing balanced in my thoughts:
    "It's quite too late to think of nay." —

My bridegroom answered in his turn,
    Myself had almost answered "yea:"
When through the flashing nave I heard   15
    A struggle and resounding "nay."

Bridemaids and bridegroom shrank in fear,
    But I stood high who stood at bay:
"And if I answer yea, fair Sir,
    What man art thou to bar with nay?"   20

He was a strong man from the north,
    Light-locked, with eyes of dangerous grey:
"Put yea by for another time
    In which I will not say thee nay."

He took me in his strong white arms,   25
    He bore me on his horse away
O'er crag, morass, and hairbreadth pass,
    But never asked me yea or nay.

He made me fast with book and bell,
    With links of love he makes me stay;   30

Till now I've neither heart nor power
Nor will nor wish to say him nay.

1856

39 The Sailing of the Sword

William Morris (1834–96)

Across the empty garden-beds,
   When the Sword went out to sea,
I scarcely saw my sisters' heads
   Bowed each beside a tree.
I could not see the castle leads,   5
   When the Sword went out to sea,

Alicia wore a scarlet gown,
   When the Sword went out to sea,
But Ursula's was russet brown:
   For the mist we could not see   10
The scarlet roofs of the good town,
   When the Sword went out to sea.

Green holly in Alicia's hand,
   When the Sword went out to sea;
With sere oak-leaves did Ursula stand;   15
   O! yet alas for me!
I did but bear a peel'd white wand,
   When the Sword went out to sea.

O, russet brown and scarlet bright,
   When the Sword went out to sea,   20
My sisters wore; I wore but white:
   Red, brown, and white, are three;
Three damozels; each had a knight,
   When the Sword went out to sea.

Sir Robert shouted loud, and said:
  When the Sword went out to sea,
Alicia, while I see thy head,
  What shall I bright for thee?
O, my sweet Lord, a ruby red:
  The Sword went out to sea.

Sir Miles said, while the sails hung down,
  When the Sword went out to sea,
O, Ursula! while I see the town,
  What shall I bring for thee?
Dear knight, bring back a falcon brown:
  The Sword went out to sea.

But my Roland, no word he said
  When the Sword went out to sea,
But only turn'd away his head;
  A quick shriek came from me:
Come back, dear lord, to your white maid.
  The Sword went out to sea.

The hot sun bit the garden-beds
  When the Sword came back from sea;
Beneath an apple-tree our heads
  Stretched out toward the sea;
Grey gleam'd the thirsty castle-leads,
  When the Sword came back from sea.

Lord Robert brought a ruby red,
  When the Sword came back from sea;
He kissed Alicia on the head:
  I am come back to thee;
'Tis time, sweet love, that we were wed,
  Now the Sword is back from sea!

Sir Miles he bore a falcon brown,
  When the Sword came back from sea;
His arms went round tall Ursula's gown:
  What joy, O love, but thee?
Let us be wed in the good town,
  Now the Sword is back from sea!

My heart grew sick, no more afraid,
When the Sword came back from sea;
Upon the deck a tall white maid
Sat on Lord Roland's knee;
His chin was press'd upon her head, 65
When the Sword came back from sea!

1858

40   Margaret's Bridal Eve

George Meredith (1828–1909)

I

The old grey mother she thrummed on her knee:
There is a rose that's ready;
And which of the handsome young men shall it be?
There's a rose that's ready for clipping.

My daughter, come hither, come hither to me: 5
There is a rose that's ready;
Come, point me your finger on him that you see:
There's a rose that's ready for clipping.

O mother, my mother, it never can be:
There is a rose that's ready; 10
For I shall bring shame on the man marries me:
There's a rose that's ready for clipping.

Now let your tongue be deep as the sea:
There is a rose that's ready;
And the man'll jump for you, right briskly will he: 15
There's a rose that's ready for clipping.

Tall Margaret wept bitterly:
There is a rose that's ready;
And as her parent bade did she:

There's a rose that's ready for clipping.

O the handsome young man dropped down on his knee:
There is a rose that's ready;
Pale Margaret gave him her hand, woe's me!
There's a rose that's ready for clipping.

II

O mother, my mother, this thing I must say:
There is a rose in the garden;
Ere he lies on the breast where that other lay:
And the bird sings over the roses.

Now, folly, my daughter, for men are men:
There is a rose in the garden;
You marry them blindfold, I tell you again:
And the bird sings over the roses.

O mother, but when he kisses me!
There is a rose in the garden;
My child, 'tis which shall sweetest be!
And the bird sings over the roses.

O mother, but when I awake in the morn!
There is a rose in the garden;
My child, you are his, and the ring is worn:
And the bird sings over the roses.

Tall Margaret sighed and loosened a tress:
There is a rose in the garden;
Poor comfort she had of her comeliness:
And the bird sings over the roses.

My mother will sink if this thing be said:
There is a rose in the garden;
That my first betrothed came thrice to my bed:
And the bird sings over the roses.

He died on my shoulder the third cold night:
There is a rose in the garden;
I dragged his body all through the moonlight:
And the bird sings over the roses.

But when I came by my father's door:
There is a rose in the garden;
I fell in a lump on the stiff dead floor:
And the bird sings over the roses.

O neither to heaven, nor yet to hell:
There is a rose in the garden;
Could I follow the lover I loved so well!
And the bird sings over the roses.

III

The bridesmaids slept in their chambers apart:
There is a rose that's ready;
Tall Margaret walked with her thumping heart:
There's a rose that's ready for clipping.

The frill of her nightgown below the left breast:
There is a rose that's ready;
Had fall'n like a cloud of the moonlighted West:
There's a rose that's ready for clipping.

But where the West-cloud breaks to a star:
There is a rose that's ready;
Pale Margaret's breast showed a winding scar:
There's a rose that's ready for clipping.

O few are the brides with such a sign!
There is a rose that's ready;
Though I went mad the fault was mine:
There's a rose that's ready for clipping.

I must speak to him under this roof to-night:
There is a rose that's ready;
I shall burn to death if I speak in the light:
There's a rose that's ready for clipping.

O my breast!   I must strike you a bloodier wound:
There is a rose that's ready;
Than when I scored you red and swooned:
There's a rose that's ready for clipping.

I will stab my honour under his eye:

There is a rose that's ready;
Though I bleed to the death, I shall let out the lie:
There's a rose that's ready for clipping.

O happy my bridesmaids! white sleep is with you!
There is a rose that's ready; 90
Had he chosen among you he might sleep too!
There's a rose that's ready for clipping.

O happy my bridesmaids! your breasts are clean:
There is a rose that's ready;
You carry no mark of what has been! 95
There's a rose that's ready for clipping.

IV

An hour before the chilly beam:
Red rose and white in the garden;
The bridegroom started out of a dream:
And the bird sings over the roses. 100

He went to the door, and there espied:
Red rose and white in the garden;
The figure of his silent bride:
And the bird sings over the roses.

He went to the door, and let her in: 105
Red rose and white in the garden;
Whiter looked she than a child of sin:
And the bird sings over the roses.

She looked so white, she looked so sweet:
Red rose and white in the garden; 110
She looked so pure he fell at her feet:
And the bird sings over the roses.

He fell at her feet with love and awe:
Red rose and white in the garden;
A stainless body of light he saw: 115
And the bird sings over the roses.

O Margaret, say you are not of the dead!
Red rose and white in the garden;

My bride! by the angels at night are you led?
And the bird sings over the roses.

I am not led by the angels about:
Red rose and white in the garden;
But I have a devil within to let out:
And the bird sings over the roses.

O Margaret! my bride and saint!
Red rose and white in the garden;
There is on you no earthly taint:
And the bird sings over the roses.

I am no saint, and no bride can I be:
Red rose and white in the garden;
Until I have opened my bosom to thee:
And the bird sings over the roses.

To catch at her heart she laid one hand:
Red rose and white in the garden;
She told the tale where she did stand:
And the bird sings over the roses.

She stood before him pale and tall:
Red rose and white in the garden;
Her eyes between his, she told him all:
And the bird sings over the roses.

She saw how her body grew freckled and foul:
Red rose and white in the garden;
She heard from the woods the hooting owl:
And the bird sings over the roses.

With never a quiver her mouth did speak:
Red rose and white in the garden;
O when she had done she stood so meek!
And the bird sings over the roses.

The bridegroom stamped and called her vile:
Red rose and white in the garden;
He did but waken a little smile:
And the bird sings over the roses.

The bridegroom raged and called her foul:
Red rose and white in the garden;
She heard from the woods the hooting owl:
And the bird sings over the roses.

He muttered a name full bitter and sore:
Red rose and white in the garden;
She fell in a lump on the still dead floor:
And the bird sings over the roses.

O great was the wonder, and loud the wail:
Red rose and white in the garden;
When through the household flew the tale:
And the bird sings over the roses.

The old grey mother she dressed the bier:
Red rose and white in the garden;
With a shivering chin and never a tear:
And the bird sings over the roses.

O had you but done as I bade you, my child!
Red rose and white in the garden;
You would not have died and been reviled:
And the bird sings over the roses.

The bridegroom he hung at midnight by the bier:
Red rose and white in the garden;
He eyed the white girl thro' a dazzling tear:
And the bird sings over the roses.

O had you been false as the women who stray:
Red rose and white in the garden;
You would not be now with the Angels of Day!
And the bird sings over the roses.

1862

41 The King's Daughter

A. C. Swinburne (1837–1909)

We were ten maidens in the green corn,
   Small red leaves in the mill-water;
Fairer maidens never were born,
   Apples of gold for the king's daughter.

We were ten maidens by a well-head,   5
   Small white birds in the mill-water:
Sweeter maidens never were wed,
   Rings of red for the king's daughter.

The first to spin, the second to sing,
   Seeds of wheat in the mill-water;   10
The third may was a goodly thing,
   White bread and brown for the king's daughter.

The fourth to sew and the fifth to play,
   Fair green weed in the mill-water;
The sixth may was a goodly may,   15
   White wine and red for the king's daughter.

The seventh to woo, the eighth to wed,
   Fair thin reeds in the mill-water;
The ninth had gold work on her head,
   Honey in the comb for the king's daughter.   20

The ninth had gold work round her hair,
   Fallen flowers in the mill-water;
The tenth may was goodly and fair,
   Golden gloves for the king's daughter.

We were ten maidens in a field green,   25
   Fallen fruit in the mill-water;
Fairer maidens never have been,
   Golden sleeves for the king's daughter.

By there comes the king's young son,
   A little wind in the mill-water;   30

"Out of ten maidens ye'll grant me one,"
   A crown of red for the king's daughter.

"Out of ten mays ye'll give me the best,"
   A little rain in the mill-water;
A bed of yellow straw for all the rest,
   A bed of gold for the king's daughter.

He's ta'en out the goodliest,
   Rain that rains in the mill-water;
A comb of yellow shell for all the rest,
   A comb of gold for the king's daughter.

He's made her bed to the goodliest,
   Wind and hail in the mill-water;
A grass girdle for all the rest,
   A girdle of arms for the king's daughter.

He's set his heart to the goodliest,
   Snow that snows in the mill-water;
Nine little kisses for all the rest,
   An hundred fold for the king's daughter.

He's ta'en his leave at the goodliest,
   Broken boats in the [m]ill-water,
Golden gifts for all the rest,
   Sorrow of heart for the king's daughter.

"Ye'll make a grave for my fair body,"
   Running rain in the mill-water;
"And ye'll streek my brother at the side of me,"
   The pains of hell for the king's daughter.

1866

42 Stratton Water

Dante Gabriel Rossetti (1828–82)

"O have you seen the Stratton flood
   That's great with rain to-day?
It runs beneath your wall, Lord Sands,
   Full of the new-mown hay.

"I led your hounds to Hutton bank
   To bathe at early morn:
They got their bath by Borrowbrake
   Above the standing corn."

Out from the castle-stair Lord Sands
   Looked up the western lea;
The rook was grieving on her nest,
   The flood was round her tree.

Over the castle-wall Lord Sands
   Looked down the eastern hill:
The stakes swam free among the boats,
   The flood was rising still.

"What's yonder far below that lies
   So white against the slope?"
"O it's a sail o' your bonny barks
   The waters have washed up."

"But I have never a sail so white,
   And the water's not yet there."
"O it's the swans o' your bonny lake
   The rising flood doth scare."

"The swans they would not hold so still,
   So high they would not win."
"O it's Joyce my wife has spread her smock
   And fears to fetch it in."

"Nay, knave, it's neither sail nor swans,
   Nor aught that you can say;

For though your wife might leave her smock,
   Herself she'd bring away."

Lord Sands has passed the turret-stair,
   The court, and yard, and all;
The kine were in the byre that day,
   The nags were in the stall.

Lord Sands has won the weltering slope
   Whereon the white shape lay:
The clouds were still above the hill,
   And the shape was still as they.

Oh pleasant is the gaze of life
   And sad is death's blind head;
But awful are the living eyes
   In the face of one thought dead!

"In God's name, Janet, is it me
   Thy ghost has come to seek?"
"Nay, wait another hour, Lord Sands, —
   Be sure my ghost shall speak."

A moment stood he as a stone,
   Then grovelled to his knee.
"O Janet, O my love, my love,
   Rise up and come with me!"
"O once before you bade me come,
   And it's here you have brought me!

"O many's the sweet word, Lord Sands,
   You've spoken oft to me;
But all that I have from you to-day
   Is the rain on my body.

"And many's the good gift, Lord Sands,
   You've promised oft to me;
But the gift of yours I keep to-day
   Is the babe in my body.

"O it's not in any earthly bed
   That first my babe I'll see;

For I have brought my body here
      That the flood may cover me."

His face was close against her face,
    His hands of hers were fain:
O her wet cheeks were hot with tears,
    Her wet hands cold with rain.

"They told me you were dead, Janet, —
    How could I guess the lie?"
"They told me you were false, Lord Sands, —
    What could I do but die?"

"Now keep you well, my brother Giles, —
    Through you I deemed her dead!
As wan as your towers seem to-day,
    To-morrow they'll be red.

"Look down, look down, my false mother,
    That bade me not to grieve:
You'll look up when our marriage fires
    Are lit to-morrow eve:

"O more than one and more than two
    The sorrow of this shall see:
But it's to-morrow, love, for them, —
    To-day's for thee and me."

He's drawn her face between his hands
    And her pale mouth to his:
No bird that was so still that day
    Chirps sweeter than his kiss.

The flood was creeping round their feet.
    "O Janet, come away!
The hall is warm for the marriage-rite,
    The bed for the birthday."

"Nay, but I hear your mother cry,
    'Go bring this bride to bed!
And would she christen her babe unborn,
    So wet she comes to wed?'

"I'll be your wife to cross your door
    And meet your mother's e'e.
We plighted troth to wed i' the kirk,
    And it's there you'll wed with me."

He's ta'en her by the short girdle
    And by the dripping sleeve:
"Go fetch Sir Jock my mother's priest, —
    You'll ask of him no leave.

"O it's one half-hour to reach the kirk
    And one for the marriage-rite;
And kirk and castle and castle-lands
    Shall be our babe's to-night."

"The flood's in the kirkyard, Lord Sands,
    And round the belfry-stair."
"I bade you fetch the priest," he said,
    "Myself shall bring him there.

"It's for the lilt of wedding bells
    We'll have the hail to pour,
And for the clink of bridle-reins
    The plashing of the oar."

Beneath them on the nether hill
    A boat was floating wide:
Lord Sands swam out and caught the oars
    And rowed to the hill-side.

He's wrapped her in a green mantle
    And set her softly in;
Her hair was wet upon her face,
    Her face was grey and thin;
And "Oh!" she said, "lie still, my babe,
    It's out you must not win!"

But woe's my heart for Father John
    As hard as he might pray,
There seemed no help but Noah's ark
    Or Jonah's fish that day.

The first strokes that the oars struck
   Were over the broad leas;
The next strokes that the oars struck   135
   They pushed beneath the trees;

The last stroke that the oars struck,
   The good boat's head was met,
And there the gate of the kirkyard
   Stood like a ferry-gate.   140

He's set his hand upon the bar
   And lightly leaped within:
He's lifted her to his left shoulder,
   Her knees beside his chin.

The graves lay deep beneath the flood   145
   Under the rain alone;
And when the foot-stone made him slip,
   He held by the head-stone.

The empty boat thrawed i' the wind,
   Against the postern tied.   150
"Hold still, you've brought my love with me,
   You shall take back my bride."

But woe's my heart for Father John
   And the saints he clamoured to!
There's never a saint but Christopher   155
   Might hale such buttocks through!

And "Oh!" she said, "on men's shoulders
   I well had thought to wend,
And well to travel with a priest,
   But not to have cared or ken'd.   160

"And oh!" she said, "it's well this way
   That I thought to have fared, —
Not to have lighted at the kirk
   But stopped in the kirkyard.

"For it's oh and oh I prayed to God,   165
   Whose rest I hoped to win,

That when to-night at your board-head
    You'd bid the feast begin,
This water past your window-sill
    Might bear my body in."   170

Now make the white bed warm and soft
    And greet the merry morn.
The night the mother should have died,
    The young son shall be born.

1869

43   *King Henry's Hunt*

William Allingham (1824–89)

King Henry stood in Waltham Wood,
    One morn in merry May-time;
Years fifteen hundred thirty-six,
    From Christ, had roll'd away time.

King Henry stood in Waltham Wood,   5
    All young green, sunny-shady.
He would not mount his pawing horse,
    Though men and dogs were ready.

"What ails his Highness?   Up and down
    In moody sort he paceth;   10
He is not wont to be so slack,
    Whatever game he chaseth."

He paced and stopp'd; he paced and turn'd;
    At times he inly mutter'd;
He pull'd his girdle, twitch'd his beard;   15
    But not one word he utter'd.

The hounds in couples nosed about,

  Or on the sward lay idle;
The huntsmen stole a fearful glance,
  While fingering girth or bridle.

  Among themselves, but not too loud,
   The young lords laugh'd and chatter'd,
Or broke a branch of hawthorn-bloom,
  As though it nothing matter'd.

King Henry sat on a fell'd oak,
  With gloomier eyes and stranger;
His brows were knit, his lip he bit;
  To look that way was danger.

Mused he on Pope and Emperor?
  Denied them and defied them?
Or traitors in his very realm
  Complotting? — woe betide them!

Suddenly on the southern breeze,
  Distinct though distant, sounded
A cannon shot, — and to his feet
  The King of England bounded.

"My horse!" he shouts, — "Uncouple now!"
  And all were quickly mounted.
A hind was found; man, horse, and hound
  Like furious demons hunted.

Fast fled the deer by grove and glade,
  The chase did faster follow;
And every wild-wood alley rang
  With hunter's horn and hollo.

Away together stream'd the hounds;
  Forward press'd every rider.
You're free to slay a hind in May,
  If there's no calf beside her.

King Harry rode a mighty horse,
  His Grace being broad and heavy,
And like a stormy wind he crash'd

Through copse and thicket leavy.

He rode so hard, and roar'd so loud,
    All men his course avoided;
The fiery steed, long held on fret,
    With many a snort enjoy'd it.

The hind was kill'd, and down they sat
    To flagon and to pasty.
"Ha, by Saint George, a noble Prince
    Tho' hot, by times, and hasty."

Lord Norfolk knew, and other few,
    Wherefore that chase began on
The signal of a gun far off,
    One growl of distant cannon, —

And why so jovial grew his Grace,
    That erst was sad and sullen.
With that boom from the Tower, had fall'n
    The head of fair Anne Bullen.

Her neck, which Henry used to kiss,
    The bloody axe did sever;
Their little child, Elizabeth,
    She'll see no more for ever.

Gaily the King rides west away;
    Each moment makes his glee more;
To-morrow brings his wedding-day
    With beautiful Jane Seymour.

The sunshine falls, the wild-bird calls,
    Across the slopes of Epping;
From grove to glade, through light and shade,
    The troops of deer are stepping.

1877

44 After Dilettante Concetti

Henry Duff Traill (1842–1900)

"Why do you wear your hair like a man,
                Sister Helen?
This week is the third since you began."
"I'm writing a ballad; be still if you can,
                Little brother.
      (O Mother Carey, mother!
What chickens are these between sea and heaven?)"

"But why does your figure appear so lean,
                Sister Helen?
And why do you dress in sage, sage green?"
"Children should never be heard, if seen,
                Little brother?
      (O Mother Carey, mother!
What fowls are a-wing in the stormy heaven!)"

"But why is your face so yellowy white,
                Sister Helen?
And why are your skirts so funnily tight?"
"Be quiet, you torment, or how can I write,
                Little Brother?
      (O Mother Carey, mother!
How gathers thy train to the sea from the heaven!)"

"And who's Mother Carey, and what is her train,
                Sister Helen?
And why do you call her again and again?"
"You troublesome boy, why that's the refrain,
                Little brother.
      (O Mother Carey, mother!
What work is toward in the startled heaven?)"

"And what's a refrain?   What a curious word,
                Sister Helen!
Is the ballad you're writing about a sea-bird?"
"Not at all; why should it be?   Don't be absurd,
                Little brother.

After Dilettante Concetti

(O Mother Carey, mother!
Thy brood flies lower as lowers the heaven.)"   35

    (A big brother speaketh:)

"The refrain you've studied a meaning had
                  Sister Helen!
It gave strange force to a weird ballàd,
But refrains have become a ridiculous 'fad'
                  Little brother.   40
    And *Mother Carey, mother,*
Has a bearing on nothing in earth or heaven.

"But the finical fashion has had its day,
                  Sister Helen.
And let's try in the style of a different lay   45
To bid it adieu in poetical way,
                  Little brother.
    So, Mother Carey, mother!
Collect your chickens and go to — heaven."

    (A pause. Then the big brother singeth, accompanying
    himself in a plaintive wise on the triangle:)

"Look in my face. My name is Used-to-was;   50
    I am also called Played-out and Done-to-death,
       And It-will-wash-no-more. Awakeneth
Slowly, but sure awakening it has,
The common-sense of man; and I, alas!
    The ballad-burden trick, now known too well,   55
       Am turned to scorn, and grown contemptible —
A too transparent artifice to pass.

"What a cheap dodge I am! The cats who dart
    Tin-kettled through the streets in wild surprise   60
       Assail judicious ears not otherwise;
And yet no critics praise the urchin's 'art,'
Who to the wretched creature's caudal part
    Its foolish empty-jingling 'burden' ties."

1882

45 The Ballad of the Wayfarer

Robert W. Buchanan (1841–1901)

    O'er the cheerless common,
      Where the bleak winds blow,
    Wanders the wan Woman;
    Waysore and weary,
      Through the dark and dreary 5
        Drift-bed of the Snow.
On her pale pinch'd features snowing 'tis and sleeting,
By her side her little Son runs with warm heart beating,
Clinging to her wet robe, while she wails repeating:
    'Further, my child, further — further let us go!' 10

    Fleet the Boy doth follow,
      Wondering at her woe;
    On, with footfall hollow,
    O'er the pathway jagged
      Crawls she wet and ragged, 15
        Restless and slow.
'Mother!' now he murmurs, mid the tempest's crying,
'Mother, rest a little — I am faint with flying —
Mother, rest a little!'   Still she answers sighing,
    'Further, child, and faster — further let us go!['] 20

    But now she is sitting
      On a stone, and lo!
    Dark her brows are knitting,
    While the Child, close clinging
      To her raiment wringing, 25
        Shivers at the snow.
'Tell me of my *father!* for I never knew him
Is he dead or living, are we flying to him?'
'Peace, my child!' she answers, and the voice thrills through him;
    'When we wander further — further! — thou shalt know.' 30

    (Wild wind of December,
      Blow, wind, blow! —)
    'Oh, but I remember!
    In my mind I gather

Pictures of my father,
    And a gallant show.
Tell me, mother, tell me — did we always wander?
Was the world once brighter? In some town out yonder
Dwelt we not contented?' Sad she seems to ponder,
    Sighing 'I will tell thee — when we further go.'

'Oh, but Mother, listen!
    We were rich, I know!
    (How his bright eyes glisten!)
    We were merry people,
    In a town with a steeple,
        Long, long ago;
In a gay room dwelling, where your face shone brightly,
And a brave man brought us food and presents nightly,
Tell me, 'twas my father?' Now her face looms whitely,
    While she shivers moaning, 'Peace, let us go!'

    How the clouds gather!
        How the winds blow!
    '*Who* was my father?
    Was he Prince or Lord there,
    With a train and a sword there?
        Mother, I *will* know! —
I have dreamt so often of those gallant places;
There were banners waving — I could see the faces —
Take me to my father!' cries he with embraces,
    While she shivers moaning, 'No, child, no!'

    While the child is speaking,
        Forth the moon steals slow,
    From the black cloud breaking,
    Shining white and eerie
    On the wayside weary,
        Shrouded white in snow.
On the heath behind them, 'gainst the dim sky lying,
Looms the Gallows blackly, in the wild wind sighing.
To her feet the woman springs! with fierce shriek crying —
    'See! Oh, God in heaven! . . . Woe, child, woe!'

        (Blow, wind of December,
            Blow, wind, blow! —)

    '*Thou* canst not remember —
    Thou wert but a blossom
    Suckled on my bosom, 75
        Years, years ago!
Thy father stole to feed us; our starving faces stung him;
In yonder town behind us, they seized him and they hung him!
They murdered him on Gallows-Tree, and to the ravens flung him!
    Faster, my child, faster — faster let us go!' 80

1882

46   The Bridge of Death

Andrew Lang (1844–1912)

'The dance is on the Bridge of Death
    And who will dance with me?'
'There's never a man of living men
    Will dare to dance with thee.'

Now Margaret's gone within her bower 5
    Put ashes in her hair,
And sackcloth on her bonnie breast,
    And on her shoulders bare.

There came a knock to her bower door,
    And blithe she let him in; 10
It was her brother from the wars,
    The dearest of her kin.

'Set gold within your hair, Margaret,
    Set gold within your hair;
And gold upon your girdle band, 15
    And on your breast so fair.

'For we are bidden to dance to-night,
    We may not bide away;

This one good night, this one fair night,
    Before the red new day.'

'Nay, no gold for my head, brother,
    Nay, no gold for my hair;
It is the ashes and dust of earth
    That you and I must wear.

'No gold work for my girdle band,
    No gold work on my feet;
But ashes of the fire, my love,
    But dust that the serpents eat.'

They danced across the Bridge of Death
    Above the black water,
And the marriage bell was tolled in hell
    For the souls of him and her.

1872

47   The Ballad of Moll Magee

William Butler Yeats (1865–1939)

Come round me, little childer;
There, don't fling stones at me
Because I mutter as I go;
But pity Moll Magee.

My man was a poor fisher
With shore lines in the say;
My work was saltin' herrings
The whole of the long day.

And sometimes from the saltin' shed
I scarce could drag my feet,
Under the blessed moonlight,

Along the pebbly street.

I'd always been but weakly,
And my baby was just born;
A neighbour minded her by day,
I minded her till morn.

I lay upon my baby;
Ye little childer dear,
I looked on my cold baby
When the morn grew frosty and clear.

A weary woman sleeps so hard!
My man grew red and pale,
And gave me money, and bade me go
To my own place, Kinsale.

He drove me out and shut the door,
And gave his curse to me;
I went away in silence,
No neighbour could I see.

The windows and the doors were shut,
One star shone faint and green,
The little straws were turnin' round
Across the bare boreen.

I went away in silence:
Beyond old Martin's byre
I saw a kindly neighbour
Blowin' her mornin' fire.

She drew from me my story —
My money's all used up,
And still, with pityin', scornin' eye,
She gives me bite and sup.

She says my man will surely come
And fetch me home agin;
But always, as I'm movin' round,
Without doors or within,

Pilin' the wood or pilin' the turf, 45
Or goin' to the well,
I'm thinkin' of my baby
And keenin' to mysel'.

And sometimes I am sure she knows
When, openin' wide His door, 50
God lights the stars, His candles,
And looks upon the poor.

So now, ye little childer,
Ye won't fling stones at me;
But gather with your shinin' looks 55
And pity Moll Magee.

1889

48 The Last Rhyme of True Thomas

Rudyard Kipling (1865–1936)

The King has called for priest and cup,
    The King has taken spur and blade
To dub True Thomas a belted knight,
    And all for the sake of the songs he made.

They have sought him high, they have sought him low, 5
    They have sought him over down and lea.
They have found him by the milk-white thorn
    That guards the Gates of Faerie.

'Twas bent beneath and blue above:
    Their eyes were held that they might not see 10
The kine that grazed beneath the knowes,
    Oh, they were the Queens of Faerie!

"Now cease your song," the King he said,

"Oh, cease your song and get you dight
"To vow your vow and watch your arms,
   "For I will dub you a belted knight.

"For I will give you a horse o' pride,
    "Wi' blazon and spur and page and squire;
"Wi' keep and tail and seizin and law,
    "And land to hold at your desire."

True Thomas smiled above his harp,
    And turned his face to the naked sky,
Where, blown before the wastrel wind,
    The thistle-down she floated by.

"I ha' vowed my vow in another place,
    "And bitter oath it was on me.
"I ha' watched my arms the lee-long night,
    "Where five-score fighting men would flee.

"My lance is tipped o' the hammered flame,
    "My shield is beat o' the moonlight cold;
"And I won my spurs in the Middle World,
    "A thousand fathom beneath the mould.

"And what should I make wi' a horse o' pride,
    "And what should I make wi' a sword so brown,
"But spill the rings of the Gentle Folk
    "And flyte my kin in the Fairy Town?

"And what should I make wi' blazon and belt,
    "Wi' keep and tail and seizin and fee,
"And what should I do wi' page and squire
    "That am a king in my own countrie?

"For I send east and I send west,
    "And I send far as my will may flee,
"By dawn and dusk and the drinking rain,
    "And syne my Sendings return to me.

"They come wi' news of the groanin' earth,
    "They come wi' news of the roarin' sea.
"Wi' word of Spirit and Ghost and Flesh,

"And man, that's mazed among the three."

The King he bit his nether lip,
    And smote his hand upon his knee:
"By the faith of my soul, True Thomas," he said,
    "Ye waste no wit in courtesie!

"As I desire, unto my pride,
    "Can I make Earls by three and three,
"To run before and ride behind
    "And serve the sons o' my body."

"And what care I for your row-foot earls,
    "Or all the sons o' your body?
"Before they win to the Pride o' Name,
    "I trow they all ask leave o' me.

"For I make Honour wi' muckle mouth,
    "As I make Shame wi' mincing feet,
"To sing wi' the priests at the market-cross,
    "Or run wi' the dogs in the naked street.

"And some they give me the good red gold,
    "And some they give me the white money,
"And some they give me a clout o' meal,
    "For they be people of low degree.

"And the song I sing for the counted gold
    "The same I sing for the white money,
"But best I sing for the clout o' meal
    "That simple people given me."

The King cast down a silver groat,
    A silver groat o' Scots money,
"If I come wi' a poor man's dole," he said,
    "True Thomas, will ye harp to me?"

"Whenas I harp to the children small,
    "They press me close on either hand.
"And who are you," True Thomas said,
    "That you should ride while they must stand?

"Light down, light down from your horse o' pride,
   "I trow ye talk too loud and hie,
"And I will make you a triple word,
   "And syne, if ye dare, ye shall 'noble me."

He has lighted down from his horse o' pride,
   And set his back against a stone.
"Now guard you well," True Thomas said,
   "Ere I rax your heart from your breast-bone!"

True Thomas played upon his harp,
   The fairy harp that couldna lee,
And the first least word the proud King heard,
   It harpit the salt tear out o' his e'e.

"Oh, I see the love that I lost long syne,
   "I touch the hope that I may not see,
"And all that I did of hidden shame,
   "Like little snakes they hiss at me.

"The sun is lost at noon — at noon!
   "The dread of doom has grippit me.
"True Thomas, hide me under your cloak,
   "God wot, I'm little fit to dee!"

'Twas bent beneath and blue above —
   'Twas open field and running flood —
Where, hot on heath and dyke and wall,
   The high sun warmed the adder's brood.

"Lie down, lie down," True Thomas said,
   "The God shall judge when all is done,
"But I will bring you a better word
   "And lift the cloud that I laid on."

True Thomas played upon his harp,
   That birled and brattled to his hand,
And the next least word True Thomas made,
   It garred the King take horse and brand.

"Oh, I hear the tread o' the fighting-men,
   "I see the sun on splent and spear.

"I mark the arrow outen the fern
    "That flies so low and sings so clear!

"Advance my standards to that war,
    "And bid my good knights prick and ride;
"The gled shall watch as fierce a fight
    "As e'er was fought on the Border-side!"

'Twas bent beneath and blue above,
    'Twas nodding grass and naked sky,
Where, ringing up the wastrel wind,
    The eyass stooped upon the pye.

True Thomas sighed above his harp,
    And turned the song on the midmost string;
And the last least word True Thomas made,
    He harpit his dead youth back to the King.

"Now I am prince, and I do well
    "To love my love withouten fear;
"To walk with man in fellowship,
    "And breathe my horse behind the deer.

"My hounds they bay unto the death,
    "The buck has couched beyond the burn,
"My love she waits at her window
    "To wash my hands when I return.

"For that I live am I content
    "(Oh!   I have seen my true love's eyes)
"To stand with Adam in Eden-glade,
    "And run in the woods o' Paradise!"

'Twas naked sky and nodding grass,
    'Twas running flood and wastrel wind,
Where, checked against the open pass,
    The red deer turned to wait the hind.

True Thomas laid his harp away,
    And louted low at the saddle-side;
He has taken stirrup and hauden rein,
    And set the King on his horse o' pride.

"Sleep ye or wake," True Thomas said,
    "That sit so still, that muse so long?   150
"Sleep ye or wake? — till the Latter Sleep
    "I trow ye'll not forget my song.

"I ha' harpit a Shadow out o' the sun
    "To stand before your face and cry;
"I ha' armed the earth beneath your heel,   155
    "And over your head I ha' dusked the sky.

"I ha' harpit ye up to the Throne o' God,
    "I ha' harpit your midmost soul in three.
"I ha' harpit ye down to the Hinges o' Hell,
    "And — ye — would — make — a Knight o' me!"   160

1893

49   A Ballad of a Nun

John Davidson (1857–1909)

From Eastertide to Eastertide
    For ten long years her patient knees
Engraved the stones — the fittest bride
    Of Christ in all the diocese.

She conquered every earthly lust;   5
    The abbess loved her more and more;
And, as a mark of perfect trust,
    Made her the keeper of the door.

High on a hill the convent hung
    Across a duchy looking down,   10
Where everlasting mountains flung
    Their shadows over tower and town.

The jewels of their lofty snows

A Ballad of a Nun

In constellations flashed at night;
Above their crests the moon arose;
   The deep earth shuddered with delight.

Long ere she left her cloudy bed,
   Still dreaming in the orient land,
On many a mountain's happy head
   Dawn lightly laid her rosy hand.

The adventurous sun took Heaven by storm;
   Clouds scattered largesses of rain;
The sounding cities rich and warm,
   Smouldered and glittered in the plain.

Sometimes it was a wandering wind,
   Sometimes the fragrance of the pine,
Sometimes the thought how others sinned,
   That turned her sweet blood into wine.

Sometimes she heard a serenade
   Complaining sweetly far away:
She said, "A young man woos a maid";
   And dreamt of love till break of day.

Then would she ply her knotted scourge
   Until she swooned; but evermore
She had the same red sin to purge,
   Poor, passionate keeper of the door!

For still night's starry scroll unfurled,
   And still the day came like a flood:
It was the greatness of the world
   That made her long to use her blood.

In winter-time when Lent drew nigh,
   And hill and plain were wrapped in snow,
She watched beneath the frosty sky
   The nearest city nightly glow.

Like peals of airy bells outworn
   Faint laughter died above her head
In gusts of broken music borne:

"They keep the Carnival," she said.

Her hungry heart devoured the town:
   "Heaven save me by a miracle! 50
Unless God sends an angel down,
   Thither I go though it were Hell."

She dug her nails deep in her breast,
   Sobbed, shrieked, and straight withdrew the bar:
A fledgling flying from the nest, 55
   A pale moth rushing to a star.

Fillet and veil in strips she tore;
   Her golden tresses floated wide;
The ring and bracelet that she wore
   As Christ's betrothed, she cast aside. 60

"Life's dearest meaning I shall probe;
   Lo!   I shall taste of love at last!
Away!"   She doffed her outer robe,
   And sent it sailing down the blast.

Her body seemed to warm the wind; 65
   With bleeding feet o'er ice she ran:
"I leave the righteous God behind;
   I go to worship sinful man."

She reached the sounding city's gate;
   No question did the warder ask: 70
He passed her in: "Welcome, wild mate!"
   He thought her some fantastic mask.

Half-naked through the town she went;
   Each footstep left a bloody mark;
Crowds followed her with looks intent; 75
   Her bright eyes made the torches dark.

Alone and watching in the street
   There stood a grave youth nobly dressed;
To him she knelt and kissed his feet;
   Her face her great desire confessed. 80

A Ballad of a Nun

Straight to his house the nun he led:
  "Strange lady, what would you with me?"
"Your love, your love, sweet lord," she said;
  "I bring you my virginity."

He healed her bosom with a kiss;   85
  She gave him all her passion's hoard;
And sobbed and murmured ever, "This
  Is life's great meaning, dear, my lord.

"I care not for my broken vow,
  Though God should come in thunder soon;   90
I am sister to the mountains now,
  And sister to the sun and moon."

Through all the towns of Belmarie,
  She made a progress like a queen.
"She is," they said, "whate'er she be,   95
  The strangest woman ever seen.

"From fairyland she must have come,
  Or else she is a mermaiden."
Some said she was a ghoul, and some
  A heathen goddess born again.   100

But soon her fire to ashes burned;
  Her beauty changed to haggardness;
Her golden hair to silver turned;
  The hour came of her last caress.

At midnight from her lonely bed   105
  She rose, and said: "I have had my will."
The old ragged robe she donned, and fled
  Back to the convent on the hill.

Half-naked as she went before,
  She hurried to the city wall,   110
Unnoticed in the rush and roar
  And splendour of the Carnival.

No question did the warder ask:
  Her ragged robe, her shrunken limb,

Her dreadful eyes! "It is no mask;
    It is a she-wolf, gaunt and grim!"

She ran across the icy plain;
    Her worn blood curdled in the blast;
Each footstep left a crimson stain;
    The white-faced moon looked on aghast.

She said between her chattering jaws,
    "Deep peace is mine, I cease to strive;
Oh, comfortable convent laws,
    That bury foolish nuns alive!

"A trowel for my passing-bell,
    A little bed within the wall,
A coverlet of stones; how well
    I there shall keep the Carnival!"

Like tired bells chiming in their sleep,
    The wind faint peals of laughter bore;
She stopped her ears and climbed the steep,
    And thundered at the convent door.

It opened straight: she entered in,
    And at the wardress' feet fell prone:
"I come to purge away my sin,
    Bury me, close me up in stone."

The wardress raised her tenderly;
    She touched her wet and fast-shut eyes;
"Look, sister; sister, look at me;
    Look; can you see through my disguise?"

She looked and saw her own sad face,
    And trembled, wondering, "Who art thou?"
"God sent me down to fill your place:
    I am the Virgin Mary now."

And with the word, God's mother shone:
    The wanderer whispered, "Mary, hail!"
The vision helped her to put on
    Bracelet and fillet, ring and veil.

"You are sister to the mountains now,
    And sister to the day and night; 150
Sister to God;" and on the brow
    She kissed her thrice, and left her sight.

While dreaming in her cloudy bed,
    Far in the crimson orient land,
On many a mountain's happy head 155
    Dawn lightly laid her rosy hand.

1894

50 The Carpenter's Son

A. E. Housman (1859–1936)

"Here the hangman stops his cart:
Now the best of friends must part.
Fare you well, for ill fare I:
Live, lads, and I will die.

"Oh, at home had I but stayed 5
'Prenticed to my father's trade,
Had I stuck to plane and adze,
I had not been lost, my lads.

"Then I might have built perhaps
Gallows-trees for other chaps, 10
Never dangled on my own,
Had I but left ill alone.

"Now, you see, they hang me high,
And the people passing by
Stop to shake their fists and curse; 15
So 'tis come from ill to worse.

"Here hang I, and right and left

Two poor fellows hang for theft:
All the same's the luck we prove,
Though the midmost hangs for love.

"Comrades all, that stand and gaze,
Walk henceforth in other ways;
See my neck and save your own:
Comrades all, leave ill alone.

"Make some day a decent end,
Shrewder fellows than your friend.
Fare you well, for ill fare I:
Live, lads, and I will die."

1895

51 Screaming Tarn

Robert Bridges (1844–1930)

The saddest place that e'er I saw
   Is the deep tarn above the inn
That crowns the mountain-road, whereby
   One southward bound his way must win.

Sunk on the table of the ridge
   From its deep shores is nought to see:
The unresting wind lashes and chills
   Its shivering ripples ceaselessly.

Three sides 'tis banked with stones aslant,
   And down the fourth the rushes grow,
And yellow sedge fringing the edge
   With lengthen'd image all arow.

'Tis square and black, and on its face
   When noon is still, the mirror'd sky

Looks dark and further from the earth
   Than when you gaze at it on high.

At mid of night, if one be there,
   — So say the people of the hill —
A fearful shriek of death is heard,
   One sudden scream both loud and shrill.

And some have seen on stilly nights,
   And when the moon was clear and round,
Bubbles which to the surface swam
   And burst as if they held the sound. —

'Twas in the days ere hapless Charles
   Losing his crown had lost his head,
This tale is told of him who kept
   The inn upon the watershed:

He was a lowbred ruin'd man
   Whom lawless times set free from fear:
One evening to his house there rode
   A young and gentle cavalier.

With curling hair and linen fair
   And jewel-hilted sword he went;
The horse he rode he had ridden far,
   And he was with his journey spent.

He asked a lodging for the night,
   His valise from his steed unbound,
He let none bear it but himself
   And set it by him on the ground.

'Here's gold or jewels,' thought the host,
   'That's carrying south to find the king.'
He chattered many a loyal word,
   And scraps of royal airs gan sing.

His guest thereat grew more at ease
   And o'er his wine he gave a toast,
But little ate, and to his room
   Carried his sack behind the host.

'Now rest you well,' the host he said,
    But of his wish the word fell wide; 50
Nor did he now forget his son
    Who fell in fight by Cromwell's side.

Revenge and poverty have brought
    Full gentler heart than his to crime;
And he was one by nature rude, 55
    Born to foul deeds at any time.

With unshod feet at dead of night
    In stealth he to the guest-room crept,
Lantern and dagger in his hand,
    And stabbed his victim while he slept. 60

But as he struck a scream there came,
    A fearful scream so loud and shrill:
He whelm'd the face with pillows o'er,
    And lean'd till all had long been still.

Then to the face the flame he held 65
    To see there should no life remain: —
When lo! his brutal heart was quell'd:
    'Twas a fair woman he had slain.

The tan upon her face was paint,
    The manly hair was torn away, 70
Soft was the breast that he had pierced;
    Beautiful in her death she lay.

His was no heart to faint at crime,
    Tho' half he wished the deed undone.
He pulled the valise from the bed 75
    To find what booty he had won.

He cut the straps, and pushed within
    His murderous fingers to their theft.
A deathly sweat came o'er his brow,
    He had no sense nor meaning left. 80

He touched not gold, it was not cold,
    It was not hard, it felt like flesh.
He drew out by the curling hair

Screaming Tarn

A young man's head, and murder'd fresh;

A young man's head, cut by the neck.
    But what was dreader still to see,
Her whom he had slain he saw again,
    The twain were like as like can be.

Brother and sister if they were,
    Both in one shroud they now were wound, —
Across his back and down the stair,
    Out of the house without a sound.

He made his way unto the tarn,
    The night was dark and still and dank;
The ripple chuckling neath the boat
    Laughed as he drew it to the bank.

Upon the bottom of the boat
    He laid his burden flat and low,
And on them laid the square sandstones
    That round about the margin go.

Stone upon stone he weighed them down,
    Until the boat would hold no more;
The freeboard now was scarce an inch:
    He stripp'd his clothes and push'd from shore.

All naked to the middle pool
    He swam behind in the dark night;
And there he let the water in
    And sank his terror out of sight.

He swam ashore, and donn'd his dress,
    And scraped his bloody fingers clean;
Ran home and on his victim's steed
    Mounted, and never more was seen.

But to a comrade ere he died
    He told his story guess'd of none:
So from his lips the crime returned
    To haunt the spot where it was done.

1899

52 The Yarn of the Loch Achray

John Masefield (1878–1967)

The *Loch Achray* was a clipper tall
With seven-and-twenty hands in all.
Twenty to hand and reef and haul,
A skipper to sail and mates to bawl
"Tally on to the tackle-fall, 5
Heave now 'n' start her, heave 'n' pawl!"
    Hear the yarn of a sailor,
    An old yarn learned at sea.

Her crew were shipped and they said "Farewell,
So-long, my Tottie, my lovely gell; 10
We sail to-day if we fetch to hell,
It's time we tackled the wheel a spell."
    Hear the yarn of a sailor,
    An old yarn learned at sea.

The dockside loafers talked on the quay 15
The day that she towed down to sea:
"Lord, what a handsome ship she be!
Cheer her, sonny boys, three times three!"
And the dockside loafers gave her a shout
As the red-funnelled tug-boat towed her out; 20
They gave her a cheer as the custom is,
And the crew yelled "Take our loves to Liz —
Three cheers, bullies, for old Pier Head
'N' the bloody stay-at-homes!" they said.
    Hear the yarn of a sailor, 25
    An old yarn learned at sea.

In the grey of the coming on of night
She dropped the tug at the Tuskar Light,
'N' the topsails went to the topmast head
To a chorus that fairly awoke the dead. 30
She trimmed her yards and slanted South
With her royals set and a bone in her mouth.
    Hear the yarn of a sailor,
    An old yarn learned at sea.

She crossed the Line and all went well,
They ate, they slept, and they struck the bell
And I give you a gospel truth when I state
The crowd didn't find any fault with the Mate,
But one night off the River Plate.
    Hear the yarn of a sailor,
    An old yarn learned at sea.

It freshened up till it blew like thunder
And burrowed her deep, lee-scuppers under.
The old man said, "I mean to hang on
Till her canvas busts or her sticks are gone" —
Which the blushing looney did, till at last
Overboard went her mizzen-mast.
    Hear the yarn of a sailor,
    An old yarn learned at sea.

Then a fierce squall struck the *Loch Achray*
And bowed her down to her water-way;
Her main-shrouds gave and her forestay,
And a green sea carried her wheel away;
Ere the watch below had time to dress
She was cluttered up in a blushing mess.
    Hear the yarn of a sailor,
    An old yarn learned at sea.

She couldn't lay-to nor yet pay-off,
And she got swept clean in the bloody trough;
Her masts were gone, and afore you knowed
She filled by the head and down she goed.
Her crew made seven-and-twenty dishes
For the big jack-sharks and the little fishes,
And over their bones the water swishes.
    Hear the yarn of a sailor,
    An old yarn learned at sea.

The wives and girls they watch in the rain
For a ship as won't come home again.
"I reckon it's them head-winds," they say,
"She'll be home to-morrow, if not to-day.
I'll just nip home 'n' I'll air the sheets
'N' buy the fixins 'n' cook the meats

As my man likes 'n' as my man eats."
So home they goes by the windy streets,
Thinking their men are homeward bound 75
With anchors hungry for English ground,
And the bloody fun of it is, they're drowned!
   Hear the yarn of a sailor,
   An old yarn learned at sea.

1902

53 *A Sunday Morning Tragedy*
     (*circa* 186–)

Thomas Hardy (1840–1928)

I bore a daughter flower-fair,
In Pydel Vale, alas for me;
I joyed to mother one so rare,
But dead and gone I now would be.

Men looked and loved her as she grew, 5
And she was won, alas for me;
She told me nothing, but I knew,
And saw that sorrow was to be.

I knew that one had made her thrall,
A thrall to him, alas for me; 10
And then, at last, she told me all,
And wondered what her end would be.

She owned that she had loved too well,
Had loved too well, unhappy she,
And bore a secret time would tell, 15
Though in her shroud she'd sooner be.

I plodded to her sweetheart's door
In Pydel Vale, alas for me:

I pleaded with him, pleaded sore,
To save her from her misery.

He frowned, and swore he could not wed,
Seven times he swore it could not be;
"Poverty's worse than shame," he said,
Till all my hope went out of me.

"I've packed my traps to sail the main" —
Roughly he spake, alas did he —
"Wessex beholds me not again,
'Tis worse than any jail would be!"

— There was a shepherd whom I knew,
A subtle man, alas for me:
I sought him all the pastures through,
Though better I had ceased to be.

I traced him by his lantern light,
And gave him hint, alas for me,
Of how she found her in the plight
That is so scorned in Christendie.

"Is there an herb. . . . ?"   I asked.   "Or none?"
Yes, thus I asked him desperately.
"— There is," he said; "a certain one. . . . "
Would he had sworn that none knew he!

"To-morrow I will walk your way,"
He hinted low, alas for me. —
Fieldwards I gazed throughout next day;
Now fields I never more would see!

The sunset-shine, as curfew strook,
As curfew strook beyond the lea,
Lit his white smock and gleaming crook,
While slowly he drew near to me.

He pulled from underneath his smock
The herb I sought, my curse to be —
"At times I use it in my flock,"
He said, and hope waxed strong in me.

"'Tis meant to balk ill-motherings" —
(Ill-motherings! Why should they be?) —
"If not, would God have sent such things?"
So spoke the shepherd unto me.

That night I watched the poppling brew,
With bended back and hand on knee:
I stirred it till the dawnlight grew,
And the wind whiffled wailfully.

"This scandal shall be slain," said I,
"That lours upon her innocency:
I'll give all whispering tongues the lie;" —
But worse than whispers was to be.

"Here's physic for untimely fruit,"
I said to her, alas for me,
Early that morn in fond salute;
And in my grave I now would be.

— Next Sunday came, with sweet church chimes
In Pydel Vale, alas for me:
I went into her room betimes;
No more may such a Sunday be!

"Mother, instead of rescue nigh,"
She faintly breathed, alas for me,
"I feel as I were like to die,
And underground soon, soon should be."

From church that noon the people walked
In twos and threes, alas for me,
Showed their new raiment — smiled and talked,
Though sackcloth-clad I longed to be.

Came to my door her lover's friends,
And cheerly cried, alas for me,
"Right glad are we he makes amends,
For never a sweeter bride can be."

My mouth dried, as 'twere scorched within,
Dried at their words, alas for me:

More and more neighbours crowded in,
(O why should mothers ever be!)

"Ha-ha!   Such well-kept news!" laughed they,
Yes — so they laughed, alas for me.
"Whose banns were called in church to-day?" —
Christ, how I wished my soul could flee!

"Where is she?   O the stealthy miss,"
Still bantered they, alas for me,
"To keep a wedding close as this . . . . "
Ay, Fortune worked thus wantonly!

"But you are pale — you did not know?"
They archly asked, alas for me,
I stammered, "Yes — some days — ago,"
While coffined clay I wished to be.

"'Twas done to please her, we surmise?"
(They spoke quite lightly in their glee)
"Done by him as a fond surprise?"
I thought their words would madden me.

Her lover entered.   "Where's my bird? —
My bird — my flower — my picotee?
First time of asking, soon the third!"
Ah, in my grave I well may be.

To me he whispered: "Since your call —"
So spoke he then, alas for me —
"I've felt for her, and righted all."
— I think of it to agony.

"She's faint to-day — tired — nothing more —"
Thus did I lie, alas for me. . . .
I called her at her chamber door
As one who scarce had strength to be.

No voice replied.   I went within —
O women! scourged the worst are we. . . .
I shrieked.   The others hastened in
And saw the stroke there dealt on me.

There she lay — silent, breathless, dead,
Stone dead she lay — wronged, sinless she! —
Ghost-white the cheeks once rosy-red:
Death had took her.   Death took not me.

I kissed her colding face and hair,   125
I kissed her corpse — the bride to be! —
My punishment I cannot bear,
But pray God *not* to pity me.

1904

54   The Ghost

Walter de la Mare (1873–1956)

'Who knocks?'   'I, who was beautiful,
  Beyond all dreams to restore,
I, from the roots of the dark thorn am hither,
  And knock on the door.'

'Who speaks?'   'I — once was my speech   5
  Sweet as the bird's on the air.
When echo lurks by the waters to heed;
  'Tis I speak thee fair.'

'Dark is the hour!'   'Ay, and cold.'
  'Lone is my house.'   'Ah, but mine?'   10
'Sight, touch, lips, eyes yearned in vain.'
  'Long dead these to thine . . .'

Silence.   Still faint on the porch
  Brake the flames of the stars.
In gloom groped a hope-wearied hand   15
  Over keys, bolts, and bars.

A face peered.   All the grey night

In chaos of vacancy shone;
Nought but vast sorrow was there —
The sweet cheat gone.

1918

55 The Murder on the Downs

William Plomer (1903–73)

Past a cow and past a cottage,
Past the sties and byres,
Past the equidistant poles
Holding taut the humming wires,

Past the inn and past the garage,
Past the hypodermic steeple
Ever ready to inject
The opium of the people,

In the fresh, the Sussex morning,
Up the Dangerous Corner lane
Bert and Jennifer were walking
Once again.

The spider's usual crochet
Was caught upon the thorns,
The skylark did its stuff,
The cows had horns.

'See,' said Bert, 'my hand is sweating.'
With her lips she touched his palm
As they took the path above the
Valley farm.

Over the downs the wind unveiled
That ancient monument the sun,

And a perfect morning
Had begun.

But summer lightning like an omen
Carried on a silent dance
On his heart's horizon, as he
Gave a glance

At the face beside him, and she turned
Dissolving in his frank blue eyes
All her hope, like aspirin.
On that breeding-place of lies

His forehead, too, she laid her lips.
'Let's find a place to sit,' he said.
'Past the gorse, down in the bracken
Like a bed.'

Oh the fresh, the laughing morning!
Warmth upon the bramble brake
Like a magnet draws from darkness
A reviving snake:

Just an adder, slowly gliding,
Sleepy curving idleness,
On the Sussex turf now writing
SOS.

Jennifer in sitting, touches
With her hand an agaric,
Like a bulb of rotten rubber
Soft and thick,

Screams, withdraws, and sees its colour
Like a leper's liver,
Leans on Bert so he can feel her
Shiver.

Over there the morning ocean,
Frayed around the edges, sighs,
At the same time gaily twinkles,
Conniving with a million eyes

At Bert whose free hand slowly pulls
A rayon stocking from his coat,
Twists it quickly, twists it neatly,
Round her throat.

'Ah, I knew that this would happen!'
Her last words: and not displeased
Jennifer relaxed, still smiling
While he squeezed.

Under a sky without a cloud
Lay the still unruffled sea,
And in the bracken like a bed
The murderee.

1936

56 The Enchanted Knight

Edwin Muir (1887–1959)

Lulled by La Belle Dame Sans Merci he lies
   In the bare wood below the blackening hill.
The plough drives nearer now, the shadow flies
   Past him across the plain, but he lies still.

Long since the rust its gardens here has planned,
   Flowering his armour like an autumn field.
From his sharp breast-plate to his iron hand
   A spider's web is stretched, a phantom shield.

When footsteps pound the turf beside his ear
   Armies pass through his dream in endless line,
And one by one his ancient friends appear;
   They pass all day, but he can make no sign.

When a bird cries within the silent grove

The long-lost voice goes by, he makes to rise
And follow, but his cold limbs never move, 15
And on the turf unstirred his shadow lies.

But if a withered leaf should drift
    Across his face and rest, the dread drops start
Chill on his forehead.   Now he tries to lift
    The insulting weight that stays and breaks his heart. 20

1937

57   Miss Gee

W. H. Auden (1907–73)

(*Tune, St. James' Infirmary*)

Let me tell you a little story
    About Miss Edith Gee,
She lived in Clevedon Terrace
    At Number 83.

She'd a slight squint in her left eye, 5
    Her lips they were thin and small,
She had narrow sloping shoulders
    And she had no bust at all.

She'd a velvet hat with trimmings,
    And a dark grey serge costume, 10
She lived in Clevedon Terrace
    In a small bed-sitting-room.

She'd a purple mac' for wet days,
    A green umbrella too to take,
And a bicycle with shopping basket 15
    And a harsh back-pedal brake.

The Church of Saint Aloysius
    Was not so very far,
She did a lot of knitting,
    Knitting for that Church bazaar.

Miss Gee looked up at the starlight,
    Said: Does anyone care
That I live in Clevedon Terrace
    On a hundred pounds a year?

She dreamt a dream one evening
    That she was the Queen of France,
And the Vicar of Saint Aloysius
    Asked Her Majesty to dance.

But a storm blew down the palace,
    She was biking through a field of corn,
And a bull with the face of the Vicar
    Was charging with lowered horn.

She could feel his hot breath behind her,
    He was going to overtake,
And the bicycle went slower and slower
    Because of that back-pedal brake.

Summer made the trees a picture,
    Winter made them a wreck.
She bicycled down to the evening service
    With the clothes buttoned up to her neck.

She passed by the loving couples,
    She turned her head away,
She passed by the loving couples,
    And they didn't ask her to stay.

Miss Gee sat down in the side-aisle,
    She heard the organ play,
And the choir it sang so sweetly
    At the ending of the day,

The Vicar stood up in the pulpit,
    He took away her breath,

He took as the text for his sermon;
   "The Wages of Sin is Death."

Miss Gee knelt down in the side-aisle,
   She knelt down on her knees:
"Lead me not into temptation
   But make me a good girl please."

The days and nights went by her
   Like waves round a Cornish wreck,
She bicycled down to the doctor
   With the clothes buttoned up to her neck.

She bicycled down to the doctor,
   She rang the surgery bell,
'O, doctor, I've a pain inside me,
   And I don't feel very well.'

Doctor Thomas looked her over,
   And then he looked some more,
Walked over to his wash-basin,
   Said: 'Why haven't you come before?'

Doctor Thomas looked her over,
   He shook his well-groomed head,
'You've a cancer on your liver,
   Miss Gee, you'll soon be dead.'

Doctor Thomas sat down to dinner,
   Said to his wife: 'My dear,
I've just seen Miss Gee this evening
   And she's a gonner, I fear.'

They took Miss Gee to hospital,
   She lay there a total wreck,
Lay in the ward for women
   With the bedclothes right up to her neck.

They put her on the table,
   The students began to laugh,
And Mr. Rose, the surgeon,
   He cut Miss Gee in half.

Mr. Rose he turned to his students,
    Said: 'Gentlemen, if you please,
We seldom meet a sarcoma
    As far advanced as this.'

They took her off the table,
    They wheeled away Miss Gee
Down to another department
    Where they study anatomy.

They hung her from the ceiling,
    Yes, they hung up Miss Gee,
And a couple of Oxford Groupers
    Carefully dissected her knee.

1937

58   *A Subaltern's Love-song*

John Betjeman (1906–84)

Miss J. Hunter Dunn, Miss J. Hunter Dunn,
Furnish'd and burnish'd by Aldershot sun,
What strenuous singles we played after tea,
We in the tournament — you against me!

Love-thirty, love-forty, oh! weakness of joy,
The speed of a swallow, the grace of a boy,
With carefullest carelessness, gaily you won,
I am weak from your loveliness, Joan Hunter Dunn.

Miss Joan Hunter Dunn, Miss Joan Hunter Dunn,
How mad I am, sad I am, glad that you won.
The warm-handled racket is back in its press,
But my shock-headed victor, she loves me no less.

Her father's euonymus shines as we walk,

And swing past the summer-house, buried in talk,
And cool the verandah that welcomes us in
To the six-o'clock news and a lime-juice and gin.

Tho scent of the conifers, sound of the bath,
The view from my bedroom of moss-dappled path,
As I struggle with single-end evening tie,
For we dance at the Golf Club, my victor and I.

On the floor of her bedroom lie blazer and shorts
And the cream-coloured walls are be-trophied with sports,
And westering, questioning settles the sun
On your low-leaded window, Miss Joan Hunter Dunn.

The Hillman is waiting, the light's in the hall,
The pictures of Egypt are bright on the wall,
My sweet, I am standing beside the oak stair
And there on the landing's the light on your hair.

By roads "not adopted," by woodlanded ways,
She drove to the club in the late summer haze,
Into nine-o'clock Camberley, heavy with bells
And mushroomy, pine-woody, evergreen smells.

Miss Joan Hunter Dunn, Miss Joan Hunter Dunn,
I can hear from the car-park the dance has begun.
Oh! full Surrey twilight! importunate band!
Oh! strongly adorable tennis-girl's hand!

Around us are Rovers and Austins afar,
Above us, the intimate roof of the car,
And here on my right is the girl of my choice,
With the tilt of her nose and the chime of her voice,

And the scent of her wrap, and the words never said,
And the ominous, ominous dancing ahead.
We sat in the car park till twenty to one
And now I'm engaged to Miss Joan Hunter Dunn.

1945

59 *The Foreboding*

Robert Graves (1895–1985)

Looking by chance in at the open window
I saw my own self seated in his chair
With gaze abstracted, furrowed forehead,
    Unkempt hair.

I thought that I had suddenly come to die,
    That to a cold corpse this was my farewell,
Until the pen moved slowly upon paper
    And tears fell.

He had written a name, yours, in printed letters:
    One word on which bemusedly to pore —
No protest, no desire, your naked name,
    Nothing more.

Would it be tomorrow, would it be next year?
    But the vision was not false, this much I knew;
And I turned angrily from the open window
    Aghast at you.

Why never a warning, either by speech or look,
    That the love you cruelly gave me could not last?
Already it was too late: the bait swallowed,
    The hook fast.

1953

60 *Ballad of the Three Coins*

Vernon Watkins (1906–67)

I know this road like the back of my hand

From birth to the lonely sea
With a windblown dog and a bottle of sand,
And I count my curses three.

The birds of the sea hang high in the air
And the land-birds crowd the tree.
I go, they cannot tell me where,
But their cries were torn from me.

A mile beyond Red Chamber
Flashes a light of broken skies.
The mother-of-pearl of the winkle-shell
Runs back to drowned men's eyes.

I take this first of the paths which run
Seaward from the thorny wood.
Flocks of starlings darken the sun,
And the moon is in my blood.

Swollen shoes, a pole and a pack,
And three considered coins;
A pain in the head, a pain in the back,
And a great pain in the groins.

They say the dawn brings learning
And the midnight, love.
The sun and the moon should teach me;
The stars should dig my grave.

But the bones that are I are the bones of a man
Walking between two lives.
The three coins of the Furies
Leap on the road of knives.

 The first coin spins in the light of Dawn.
 I see it glint and burn.
 There is eager thought in those patient eyes.
 Athene, O, your turn.

  'Go to the field and you will find
  A woman milking a cow.'
  Beautiful dawn, instruct me:

Ballad of the Three Coins

    Dawn, and the olive-bough.

I passed a field where they buried a man.
A dark priest in a cowl
Prayed above his body,
And over him swept an owl.

Then I came, I came to a five-barred gate
Where a slow sight held me still.
A woman was gripping the teats of a cow,
A bucket waiting to fill.

The curse of Earth is the curse of the beggar.
Intellect breaks his sleep.
No books in the world will slake that thirst,
So swift it is, and deep.

I raised the white milk high on my head
Where it shone like Solomon's crown.
That world would have stood for ever,
But the second coin pulled me down.

    The second coin spins in the light of Noon.
    I see it glint and burn.
    There is jealous arrogance in those eyes.
    This is Juno's turn.

        'Go to the stream and you will find
        A queen where the light is strong.'
        Beautiful noon, instruct me:
        Noon, and the cuckoo's song.

I went, I went to the faltering stream,
And a rare sight held me back.
A woman bathed from the water's edge,
Stopped me in my track.

I fixed my eyes on her.   At once
Jealousy ran through my blood.
Her proud beauty was the sun's,
Her brood the eagle's brood.

I could not cross the stepping-stones
For jealousy jumped on my back.
I cursed the crone on my great back-bone.
I cursed her white and black.

O stint and glint of the jealous flint,
O pride of the flashing crown!
What was the good of a haughty queen?
A beggar cannot lie down.

At last I managed my way across
That crooked, evil stream,
And I found a stone with a little green moss
And a lost, illegible name.

I stretched my legs and my heart was still;
I fixed my eyes on a tree;
When the third great pain got hold of me,
The worst of those bad three.

O let me be, you women!
O my coins were curses three.
The first I carried, the second I buried.
The third I'll cast to the sea.

    The third coin spins in the Starlight.
    O where are the first two gone?
    Come down, engendering darkness.
    A wild dog leads me on.

    What rest is there on the love-starved Earth
    When the sea is starved for love?
    Beautiful Night, instruct me:
    Night, and the turtle-dove.

        'Run down, run down to the yellow-white foam,
        A naked girl you will see
        Who will take that last coin from you,
        The worst of those bad three.'

To the beach I went, I went to the rock,
I stood where the limpets clung.

The salt blood sprang at my heart's great knock,
And now the salt wind stung.

What have I come to win from death
Girding up my loins?
Swollen shoes, a pole and a pack,
And the last of three bad coins.

What if, when I come to the yellow-white foam,
Nothing I can see
But a bottle up to its neck in sand
And a wet dog peeled by the sea?

O what of Athene's halo
And what of Solomon's crown?
And what of Juno's jealous love?
A beggar cannot lie down.

But now by the yellow-white foam I stand,
And all is altered, all is changed,
All that logic of the land
Ravished and deranged.

The barren bears the fruits of the Earth
And the fruit bears barrenness.
The sun and the moon know nothing,
And between them I know less.

1954

解説と語註

Abbreviations

Ehrenpreis Anne Henry Ehrenpreis, ed., *The Literary Ballad*, London, 1966.

ESPB Francis James Child, ed., *The English and Scottish Popular Ballads*, 10 vols., Boston, 1882–98. Unless otherwise stated, quotations from traditional ballads are from this edition, and Child's version category in *ESPB* is indicated by the number and letters in parentheses as in (Child 10A).

Friedman Albert B. Friedman, *The Ballad Revival: Studies in the Influence of Popular on Sophisticated Poetry*, Chicago, 1961.

Minstrelsy Sir Walter Scott, ed., *Minstrelsy of the Scottish Border*, ed. Thomas Henderson, London, 1931.

Reliques Thomas Percy, ed., *Reliques of Ancient English Poetry: Consisting of Old Heroic Ballads, Songs, and Other Pieces of Our Earlier Poets; Together with Some Few of Later Date*, 3 vols., with memoir and critical dissertation by the Rev. George Gilfillan, Edinburgh, 1858. A rpt. entire from Percy's last edition of 1794.

Wheatley Thomas Percy, ed., *Reliques of Ancient English Poetry*, 3 vols, ed. Henry B. Wheatley, New York, 1966. An unabridged and unaltered republication of the work originally published by Swan Sonneschein, Lebas, and Lowrey in 1886.

1　Hardyknute

Lady Elizabeth Wardlaw（1677–1727）作，1719 年。
　彼女は初め，これを自分の創作ではなくて，ある紙切れに書かれていた古いバラッドの断片だと主張した。Thomas Percy がこれを出版した時には，作者が Wardlaw 夫人であろうということについては言及しているものの，なお確定できていなかった。また，ある時期，同じ Wardlaw 夫人が民衆の名作バラッド "Sir Patrick Spens"（Child 58）の作者ではないかと主張されたことは面白い。"Hardyknute" の作者は明らかに "Sir Patrick Spens" をよく知っていた。それまでのバラッド詩がすべてブロードサイド・バラッドの模倣であったのに対して，"Hardyknute" は初めて口承バラッドを模した作品であった。各スタンザは 8 行編成になっているが，4 行ずつが $abcb$ と押韻し，各行弱強 4 歩格と 3 歩格を繰り返す典型的なバラッド・スタンザで構成されている。
　作品の背景となった時代は，スコットランド王アレグザンダー三世（r. 1241–86）の治世である（この王の世継をめぐる遭難事故を "Sir Patrick Spens" はうたっている）。1262 年，アレグザンダー三世はスコットランド西方諸島を支配するノルウェー軍からスカイ島を奪回。翌 63 年，200 隻の船と 15,000 の軍勢を率いたノルウェー軍は 8 月の終わり，ケレラに集結，ロッホ・ローモンドまで侵入しながらも，アレグザンダー三世の防御の砦は堅く，10 月 2 日，スコットランドにとっては「神風」ともいうべき暴風雨に見舞われ，ノルウェーの艦隊はクライド川に潰滅する。この 10 月 2 日の戦いが「ラーグの戦い」と呼ばれるものであるが，この勝利によってアレグザンダー三世は 65 年にはマン島を含む全西方諸島を掌中に収める。
　無名の船乗りを主人公とする "Sir Patrick Spens" の背景は，戦いの終息の後の平和の時代であった。一方，"Hardyknute" の背景は「ラーグの戦い」そのものであり，主人公が武将であることも，また，当然であったと言えよう。勝利を導いた王はもちろんアレグザンダー三世であった。しかし，若き主君を助けた勝利の立役者は Alexander Stewart（1214–83; the 4th Steward of Scotland）であったと言われている。時に Stewart 49 歳。作品での主人公ハーディクヌートはこの立役者 Alexander Stewart に見立てられている。
　この詩の最大の創作意図は主人公の年齢設定にある。オープニング・スタンザは，戦いに明け暮れた人生の後，今は静かに余生を送る 70 歳のハーディクヌートの紹介で始まる。しかし作者は，王の命令が絶対であった時代を生きた男の運

命を，"Sir Patrick Spens" と巧みに重ねながら，呼び戻された戦場での敗北ではなくて，後に残した妻子の悲劇という形でクローズアップしてみせる。個人の心情に立ち入ってトータルな人生の悔いを語るというような姿勢は，伝承バラッドには無縁のものであった。作者が女性であったことが，「妻と美しい娘フェアリーを顧みず……」という老雄の最後の悔いを一段と説得力あるものにしている。

8	**fae:** foe.
10	**ha's:** halls.
15	**marrow:** equal.
16	**ELENOR the queen:** Eleanor of Provence (d. 1291), queen of Henry III of England, mother of Margaret, queen of Alexander III.
20	**bot:** without.
27	**gimp:** slender.
40	**Drinking the blood-red wine:** cf. 'The king sits in Dumferling toune, / Drinking the blude-reid wine' ("Sir Patrick Spens", Child 58A, 1–2).
62	**sae shill:** so shrill.
73	**Late, late yestreen:** cf. 'Late late yestreen I saw the new moone, / Wi the auld moone in hir arme' ("Sir Patrick Spens", 25–26).
	yestreen: yesterday evening.
82	**leel:** well-aimed, hitting the mark.
85	**Brade:** broad.
87	**anes:** once.
93	**harnisine:** harness.
107	**twirtle twist:** spiral twist.
116	**mane:** moan.
130	**Full lowns the shynand day:** meaning 'full calm the shining day becomes,' words intended to cheer up the young knight.
131	**menzie:** retinue. Cf. 'menzie' (156) as a body of troops.
145	**Syne:** then.
	hynd: away.
148	**sey'd:** tried.
150	**Caledon:** Scotland.
155	**Quhair:** where.
157	**feirs:** companions.
158	**revers:** opponents.
162	**rude:** rood, the holy Cross.
171	**meit:** meet, appropriate.
173	**stoup of weir:** support in times of war.
185	**sindle:** seldom, rarely.
194	**mense the faught:** engage in combat.

196 **unsonsie:** unfortunate.
207 **quat:** gave up.
213 **ettled at:** took aim at.
217 **jupe:** tunic.
219 **quhilk:** which.
236 **heght:** vowed, promised.
240 **garr'd:** made.
251 **darr'd:** dared to hit.
263 **Wha:** who.
268 **jear:** jeer.
276 **Sure taiken he was fey:** a certain token that he is fated to die.
277 **Swith:** at once.
286 **mease:** pacify.
　　bruik: enjoy.
288 **luik:** look.
289 **walowit:** pale.
297 **On Norways coast the widowit dame . . . :** cf. 'O lang, lang may their ladies sit, / Wi thair fans into their hand, / Or eir they se Sir Patrick Spence / Cum sailing to the land' ("Sir Patrick Spens", 33–36).

2　Sweet William's Farewell to Black-Ey'd Susan

John Gay (1685–1732) 作，*Poems on Several Occasions* (1720) 収録。
　この詩集によって 1,000 ポンドを超える収入を得た Gay は，それをそっくり南洋貿易会社に投資するが，有名な 'South Sea Bubble' で挫折する。しかし Alexander Pope や Jonathan Swift ら友人たちの援助で徐々に立ち直り，Swift から盗賊たちを主人公にする 'Newgate pastoral' を書くように勧められて出来たのがかの有名な *The Beggar's Opera* (1728) である。初演の舞台となった Lincoln's Inn Fields Theatre のオーナーは John Rich (?1692–1761) であったが，"*The Beggar's Opera* made Rich gay and Gay rich." と当時言いはやされた。
　このオペラの前口上で，乞食が登場して次のように述べる。

> This piece I own was originally writ for the celebrating the marriage of James Chanter and Moll Lay, two most excellent ballad-singers. . . . I hope I may be forgiven that I have not made my opera throughout unnatural, like those in vogue; for I have no recitative; excepting this, as I have consented to have neither Prologue nor Epilogue, it must be allowed an opera in all its forms. [*Eighteenth-Century Plays*, selected with an introduction by John Hampden (London, 1928) 111]

解説と語註　209

　Gay は，当時ロンドンの舞台を席巻していたイタリアオペラに対抗して，イギリス伝統のバラッドによる 'ballad opera' を目指したのである。流行のブロードサイド・バラッドのメロディに合わせて，Gay は数々の自作のバラッドを登場人物にうたわせた。Albert B. Friedman は 'ballad opera' の貢献について，'One certain result of the ballad opera's popularity was the removal of some of the opprobrium that attached to the term "ballad"' (Friedman 167) と述べているが，イタリアオペラを 'unnatural' と感じ，自分たちの中にうたい継がれてきたバラッドこそ 'natural' なものとして採用した点に，その後 William Wordsworth らが指摘するバラッドの魅力に触れた先見性があったと言えよう。

　表題の作品は，「幸福なる再会」を約束する点で 18 世紀中葉に流行した感傷的なバラッド詩の先駆けともなったものであるが，全編を通した愛の誇張表現は 20 世紀の詩人 W. H. Auden のバラッド詩 "As I Walked Out One Evening" (1938) にも実によく通じる一種の 'burlesque' としても読める。6 歳で両親を失い丁稚奉公に出た Gay は生涯「美装と贅沢な生活」[cf. Robert Chambers, *Cyclopædia of English Literature* (London, 1858) 1: 589] に憧れていたそうで，彼のバラッド・オペラ同様，その諧謔性は庶民感覚あふれるものであった。ウェストミンスター寺院に眠る Gay の自作の墓碑銘に

　　　　　　　　Life is a jest, and all things show it;
　　　　　　　　I thought so once, and now I know it.

とある。虚実の間(あわい)に人生ありである。

　1　**the *Downs*:** the part of the sea within the Goodwin Sands, off the east coast of Kent, a famous rendezvous for ships.

3　The Braes of Yarrow

William Hamilton (1704–54) 作。初出は Allan Ramsay 編纂の *The Tea-Table Miscellany* (1723) において。

　元歌となった "The Braes o Yarrow" (Child 214) は，家族から認められない夫 (版によっては，恋人) がヤロー川の土手で女の兄弟たちとの決闘の末に果ててゆくという物語であるが，このバラッド詩では決闘はすでに終わっていて，ハミルトンが 'A' と名付けた男 (恋人を殺した男) が残された女 ('C') を口説いて，自分と結婚してヤローの村を出てゆこうと誘っているという内容である。'B' は事件とはまったく無関係な単なる第三者で，問いを発することによって，それに対す

る回答から徐々に内容を明らかにする役回りを演じている。
　第7スタンザから第8スタンザの2行目までは 'B' の台詞とは示されていないが，明らかにそうである。視線が辺りの情景に向かって動きながら，事件をめぐる質問者の意識が移動してゆく。第8スタンザ後半から第15スタンザまで続く 'A' のモノローグは，質問者の意識の位相に呼応するかのごとく，話者の意識の動きを伝える。第17スタンザで初めて 'C' が登場する。以下，最終スタンザの一つ前まで，今度は一方的に女が語る。ここでも女の意識の位相が展開する。第25スタンザ (97ff) から雰囲気は一変する。一般的に伝承バラッドでは，死んだ恋人は「肉体を持った亡霊」('corporeal revenant') として生きている恋人の前に現れるが，ここでは，女は死んだ恋人の亡霊を彼女の意識の中に「幻覚」('hallucination') として見ているのである。バラッド詩が模倣から逸脱してゆく場合の一つの大きな特徴である「心理化」('psychologization') を，「幻覚」という形で実現している最初の重要な例である。
　ヤロー川のほとりに 'Dryhope Tower' と呼ばれ，「ヤローの花」とうたわれた Mary Scott の館の廃墟がある。伝承の歌の中では，恋人を失った彼女は最後に悲しみに胸張り裂けて死ぬことになるが，現実には彼女は1576年に Walter Scott of Harden と結婚している。結婚前に実際にこのような恋愛事件があったのか，それとも，これは彼女をめぐって作られたまったく架空の物語なのか。Hamilton の作品における話者 'A' は，メアリが現実に結婚した人物と重なるのか。想像するに，Hamilton もその地を訪ね，ヤロー川のほとりに佇んでこの廃墟を目にし，「ヤローの花」とうたわれた彼女をめぐって，事件の後日談として作品を書いたのか。そうであれば，彼の詩に設定された三人の登場人物 'A'，'B'，'C' ともに一つの事件をめぐって様々に意識が移ってゆくその「意識の位相」とは，取りも直さずかの地に佇んだ作者自身の「意識の位相」として大いに納得がいく。Friedman はこの作品について，'The poem has much ballad-like language but a most unballad-like discursiveness.' (Friedman 160) と一言で片付けているが，この「とりとめのなさ」の実態こそ，このような伝承バラッドに向かう時の詩人の意識なのである。バラッド詩が単なる模倣から逸脱してゆくときの質的変化を Hamilton の作品は端的に示していると言える。
　(初出の *The Tea-Table Miscellany* においては登場人物 'A'，'B'，'C' は明示されていないが，話の流れを判りやすくするために話者を表記した *Reliques* 版をテキストとして採用した。)

　　　Braes: the banks of a river.
　7　**na weil:** no longer.

8　**Puing the birks:** plucking the birth twigs, especially as used for decoration.
　24　**eir:** before.
　25　**reid:** red.
　27　**weids:** garments.
　50　**gowan:** daisy.
　52　**flowan:** flows.
　79　**toofall:** to-fall, nightfall.

4　Margaret's Ghost

David Mallet（?1705-65）作。1723年に書かれ，*The Plain Dealer* 誌上（1724年7月24日号，No. 36）に匿名で発表され，のちに *Reliques* 第3巻に収録された。

　故郷スコットランドからロンドンに移った際に名前を 'Malloch' から英語式に 'Mallet' と改め，詩作品 *The Excursion*（1728）や友人 James Thomson との共作仮面劇 *Alfred*（1740），伝記 *Life of Francis Bacon*（1740）など多方面で健筆を振るったが，このスコットランド詩人の名を後世にとどめたのは表題のバラッド詩によってであった。別名 "William and Margaret" として当時大変な人気を博したこの作品について，18世紀バラッド・コレクションの最初のものである *The Tea-Table Miscellany* を編集した Ramsay は 'I know not where to seek a finer mixture of pathos and terror in the whole range of Gothic romance.'（Wheatley 3: 309）と評し，Percy のバラッド編纂に対しては極めて辛辣な批評を呈した Joseph Ritson も 'It may be questioned whether any English writer has produced so fine a ballad as *William and Margaret*.'（Wheatley 3: 309）と評しているほどであった。

　Mallet は当時実際に起こった事件に基づいた創作であると述べているが，"Fair Margaret and Sweet William"（Child 74）や "Sweet William's Ghost"（Child 77）を元歌としていることは明白である。21行目から56行目にわたる哀感あふれた亡霊の台詞は，感情表現を抑制するという伝承バラッドの最大の特質からの逸脱を示した好例である。

　27　**give up:** emit.
　61　**hyed him:** hastened.

5 Lucy and Colin

　Thomas Tickell（1685-1740）作。"Lucy and Colin, A Song, Written in Imitation of William and Margaret" の原題で，1725年，ダブリンにおいて匿名で発表された。後に，Tickell の実名で *The Musical Miscellany; Being a Collection of Choice Songs, Set to the Violin and Flute, By the Most Eminent Masters* (London, 1729) に，さらに，Robert Dodsley の *A Collection of Poems by Several Hands* (1748) に収められ，最終的に *Reliques* 第3巻に収められた。

　原題に Mallet の "William and Margaret" を模倣したとあるが，Mallet の作品が "Fair Margaret and Sweet William" (Child 74) を元歌としているように，Tickell もその元歌の伝承バラッドを知った上であることは，65行目からの「恋結び」（'love-knot'）のモチーフがうたわれるスタンザから明らかである。これは Mallet には無いもので，死んだ恋人同士がバラとイバラに変身して結ばれるという「変身」（'metamorphosis'）は伝承バラッドにおいては常套のモチーフである。一方，Tickell においては，恋結びを結ぶのは死んだ恋人同士という当事者ではなくて，彼らの墓の前で契りを結ぶ村の若い男女という第三者である。そして詩人は彼らに，誓いを裏切らないようにと忠告する。類似のモチーフを利用しながら，教訓性を織り込んでゆくバラッド詩の好例である。一言で言えば，伝承の変身物語に対して，Tickell の作品は復讐物語である。

　死んだルーシーと対面した時のコリンの描写も，模倣からの逸脱を端的に表している。'Confusion, shame, remorse, despair / At once his bosom swell: / The damps of death bedew'd his brow, / He shook, he groan'd, he fell.' (53-56) という抽象的・散文的表現は，伝承における具体的で，かつ聴き手の想像力を豊かに刺激する表現とは好対照である。例えば，"Lord Thomas and Fair Annet" (Child 73) において，アネットは貧しさのゆえに裏切られ，死んだのち，24人の騎士と貴婦人を従え，真珠をちりばめた帯を腰に巻き，女王のように着飾って恋人の結婚式に現れるのに対して，Tickell におけるコリンが「鮮やかな婚礼衣装を身にまとい」(47)，ルーシーが「経帷子に身をつつみ」(48) では，ただ現実を素っ気なく表現するのみである。生と死を豊かにドラマタイズしてゆく伝承バラッドの遊戯性は詩人の模倣の中では欠落してゆく。元歌におけるウィリアムがマーガレットにくちづけするという「行為」から，抽象化された言葉に託した「苦悩」の表現への逸脱は，やがてロマン派の内向化する詩の世界に至る前奏となるものであった。

1 **Leinster:** a province in the east of Republic of Ireland.
3 **Liffy:** or Liffey, the river of the eastern part of Ireland running into Dublin Bay on the Irish Sea.

6　Admiral Hosier's Ghost

Richard Glover (1712–85) 作，1739 年。

　Leonidas (1737)，*The Athenaid* (1788) などの叙事詩で知られる Glover のもう一つの顔は国会議員であり，1739 年に *London, or the Progress of Commerce* を出版して，時の宰相 Robert Walpole の対スペイン平和外交に反対する国民感情を煽った。同じ目的をより効果的にしたのがこのバラッド詩であった。Walpole が同年 10 月，William Pitt 率いる野党とロンドン商人たちの世論に押されて不承不承に対スペイン宣戦を布告するや否や（いわゆる 'the War of Jenkins' Ear'），11 月 22 日，Edward Vernon 提督 (1684–1757) 率いる英国艦隊はスペインのアメリカ植民地主要都市であったポルトベロを奪取した。Glover はこの成功を祝す歌として表題のバラッド詩を作ったのであるが，彼の巧妙なところは，Vernon 提督を主人公にするのではなくて，その時を遡る十数年前に同じ海上で悲劇的死を遂げた別の提督をクローズアップした点にある。1726 年 4 月，Hosier 提督 (1673–1727) の艦隊がスペイン艦隊を包囲し，抵抗するものは捕捉してイギリスに曳航せよという命令のもと，スペイン領西インド諸島に派遣された。交戦してはならず，ただ威嚇するだけという状態で無為に時を過ごすうちに，4,000 人の艦隊員のほとんどが熱病に倒れ，戦艦は破損し，敵の嘲笑を受け，遂には Hosier 自身も失意のうちに命を落としたのである。

　詩人であると同時に政治家としても高名であった者がバラッド詩を書いたという点で，18 世紀前半におけるバラッドの地位向上に大いに貢献するとともに，19 世紀においても大英帝国の国威高揚に貢献して大変な人気を博し，Alfred Tennyson の "The Charge of the Light Brigade" (1854) が生まれる一因ともなった。

1 **Porto-Bello:** a small seaport on the Caribbean coast of Panama, and principal city of Spanish colonial America.
22 **the Burford:** Vernon's ship.
53 **the Bastimentos:** Spanish ships. (*OED*, citing this line.)

7　Jemmy Dawson

William Shenstone (1714–63) 作，1746 年。

　ステュアート家は，ロバート二世からジェイムズ六世に至る間 (1371–1603) スコットランドに君臨し，ジェイムズ六世がイングランドのジェイムズ一世となって以降，共和制の期間を除いてアン女王に至るまで (1603–1714) イングランド・スコットランド両国に君臨した王家であったが，アン女王をもって断絶，次のジョージ一世からヴィクトリア女王まで (1714–1901) はハノーヴァ王朝となった。表題の作品は，1746 年 7 月 30 日，ステュアート家の復権を図ったかどで逮捕され，手足を別々の馬に繋がれて八つ裂きの刑に処せられた謀反人の一人 Captain James Dawson とその恋人の物語であるが，Percy は次のような頭注を付けている。

> James Dawson was one of the Manchester rebels, who was hanged, drawn, and quartered, on Kennington-common, in the county of Surrey, July 30, 1746. This ballad is founded on a remarkable fact, which was reported to have happened at his execution. (*Reliques* 2: 302)

'Come listen to my mournful tale, / Ye tender hearts and lovers dear!' (1–2) と始まる，いわゆるブロードサイド・バラッドの形式を採っているが，愛する者の死を冷厳な目で見つめる恋人を残酷な処刑の場に配する手法は，父親と 7 人の兄弟が愛する恋人の刃で次々と倒れてゆく様を「一滴の涙も流さず」(st. 6) 見つめるマーガレットをうたう伝承バラッド "The Douglas Tragedy" (Child 7B) を彷彿させ，ブロードサイド的感傷に流されることを押しとどめる Shenstone の巧みさが窺える。

　Percy の *Reliques* 出版をうながし，様々な形での協力を惜しまなかった Shenstone は，1758 年 1 月 4 日の Percy にあてた書簡で，'You pique my Curiosity extremely by the mention of that antient Manuscript; as there is nothing gives me greater Pleasure than the *simplicity* of style & *sentiment* that is observable in old English ballads.' [*Letters of William Shenstone*, ed. Duncan Mallam (Minneapolis, 1939) 345] と述べているが，Percy の成功を見届けることなく，*Reliques* 第 1 巻の出版直前に発疹チフスで亡くなった。

35　**George:** King George II (r. 1727–60), with possible allusion to Saint George, England's patron saint.

8 The Hermit; or, Edwin and Angelina

Oliver Goldsmith（?1730–74）作，小説 The Vicar of Wakefield（1766）の中で紹介されるが，実際の制作年代は 1761 年頃と推定される。

　小説第 8 章で Mr. Burchell は，牧師の次女 Sophia に好意を寄せて一家をよく訪ねてくる。場面は，戸外での昼食のあとの団欒のひと時である。ソフィアが，互いの腕に抱かれたまま雷に打たれて死んだ二人の恋人のことを書いた John Gay の描写にとても心を打たれるものがあると言い，それに対して弟の Moses が，Ovid の Acis と Galatea の描写には及ばない，ローマの詩人は対照法をよく心得ており，人の心を動かす力はいかに巧みにその方法を駆使するかにかかっている，と述べる。二人のやりとりを聴いていたバーチェル氏は，次のように言って，彼の詩に対する考え方を主張する。

> "It is remarkable," cried Mr. Burchell, "that both the poets you mention have equally contributed to introduce a false taste into their respective countries, by loading all their lines with epithet. Men of little genius found them most easily imitated in their defects, and English poetry, like that in the latter empire of Rome, is nothing at present but a combination of luxuriant images, without plot or connexion; a string of epithets that improve the sound, without carrying on the sense. . . . I have made this remark only to have an opportunity of introducing to the company a ballad, which, whatever be its other defects, is, I think, at least free from those I have mentioned. (*The Vicar of Wakefield*, in *The Miscellaneous Works of Goldsmith* 1: 36)

このようにして紹介されたのが表題の作品であるが，このバラッド詩が Goldsmith の作品であるように，バーチェル氏の英詩に対する批判は作者自身のものであると考えられよう。

　Goldsmith の作品が，バーチェル氏の言うように華美なイメージ，形容辞を排して豊かなプロットを展開していることは認めよう。しかも，この作品は当時絶賛を博している。しかし，実はこの作品には元歌があった。*Reliques* に収められた "Gentle Herdsman, Tell to Me"（vol. 2, bk. 1, XIV）である。若者が羊飼いに道をたずね，男の身なりをしているが実は女で，かつてつれなくした恋人への罪を詫びて巡礼しているという事情を明かすところまでは，Goldsmith がそっくり取り入れている。違うのは，それぞれの歌の結末である。元歌では，すべての話を聞いて最後に羊飼いは「それでは気をつけて行かれるがよい，ごきげんよう」と言って別れる。一方 Goldsmith の方では，女の身の上話を聞いていた隠者こそ，実は，

かつて女につれなくされてこの世を捨てた，そしてもうてっきり死んだものと思われていた，恋人 Edwin その人だったということになる。これはあまりにも劇的な再会のメロドラマである。

27 **scrip:** a small bag, wallet, or satchel, *esp.* one carried by a pilgrim, a shepherd, or a beggar. (*OED*, citing this line.)
101 **the Tyne:** the river of northern England running into the North Sea at Tynemouth.
128 **Their constancy was mine:** as is mentioned in lines 125–26, the dew and the blossom on the tree *always* shine with 'inconstant' charms, and so 'their constancy' paradoxically meaning their 'inconstancy', is after all the speaker's 'own fickleness', or her 'own persistence of ignoring him'.

9 The Friar of Orders Gray

Thomas Percy (1729–1811) 作，1765 年。

　Percy は *Reliques* 第 1 巻の Book 2 全体に 'Ballads that illustrate Shakespeare' という題を付け，次のような註を記している。

> Our great dramatic poet having occasionally quoted many ancient ballads, and even taken the plot of one, if not more, of his plays from among them, it was judged proper to preserve as many of these as could be recovered, and that they might be the more easily found, to exhibit them in one collective view. This Second Book is therefore set apart for the reception of such ballads as are quoted by Shakespeare, or contribute in any degree to illustrate his writings: this being the principal point in view, the candid reader will pardon the admission of some pieces, that have no other kind of merit. (*Reliques* 1: 102)

この詩もそういう意図にそって断片を集め，自ら手を加えて一つのまとまった物語に構成したものである。ちなみに，この詩の第 3, 5 スタンザは *Hamlet* 4 幕 5 場で Ophelia がうたう次の歌から採ったものである。

> Oph. (*sings*)　How should I your true love know
> 　　　　　　　　From another one?
> 　　　　　　　By his cockle hat and staff
> 　　　　　　　And his sandal shoon.
> 　　　　　　　............................
> 　　　　　　　He is dead and gone, lady,
> 　　　　　　　　He is dead and gone,
> 　　　　　　　At his head a grass-green turf,

> At his heels a stone. (*Hamlet,* iv, v, 23–26, 29–32)

- 1 **a friar of orders gray:** a 'grey friar', member of the order of Franciscan friars, founded by St. Francis of Assisi in 1210, 'gray' coming from the colour of their habits.
- 11–12 **by his cockle hat ... sandal shoone:** 'These are the distinguishing marks of a Pilgrim. The chief places of devotion being beyond sea, the pilgrims were wont to put cockle-shells in their hats to denote the intention or performance of their devotion.' (Percy's note, *Reliques* 1: 197n)
  shoone: shoes.
- 101 **year of grace:** 'The year of probation, or noviciate' (Percy's note, *Reliques* 1: 200n).

10 Auld Robin Gray

Lady Anne Lindsay (のちに結婚して Lady Anne Barnard, 1750–1825) 作，1771 年。最初匿名で発表されると直ちに非常な人気を博し，David Herd 編纂の *Ancient and Modern Scottish Songs, Heroic Ballads, Etc.* (1776) に収められたりしたが，亡くなる 2 年前まで自分が作者であることを公表しなかった。結婚後，夫と南アフリカに渡り，英国によるケープタウン植民地化の初期の貴重な記録となる *Lady Anne Barnard at the Cape, 1797–1802* を執筆した。

彼女は，Sir Walter Scott にあてた書簡の中で，作品の成立の経緯について次のように述べている。

> There was an ancient Scotch melody, of which I was passionately fond .... I longed to ... give to its plaintive tones some little history of virtuous distress in humble life, such as might suit it. While attempting to effect this in my closet, I called to my little sister, now Lady Hardwicke, who was the only person near me, "I have been writing a ballad, my dear; I am oppressing my heroine with many misfortunes. I have already sent her Jamie to sea, and broken her father's arm, and made her mother fall sick, and given her Auld Robin Gray for her lover; but I wish to load her with a fifth sorrow within the four lines, poor thing! Help me to one." — "Steal the cow, sister Anne," said the little Elizabeth. The cow was immediately *lifted* by me, and the song completed. [J. G. Lockhart, *Memoirs of Sir Walter Scott* (London, 1900) 4: 212n]

話の筋立は伝承バラッド "James Harris (The Dæmon Lover)" (Child 243) そっくりである。しかし，結論の付け方には天地の差がある。伝承では，女は戻って来た恋人(肉体を持った亡霊)を再び愛して一緒に船出し，やがて悪魔の正体を見せた

恋人が船を真っ二つに打ち砕き，二人は諸共に海の底に沈んでゆくという，迫力満点の超自然的ドラマを展開するのに対して，恋人のことを思い続けることは罪であると納得して良き妻であろうとする主人公をうたう Lindsay の作品は，健全なる小市民的まとまりを見せている。

10 **stown:** stolen.
31 **no like:** not likely.

11 Bristowe Tragedie: or the Dethe of Syr Charles Bawdin

Thomas Chatterton (1752–70) 作，1768 年。

　Chatterton のいわゆる 'Rowley poems' の一つ。'Rowley poems' は，15 世紀のブリストルの詩人・修道士 Thomas Rowley によるものとして 1777 年に Thomas Tyrwhitt によって初めて出版された。しかし，1 年後にはオックスフォード大学詩学教授で後の桂冠詩人 Thomas Warton によって疑義が指摘され，1871 年にケンブリッジ大学教授 Walter W. Skeat 編集のいわゆる Skeat 版が出るまでその真偽が延々と論じられた。

　しかし，Chatterton の天才をいち早く認めたのはロマン派の詩人たちであった。Wordsworth はこの類稀な少年の挫折を，'I thought of Chatterton, the marvellous Boy, / The sleepless Soul that perished in his pride; // We poets in our youth begin in gladness; / But thereof come in the end despondency and madness' ("Resolution and Independence", 43–44, 48–49) とうたって共感を示し，John Keats は *Endymion* (1818) を彼に捧げた。特に Keats の場合，貧困からくる絶望のうちにわずか 18 歳で自殺して果てたこの天才に，やがて来る自らの早世を予感したのか。言葉の天才 Keats は，Chatterton の英語の純粋性について次のように書いている。

> I always somehow associate Chatterton with autumn. He is the purest writer in the English Language. He has no French idiom, or particles like Chaucer — 'tis genuine English Idiom in English words. [*The Letters of John Keats*, ed. Hyder Edward Rollins (Harvard, 1958) 2: 167]

　作品の背景はバラ戦争 (1455–85) で，1461 年ランカスター派のヘンリー六世はタウントンの戦いに破れ，国外に逃れる。ヨーク派のエドワード四世は敵方の者たちをことごとく反逆罪に問い，領地を没収し，ヘンリーを捕らえて投獄した。歌の主人公は，彼ら反逆罪に問われた者たちの一人，Sir Baldwin Fulford である。
　Chatterton の完璧なバラッド・スタンザと Chaucer 風の古風なスペリングによ

るこの作品は，中世という時代背景の雰囲気をよく伝えている。また，「人間はいずれ死に逝く運命にある」(33ff, 105ff) と繰り返し，「時代に迎合した生き方はしなかった」(147) と言って毅然として死に向かう主人公の姿には正に伝承バラッドの伝える人間の生き様に共通したものがあるが，ロマン派の詩人たちはそこに若き天才詩人と自らの生き様を重ねて共鳴したのではないか。

    Bristowe: Bristol.
1   **chaunticleer:** cock.
2   **Han:** has.
9   **quod:** said.
40 **for aie:** forever.
45 **CANYNGE:** William Canynges (?1399–1474), Mayor of Bristol.
58 **rewyn'd:** ruined.
73 **reines:** the loins as the seat of the feelings or affections.
78 **faste:** make secure.
151 **fadre:** father.
187 **choppe:** exchange.
189 **sledde:** sledge.
233 **saie:** speech.
263 **enshone:** showed.
269 **Freers:** friars.
276 **bataunt:** 'musical instrument (an invention of Chatterton's)' (Ehrenpreis 45n). Cf. *OED*, citing this line, explains 'bataunt' as the variant of 'bataud', meaning 'hastening, eager', and says it is 'misused by Chatterton'.
280 **defend:** prevent.
341 **RICHARD:** Duke of Gloucester (1452–85), younger brother of Edward IV, later King Richard III.
384 **crowen:** crows.

12 The Braes of Yarrow

John Logan (1748–88) 作，1781 年。

  Logan はスコットランドの詩人，長老派教会牧師。情熱的な説教で人気を博していたが，彼の書いた悲劇 *Runnamede* が 1783 年にエディンバラで上演されたことから信者の不興を買い，父親ゆずりの大酒癖のせいもあって，86 年に聖職を去り，ロンドンに出て文筆活動に専念した。

  本作品と同名のものに前出 Hamilton のバラッド詩があるが，Hamilton が伝承

バラッド "The Braes o Yarrow" (Child 214) を元歌としていたのに対して，Logan は "Rare Willie Drowned in Yarrow, or, the Water o Gamrie" (Child 215) を元歌としている。29〜30行目は元歌の 'She sought him east, she sought him west, / She sought him brade and narrow' (215A, 13-14) をほとんど借用しているが，結婚に反対する母親の呪いによって増水した川で息子が溺れ死ぬという元歌のモチーフはLoganにあってはまったく姿を消し，恋人を失った語り手の悲しみだけがクローズアップされている。詩人のねらいは，全48行中44行を占めるモノローグを通して語り手の悲しみを伝えることにあった。事件を語る伝承バラッドの迫力が消え，バラッド詩が心理的・主観的になっていった点で Hamilton と共通する。

なお，Wordsworth の "Yarrow Visited" (1814) に次の一節がある。

> Where was it that the famous Flower
> Of Yarrow Vale lay bleeding?
> His bed perchance was yon smooth mound
> On which the herd is feeding:
> And haply from this crystal pool,
> Now peaceful as the morning,
> The Water-wraith ascended thrice —
> And gave his doleful warning. (25-32)

この作品は，1814年に二度目のスコットランド旅行をした際のものであるが，最初の旅行の時に作られた "Yarrow Unvisited" (1803) の頭註にあるように，いずれの作品においてもヤロー川訪問に際して Wordsworth の念頭には Hamilton の作品があったことは明らかである。しかし，上記引用最後の2行は明らかに Logan の23〜24行から来たものであり，Wordsworth には Logan の作品も同時に念頭にあったことがわかり，大変興味深い。

12　**'squire:** attend a lady.

13　The Diverting History of John Gilpin

William Cowper (1731–1800) 作。最初匿名で *The Public Advertiser* 紙の1782年11月14日号に，「"Chevy Chace"の曲に合わせて」として掲載された。

作品はたちまち大人気を博して，ブロードサイドやチャップ・ブックに収められて売り歩かれた。のちに，自分の書く詩があまりにもユーモアに欠けると批判された Cowper は，たまには楽しく書けるのだということを知らしめるために自

解説と語註　　　　　　　　　221

分がこの有名なバラッドの作者であることを明らかにした。

　子供の頃から気質的に過敏であった Cowper は，生涯に何度も激しい憂鬱症に悩まされ，自殺を試みている。いとこの Theodore Cowper との結婚がかなわなかったことなども輪をかけて，Cowper は，自分が神から見捨てられた子であると強く感じるようになる。そうした中で，1765 年から Morley Unwin 牧師の家に寄宿することになり，牧師の死後，未亡人の Mary と以後の生涯を一緒に過ごす。その間にも憂鬱症と自殺未遂は繰り返される。一時，福音主義派牧師 John Newton の家に身を寄せるが，再び Mary の元に戻り，しばらく静かな精神状態が続く。その間に Mary に励まされて，"The Progress of Error"，"Hope" その他の諷刺詩を書き，1782 年に最初の詩集を出版する。表題の作品は，その同じ時期のものであるが，隣人の Lady Austen がある夜のパーティで，Cowper の気を晴らすために語った話に基づいている。Cowper はこの話が大いに気に入って，その夜のうちに一気にこれを書き上げたという。

　結婚 20 周年記念の祝いのもくろみは，文字通りワインと帽子とかつらと共に吹っ飛んで，ロンドンの町中から Edmonton まで 8 マイル，さらにその先の Ware まで 18 マイルとして片道 26 マイル，往復 52 マイル，80 キロを越える道のりを暴れ馬にしがみついて疾走するジョン・ギルピンの姿は当時のロンドンっ子を大いに喜ばせたかも知れないが，些細な庶民の幸せと平安を願う Cowper の泣き笑いの顔も見えてきて，複雑である。どじな庶民の哀感をうたうユーモアあふれる伝承バラッドの真髄を Cowper は実によく理解していたのである。

　3　**train-band:** a trained company of citizen soldiery, organized in London and other parts in the 16th, 17th, and 18th centuries. (*OED*, citing this line.)
　11　**Edmonton:** the municipal borough in the county of Middlesex, eight miles north of London. 'The "Bell at Edmonton" has become famous by association with the adventures of John Gilpin, the hero of Cowper's poem' (*Encyclopedia Americana*).
　23　**calender:** one who presses cloth, paper, etc., under rollers for the purpose of smoothing or glazing. (*OED*, citing this line.)
　44　**Cheapside:** the historical district and street of London, extending eastward from St. Paul's Cathedral to the Poultry, and to the Mansion House.
133　**Islington:** inner borough of Greater London, 2 miles north of St. Paul's.
135　**the Wash:** a stream running across a road. (*OED*, citing this line.)
152　**Ware:** the east district in the county of Hertfordshire.
178　**pin:** mood.
236　**hue and cry:** outcry calling for the pursuit of a felon, raised by the party aggrieved, by a constable, etc. (*OED*, citing this line.)

14　Cumnor Hall

William Julius Mickle（1735–88）作。Thomas Evans 編纂の *Old Ballads*（1784）に収録。

　Scott の小説 *Kenilworth*（1821）に題材を提供したことで有名なこの作品の語り手は，エリザベス一世の寵愛を受けた Robert Dudley, Earl of Leicester（?1532–88）の隠し妻 Amy Robsart である。題名となっている 'Cumnor Hall' はオックスフォード近郊の屋敷で，そこに幽閉されていた彼女は，後に Leicester 伯によって殺害されたと言い伝えられている。

　全 120 行中 3 分の 2 を占める語り手のモノローグは，伝承バラッドでは考えられない形式であり，18 世紀バラッド詩の一つの特徴である感傷主義に荷担しているが，訪れぬ恋人を待つという主題は，Keats の "Isabella"（1818），Tennyson の "Mariana"（1830）や "Mariana in the South"（1832）に引き継がれてゆく。他方，悲しみにやつれて死んでゆくという伝承バラッド的終息にゴシック的雰囲気が加味されて，やがて来る 'Gothic horror-ballads' の先鞭をつけた作品でもある。

　　8　**pile:** a small tower.
　 12　**privitie:** seclusion.
　 43　**eastern flow'rs:** sunflowers（?）
　 48　**gaudes:** ostentatious, but lesser beauties.

15　A Red, Red Rose

Robert Burns（1759–96）作，1794 年。

　Burns はスコットランドの古今の歌を集めた James Johnson 編纂の *The Scots Musical Museum*（1787–1803）への協力を求められ，それに寄稿する歌の蒐集，改作，創作に終生情熱をそそぎ，表題作や "Auld Lang Syne" その他多くの名作を残した。

　表題作をめぐっても，元歌となったと推測される多くの 'street ballads' が紹介されているが，ここでは Robert Chambers が紹介しているものの一節と，J. H. Fowler が Francis T. Palgrave 編纂の *Golden Treasury*（1861）に付けた註の中で指摘しているものの一部を紹介しよう。

> "O fare thee well, my own true love,
>   O fare thee well awhile;
> But I'll come back and see thee, love,
>   Though I go ten thousand mile."
>   [*The Life and Works of Robert Burns*, ed. Robert
>   Chambers (Edinburgh, 1851–52) 4: 68]

> "Her cheeks are like the roses
>   That blossom fresh in June.
> O, she's like a new-strung instrument
>   That's newly put in tune."

> "The seas they shall run dry,
>   And rocks melt into sands;
> Then I'll love you still, my dear,
>   When all those things are done."
>   [J. H. Fowler, *Notes to Palgrave's Golden Treasury
>   of Songs and Lyrics* (London, 1904) 134]

様々な元歌があると推測される Burns の作品評価について，Fowler は次のように述べている。

> The superiority of Burns' poem to these rude originals is obvious. We may give to him the praise that was given to Virgil, who borrowed freely from the old Italian poets: "he has touched nothing that he has not adorned." And if any reader finds in the fame of this lyric an injustice to Burns' nameless predecessors, he should reflect that the tiny seeds of poetry that lay hidden in their work would long ago have perished from memory if the touch of Burns' genius had not quickened them into lovely flowers. (Fowler 134)

無数の伝承バラッド再生の一翼をになって，Burns はスコットランドで最も愛される詩人となった。

16　Fair Elenor

William Blake (1757–1827) 作，*Poetical Sketches* (1783) 収録。
　本作品に見られる 'abrupt opening' の手法は伝承バラッドでおなじみのものである。また亡霊や死体が死の真相を語る伝承バラッドとしては "Fair Margaret and Sweet William" (Child 74), "Sweet William's Ghost" (Child 77), "Young Benjie"

(Child 86) などが挙げられる。しかしこの作品における死者の告白は，死の真相に対する驚きよりも，むしろ，生首が語ることに対する恐怖を掻き立てる。ここには死者が生者と同様に描かれる伝承バラッドとは全く異なる世界が存在している。W. H. Stevenson はこのような "Fair Elenor" に表れるゴシック的怪奇趣味について次のように述べている。

> This poem and *Gwin* embody the full Gothic strain deriving from the ballads and Walpole's *The Castle of Otranto*, at this time fashionable and becoming more and more popular. This poem has all the classical Gothic elements (later to be used e.g. by Coleridge in *Christabel* and Keats in *Isabella*) — midnight, a fair maiden, a castle, vault, a horrific bloody head, ghostly voices, and a macabre ending. [*Blake: The Complete Poems*, ed. W. H. Stevenson (London, 1971) 6]

本作品において，Blake は伝統的手法をベースにしながら，ロマン派的な美しさ，すなわち Keats の "Isabella" (1818) にも表されるような死への憧憬に，ゴシック的な要素を加味することで，彼独自の世界を築いている。

   2 **give up:** emit.
 20 **froze:** frozen.
 38 **erst:** not long ago.

17 William and Helen

Sir Walter Scott (1771–1832) 作，1796 年。

  Scott は 'In my youth I had been an eager student of Ballad Poetry' (*Minstrelsy* 553) と書いているように，13 歳のときに Percy の *Reliques* に出会い，時間を忘れて読みふけった。1802 年に彼は *Minstrelsy of the Scottish Border* を出版するが，そのひとつの契機となったのが表題の作品の原詩である Gottfried August Bürger (1747–94) の "Lenore" (1773) である。"Lenore" は 1793 年頃イギリスに紹介された。Miss Letitia Aikin は William Taylor 訳の "Ellenore" をエディンバラの Dugald Stewart 宅で朗読したが，Scott はその席には居合わせなかった。友人からその話を聞いた彼は Bürger の原詩を手に入れて自らも英訳を試み，Bürger のほかの作品とあわせて *The Case, and William and Helen: Two Ballads from the German of Gottfried A. Bürger* として表題の訳詩を出版した。

  死んだ男が後に残した恋人のもとを訪れるという話の筋は，伝承バラッドにも多く見られ，例として "Sweet William's Ghost" (Child 77) などが挙げられる。伝

承と類似のテーマを使いながら本作品を特徴付けているのは独特の軽快さであり，この点について Henry Cockburn は次のように述べている．

> Walter Scott's vivacity and force had been felt since his boyhood by his comrades, and he had disclosed his literary inclinations by some translation of German ballads, and a few slight pieces in the Minstrelsy of the Scottish Border . . . . [Henry Cockburn, *Memorials of His Time* (Edinburgh, 1856), in *Scott*, ed. Fiona Robertson (*Lives of the Great Romantics II*, vol. 3, London, 1997) 302]

Cockburn が指摘する Scott の 'vivacity and force' は音の効果によく表れている．第 10 スタンザからの [g] [d] [b] の繰り返しはヘレンの胸の苦しみを伝え，第 24 スタンザからは 'crash'，'clatter'，'clank'，'tap' などの単語で真夜中の静けさを破る音を表し，読者を物語に惹きつけている．特に第 36 スタンザからの二人の墓場への道中の描写は，素朴な単語がリズムよく何度も繰り返され，ウィリアムの変わり果てた姿が描かれる最終場面に向けて一気に緊張感を高める働きをしている．Scott は，子から孫へと受け継がれてゆく口承文学を，文字をもたない貧しい民衆にとっての世襲財産のようなものだと考えていた．本作品に見られるこのような音の演出は，口承ゆえの音の効果を Scott が念頭に置いていたことを示すものである．

また，Scott のゴシック・ロマンス的傾向は，最終場面におけるウィリアムの死体の描写によく表れている．甲冑の下から現れる骸骨や骨に残る朽ちた肉は，M. G. Lewis を思わせる．

- 38 **lorn:** abandoned.
- 49 **pater noster:** the Lord's prayer.
- 64 **O hallow'd be thy woe!:** cf. 'hallowed be thy name' (The Lord's Prayer, *Matthew* 6. 9).
- 123 **wight:** strong.
- 125 **boune:** set out.
- 126 **barb steed:** barbary horse.
- 203 **a fetter dance:** invoking the criminal's swinging legs as he hangs on the gallows.
- 222 **The sand will soon be run:** our time will soon be up.

18 Alonzo the Brave and Fair Imogine

M. G. Lewis (1775–1818) 作．1796 年に出版されたゴシック小説 *Ambrosio, or the Monk* (のちに *The Monk* と改題)に挿入されている．

Lewisはドイツの'horror-romanticism'を英文学に本格的に持ち込み，1801年に*Tales of Wonder*を出版した。*Tales of Terror*と共に二巻組みで出版されたこの詩集には，グロテスクな色合いの濃い作品が多く集められ，Goetheの"Fisher"などの翻訳のほか，ルーン文字で書かれたバラッドの翻訳やイギリスの古いバラッドが収録された。Lewisは当時流行の'Gothic horror-ballads'を集めたが，そこには恐怖や醜悪なものに対する人間の本能的興味が表されている。'Gothic horror-ballads'は大流行となり，Samuel Taylor Coleridge, George Gordon Byron, Percy Bysshe Shelleyへと受け継がれていった。

　*Tales of Wonder*出版の数年前に書かれた本作品について，Joseph James Irwinは，この詩にはゴシック・ロマンスに必要な要素がすべて含まれていると指摘する [cf. Joseph James Irwin, *M. G. "Monk" Lewis* (Boston, 1976) 101]。また，Sukumar Duttは作品のモチーフをBürgerの"Lenore"に由来すると指摘しているが [cf. Sukumar Dutt, *The Supernatural in English Romantic Poetry* (Calcutta, 1938) 139]，裏切られた男が亡霊となって現れ，不実な恋人を罰するというモチーフは伝承の"The Daemon Lover" (Child 243) にも見られる。Lewisは古くからある話の筋を用いながら，更にゴシックという要素を組み込んでいる。Duttは'The horror is concentrated in the appearance of the ghost which is typical of Lewis's ghostly creations.' (Dutt 140) と指摘し，Lewisの作品に緊張感が生まれるのは，Clara Reeve (1729–1807) の恐怖小説に代表されるような，呪文や魔法による亡霊の呼び出しという手法をとらなかったためだとしている。確かに，ごく普通の披露宴の席に裏切られた男の亡霊が突然現れるという描写は，呪文などによって亡霊を呼び出すという設定よりも読者の意表を突き，緊張感を高めているが，呪文によらない亡霊の出現や肉体を持った亡霊 ('corporeal revenant') は，実は伝承バラッドにおなじみの手法である。しかし，Lewisの独創性が発揮されるのは亡霊となった騎士の描写にある。生前と同じ姿で現れる伝承世界の亡霊とは異なり，Lewisの亡霊の肉体は朽ち果てている。読者はその姿にぞっとしながらも，目を離せぬまま，毎晩繰り返される亡霊たちの饗宴を目撃する。この恐怖感の演出こそ，Duttの言う'the dark reverse side of mediaeval life' (Dutt 143) を映し出す鏡であり，Lewisの真髄である。

39　**His air was terrific:** his appearance was terrifying.
51　**cheer:** celebration.

19　Giles Jollup the Grave, and Brown Sally Green

M. G. Lewis 作，1801 年。

　Irwin は Lewis がゴシック的世界を描きながらも常にユーモアのセンスを兼ね備えていたことを指摘したのちに，この作品について次のような解説を加えている。

> Lewis's humor can be turned on himself. . . . Lewis provides amusing details, particularly the description of the ghost of Giles, pea-green and blue, with snuff-stained cravat and ruffles, dirty apron, wig back-side front and, when wig is removed, a bare skull, not "fit to be seen." There is also the wolfish eating of Sally at the bridal feast and the active ghosts in the brewhouse. The whole thing is Gothic in machinery but it is nevertheless an absurd bit of fun. (Irwin 108)

Lewis 自身は，以下のような頭注をつけて，この作品が前作 "Alonzo the Brave and Fair Imogine" のパロディであることを明らかにしている。

> This is a Parody upon the foregoing Ballad. I must acknowledge, however, that the lines printed in italics, and the idea of making an apothecary of the knight, and a brewer of the baron, are taken from a parody which appeared in one of the newspapers, under the title of "Pil-Garlic the Brave and Brown Celestine." [*Tales of Wonder*, ed. M. G. Lewis (London, 1801) 1: 26]

他の作品のパロディ化の例としては，伝承バラッドにも "The Three Ravens" (Child 26) とそのパロディ "The Twa Corbies" (Child 26, headnote) があるが，伝承バラッドにおけるパロディが現実の冷酷さを浮き彫りにしているのとは異なり，Lewis のパロディは滑稽さに焦点を当てている。

2　**Hob-a-nobb'd:** hobnobbed, socialized. (*OED*, citing this line.)
　　marasquin: maraschino, a liqueur distilled from the marasca cherry.
7　*physic***:** to dose or treat with physic or medicine.
8　**hop:** party.
　　Mayor's show: annual street celebration.
20　**rhubarb:** purgative rootstock used for medicinal purposes.
53　**phiz:** face.
54　**Adzooks:** cry of surprise or shock, 'God sickens you'.

20 Goody Blake, and Harry Gill

William Wordsworth (1770–1850) 作，1798 年。
　Wordsworth は，Percy の *Reliques* に大きな感銘を受け，次のように書いている。

> I have already stated how much Germany is indebted to [Percy's *Reliques*]; and for our own country, its poetry has been absolutely redeemed by it. I do not think that there is an able writer in verse of the present day who would not be proud to acknowledge his obligations to the Reliques; I know that it is so with my friends; and, for myself, I am happy in this occasion to make a public avowal of my own. ["Essay, Supplementary to the Preface" (1815), *The Prose Works of William Wordsworth*, ed. W. J. B. Owen, and Jane Worthington Smyser (Oxford, 1974) 3: 78]

　Wordsworth は伝承バラッドの持つ素朴さに魅力を感じ，*Lyrical Ballads* (1798) の序文において，'poetic diction' を排し簡素な表現で詩を書くことを宣言した。*Lyrical Ballads* を編むにあたり，タイトルに 'ballad' を付していることからも伝承バラッドが Wordsworth に与えた影響が大きかったことが窺える。
　本作品は，'abrupt opening' や淡々とした語りなどの伝承バラッドの手法を用いながらも，伝承バラッドとは別種の世界を展開している。伝承バラッドとの違いを生む理由のひとつとして，Mary Jacobus が指摘する 'moral context' が挙げられる [cf. Mary Jacobus, *Tradition and Experiment in Wordsworth's Lyrical Ballads (1798)* (Oxford, 1976) 235]。欲に目がくらんで天罰を受けるエピソードは伝承バラッドにも見られるが，この作品の，慈善の精神を欠いたために罰を受けるという設定にはキリスト教文化の色濃い影響が見られる。Wordsworth は，バラッドという形式を用いながらも，神や罰を描くことで，バラッドの世界とは全く別種の世界を生き生きと描いている。妖精や呪術の世界に突然飛び込んで来たキリスト教という異文化をも大きく包み込む，バラッド世界の奥深さを感じさせる作品である。

29　**Dorsetshire:** a county in the south-west of England.
32　**by wind and tide:** with difficulty.
39　*canty*: gay.

21 Bishop Bruno

Robert Southey (1774–1843) 作, 1798 年。

　Southey は 1808 年から 30 年間 *Quarterly Review* 誌の専属寄稿家として働き, 1813 年には桂冠詩人に就任している。Byron と折り合いが悪く, *A Vision of Judgement* (1821) で彼を激しく攻撃しているが, 一方 Byron も *Don Juan* (1819–24) の中で Southey を偽善者として諷刺している。

　代表作 *The Curse of Kehama* (1810) などの叙事詩を残しているが, 彼の才能が遺憾なく発揮されたのはむしろ短編詩やバラッド詩の中においてである。この点について, Herman Merivale は次のように述べている。

> The spirit of the poet is to be found in his minor pieces, the more vigorous and less trained offspring of his genius. First and foremost among these are his ballads. In them he is really an original and a creative writer. ["Herman Merivale on Southey's poetry", *Edinburgh Review* (January 1839, lxviii, 354–76), *Robert Southey: The Critical Heritage*, ed. Lionel Madden (London, 1972) 406]

William Taylor も Southey がバラッド作品に優れた才能を発揮していると指摘した上で, 'The cleanly simplicity of the good old time adheres to his thoughts and to his expressions.' ("William Taylor, unsigned review", *Annual Review* (1806, iv, 579–81), *Southey: Critical Heritage* 115) と述べている。

　Taylor の指摘通り, 本作品は筋, 描写ともに単純明快である。簡素な死神の言葉と司教の描写の繰り返しは, 伝承バラッドにおけるリフレインと同様に, 物語の最終場面に向けて不安と期待を高める役割を果たしている。

　作品中に現れる Bishop Bruno は 925 年ドイツ王ヘンリー一世の息子として生まれ, オットー一世の弟にあたる。聖職者として模範的な人であり, ケルン司教と神聖ローマ帝国の共同摂政を務めた。965 年 10 月 11 日, 派遣されたフランスの饗宴の席で謎に包まれた死をとげた。この死の事情は伝説化され, Southey はこの伝説を元に本作品を書いている。

22 Love

Samuel Taylor Coleridge (1772–1834) 作。この詩は 1799 年 12 月 21 日, "Introduction to the Tale of the Dark Ladie" として *Morning Post* 誌に掲載された。その後

"Love" として 1800 年の *Lyrical Ballads* に収録された。

1799 年に Coleridge は Sara Hutchinson と出会い，1810 年までの 10 年間に，彼女に対する思いを Asra という女性を創作して詩の中に書き残している。本作品はそのような 'The Asra Poems' のうちの最初期のものである。作品中の Genevieve が Sara を指すのかどうか定かではないが，Coleridge 自身の感情が織り込まれていることは間違いない。

Friedman は Coleridge のバラッド詩について 'Coleridge has entirely sacrificed ballad impersonality.' (Friedman 278) と指摘しているが，この作品でも語り手の感情が描かれ，伝承バラッドの個性と感情を排した描写とは全く異なる世界を展開している。しかし彼が描こうとしたのは単なる男女の恋の物語ではない。William Hazlitt は Coleridge における過去と現在の連続について，次のように述べている。

> Mr. Coleridge has "a mind reflecting ages past:" his voice is like the echo of the congregated roar of the "dark rearward and abyss" of thought. [William Hazlitt, *The Spirit of the Age: or Contemporary Portraits* (London, 1825), *The Selected Writings of William Hazlitt*, ed. Duncan Wu (London, 1998) 7: 98]

古く伝承バラッドの時代の人々は，心の奥底の暗闇を妖精たちが生きる異界として表現してきた。時代は変わっても，この暗闇は人間の内に存在し続けている。Coleridge はこの異界から湧き上がる感情を 'his sacred flame' (4) として捉え，作品に写し取ったと言える。

14 **The statue of the arméd knight:** 'In the church at Sockburn there is a recumbent statue of an "armed knight" (of the Conyers family) . . . . ' [*Coleridge: Poetical Works*, ed. Ernest Hartley Coleridge (Oxford, 1967) 331n] The Hutchinsons had a farm in Sockburn. [Cf. Patricia M. Adair, *The Waking Dream* (London, 1967) 184]

23 Beth Gêlert; or, The Grave of the Greyhound

William Robert Spencer (1769–1834) 作，1800 年。

Spencer はバラッドに通じ，Bürger の "Lenore" の英訳もしている。本作品は最初，北ウェールズで 1800 年に発行されたブロードサイド紙に掲載され，ウェールズ語による古いバラッドの英語訳と信じられて人気を博した。Spencer はこの詩が収められた *Poems* (1811) に次のような註を付けている。

> The story of this ballad is traditionary in a village at the foot of Snowdon, where

Llewelyn the great had a house. The Greyhound, named Gêlert, was given him by his father-in-law, King John, in the year 1205, and the place to this day, is called Beth-Gêlert, or the grave of Gêlert. [*The Oxford Book of Narrative Verse*, ed. Iona and Peter Opie (Oxford, 1983) 391–92]

Spencer は Edward Jones の *Musical Relicks of the Welsh Bards* の第2版 (1794) から物語の背景を借用しているそうであるが，ウェールズに古くから伝わる物語とケルト民族の首長 Llyewelyn ap Iorwerth，舞台としての Beth-Gêlert とは何ら関係の無い，Jones のフィクションであった。しかし，赤ん坊の惨殺を思わせる無残な光景，33行目からの血のついた犬の口や牙，空の赤ん坊のベッド，壁や床に点々とついた血を淡々と列挙する描写や，61行目からの狼の死体の出現による突然の展開は，ゴシック・バラッドの色合いを十分に備えている。

    Beth Gêlert: the anglicized spelling for the original Welsh Beddgelert, 6 km south of Snowdon.
4   **Llewelyn:** Llyewelyn ap Iorwerth (?-1240), chieftain of Gwynedd, who controlled most of Wales in the early 13th century.
23   **Snowdon:** mountain in north Wales.

24   The Elfin-King

John Leyden (1775–1811) 作。Lewis 編纂の *Tales of Wonder* (1801) に収められた。
　スコットランドの詩人，考古学者，医者，東洋学者であった Leyden は，'border ballad' にも深い興味を抱いた。彼は Scott と交友があり，*Minstrelsy* に多くの題材を提供した。Scott は Leyden の才能を高く評価し，*Lord of the Isles* (1815) では彼の奇才を称え，早すぎた死を悼んでいる。
　三つ葉のお守りを持っていなかった騎士は，妖精の騎士に出会い，魅入られてついて行ってしまう。緑の輪の中に入り，出された飲み物を飲むという禁忌を犯した騎士は自らも妖精となってしまうが，聖クレアの賢い助言によって人間に戻される。妖精にまつわる迷信は様々なものがあるが，草原や森に突然現れる緑の輪は妖精が踊った跡であり，輪の中に入ったり輪を踏んだりすると異界に入り込み，帰って来られなくなると信じられていた。
　妖精による呪詛と，そこからの解放というテーマは伝承バラッド "Tam Lin" (Child 39) にも見られる。伝承で描かれる，イモリやカエルに姿が変わっても決して恋人を離さず，ついには Tam Lin を元の騎士の姿に戻す Janet の真摯な愛は，読者に素朴な喜びを与えてくれる。一方 Leyden の場合には，与えられる試練が

伝承バラッドのものとは異なる恐怖をかきたてる。後ろから語りかける恋人のすすり泣きの声にも振り向かず，足下の生首を踏みつけ，そこから湧き上がる母の声を振り切ったうえで人間界に帰る騎士の必死の形相は，読者に複雑な感情を抱かせる。ここに人間の内面を深く掘り下げ，グロテスクなまでに心の諸相を描くようになったロマン派詩人の姿を見ることができる。Dutt は Leyden の作品について 'His vigour and originality save him from the fatuity of lifeless imitation' (Dutt 87–88) と指摘しているが，本作品におけるバラッドからのテーマの借用とロマン派的内面描写の導入が，Leyden の作品に深みを与えている。

5	**strath:**	wild valley.
14	**faulchion:**	falcon.
16	**the holy Trefoil:**	clover, a symbol of the cross. St. Patrick explained the concept of the Trinity in Christianity using a trefoil he found growing at his feet.
25	**the streamer's light:**	the Aurora Borealis. [Cf. 'the streamers red' (117) (*OED*, citing this line.)]
46	**wassel crew:**	revellers. Cf. 'wassail' means the liquor in which healths were drunk, esp. the spiced ale used in Twelfth-night and Christmas-eve celebration. Cf. 'wassel ale' (56).
48	**watchet blue:**	light blue.
49	**windlestrae:**	windlestraw.
52	**morrice:**	morris dance.
53	**feere:**	fere, friend.
74	**ezlar:**	ashlar.
82	**heath-ale:**	a traditional beverage said to have been brewed from heather. (*OED*, citing this line.)
152	**elritch:**	eldritch, weird.

25　Oscar of Alva

George Gordon Byron (1788–1824) 作，1806 年に制作され，翌年 *Hours of Idleness* に収録。

　この作品は James Macpherson の *Ossian* (1760–63) を元に作られたとされるが，弟が兄の幸福を羨むというテーマは，古くは旧約聖書の中のヤコブとエサウの物語に遡ることができ，性格描写は異なるが，二人の容姿の描写にその影響が見られる。また伝承バラッドにおいては "The Twa Sisters" (Child 10) や "The Twa Brothers" (Child 49) に類似のテーマが見られ，作者 Byron が伝統的なテーマを扱った

ことが分かる。

　文体にも伝承バラッドとの類似がある。この詩には感情を表す語句はほとんど見られない。物語にぐんぐんと引き込まれてゆくのは，伝承バラッドに特徴的な淡々とした語り口調のためであろう。栄えていたクラン一家が弟の嫉妬が元で滅びてゆく悲劇は，その地に吹く風とともに描かれる。ここで描かれる風は物語の持つ悲劇性に同調するだけでなく，登場人物の心情，語り手の息遣い，さらには読者の心理にまでも共鳴している。詩の中に吸い込まれるように感じる読者と作品との一体感は，語りの伝統と自然描写に見られる作者の計算の上に成り立つものである。

　淡々とした語りの口調は，彼の好みでもあった。Leslie A. Marchand は Byron の文体について以下のように紹介している。

> His favourite sources were Scott and Shakespeare, Sheridan and Goldsmith, and the Restoration and eighteenth-century dramatists, even obscure ones. His preference was not for high-sounding rhetoric but for a catch phrase, or the speech of some minor character which could be twisted for his use. [*Byron's Letters and Journals*, ed. Leslie A. Marchand (London, 1973) 1: 2]

ここで指摘されているように，彼はもともと典雅な文体よりも印象の強い簡素な言葉を好んだ。粗雑さはあっても明確な文体で政治，宗教，道徳上の偽善を常に攻撃したために，彼の詩は一般民衆から広く受け入れられた。

42　**its piercing note:** cf. 'Lord Byron falls into a very common error, that of mistaking *pibroch*, which means a particular sort of tune, for the instrument on which it is played, the bagpipe.' [*The Poetical Works of Lord Byron*, ed. Thomas Moore, et. al. (London, 1846) 390n]

220　**beltane:** 'Beltane Tree, a Highland festival on the first of May, held near fires lighted for the occasion. *Beal-tain* means the fire of Baal, and the name still preserves the primeval origin of this Celtic superstition. ' (*The Poetical Works of Lord Byron* 392n)

256　**terrific:** terrifying.

26　Sir David Graeme

James Hogg (1770–1835) 作，1807 年。

　Hogg はスコットランド南東部のエトリックに生まれ，幼い時から羊飼いをしていたために，のちに詩人として世に知られるようになった際に 'Ettrick Shepherd'

と呼ばれるようになった。Scott によって詩人としての才能を認められ，Scott 編纂の *Minstrelsy* に題材を提供した。初期の作品は *The Mountain Bard* (1807) にまとめられ，表題の作品も同詩集に収められている。

　死んだ騎士，忠実な猟犬，死肉を食らう鳥，死んだ恋人のもとに来る乙女など，この作品が伝承バラッドの "The Three Ravens" (Child 26) や "The Twa Corbies" (Child 26, headnote) を念頭に置いて書かれたことは明らかである。また，物語最終部で語られる娘の兄弟が恋人を殺したという設定には，"The Braes o Yarrow" (Child 214) などの影響が見られる。Hogg のバラッドに対する造詣の深さには母親からの影響が大きい。Thomas Thomson はその点について次のように指摘する。

> [T] he education of his boyhood had been chiefly oral; it was from a mother's voice rather than from books and schoolmasters, that he had derived what he knew, and laid the foundation of his subsequent progress and acquirements. She had stored his early memory with the rude, but vitally poetic and inspiring ballads of the Border, which were still fresh in his heart, and with the indelible character of those first impressions out of which the future man is moulded; so that, when his attempts in poetry commenced, they not only communicated the impulse, but served as guides and exemplars. [*The Works of Ettrick Shepherd*, with a Memoir of the Author by the Rev. Thomas Thomson (London, 1876) xiv-xv]

また Hogg 自身もこの作品の第 1 スタンザについて，'I borrowed the above line from a beautiful old rhyme which I have often heard my mother repeat' (*Works of Ettrick Shepherd* 62n) と述べている。この言葉からは，一詩人としてバラッド風の詩作を試みると同時に，母から子へ，子から孫へと脈々と語り継がれる伝承バラッドの大きな流れの一時点を文字にとどめようとする，バラッド詩人としての姿勢も窺われる。

1　**dow:** dove.
2　**ayont:** beyond.
7　**lookit:** looked.
　　war boun': was bound.
13　**starns:** stars.
19　**Dryfe:** 'the river Dryfe forms the south-east district of Annandale; on its banks the ruins of the tower of Graeme still remain in considerable uniformity.' (*Works of Ettrick Shepherd* 62n)
25　**grat:** wept.
29　**Keilder fell:** 'Keilder Fells are those hills which lie eastward of the sources of North Tyne.' (*Works of Ettrick Shepherd* 62n)
34　**laverock:** lark.

	hiche: high.
	attour: above.
44	**fause:** false.
50	**aince:** formerly.
54	**letten:** let.
61	**ahiche:** high (*adv.*).
62	**"cur-dow":** bad dove.
72	**fauldit:** folded.
78	**humpling:** humped.
83	**howe ee:** hollow eye.
87	**coured:** bent.
88	**slunkered:** walked.
95	**wilye:** decorative.
98	**dowie:** dreary.
100	**dreepit:** dripped.
102	**darena:** dares not.
105	**ae:** one.
108	**paukie:** sly.
112	**kythed:** proclaimed.
124	**sirple:** slip out.
133	**swaird:** turf.
135	**wul-weird:** bad luck.
141	**een:** eyes.
143	**glisked:** glimpsed.

27　Lord Ullin's Daughter

Thomas Campbell (1777–1844) 作，1809 年。

　ヒロインは親に結婚を反対されて家を逃げ出すが，行く手を河の急な流れに阻まれ，ついには流れに飲まれて命を落としてしまう。"The Braes o Yarrow"（Child 214）などの伝承バラッドを思い起こさせるモチーフが次々に使われ，Friedman は本作品を "The Douglas Tragedy"（Child 7）の 'a sentimentalized version'（Friedman 326）と位置付けている。

　しかしこの作品が伝承バラッドと大きく異なるのは，娘を失った父親の悲しみが最終場面でクローズアップされることであろう。激流に流されながら助けを求めて伸ばす娘の手は 'lovely hand'（47）と描かれ，'Come back! come back!'（49），'My daughter! oh my daughter!'（52）という父親の悲痛な叫びに，いっそうの哀れ

さを加えている。"The Mother's Malison"（Child 216）に描かれるような，呪いによって洪水を起こして息子と恋人をおぼれさせる伝承バラッドの無慈悲な母親の姿とは異なり，ここでの父親はあくまで自然の前に無力である。自然さえも支配する母親の呪いの強大な力や，わが子にまで向けられた憎しみは存在しない。伝承バラッドの持ち味である呪術性や淡々とした口調が失われる一方で，本作品で描かれる父親の悲しみと無力さは，伝承には無い感傷性を示している。Campbellは伝承バラッドの物語を忠実に再現しながらも，自然に対する人間の無力さや肉親に対する愛情という現実を物語に盛り込むことに成功していると言える。

7　**Ulva's isle:** an island of the Inner Hebrides, Scotland, west of Mull, about 5 miles in length.

28　Sister Rosa: a Ballad

Percy Bysshe Shelley（1792–1822）作。Shelley はイートン校在学中にロマンス *Zastrozzi: A Romance*（1810）や *St. Irvyne or the Rosicrucian*（1811）を制作したが，本作品はこの *St. Irvyne* の中でうたわれたバラッドである。

　Scott や Byron など数多くのロマン派詩人が Bürger の "Lenore" に影響を受けたが，Shelley も例外ではない。彼は自筆の写しを持ち，クリスマスには子供たちに語って聞かせたほど "Lenore" を好んだが，本作品の第 15 スタンザは Bürger からの引用である。

　'Abrupt opening' など伝承バラッドを思い起こさせる技法も使われている。特に淡々とした物語の流れは，月明かりのうすら寒い墓場という場面設定とあいまって，静かな雰囲気を物語に与えている。

　本作品に伝承バラッドとは異なる特色を与えているのは，第 7 スタンザの 'the horrors of hell / Were delights to his agonized pain' に象徴されるものである。ロマン派詩人は感情を鋭く捉え，高揚させ，混合することで，究極の恍惚へと純化させていった。Mario Praz は美や喜びにつながっていくこのような苦悩の世界を 'Romantic agony' として説明したが，本作品において Shelley も恐怖や苦痛と喜びとの混交によってロマン派詩人としての特徴を表している。

　一方で彼は，Lewis の影響を強く受けていた。修道僧，尼僧，暗くじめじめとした墓，死んだ恋人の半ば蛆虫に喰われた眼球，肉が落ちて骨となった手などの描写に，その影響が見られる。これらの描写から本作品は当時流行の 'Gothic horror-ballads' の伝統の中に位置付けられるだろう。しかし，本作品中ではゴシッ

ク的色彩は淡々とした語りによってその毒々しさを抑えられている。また 35〜36 行目などに見られるような情景描写は作品に美しさを与えており，ロマン派的美とゴシック的グロテスクが調和している。本作品において Shelley は，バラッドの感情を排した世界と，ロマン派の美の世界，ゴシックの恐怖の世界を見事に融合させたと言える。

29 La Belle Dame sans Merci

John Keats (1795–1821) 作，1819 年。

　騎士が妖精から異界に連れ去られ，再び人間界に戻るというモチーフは，伝承バラッド "Thomas Rhymer" (Child 37) などから得たものである。しかし Keats における魅惑的な妖精の娘と魅了される騎士という設定は "Thomas Rhymer" には見られず，むしろ中世のロマンス *Tomas off Ersseldoune* (?1410) の内容に近い。多読であった Keats らしく，本作品にはバラッドやロマンス以外にも様々な詩人からの影響がうかがえる。Miriam Allott は，バラッド以外に，Spenser, Dante, Milton, Allain Chartier などの影響や彼らの作品からの描写の借入を，ほぼ毎スタンザに指摘している [cf. *The Poems of John Keats*, ed. Miriam Allott (London, 1970) 500–06]。しかしこの作品が優れているのは，先人の作った物語や様々な描写を取り入れながらも，ちぐはぐになることなく一つの美しい世界を作り上げていることである。

　物語は伝承バラッドによく見られる唐突とも思える語り手の質問から始まる。しかしその後には，伝承とはまったく異なる世界が描かれている。このことについて Friedman は次のように指摘している。

> The initial query, a ballad formality — "O what can ail thee, knight-at-arms?" — is not preparatory to sanguine action in ballad fashion. It elicits instead a subjective description of an obscure, languid state of anguish. (Friedman 300)

Friedman の指摘する伝承バラッドと Keats の作品との違いは，騎士の描写に最もよく表れている。Keats の騎士は精神的には非常に苦悩しながらも，肉体的にはただささまよっているだけである。読者は活発な精神世界と不活発な肉体世界の分離を騎士の中に見いだす。このような騎士の状態を Charles I. Patterson, Jr. は 'He is pitiably suspended between two worlds.' [Charles I. Patterson, Jr., *The Daemonic in the Poetry of John Keats* (Urbana, 1970) 135–36] と指摘している。この不安定な騎士の状態は，スゲは枯れ鳥も鳴かない湖畔という情景描写とも重なって，作品全

体に物憂げな雰囲気を与えている。

22 **fragrant zone:** girdle of flowers.

30　Mary's Ghost

Thomas Hood（1799–1845）作，1827 年。

　Hood は機知を好み，漫画や雑文をよく書いた。言葉遊びやユーモアは，病弱だった彼に病の苦しみを忘れさせる手段であったかもしれない。1826 年に *Whims and Oddities* を世に出すが，批評家たちは彼の 'pun' に否定的だった。その一方で大衆からは喜んで受け入れられ，この本は再版を重ねた。

　本作品は題名が示すとおり "Sweet William's Ghost"（Child 77）のパロディと考えられる。真夜中，枕元に死んだ恋人の亡霊が現れて話しかけるというバラッドの伝統的な内容を土台としながら，ここで Hood は亡霊となったメアリーに，墓が墓泥棒に暴かれ，死体はばらばらにされて医師の手に渡ったことを語らせている。これは死体や死そのものに対する畏れを忘れつつあった当時の人々の価値観や科学に対する批判を込めたものだろう。幾人もの医者が体の部位をまるで機械の部品のように扱う様は，長い間病床に伏した自身の体験から生まれたのかもしれない。

　伝承バラッドのモチーフと様式を十分に残しながらも，その中に様々な言葉遊びや諷刺を盛り込むスタイルに Hood の機知がよく表れている。しかしその一方で，一つのストーリーに対する様々なパロディの創作は伝承バラッドの時代からよく見られたことであり，このことを考慮に入れると，Hood は伝承バラッドの形式のみならず，その精神までも受け継いだと言える。

11 **long home:** coffin.
18 **chary:** carefully.（*OED*, citing this line.）
20 **boned:** stolen.
36 **Pickford's:** the famous furniture removal company.

31　Porphyria's Lover

Robert Browning（1812–89）作。初出は 1836 年 *Monthly Repository* 誌において。

当時この作品には "Johannes Agricola in Meditation" と共に "Madhouse Cells" の名が与えられていたが，1863 年に一篇の詩として独立した。

"Porphyria's Lover" について注目すべきは，代表作 Men and Women (1855) や The Ring and the Book (1868–69) に用いられ，彼独特の手法として知られる 'dramatic monologue' が初めて試みられたとされる点であろう。主人公が恋人を殺めてゆく過程を，本人の視点に立って詳細に，そして繊細に語ってゆくという描き方は，伝承バラッドに慣れ親しんだ読者にとっては衝撃的である。ことに43～44 行の官能性は印象深い。

批評家 Ian Jack は Browning を 'the born story-teller' [Ian Jack, Browning's Major Poetry (Oxford, 1973) 93] であると評価しており，ストーリーを語るというバラッドこそ彼の真面目と言える。しかしその一方で，代表作に見られるような詩人の人間心理に対する深い洞察力が，この作品においても発揮されていることも無視できない。このことについて，Ian Jack は以下のように指摘している。

> Browning was particularly interested in insanity and every sort of mental imbalance, but when one of his dramatis personae is lying the poet usually or always makes it quite clear. Sometimes he explicitly draws our attention to the unbalanced condition of his speaker: if 'Porphyria's Lover' had not at one point been labelled as one of two 'Madhouse Cells' critics might claim greater liberty of interpretation than is now reasonable. More often, however, Browning tells us what we need to know about the psychological condition of his speaker by subtler means, and in particular by the movement of the verse which he makes him speak. The speaker in 'Porphyria's Lover' is obviously (to put it mildly) over-excited. (Jack 94)

ストーリーを語ることに留まらず，人間の内面に関心を持ち，分析を試み，これを主題に置いたことこそ，近代人たる Browning の特質であり，そこに伝承バラッドと詩人の手によるバラッド詩との大いなる相違点が窺われよう。

ちなみに Porphyria の名の由来について批評家 Daniel Karlin は，詩人がそう認識していたかどうかは定かでないと断りながらも，古のある種の蛇の名であると指摘して彼女の魔性をほのめかし，興味深い作品解釈を提案している [cf. Daniel Karlin, Browning's Hatreds (Oxford, 1993) 210]。

32　The Lord of Burleigh

Alfred Tennyson (1809–92) 作，1833–34 年。

幼い頃から Scott の Minstrelsy を諳んじていたと言われる Tennyson は伝承バ

ラッドに精通しており，バラッドの技法を巧みに用いた作品を数多く書き残している。ここに取り上げた詩は1791年に貴族John Jonesと結婚した農夫の娘Sarah Hogginsの実話を元にして書かれたものである。24年というあまりにも短い生涯をとじた彼女であるが，生前は貴族夫人として多くの人々に愛され，複数の文人の筆により後世にその姿を残された。1822年にHazlittが *New Monthly Magazine* 誌において彼女の話を伝えており，それが再録された *The Picture Galleries in England* (1824) をTennysonは読んでいた。またThomas Mooreは "You Remember Ellen" (1820) という題の詩に彼女の生涯をうたっているが，アレンジを施して結末を幸せなものにしている。Tennysonの "The Lord of Burleigh" は前半63行目までが現在形，64行目以降が過去形で書かれており，この異なる時制は彼女の幸福な恋愛時代と不幸な結婚生活とにそれぞれ対応している。詩人がこうした構造をとったことには，不幸を過去のものとし，ヒロインに永遠の幸福の日々を与えようという思惑が感じられる。

この詩についてEdward FitzGeraldは，'When this poem was read from MS in 1835 I remember the Author doubting if it were not too familiar with its "Let us see the handsome houses, etc.," for public Taste.' [Christopher Ricks, ed., *The Poems of Tennyson* (London, 1969) 603] と記録しているが，自身の作品が「あまりに陳腐」なのではないかとの言葉には，常に時勢を考慮し，その時々の大衆の趣味を敏感に感じ取り詩作に反映させようとする詩人の職業意識と試行錯誤とが窺える。

伝承バラッドにおいても，物乞いに変装した貴族の男が娘に求婚し，結婚後初めて自分の正体を明かすという物語は "Lizie Lindsay" (Child 226) や "The Beggar-Laddie" (Child 280) の他，多くうたわれているが，身分違いの結婚をしたために心身ともにやつれ衰える女の苦労をうたうTennysonの筆致は，伝承の範疇を越えている。

92 **Burleigh-house:** Burleigh House dates back to 1587 and is situated in Northamptonshire.
Stamford-town: south Kestevan district, county of Lincolnshire.

33 The Execution of Montrose

William Edmondstoune Aytoun (1813–65) 作，1844年。

Aytounは1858年に編集・出版した *The Ballads of Scotland* の中で，様々な時代の変化を乗り越えてスコットランドの歴史を語り継ぐバラッドの役割について，

次のように述べている。

> It should always be remembered that these ballads were essentially the property of the people, and were not composed to be read, but to be recited or sung. Hence, perhaps, their popularity, which is sufficiently vouched for by the fact that they have been so wonderfully preserved. . . . For such changes, though tending essentially towards the production of the ballad, especially in the historical department, cannot possibly be favourable to its preservation; and no stronger proof of the intense nationality of the people of Scotland can be found than this — that the songs commemorative of our earlier heroes have outlived the Reformation, the union of the two Crowns, the civil and religious wars of the Revolution, and the subsequent union of the kingdoms, and, at a comparatively late period, were collected from the oral traditions of the peasantry. [William Edmondstoune Aytoun, ed., *The Ballads of Scotland* (Edinburgh, 1858) 1: liii-liv]

ここに取りあげる "The Execution of Montrose" は、そうした伝承バラッドの存在意義を自らのバラッド詩にも担わせようという壮大な試みであったと言える。

James Graham, 5th Earl and 1st Marquis of Montrose (1612-50) は、チャールズ一世に忠誠を誓い戦ったスコットランドの英雄である。王の処刑後、救いを求めた Neil Macleod of Assynt の裏切りに遭い、捕らえられ、エディンバラにおいて処刑される。モントローズの武勇は数篇の伝承バラッドの中に華々しくうたわれている。しかしその最期については、"The Gallant Grahams" の第21スタンザに次のようにうたわれるのみである。

> And the laird of Assint has seized Montrose,
>   And had him into Edinburgh town;
> And frae his body taken the head,
>   And quartered him upon a trone. (81-84)

"The Execution of Montrose" の第2スタンザで老人が語る 'But never have I told thee yet / How the Great Marquis died' という言葉の中に、伝承バラッドでは触れられることのなかった英雄の死に様をうたう意義が示唆されている。

1 **Evan Cameron:** the historical Cameron was a Scottish Highland chieftain, a strong supporter of the Stuart monarchs.
14 **Lochaber:** district at the 'mouth of the lochs' of southern Inverness-shire.
19 **the Campbell clan:** Archibald Campbell, 1st Marquis and 8th Earl of Argyle (1598-1661) was the leader of Scotland's anti-Royalist party and was the principal enemy of Montrose.
20 **Inverlochy:** south-west of Inverness.

21　**Dundee:** the city and seaport of Tayside, eastern Scotland.
22　**the Lindsays:** the Lindsay clan.
37　**Watergate:** the old entrance to Canongate, Edinburgh.
53　**the Whig:** after the execution of Charles I the Whig party split into two factions; one supported Charles II and the other was anti-Royalist, or 'Whig'.
59　**Covenanting carles:** the signers of the National Covenant (1638) to defend Presbyterianism in the face of Charles I's attempts to institute an alternative liturgy in Scottish churches.
77　**a woman's voice:** 'Lady Jean Gordon, Lord Haddington's widow, Argyle's niece and Hurtley's daughter, is said to have laughed shrilly and shouted a word of insult from the balcony where she sat.' [John Buchan, *Montrose* (1928; London, 1931) 369]
81　**the Græme:** James Graham, Marquis of Montrose, the condemned protagonist.
99　**Dunedin:** Edinburgh.
110　**the solemn hall:** Parliament House.
117　**Warristoun:** Archibald Johnston, Lord Warristoun (1611–63), a supporter of Argyle.
147　**levin-bolt:** lightning bolt.
193　**Geneva ministers:** of the Presbyterian faith.

34　The Knight and the Lady

William Makepeace Thackeray (1811–63) 作, 1848 年。

　Thackeray と言えば *The Book of Snobs* (1847) や *Vanity Fair* (1848) といった諷刺精神溢れる散文作品がよく知られているが, 彼がケンブリッジ大学トリニティ・カレッジをたった一年で退学した理由は, 散文ではなく詩の制作に耽り勉学を怠ったためである。彼はヴィクトリア朝時代に最も多くのバラッド詩を書いた詩人の一人でもあった。批評家 Leslie Stephen が 'His poetry was evidently regarded by himself as an amusement, and he did not value the results sufficiently to labour after any high polish or to attempt any exalted task.' [Leslie Stephen, "Thackeray's Writings: An Historical and Critical Essay", *Thackeray: The Critical Heritage*, ed. Geoffrey Tillotson and Donald Hawes (London, 1968) 381] と指摘するように, 彼の詩作品が「娯しみ」をその旨としていることは, ここに挙げたバラッド詩においても証明される。彼は 'Charity and Humour' と題された講演の中で次のように述べている。

　　Humour! humour is the mistress of tears; she knows the way to the *fons lachrymarum*, strikes in dry and rugged places with her enchanting wand, and bids the fountain gush and sparkle. She has refreshed myriads more from her natural springs than ever tragedy has watered from her pompous old urn. [W. M. Thackeray, *The English Humourists and The Four Georges, Essays and Belles Lettres*, ed. Ernest Rhys (London, 1912) 280]

幼くして父を亡くしたことに起因する母親への過剰な愛情と発狂した妻との別居のために，生涯女性に対する正常な情動を育み得なかったと言われる Thackeray であるが，ユーモアをもって人生を受け入れる人生観を詩作に生かすことには十分成功しているようだ。年老いてもなお好色衰えぬ Sir John の甲斐甲斐しさは，'knight' にはおよそ似つかわしくないほど滑稽であるが，それに続く結末はこれによってますます惨めさを増す。ユーモラスであるからこそ哀しくもあり，あまりに哀れだからこそ笑いを誘う。そんな人生悲喜劇をうたうには，ノン・スタンダードな英語とバラッドという形式がいかにも相応しい。

    2 **King Bladud:** the legendary founder of Bath.
  15 **the Shons-Eleesy:** Champs Élysées.
  16 **the Roo de Rivolee:** rue de Rivoli.

35 The Two Brothers

Lewis Carroll (1832–98) 作，1853 年。

　代表作 *Alice's Adventures in Wonderland* (1865) や続編 *Through the Looking-Glass and What Alice Found There* (1871) の中で Carroll は，パロディや言葉遊びに関する卓越したセンスを広く世に知らしめたが，その才能はまた彼の詩作においても大いに発揮されている。Carroll はヴィクトリア朝時代に流行した子供の躾を目的とする詩篇を数多くパロディ化しているが，中でも，ここに取りあげた "The Two Brothers" は伝承バラッドのパロディとしての側面の強いものである。複数の伝承バラッドが断片的にモチーフとして利用され，それらがまるでパズルのように組み合わされている。

　"The Two Brothers" は，脈絡のない物語の展開，言葉遊びによってすれ違う兄弟の会話，姉の登場による突然の終結，どれをとってもナンセンス文学の大家 Carroll の面目躍如たる作品と言える。彼の 'serious poetry' と 'comic poetry'，つまり 'nonsense verse' を比較して，批評家 Richard Kelly は次のように指摘する。

> These poems are rebellious in the way that children are. They are visceral, instinctive, and free, in their confrontation of authority and convention. While they assume

the poetic forms and meters of traditional English poetry, they undermine that tradition by their comic tone, bizarre logic, and unsettling assumptions. Carroll's nonsense verse embodies his primal feelings about the possible meaninglessness of life, his repressed violence and sexuality, and his growing awareness that order and meaning within the context of a poem do not necessarily reflect a corresponding order in the terrifying void of cosmic reality. [Richard Kelly, *Lewis Carroll*, rev. ed. (Boston, 1990) 31–32]

既成の価値観が崩壊し，人々を取り巻くものごとが意味を失ったヴィクトリア朝時代。そんな時代が必要とした新しい価値観の構築への希求と，どもり癖や特殊な性嗜好のために社会に馴染むことのできなかったと伝えられる Carroll の個人的事情とが，「ナンセンス」であることにより真実を描き出すという Carroll 作品を生み出したのである。

1–6 cf. "The Twa Brothers" (Child 49A)

> There were twa brethren in the north,
>   They went to the school thegither;
> The one unto the other said,
>   Will you try a warsle afore? (1–4)

15–18 cf. "The Twa Sisters" (Child 10C)

> The youngest stude upon a stane,
>   *Binnorie, O Binnorie*
> The eldest came and pushed her in.
>   *by the bonny mill-dams of Binnorie* (25–28)

26 **Tees:** a river of north-east of England, rising on the east side of Cross Fell and flowing to the North Sea.
28 **you didn't had ought ter:** you shouldn't do that.
117–20 cf. "Lord Randal" (Child 12A)

> 'What d'ye leave to your mother, Lord Randal, my son?
> What d'ye leave to your mother, my handsome young man?'
> 'Four and twenty milk kye; mother, mak my bed soon,
> For I'm sick at the heart, and I fain wad lie down.' (25–28)

125–40 cf. "Edward" (Child 13B)

> 'Why dois your brand sae drap wi bluid,
>   Edward, Edward,
>   ....
> 'O I hae killed my hauke sae guid,

解説と語註   245

> Mither, mither,
>
> ....
>
> 'Your haukis bluid was nevir sae reid,
> 　　　　　　　Edward, Edward,
>
> ....
>
> 'O I hae killed my reid-roan steid,
> 　　　　　　　Mither, mither,
>
> ....
>
> 'Your steid was auld, and ye hae gat mair,
> 　　　　　　　Edward, Edward,
>
> ....
>
> 'O I hae killed my fadir deir,
> 　　　　　　　Mither, mither,
> O I hae killed my fadir deir,
> 　　　　　　　Alas, and wae is mee O!'
>
> ....
>
> 'Ile set my feit in yonder boat,
> 　　　　　　　Mither, mither,
> Ile set my feit in yonder boat,
> 　　　　　　　And Ile fare ovir the sea O.' (1–32)

141–44　cf. "Lizie Wan" (Child 15A)

> 'And when will thou come hame again,
> 　O my son Geordy Wan?'
> 'The sun and the moon shall dance on the green
> 　That night when I come hame.' (45–48)

145–48　cf. "Prince Robert" (Child 87A)

> She's turn'd her back unto the wa,
> 　And her face unto a rock,
> And there, before the mother's face,
> 　Her very heart it broke. (69–72)

36　Ballad of Earl Haldan's Daughter

Charles Kingsley (1819–75) 作，1854 年。
　Larry K. Uffelman は Kingsley のバラッドへの関心の強さについて，次のように指摘している。

As is evident, Kingsley valued poems characterized by simplicity, "clearness," "finished melody," and established form. Ballads and brief lyrics were therefore suited both to his taste and to his talent. The ballad, unmarked by arresting figures of speech or novel turns of phrase, simple in setting and characterization, and focused on a single dramatic incident, appealed to him. [Larry K. Uffelman, *Charles Kingsley* (Boston, 1979) 126]

ここに取り上げた作品にも，彼のバラッドに対する造詣の深さが認められる。この作品のように女性の高慢さを主題とする伝承バラッドとしては "Proud Lady Margaret" (Child 47) が例に挙げられる。マーガレットは，自分に求愛を断られて自ら命を絶つ男たちが後を絶たないにも拘らず，新たな求愛者が名乗りをあげれば自分に相応しいかどうか試練を与え続ける。しかし，ある日兄の亡霊によって戒められるという話である。

このバラッド詩は，Kingsley の代表作の一つである海洋冒険小説 *Westward Ho!* (1855) の中で，美女 Rose Salterne によってうたわれたものである。随所に伝承バラッドやバラッド詩が散りばめられたこの作品は，英国とスペインが戦いを繰り広げていたエリザベス朝時代が舞台となっている。前半は主人公の青年，デボンシャーの Amyas Leigh が Francis Drake 提督に従って世界中を旅する様が描かれる。後半はスペイン人捕虜 Don Guzman に連れ去られたローズの奪還とその失敗，ガズマンへの復讐と決着とに，主人公や彼の兄 Frank，その他多くの男たちのローズへの恋心を絡ませ，この愛国的な物語を華麗にドラマタイズしている。

ガズマンの激しい愛情に心を乱されたローズが，晩餐の席でこの歌をうたうことを求められた時の様子を以下に引用してみよう。

It was a loud and dashing ballad, which chimed in but little with her thoughts; and Frank had praised it too, in happier days long since gone by. She thought of him, and of others, and of her pride and carelessness; and the song seemed ominous to her: and yet for that very reason she dared not refuse to sing it, for fear of suspicion where no one suspected; and so she began per force[.] [Charles Kingsley, *Westward Ho!* (New York, 1855) 279]

ローズはこの歌に我が身を照らし合わせる。ここで読者は，このバラッド詩を単独で読んだ時とは全く違う印象を，小説の中におかれたこの詩に対して持つことであろう。彼女が託した感情を通してこの詩を読むことは，バラッドのヒロインにも同情の余地を生み，作品鑑賞に臨み複数の視点を提示してくれる。

6 **marriage fee:** a gift from a man to his love.

37　The Ballad of Keith of Ravelston

Sydney Thompson Dobell（1824–74）作，1856 年。

　Dobell は，感情を仰々しく表現することを特徴とする「痙攣派」（'Spasmodic School'）の代表的詩人である。この一派の評判は，彼らを「痙攣派」と名付けた Aytoun の批判，および痙攣派を痛烈に諷刺した彼の詩劇 *Firmilian*（1854）の出現によって地に落ちたと言われており，詩人 Dobell に対する評価も関心も極めて低いまま今日に至っている。当時 Dobell を最も高く評価していたのは Dante Gabriel Rossetti であった。James Smetham は 1868 年 10 月号の *London Quarterly Review* 誌に寄稿した書評の中でこの詩を取り上げ，'We remember a picture by Dante Rossetti called *How They Met Themselves*, which breathes the same mysterious import....' [qtd. *Letters of Dante Gabriel Rossetti*, ed. Oswald Doughty and John Robert Wahl（Oxford, 1965）2: 670n] と指摘した。これに応えて Rossetti は 10 月 27 日，Smetham に宛てて次のように記している。

> I was specially delighted with what you say about Dobell's *Keith of Ravelston*, not only because you have so flatteringly lugged in my name in connection with it, but because I have always regarded that poem as being one of the finest of its length by any modern poet — ranking with Keats's *La Belle Dame sans Merci*, and the other masterpieces of the condensed and hinted order so dear to imaginative minds. What a pity it is that Dobell generally insists on being so long winded when he can write like that! (*Letters of Rossetti* 2: 670–71)

最高の詩人と敬愛する Keats に比肩すると述べた Rossetti の，この詩に対する熱狂ぶりが窺われる。

　"The Ballad of Keith of Ravelston" は "A Nuptial Eve" という長編詩の一場面に，うら若い乙女がリュートに合わせて歌う 'a dim sad legend old' として登場するものである。Keith of Ravelston と出会ってしまったため，亡霊として永久にこの世に留まることを強いられた乙女の物語が，抑制された叙情性をもってうたわれている。作品の後に残る余韻は，'O, Keith of Ravelston, / The sorrow of thy line!' というリフレインによってもたらされるところが大きい。Rossetti が特に好んだのはこのリフレインであったが，これについては Ehrenpreis もまた，'Dobell prefers to limit his refrain — which is largely responsible for creating the never-disclosed mystery of his tale — to five of his eleven stanzas....' (Ehrenpreis 17) と述べており，ここでも抑制された表現方法が評価されている。

31 **burnie:** brooklet. Cf. 'burn' (40).

38 Love from the North

Christina Georgina Rossetti (1830–94) 作，1856 年。

　敬虔なクリスチャンであり多くの信仰詩を書き残した Christina について，伝記作家たちは，奔放な兄 Dante Gabriel Rossetti とは対照的な，表に出ることをあまり好まぬ物静かで清らかな人物像を伝えている。中でも Fredegond Shove が批評書の序文に置いた "Christina Rossetti — the name is like a song itself." [Fredegond Shove, *Christina Rossetti: A Study* (Cambridge, 1931) ix] という言葉は，そんな彼女のイメージを端的に言い表している。しかし実際の彼女は，物静かな態度の中に新しい女性の性質を秘めており，それは兄 Gabriel 率いるラファエル前派の作風に影響を受けたことの他に，彼女生来の性質の激しさに起因していたようにも見受けられる。

　ここに取り上げた作品と同じく花嫁略奪をうたったバラッド詩には，Scott の "Young Lochinvar" (1808) がある。伝承バラッド "Katherine Janfarie" (Child 226) を元歌とするこのバラッド詩は，伊達男ロッキンバーがダンスをしながら花嫁を婚礼の場から巧みに略奪する様を軽快にうたう。これに対して "Love from the North" のヒロインが一人称で語る心情は深刻なものであり，そこに軽快さはない。

　時代の風潮に敏感に反応する，しっかりと外を向いた Christina の詩人像について，Isobel Armstrong は次のように指摘する。

> She claimed, not only the freedom of the unmarried woman to express her sexuality, but also the freedom to be absurd, undignified, if feminine sexuality necessitated this. [Isobel Armstrong, *Victorian Poetry: Poetry, poetics and politics* (London, 1993) 344]

彼女は同時代の女性たちが感じていたジレンマを直接的に表現するという強さを持ち合わせていたのである。Armstrong は更に，'ballads about prohibition, possession, rivalry, the rigour of the law, bonds and legal forms . . . testify to her awareness of the social and economic circumstances of women.' (Armstrong 346) と述べている。

　しかし，「結婚」が女性の求めるべき目的である現状を諷刺しつつも，このヒロインはあくまでも状況の変化を「待つ」ばかりである。「待つ」ことしか許されなかったヴィクトリア朝時代の女性としては，これが最大限の反逆であったのだろうか。いずれにしても，バラッドはこのような個人的な思惑をヴェールの向こうに隠すのに最適な詩型であり，それを選ぶことによって Christina は表面的

には慎みと謙譲の美徳を保ち続けることができたのである。

39　The Sailing of the Sword

William Morris（1834–96）作，1858年。

　Morris は伝承バラッドを最良の詩型であると讃え，自らも多くのバラッド詩を書き残している。代表作には "Shameful Death"（1858）や "Two Red Roses across the Moon"（1858）などが挙げられる。彼のバラッド詩は全編に溢れる中世趣味が最大の特徴であり，それは文筆家，装飾家，工芸家等々として彼の手がけた多くの作品にも共通するものであった。

　ここに挙げた "The Sailing of the Sword" は，Ehrenpreis が 'The comparison that is sometimes made between Morris's poetry and the tapestries he designed is appropriate to this strongly pictorial poem.'（Ehrenpreis 161）と指摘するように，絵画を思わせる豊かな色に彩られた作品であり，また，あたかもタペストリーの紋様のごとく織り込まれた規則的なリフレインは，娘の哀れな運命を淡々と綴る。

　詩集 The Defence of Guenevere and Other Poems に収められている作品はみな中世趣味に溢れているが，その中にあるヴィクトリア朝的なるものについて Armstrong は次のように指摘している。

> The position of women in these poems is contradictory and paradoxical. They are disempowered and passive, waiting, longing and dependent on vicarious male action for representation or nullified by male rejection . . . . On the other hand, they exert a curiously coercive power, motivating violence even when they are seen as objects of possession . . . . (Armstrong 242)

非常に抑制された作風のため見逃されがちな点であるが，前出の Christina Rossetti と同様，Morris もまた，間違いなくヴィクトリア朝時代の新しい女性像を描くという潮流の中にあったのである。

　　5　**leads:** lead roofs.

40　Margaret's Bridal Eve

George Meredith（1828–1909）作。Modern Love, and Poems of the English Roadside（1862）に収録された。

1849年，Meredithは小説家Thomas Love Peacockの娘Mary Ellen Nichollsと最初の結婚をしたが，妻の駆け落ちにより間もなく破綻。この経験を元に代表作"Modern Love"が書かれた。詩集 *Modern Love* にはMeredithの忍耐強さから生まれる楽観主義（'hardy optimism'）が表れていると指摘するRenate Muendelは，その一方で彼のバラッド詩について次のように述べている。

> Meredith's ballads ... show the poet from a different side, which has elicited recent critical interest: preoccupied with the tragic results of unrestrained human passion, particularly sexual passion. The ballads, small in number and seldom conforming to strict balladic form, deal with the forces of jealousy, pride, suspicion, revenge, and the conflict between uxoriousness and loyalty to one's followers. Dramatizing brief, suggestive incidents, they capture the tragic essence of a human relationship gone awry and, sometimes, the rottenness of an entire culture. In addition, they point to the precariousness of human communication and to the unreliability of appearances — topics Meredith explores at greater length and with more complexity in "Modern Love" and in his novels. [Renate Muendel, *George Meredith* (Boston, 1986) 23]

叙情詩では情動を十分に抑制しえない。赤裸々で醜悪な人間悲喜劇をうたい得るのは，憎しみや悲しみ，痛みや喜びを三人称で物語り，長い人間の歴史を昇華してきたバラッドであったのだろう。

Meredithのバラッド詩は，彼が親交を持ったラファエル前派のバラッド詩の設定やリフレインと多くの類似点を持っている。また，Meredithが新婚旅行で風邪をひいた友人夫妻をMorrisのバラッド詩"Two Red Roses across the Moon"（1858）に準えて，'two red noses across a honeymoon' [*George Meredith: Letters*, vol. 1 (1844–81), ed. his son (1909–12; New York, 1968) 60] と表したのは，彼のユーモア・センスばかりでなく，互いのバラッド詩への親しみも伝える微笑ましいエピソードである。

41　The King's Daughter

A. C. Swinburne（1837–1909）作，1866年。

William A. MacInnesはSwinburneのバラッド観について次のように述べている。

> From 1858 onwards, Swinburne had the definite aim in view of re-writing certain ballads and here he utilised every available version and shred of a theme. By skilful interpolation of stanzas from various renderings and by adding or substituting his

own interpretation when necessary, he succeeded in reconstructing a number of ballads which could easily deceive the most sceptical critic of their authenticity. [A. C. Swinburne, *Ballads of the English Border*, ed. William A. MacInnes (London, 1925) viii]

彼のバラッド詩が伝承バラッドの特徴を残しつつ，独自のものとして確立されるまでの経緯を端的に示した叙述である。一方 William Michael Rossetti はこの作品の特徴を 'the abruptness and suppression of facts so characteristic of the old ballad-poetry' [William Michael Rossetti, *Swinburne's Poems and Ballads: A Criticism* (London, 1866) 61] であると述べているが，このために読者は作品鑑賞に際し臨機応変な想像力を求められるのである。

本作品の解釈については Swinburne の好んで取りあげたモチーフである「近親相姦」がキーワードとなる。第8スタンザ以降のリフレインにおける，風，雨，あられ，雪，嵐と漸次暗転する悲劇のイメージの高まりによって，近親相姦が引き起こす悲劇的結末の伏線が張られている。

本作品はその鮮やかな色彩により，読者をラファエル前派独特の絵画の世界へと導き入れる。

11　**may:** maiden.

42　Stratton Water

Dante Gabriel Rossetti (1828–82) 作，1869 年。

多くのバラッド詩を書き残した Rossetti について Lionel Stevenson は次のように指摘している。

> Folk ballads and romances of chivalry had been loved by Rossetti since his boyhood, as they were by the Romantic generation that influenced him most. Three of the poets that he admired highly, Chatterton, Coleridge, and Keats, had sought to reproduce the aloof impersonality and deceptive simplicity of medieval narrative, and Rossetti successfully followed suit.
>
> His ability to create a replica of the diction and devices of folk ballad is demonstrated in "Stratton Water;" but the happy ending is out of key both with the archetypes on which it is modeled and with the suspense so well established by the ominous approach of the flood. . . . Rossetti's ever-present sense of risibility seems to break through the remarkably successful assumption of a ballad-singer's grimness.

This was the only poem in which he confined himself strictly to the simple ballad quatrain and ballad diction. [Lionel Stevenson, *The Pre-Raphaelite Poets* (Chapel Hill, 1972) 59–60]

家族の呪いによって仲を裂かれる不幸な恋人たちをうたった伝承バラッドは，"Prince Robert" (Child 87) や "The Mother's Malison" (Child 216) など数多くあるが，これら伝承バラッドのほとんどが恋人たちの死という悲劇で終わっている。

対話形式といった伝承バラッドに特徴的な技法や「肉体を持った亡霊」('corporeal revenant') の概念，恋人たちの仲を裂こうとする家族の妨害や，また異界を暗示する緑色という色彩の使用などが，伝承バラッド独特の雰囲気を作品中に醸し出している。一方，上に引用した批評にも指摘されているように，作品には伝承バラッド的でない要素も含まれている。特に「肉体を持った亡霊」という概念については，Rossetti の生きたヴィクトリア朝時代にはそぐわないものであったのか，Janet の生死を決定する表現は曖昧であり，作品は伝承バラッド特有の明解さを欠いている。それでも Rossetti がバラッドという形式にこだわったのは，死後の恋人たちの再会が可能となる領域が，生と死の境を曖昧なままに捉える中世や伝承バラッドといったプリミティブな世界のみにあったからではなかろうか。

132 **Jonah's fish:** the great fish appointed by God to swallow up Jonah who disobeyed His will. (*Jonah* 1.17)
149 **thrawed:** swayed. (*OED*, citing this line.)
155 **Christopher:** the patron saint of travellers, generally represented as carrying the Christ Child on his back.

43 King Henry's Hunt

William Allingham (1824–89) 作，1877 年。

アイルランドに生まれ 1863 年ロンドンに移った Allingham について，Arthur Hughes は次のように語ったという。

> D. G. [Rossetti], and I think [William Allingham] himself, told me, in the early days of our acquaintance, how, in remote Ballyshannon, where he was a clerk in the customs, in evening walks he would hear the Irish girls at their cottage doors singing old ballads, which he would pick up. If they were broken or incomplete, he would add to them or finish them; if they were improper, he would refine them. He could not get them sung till he got the Dublin 'Catnach' of that day to print them, on long strips of blue paper, like old songs; and if about the sea, with the old rough woodcut of a

ship on the top. He either gave them away or they were sold in the neighbourhood. Then, in his evening walks, he had at last the pleasure of hearing some of his own ballads sung at the cottage doors by the crooning lasses, who were quite unaware that it was the author who was passing by. [George Birkbeck Hill, Introduction to *Letters of Dante Gabriel Rossetti to William Allingham 1854–1870* (London, 1897) xxiii-xxiv]

このように彼のバラッド詩人としての素地はアイルランド風土に負うところが大である。またHughesの伝えるこのエピソードは，バラッド詩人冥利につきるところであろう。しかしここに取りあげた作品は，Friedmanが 'William Allingham ... was prone to English elegance and preferred English imagery and mythology to the Irish.' (Friedman 317–18) と指摘するほど英国情緒に魅了されていた詩人らしく，題材はアイルランドから全く離れ，古い英国王室の歴史の一幕の高貴と冷酷とを一切の情緒を退けて描いている。

ヘンリー八世のキャサリン王妃との離婚とアン・ブリンとの再婚については，Shakespeareの史劇 *Henry VIII* によく知られるが，"King Henry's Hunt"はその後日譚にあたる物語である。ヘンリーとキャサリンの離婚の原因は後継者たる男児に恵まれなかったことであると言われている。しかしアンもまた男児に恵まれることなく，1536年不義の廉で処刑される。ちなみに処刑執行の11日後ヘンリーの三番目の妻となるジェーン・シーモアは，この時既に後のエドワード六世となる男児を宿していたという。賢女キャサリンの気高さを対照させることによってシニカルな態度でヘンリー王の偽善を批判するShakespeare作品に対して，Allingham作品は伝承バラッドの定石どおり感傷性を排した筆致であり，特定の登場人物にあからさまな肩入れをすることもない。

1 **Waltham Wood:** Waltham Forest in the boroughs of Chingford, Walthamstow, and Leyton.
61 **Lord Norfolk:** Thomas Howard, 3rd Duke of Norfolk (1473–1554), uncle of Anne Boleyn. Norfolk presided as lord high steward at his niece's trial and execution.
68 **Anne Bullen:** Anne Boleyn, second queen consort of Henry VIII. After the final separation from Catherine, Henry secretly married Anne who had already become pregnant. In September 1533 she gave birth to a daughter, the future Elizabeth I.
71 **Elizabeth:** queen of England from 1558 to 1603.
76 **Jane Seymour:** third queen of Henry VIII.
78 **Epping:** Epping Forest, a royal hunting ground in Essex.

44　After Dilettante Concetti

Henry Duff Traill（1842–1900）作，1882年。

　ジャーナリストであったTraillは，一方で *Recaptured Rhymes*（1882）や *Saturday Songs*（1890）といった諷刺詩集を著した文人としても知られている。

　'After' は「〜流の」，'Dilettante' は「芸術愛好家」，'Concetti' は「コンシート」を意味する。伝承バラッドのリフレインの意義は様々あり，聴衆との一体感を生み出す効果もその一つに数えられるが，文字文学が発達した近代以降，リフレインは詩人が紙上で凝らす一技巧となった。特にTraillにやや先立つ時代，Tennysonやラファエル前派の詩人たちはリフレインに並々ならぬ興味を持ち，独自の展開を試み，文壇に一種の「リフレイン・ブーム」をもたらした。そのブームが去った時，格好の標的となったのはその代表格とも言えるDante Gabriel Rossettiであり，この 'After Dilettante Concetti' は題の示すごとく，正に彼に対する痛烈な諷刺作品であった。

　しかしその遊び心の豊かさはどうだろう。この作品は，49行目までがRossettiの "Sister Helen"（?1851）を，50行目以降が同じく彼のソネット "A Superscription"（1869）を土台にしたパロディ詩である。そこにはヴィクトリア朝人の本質とも言うべきユーモア精神が満ち満ちている。その明るさ，軽妙さのため，我々はTraillのうちに，彼自身が批判しているものに対する愛情，執着といった感情を見いだすのである。この作者はバラッドにたいへん精通しており，"Sister Helen" や "A Superscription" 以外のRossettiのバラッド詩やソネットをよく読み込んでいるという印象を受けるのである。

　また，11行目の 'Children should never be heard, if seen' は15世紀からある言葉ではあったが，「お行儀良さ」が異常なまでに求められたヴィクトリア朝時代の子供たちにはうんざりするほど耳に馴染んだフレーズであった。このような躾の言葉は，Carrollも "Punctuality"（1845）や "My Fairy"（1845）といった詩作品の中で度々パロディ化している。

　　1–49　cf. "Sister Helen"

> 'Why did you melt your waxen man,
> 　　　　Sister Helen?
> To-day is the third since you began.'
> 'The time was long, yet the time ran,

Little brother.'
(*O Mother, Mary Mother,*
Three days to-day, between Hell and Heaven!) (st.1)

50–63 cf. "A Superscription"

   Look in my face; my name is Might-have-been;
    I am also called No-more, Too-late, Farewell
    Unto thine ear I hold the dead-sea shell
   Cast up thy Life's foam-fretted feet between;
   Unto thine eyes the glass where that is seen
    Which had Life's form and Love's, but by my spell
    Is now a shaken shadow intolerable,
   Of ultimate things unuttered the frail screen.

   Mark me, how still I am! But should there dart
    One moment through thy soul the soft surprise
    Of that winged Peace which lulls the breath of sighs, —
   Then shalt thou see me smile, and turn apart
   Thy visage to mine ambush at thy heart
    Sleepless with cold commemorative eyes.

58 **dodge:** one who eludes or cheats.

45 The Ballad of the Wayfarer

Robert W. Buchanan (1841–1901) 作，1882 年。

 Buchanan の名を今日にまで知らしめている一番の要因は，彼がラファエル前派に対して行った攻撃であろう。彼は，1866 年 8 月に *Spectator* 誌に寄せた 'The Session of the Poets' において Swinburne を，71 年 10 月に *Contemporary Review* 誌に寄せた 'The Fleshly School of Poetry' においてラファエル前派，特に Dante Gabriel Rossetti を，野卑であるとして激しく非難した。自分の詩作を「あまりに個人的でありすぎる」と責められた Rossetti は，Buchanan の 'Thomas Maitland' という偽名を用いるという姑息さにも大いに憤慨し，2 カ月後の 12 月に *Athenaeum* 誌に発表した 'The Stealthy School of Criticism' で反論を展開した。反撃は一応の成功をおさめたが，しかし 72 年 6 月の彼の自殺未遂は Buchanan の悪意に満ちた攻撃が原因であったとも言われている。

 こうした次第で 'The Fleshly School of Poetry' は攻撃文として甚だ悪名高い批

評ではあるが，そこには Buchanan の詩に対する基本的姿勢をよく伝える箇所がある。

> Poetry is perfect human speech, and there archaisms are the mere fiddlededeeing of empty heads and hollow heart [sic]. . . . The soul's speech and the heart's speech are clear, simple, natural, and beautiful, and reject the meretricious tricks to which we have drawn attention. [Robert Buchanan, "The Fleshly School of Poetry: Mr. D. G. Rossetti", *An Anthology of Pre-Raphaelite Writings*, ed. Carolyn Hares-Stryker (Sheffield, 1997) 245]

Buchanan の考える詩が，正にバラッドのあり方に一致することを示す言葉である。「個人的でない」詩を実現していたという理由から Shakespeare を高く評価する Buchanan にとって，同じ理由からバラッドという形式は非常に具合がよかったのであろう。

　本作品の形式は，伝承バラッド "Edward" (Child 13) に見られるような母と息子との対話形式を模倣したものである。しかし貧しさ故の母子の悲劇というストーリーには，同時代の Charles Dickens などの小説にも通じる，ヴィクトリア朝社会に対する問題意識が多分に織り込まれていると考えられる。この作品にうたわれた母子の声は，当時貧困に喘いでいた人々の声ではなかったろうか。

　　4　**Waysore:** exhausted by travel.

46　The Bridge of Death

Andrew Lang (1844–1912) 作，1872 年。

　Lang はスコットランドのセルカークに生まれ，1875 年からはロンドンで詩人，評論家，伝記作家として活躍した。本作品を収めた翻訳詩集 *Ballads and Lyrics of Old France* (1872)，*Ballads in Blue China* (1880)，*Grass of Parnassus* (1888) などの詩作の他にも，共同散文訳 *Odyssey* (1879) や *Iliad* (1883) を出版したり，*The Gold of Fairnilee* (1888) や *The Blue Fairy Book* (1889) を著して，当時廃れていた 'fairy tales' への関心を復活させたりするなど，多才な文人として知られた。

　詩人としての Lang は，バラッド詩の創作に加えて，19 世紀後半から 20 世紀初頭にかけて起こったいくつかの重要なバラッド論争に参加して健筆をふるった。例えば，バラッドの起源について，吟遊詩人説をとる William Motherwell らに対抗して，F. J. Child と F. B. Gummere に賛同して共同体起源説をイギリスで最初に支持したのが Lang であった。また，Swinburne が Rossetti の "Stratton Water"

(1869) をバラッド的な言葉の簡潔さの点から賞賛したのに対し，Lang は 'nothing can be less like an old ballad than the ballads of Mr. D. G. Rossetti.' と酷評した [cf. Introduction, J. A. Farrer, *Literary Forgeries* (London, 1907) xxv]。バラッドが口承性という本来の生命を終え，蒐集記録された書物の中に新たな生命を獲得し，その担い手が民衆から研究者へと決定的に変貌した時代に，Lang はバラッド研究家として大いに貢献したのである。

　本作品では，死者となった兄と妹が中世の「死の舞踏」さながらにダンスをする。死の橋とはどこなのか，なぜ二人が死んだのかなど，状況説明が全くなされないバラッド的な唐突さが，この詩のゴシシズムを盛り上げている。「死の舞踏」は無常を説き，見るものの官能を刺激すると言われるが，この詩には，それらに加えて伝承バラッドの主要なモチーフの一つである近親相姦のトーンが重ねられている。Lang の他のバラッド詩では，"The Milk-White Doe" という，同じくフランスのフォークソングを翻訳したものがよく知られているが，そこでも近親相姦がうたわれている。

6　**ashes:** token of grief or repentance.
7　**sackcloth:** rough garment worn as a sign of penitence.

47　The Ballad of Moll Magee

William Butler Yeats（1865–1939）作。初出は *The Wanderings of Oisin and Other Poems* (1889) において。
　バラッドは詩人 Yeats の誕生とその後のアイルランド文芸復興運動に重要な役割を果たした。というのは，John O'Leary その他の編集による *Poems and Ballads of Young Ireland* (1888) の寄稿者として Yeats の文学活動は始まり，アイルランド文芸復興の推進においても，アイルランドのフォークロアおよび民族の精神こそが復興の重要な要素であると，彼は信じたからである。

> It is centuries since England has written ballads. Many beautiful poems in ballad verse have been written; but the true ballad — the poem of the populace — she has let die; commercialism and other matters have driven it away: she has no longer the conditions.
> 　For a popular ballad literature to arise, firstly are needful national traditions not hidden in libraries, but living in the minds of the populace. . . .
> 　Secondly, it is needful that the populace and the poets shall have one heart — that there shall be no literary class with its own way of seeing things and its own conven-

tions. ["Popular Ballad Poetry of Ireland" (1889), J. P. Frayne, ed., *Uncollected Prose by W. B. Yeats* (London, 1970) 1:147]

　本作品のストーリーは，Yeats 一家が 1881 年から 83 年まで住んでいたダブリン湾に面した小さな漁村ホースの教会での説教に基づいている。作品の舞台はアイルランド南部の漁村。激しい労働のために赤ん坊の上で眠り込んで殺してしまい，家を追われた Moll Magee は物乞いとなって放浪し，殺したわが子を想って嘆き続ける。このバラッド詩は Wordsworth の "The Thorn" (1798) や Thomas Hardy の "A Sunday Morning Tragedy" (1904) に共通した母親の嘆き，すなわち典型的な民衆の悲劇を描いている。

　　1　**childer:** children.
　　6　**say:** sea.
　 24　**Kinsale:** a fishing port in southern Ireland.
　 49　**she:** meaning Moll Magee's dead child.

48　The Last Rhyme of True Thomas

Rudyard Kipling (1865–1936) 作，1893 年。

　民族学者を父に，Burne-Jones の義姉を母に，ボンベイで生まれ，1882 年から 89 年までインドでジャーナリストとして活躍，その頃から作品をインドの新聞に掲載し始めた。日常語で書かれた，賛美歌と伝承バラッドの影響の色濃い作品は一般民衆に絶大な人気があり，「非公式の桂冠詩人」と言われ，1907 年にはノーベル賞を受けた。代表的な詩集は *Barrack-Room Ballads and Other Verses* (1892) であり，Shakespeare の *Henry V* 以後イギリス兵士の心情を最も的確に表現した作品として讃えられている。

　本作品は伝承バラッド "Thomas Rhymer" (Child 37) からモチーフと人物を借りている。Thomas of Erceldoune は，13 世紀に実在した予言者・詩人であり，その名声は後世まで根強く，中世から現代に至るまで詩人たちは様々なトマス譚を残しており，それらトマスを巡る一連の詩は「うた人トマスの系譜」を形成している。*Tomas off Ersseldoune* という中世ロマンスは，トマスが肉感的な妖精の女王の恋の虜となる場面が白眉である。Scott は "Thomas the Rhymer" 第 3 部 (1802–03) において，圧倒的な威力を持つトマスの予言と彼がこの世を去るストーリーを描いている。Keats は "La Belle Dame sans Merci" (1819) において，妖精の女王の虜となった騎士に永遠の懊悩を語らせている。John Davidson の "Thomas the

解説と語註　　　　　　　　　259

Rhymer" (1891) は，トマスがスコットランド王アレグザンダー三世の死を天変地異で予言するゴシック・バラッド詩である。そして Kipling は，トマスに爵位を与えようとやって来た王が，逆にトマスから真の人間性を諭される皮肉なストーリーを本作品で描いている。トマスは王の与えようとする馬や帯や刀や土地に価値を見いださない。逆に，トマスの奏でるハープと不思議な歌は，長く忘れていた恋人のことや若い頃の希望を王に思い出させ，王は呆然自失となって帰ってゆく。Kipling のトマスは，もはや妖精の女王に出会ってどぎまぎしながら異界を旅したトマスではなく，人間の奢りを諫め，世俗の権威を否定する堂々たる予言者である。

　T. S. Eliot は，一読で読者にストーリーを理解させる Kipling のバラッド的な簡潔さの追求を，次のように讃えている。

> Kipling does write poetry, but that is not what he is setting out to do. It is this peculiarity of intention that I have in mind in calling Kipling a 'ballad-writer' . . . . What is unusual about Kipling's ballads is his singleness of intention in attempting to convey no more to the simple minded than can be taken in on one reading or hearing. They are best when read aloud, and the ear requires no training to follow them easily. With this simplicity of purpose goes a consummate gift of word, phrase, and rhythm. . . .
>
> 　For Kipling the poem is something which is intended to act — and for the most part his poems are intended to elicit the same response from all readers, and only the response which they can make in common. [*A Choice of Kipling's Verse*, ed. T. S. Eliot (London, 1943) 9–11, 18]

伝承時代から広く親しまれたうた人トマスは，読者から共通の反応を得る題材としてはまことに適切である。

- 19 **keep:** daily provisions.
  tail: an area of land.
- 23 **wastrel wind:** free wind.
- 27 **lee-long:** livelong.
- 31 **Middle World:** Middle Earth, the mythical realm between heaven and hell, supposed to occupy the centre of the universe.
- 36 **flyte:** dispute.
- 57 **row-foot:** rough-foot.
- 67 **a clout o' meal:** a piece of cloth containing wheat grain.
- 88 **rax:** tear.
- 90 **lee:** lie.
- 110 **birled and brattled:** the harp's vibration as it makes music.

124 ***eyass*:** a young hawk.
***pye*:** magpie.
147 **hauden:** held.

49　A Ballad of a Nun

John Davidson (1857–1909) 作。初出は 1894 年 10 月 *The Yellow Book* 誌において。
　スコットランドのレンフルーシャーに生まれ，学校教師の仕事の傍ら 10 代から詩作を始め，後にロンドンに移って *The Yellow Book* などの雑誌に寄稿した。Davidson は Burns 色を脱して Hugh MacDiarmid に近づく現代的要素をスコットランド詩に色濃く打ち出した最初の詩人である。T. S. Eliot は Davidson のバラッド詩 "Thirty Bob a Week" (1894) における都会の描写を，次のように賞賛する。

> But I am sure that I found inspiration in the content of the poem, and in the complete fitness of content and idiom: for I also had a good many dingy urban images to reveal. Davidson had a great theme, and also found an idiom which elicited the greatness of the theme, which endowed this thirty-bob-a week clerk with a dignity that would not have appeared if a more conventional poetic diction had been employed. The personage that Davidson created in this poem has haunted me all my life, and the poem is to me a great poem for ever. [Preface by T. S. Eliot, *John Davidson: A Selection of His Poems*, ed. Maurice Lindsay, with an essay by Hugh MacDiarmid (London, 1961) xi-xii]

また，MacDiarmid は "Of John Davidson" (1932) の中で，「すばらしい光景にあいた一つの弾痕」という表現で Davidson の死を惜しんでいる。
　表題の作品は Davidson の最も有名なバラッド詩の一つであり，直接のソースは，Adelaide Anne Proctor が *Legends and Lyrics* に 1881 年に発表した "A Legend of Provence" である [cf. *The Poems of John Davidson*, ed. Andrew Turnbull (Edinburgh, 1973) 2: 485]。この作品で注目すべきは，Davidson の他の作品にも一貫したテーマであるオーソドックスなキリスト教の否定，既成の宗教へのアイロニー，ナチュラリストとしての信念が，ヒロインの尼僧の赤裸々な行動と描写の中に読みとれることである。このような現代的要素がバラッドの形式に乗せてうたわれるところに Davidson のバラッド詩の独自性がある。

93　**Belmarie:** this appears in Chaucer's *Canterbury Tales* where it is an imaginary Moorish state in Africa.

50　The Carpenter's Son

A. E. Housman（1859-1936）作。Housman が詩を書き溜めたノートに記された制作年は 1895 年 8 月，*A Shropshire Lad* の XLVII 番として 1896 年に出版された。

　A Shropshire Lad は，ラテン文学の教授であった Housman が初めて出版した詩集である。実在の地名でありながら，詩の中では架空の町とされているシュロプシャーを舞台にして，美の享受，死後の静けさへの願望，軍人的な決死の態度への憧れと蔑みなどの心情を農民の少年や兵士に語りかけるという内容で，63 篇の連作の形でうたわれている。Oscar Wilde らの世紀末芸術が流行していた時代にあって，バラッド形式を用いて簡潔な言葉で書かれたこの詩集は年ごとに人気を増し，第一次世界大戦頃には大変よく知られていた。

　Housman と 'folk poetry' あるいはバラッドとの関連を Friedman は次のように指摘する。

> Of modern poets Housman is decidedly the most thoroughly steeped in folk poetry. Those who have detected and tabulated his sources agree that "the influence of the Scottish border ballad is stronger and more pervasive than any other." The debt to folksong in all its varieties is even greater than this statement suggests, for what Housman most admired in Shakespeare's songs, Scott's lyrics, and the shorter poems of Heine, his other principal tributaries, was their folksong qualities. And if a knowledge of street ballads were more general among Housman's source-mongers, much more would be made of the resemblances between many numbers of *A Shropshire Lad* and late Victorian recruiting ballads and soldier songs. (Friedman 335-36)

　本作品の語り手である大工の息子とはキリストを暗示しており，十字架にかかって犠牲となることの空しさ，キリストへの共感，彼を見捨てる世間への蔑みをアイロニカルな筆致で描いている。

51　Screaming Tarn

Robert Bridges（1844-1930）作，初出は *New Poems*（1899）において。

　Bridges はイートン校およびオックスフォード大学コーパスクリスティ・カレッジで学んでいた頃から詩作を志していたが，市井に交わることで詩のインスピレーションは得られると考え，卒業後に新たに医学を修めて 1881 年までは医者

として働いた。Bridges の作品の人気は "On a Dead Child" (1880) に見られる日常生活の感情の的確な描写や，"London Snow" (1880) に見られる細やかな自然観察，また，作品に共通する素朴な言語の使用や理性を崇拝する人柄などによって確立された。1913 年，桂冠詩人となる。

しかし Bridges が成した最大の貢献は，伝統的な詩形と韻律の徹底した改革である。大学時代に Gerard Manley Hopkins に出会って 'sprung rhythm' の影響を受けたが，彼自身は伝統的な韻律音量分析へと向かい，'neo-Miltonics' や 'loose Alexandrines' といった韻律法を用いた。Bridges のバラッド詩はこの一連の実験の中での一つの過程と理解される。「音量」('quantity') を詩の中で重要視する立場に立った Bridges は，一行の中の長音節がストレスを置かれなくても中心的な音節となるような詩を試みたが，それは強いストレスによってごつごつとした素朴な感触を持つバラッドの韻律とは異なる。彼の音量を重視した詩の改革は，次のように評価されている。

> He preferred the more difficult path of endeavouring to restore our sense of the quantity of syllables, longs and shorts. The emancipation of English metre from the monotonous eighteenth-century pattern, effected largely by the influence of the restored interest in the ballad, had emphasized stress as the essential element, giving the utmost freedom of substitution in the foot: ... it is to [slurring or passing over the intervening syllables] that the verse of Swinburne (himself a balladist) owes its peculiar and intoxicating rhythm: ... Bridges could secure subtle effects in a stressed line .... [Herbert Grierson and J. C. Smith, *A Critical History of English Poetry* (1944; Harmondsworth, 1962) 446]

本作品は弱強四歩格で *a b c b* の韻を踏むバラッド・スタンザで作られている。清教徒革命の頃，宿の主は逗留した騎士の持っていた鞄欲しさに彼を殺害したが，殺してよく顔を見ると，騎士は女であった。しかも，財宝が入っているとばかり思っていた鞄には殺した女と瓜二つの男の生首が入っていた。このストーリーが読者のゴシック的な恐怖を喚起するよりは，むしろ悲哀を感じさせるのは，Bridges の音量の技によるのだろうか。

25 **Charles:** Charles I (r. 1625–49).
52 **Cromwell:** Oliver Cromwell (1599–1658).

52　The Yarn of the Loch Achray

John Masefield（1878–1967）作。初出は *Salt-Water Ballads*（1902）において。
　Masefield には他にも *Ballads and Poems*（1910）というバラッド詩集があるが，*Salt-Water Ballads* に含まれる作品はほとんどが海洋譚である。この種のバラッド詩は，Masefield が文筆家になる以前の，商船乗組員としての冒険に満ちた実際の経験から生まれている。イギリス南西部ヘリファドシャーに生まれた Masefield は 6 歳で母親を亡くし，親戚に預けられて成長，早くも 13 歳で見習水夫として商船に乗る。16 歳の時のチリへの航海でひどい船酔いに苦しみ，次の航海ではアメリカで下船して，職を転々としながら放浪の旅をする。その後イギリスに戻って詩を書き始めた。ブルームズベリーでの当時の仲間には Yeats や John Synge らがいた。
　世紀末の唯美主義の中にあって，Masefield は民衆の生活を題材とした物語詩を得意とした民衆詩人である。浮浪者には浮浪者の言葉を，水夫には水夫の言葉を使って描かれる庶民の生活は，物語形式の相乗効果によって一層の新鮮さとリアリティを保っている。Harry Blamires は Masefield のバラッド詩の生き生きとした特色について次のように指摘している。

> His *Salt Water Ballads* (1902) and *Ballads and Poems* (1910) contain a cluster of much-anthologised poems, rhythmically and rhetorically alive, some of them of the fresh-air-and-open-road variety, like 'The West Wind' and 'Tewkesbury Road', and some of them hailing the virtues of salt sea and saltier seamen in heart-felt acclaim or nautical bluster, like 'Sea-Fever' and 'A Ballad of John Silver'. [Harry Blamires, *Twentieth Century English Literature*, 2nd ed. (London, 1982) 13–14]

Masefield 自身，詩人としての出発点であった *Salt-Water Ballads* の巻頭を飾る "Consecration" で民衆詩人としての立場を表明し，偉人ではなく蔑まれ拒否された人々，浮浪者，出稼ぎ人，水夫たちをうたうことがこの詩集の目的である，と述べた。通常 Masefield は典型的ジョージ王朝詩人と見なされるが，民衆の生活を物語詩の形でうたう姿勢は，社会派バラッド詩人 Kingsley に近い。1930 年，桂冠詩人となる。
　本作品は船の遭難をうたっているが，華やかな船出の場面と，遭難を知らない女たちがご馳走を用意して男たちの帰りを待つ物悲しい場面が作る悲劇的コントラストは，海洋譚バラッド "Sir Patrick Spens"（Child 58）に遡る。また，変化しないリフレインを各スタンザに配置する手法は，"Sir Patrick Spens" を模倣した

Kingsley のバラッド詩 "The Three Fishers"（1851）のリフレイン 'For men must work, and women must weep' と同じく，悲劇を包み込む無常観を演出する。

- 5 **Tally:** catch hold or clap on to a rope.
- 10 **Tottie:** term of affection.
  gell: girl.
- 28 **the Tuskar Light:** the lighthouse on the Tuskar Rock located off the shore of Wexford, Ireland, in St. George's Channel.
- 39 **the River Plate:** the Río de la Plata, often called the River Plate in English, estuary in South America, flowing for 170 miles into the Atlantic Ocean between Uruguay and Argentina.
- 43 **lee-scuppers:** an opening cut in a ship's bulwarks for draining water from the deck.
- 58 **lay-to:** check the motion of a ship.
  pay-off: fall off to leeward.
- 72 **fixins:** trimmings.

53　A Sunday Morning Tragedy

Thomas Hardy（1840–1928）作，1904 年。

　人間の意志を越えてこの世を支配する無慈悲な力とそれに翻弄される人間の苦境，および生と愛が織りなす人生のアイロニーという Hardy の作品に一貫するテーマが，この詩の母と娘の悲劇にも描かれている。世間体を重んじたばかりに娘を殺してしまう母の愚かさは，代表作 Tess of the D'Urbervilles（1891）の Tess の母の愚かさと重なり合う。

　しかし，この作品のドラマティックな迫力と哀感は，このようなテーマに加えて，バラッド風のスタイルに負うところが大きい。弱強四歩格の安定したリズムに乗せて，名もない貧しい母親が事件の顛末を物語る形でストーリーは展開する。多くのスタンザで 2 行目は 'alas for me' という彼女の嘆きが繰り返され，4 行目では死ぬほどの苦しみが様々に変奏して語られており，出来事は主として 1 行目と 3 行目で展開している。また，話の流れは所々でバラッド風に飛躍し省略される。娘が身ごもるに至った事情は 6 行目の 'she was won' に集約され，詳細は語られない。母親のヒステリックな世間体への執着は 36 行目の 'That is so scorned in Christendie' と 61 行目の 'This scandal shall be slain' に表れるのみ。堕胎の煎じ薬を飲んだ娘の苦しみは 75〜76 行目で 'I feel as I were like to die, / And underground soon, soon should be' と語られるのみ。諸々の感情とストーリーの詳細は

読者の想像に委ねられる一方で、段階を追うかのごとく深められる母親の悲しみ、嘆き、後悔がドラマティックな迫力を生み出しているのである。実際、Hardy は、この作品の舞台上演を考えたこともあったと言う。

　伝承バラッドは、アイロニーと悲しみに満ちた現実を生きる平凡な庶民の世界である。悲劇の根本的な原因が母娘の貧しさにあるこの作品からは、Hardy の基本的人生観が伝承バラッドの世界のそれに近いことが窺われる。バラッドのスタイルは彼のテーマを最もよく伝えうる器であった。

- 2　**Pydel Vale:** the valley of the River Piddle near Piddlehinton, northeast of Dorchester.
- 27　**Wessex:** originally a kingdom of Anglo-Saxon England. Wessex, the celebrated fictional setting of Hardy's novels, is in the southwestern area of England.
- 36　**Christendie:** Christendom.

54　The Ghost

Walter de la Mare（1873–1956）作、1918 年。

　De la Mare は 16 歳から 20 年間石油会社で働き、年金を得るようになった 30 代中頃から執筆活動に専念する。20 代から大人と子供それぞれに向けた作品を雑誌に投稿し始める。詩の他にも、大人向け子供向けの小説、アンソロジーの編纂、Lewis Carroll や Christina Rossetti についての文芸批評など、文筆活動は多岐に渡った。

　De la Mare の作品世界は、子供時代の回想、ファンタジー、神霊現象を背景にして、日常的な事物や出来事が神秘性を帯びて描かれる非日常性が最大の特色である。モダニズムの洗礼を受けた 20 世紀初頭において、神話や幻想を扱う de la Mare の世界はいささか流行遅れに感じられたかも知れないが、彼が後世に記憶されるのは、流行に左右されない独自のテーマを支えた鮮烈なイメージと確かな技量によってである。De la Mare のイマジスト詩人に匹敵する独自のイメージと叙情的瞬間をキャッチする卓越した技量は、次のように賞賛される。

> A poetry in, but not of, the period of the reign of modernism, de la Mare's work has been admired chiefly by poets themselves. They have always prized his unfailing skill, his pointed ability to intensify a lyrical moment, and his access to the mythologies which the modern movement would either ignore, or enlist in its program of rhetorical debunking of the late nineteenth century.... His mastery of the detail of image forever fixing a moment of transformation — or, more usually, transformation just missed — is as keen as that of the Imagist poets who would have scorned the

narratives and dramatic lyrics in which he framed those images, and the lyrical forms in whose chambers they resounded. [*The Oxford Anthology of English Literature*, ed. Frank Kermode and John Hollander (1973) 2: 2036]

　本作品においても，バラッド調の対話形式による展開が生と死の境界に阻まれた恋人たちの悲しみを巧みに伝え，砕ける星明かり，闇の中で鍵をまさぐる手，灰色の夜にちらりと出現した顔といったイメージ群が残された乙女の更なる悲しみを象徴しつつ，悲しみの中に恋人の亡霊を垣間見る一瞬の至福が鮮やかに切り取られている。このような技巧とイメージによって存在を許された de la Mare の亡霊は，「肉体を持った亡霊」（'corporeal revenant'）たちが跋扈する伝承バラッドの世界から，M. G. Lewis の "Alonzo the Brave and Fair Imogine" (1796) を経て花開いたゴシック・バラッドの系譜が，20世紀にまで続いていることを証明するものでもある。

20　**The sweet cheat gone:** 'This phrase may resonate for the reader because of its use, by C. K. Scott-Moncrieff, to translate the title (*Albertine Disparue*) of one of the volumes of Proust's *Remembrance of Things Past*.' (*The Oxford Anthology of English Literature* 2: 2038n)

55　The Murder on the Downs

William Plomer (1903–73) 作，初出は *Visiting the Caves* (1936) において。

　Plomer は南アフリカでイギリス人を両親に生まれ，イギリスとアフリカを往復しながら成人した。南アで農業に従事したり，インテリ仲間と雑誌を発行したり，日本で教師をしたり，ギリシャへ放浪したりと，Plomer の前半の人生は放浪者としてのそれであった。このような，いわばバックボーンの不確かな永遠のアウトサイダーとしての生き方が，世の中の冷静な観察者としての詩人 Plomer を生み出した。

　本作品は，バラッド形式による現代社会の描写という Plomer のスタイルの確立の契機となったものである。自伝の中で Plomer は本作品の完成時に体験した非個性化について，次のように述べている。

When confronted with this, as soon as it had been completed, I felt a mingled surprise and uneasiness, as if I were being impersonated. Somebody else seemed to have written it, not the self with which I thought myself acquainted. [William Plomer, *The Autobiography* (London, 1975) 381]

Plomer の観察者的体質は，徹底した客観的描写と非個性化の醍醐味をもたらした。その後 1940 年代から 50 年代にかけて，共同体感覚を喪失した社会で物質的な利害でのみ繋がっているストレンジャーとして現代人を捉え，諧謔味と恐怖感が入り交じった，都会的で諷刺的なバラッド詩を Plomer は多く書き残しており，それらは 'the treasure of Plomer's' と呼ばれている。彼はまた，詩は「私自身と詩を聴く人，あるいは印刷された作品を読む人との間の共同作業である」と述べて，詩人と読者との共同作業としての詩作にこだわっていた [cf. *The Poet Speaks*, ed. Peter Orr (London, 1966) 176]。これは，詩の本来のあり方としての読者との共同体意識であり，彼の場合は現実の諸相，恐怖と不条理，異常と平凡が共存する現代を同時代の読者と共有するという姿勢から出て来たものである。

　本作品では殺人とも心中未遂とも言い切れない，納得ずくの恋人殺しが語られる。サセックスの夏の夜明け頃，親密そのものの様子で村から丘へ歩いている恋人たち。柔らかい羊歯の上，男はコートのポケットからレーヨンの靴下を取り出し，「わかっていたの」と呟く女の首を絞める。孕んだ女を始末するためなのか，遠からず男の命も無いことをはかなんでか，二人の置かれた状況も殺人の理由も語られないまま，不条理な殺人は完了する。豚小屋，牛小屋といった長閑な光景と注射針のように屹立する教会の尖塔のコントラスト，アスピリンと形容される女の願い，病んだ患者の肝臓のような茸，これらの医学用語を使った比喩は，この不条理な殺人に現代性とそれ故の一層の不安を与えている。

　状況の客観的観察のために物語技法を採り，時代を共有するために読者を求める Plomer のバラッド詩は，20 世紀におけるバラッド詩の展開の方向を示唆している。

56 The Enchanted Knight

Edwin Muir (1887–1959) 作，1937 年。

　20 世紀スコットランドの代表詩人 Muir の作品と文学批評の原点は，14 歳まで住んだ故郷にある。詩人自ら回想するオークニーの貧しい村は，中世以来変化が無く，人々が競い合うことも無く，伝説と民衆のうたと聖書が文化であり，そこは Muir にとってのエデンの園であった。しかし，借地農民であった一家が生活の糧を求めてイギリス一の繁栄とスラムの町グラスゴーに移り住んでからわずか 2 年の間に，両親と二人の兄が疲労と脳腫瘍で死んでしまい，Muir の楽園は完全に失われた。Muir は同時代の文学の流行を追わず，その影響も受けずに，表現という行為の確固とした基盤を追求した。また，イメージの大部分を子供時代に

見た風景や夢や神話から借用し，時と場所を超越した夢の旅を繰り返しテーマとした。このような特色を持つMuirの詩は，彼にとっての失われてしまった楽園の回復なのである。

　また，Muirの忘れてはならない功績として，バラッドを通しての現代詩批評も，故郷オークニーの賜物と言えるだろう。伝承バラッドの世界の聴き手が作品創造の重要な担い手であったという主張を通して，現代詩が無くした読者の意義をMuirは次のように訴える。

> So far as we know, these anonymous songs and ballads rose among the peasantry and were made by them. The authors, if that is what they should be called, knew nothing of poetry except by inheritance. I have heard it suggested that these songs and ballads were created communally, a theory which may have arisen from the fact that they were not only a means of communication, but also a means of participation in something belonging to and shared by everyone. The idea that they were made up by a sort of committee is absurd; one has only to turn to the great ballads to realize how absurd it is. On the other hand, if we can think of their creation in time rather than in space, we realize that there was after all a cooperation in their making, for it is clear from the many versions of them that exist that they were not merely transmitted in a passive way, but modified in their transmission, often to their advantage. It may take hundreds of years to bring a ballad to its perfection, and many generations may participate in its making, and the critical faculty cannot help coming into play.
> ［Edwin Muir, *The Estate of Poetry* (London, 1962) 11］

　本作品は，Keatsの"La Belle Dame sans Merci"（1819）で妖精の女王の虜となって懊悩する騎士の約百年後を描いたものである。鎧が錆びて身体は動かず，眠りと途切れとぎれの追憶だけに生きる騎士の傍らで，農民たちは働き，兵隊が通過する。百年の錆にまみれ忘却という恥と格闘する鎧の騎士の末路は，時と場所を超越し，黙示録的に描かれた現代人の呪縛でもある。

57　Miss Gee

W. H. Auden（1907–73）作。初出は文芸誌 *New Writing*, No. 4（1937）において。
　Audenは1930年代の混沌とした社会に対して左翼的マルクス主義的な反応を示した「30年代詩人」の一人として知られている。しかし，政治へのコミットと社会諷刺のみではなく，現実を冷静に見据える目と，政治的単純化を拒否し，人間の基本的な孤独を受け入れ，混乱した人間にとっての避難場所を求め祈る姿勢こそがAudenの詩の本質であろう。Edward Mendelsonはこのような Auden の本

解説と語註 269

質を次のように解説する。

> Auden was the first poet writing in English who felt at home in the twentieth century. He welcomed into his poetry all the disordered conditions of his time, all its variety of language and event. In this, as in almost everything else, he differed from his modernist predecessors such as Yeats, Lawrence, Eliot or Pound, who had turned nostalgically away from a flawed present to some lost illusory Eden where life was unified, hierarchy secure, and the grand style a natural extension of the vernacular. All of this Auden rejected. His continuing subject was the task of the present moment: erotic and political tasks in his early poems, ethical and religious ones later.
> [*W. H. Auden: Selected Poems*, ed. Edward Mendelson (London, 1979) ix]

本作品には Auden のこのような本領が発揮されている。'Story-telling' に徹するバラッドの様式と，時事的諷刺を込めたブロードサイド・バラッドの形式にのっとって，感傷を寄せつけないドライな視点から，都会の片隅につつましく生きる独身女性の日常の物悲しさ，屈折した性的欲求不満，人間の尊厳を剥ぎ取る現代医療，宗教運動の偽善が淡々と描かれている。苦いユーモアと現代人の悲しみが溢れた，現代版ブロードサイド・バラッドである。

13 **mac'**: mackintosh.
95 **Oxford Groupers**: members of Oxford Group, the philosophical and religious movement founded by Frank Buchman in 1921 and stressing the reform of personal and social morality.

58 A Subaltern's Love-song

John Betjeman (1906–84) 作。初出は *New Bats in Old Belfries: Poems* (1945) において。

　Betjeman はロンドン郊外ハイゲイトの実業家の家庭に生まれる。詩作の他に，イングランド各地の案内書の執筆，古い教会建築の維持保存，テレビのパーソナリティーなど，生涯にわたって多彩な活躍をした。高校時代には当時教師をしていた T. S. Eliot と，オックスフォード大学マグダレン・カレッジでは Auden や Louis MacNeice らと知り合った。1931 年，*Architectural Review* 誌に寄稿したころから文筆活動を始め，同年に最初の詩集 *Mount Zion* を出した。

　生い立ちが示しているように，中産階級の生活の諸相は Betjeman の好む詩の題材だった。その作風はウィットに富み，都会的，諷刺的であり，軽いタッチの因習喜劇的な面を持ち，地名や現代風俗がふんだんにちりばめられている。その

ような 'light verse' 的な詩風のため，19 世紀における Tennyson と同じくらいの人気があったとも言われている。しかし，そのような軽さの底に，メランコリー，恐怖，希望としての宗教の存在を読者は探り当てる。Philip Larkin は，Betjeman が注ぐ人間の営みの諸相へのこのような率直な眼差しを大いに賞讃している。

> The best criticism that has been published on Betjeman's poetry occurs in a review of *Collected Poems* by Philip Larkin (*Listen*, Spring 1959). 'The strongest and most enduring thread that runs through the contradictions of impulse in this puzzling dazzling body of work is a quite unfeigned and uninflated fascination by human beings,' [Larkin] writes and adds that 'neither the screens that he throws up of absurdity and satire, nor the amount of exploring that he does down alleys of minor interests, should prevent the recognition of his poetry's lasting quality as well as its novelty'. [*The Penguin Book of Contemporary Verse*, ed. Kenneth Allott (1950; 2nd ed. 1962) 176]

また，Betjeman の人気のもう一つの秘密は，現代詩人には珍しい，単純すぎる程明らかな韻律とリズミカルな構文にある。

本作品は，ありきたりな恋愛を描いた現代風俗のブロードサイド・バラッドである。語り手はテニスの試合に負けて相手を喜ばせることに喜びを見いだす軟弱な男性であり，ゴルフクラブのパーティに盛装して出かけ，車の中で恋人を誘惑して婚約にこぎつけるという物語が，感情を交えない淡々とした描写によって描かれる。特別な出来事は何も無い。しかし，負けてもらったことに気付かない恋人，慣れないネクタイとの格闘，もの問いたげな夕日，流行の車ヒルマンが好みという現代的嗜好，エジプトの絵画といった物語の小道具たちは，調子良い韻律に乗せられて，悲しいまでに二人の生きる「今」という時代そのものの滑稽さを暗示する。

Friedman は Betjeman を 'ironical ballad' の巨匠と呼び，ストリート・ソングのリズムを伴奏に現代風俗についてのシニカルなウィットが生み出すおかしみは，Thomas Hood の手法と同じだと指摘している (cf. Friedman 342)。1950〜60 年代にはこの軽さは受け入れられず，批評家からは無視されてきたが，その後新しい読者層を見いだしている。1972 年，桂冠詩人となる。

  2 **Aldershot:** a city in the northeast part of Hampshire.
 11 **press:** a device for keeping a tennis racket from warping when not in use.
 29 **adopted:** assumed responsibility for the maintenance.
 31 **Camberley:** a city in Surreyshire.

59　The Foreboding

Robert Graves（1895–1985）作。初出は *Poems*（1953）において。

　Graves はバラッド研究家でありバラッド詩人でもあったアイルランド人の Alfred Perceval Graves を父に，ウィンブルドンに生まれた。19 歳で第一次世界大戦に従軍し，致命傷を負って奇跡的に一命を取り留めたにもかかわらず，ちょうど 21 歳の誕生日に *The Times* で自らの死亡記事を読むという経験が詩人のトラウマとなった。しかしこの戦争体験は二つの成果を生む。一つは，戦地でバラッドが発生し短期間で洗練された歌へと変質していく，バラッドの生成の歴史を現代において体験したことである。この経験は現代のバラッド・リバイバルとして *The English Ballad: A Short Critical Survey*（1927）の序文で語られている。もう一つは，戦争が暴いた社会や文化の不確実性と帰還兵士が託つ孤立する自我との折り合いをつけるべく，*The White Goddess: A Historical Grammar of Poetic Myth*（1948）が創作されたことである。二面性を持つ白い女神の受容は生涯を通じての Graves の詩のテーマとなった。

　Graves は Muir に匹敵する 20 世紀のバラッド擁護論者の一人である。彼が詩に目を開かれたのは伝承バラッドとの出会いによってであった。

> At Penrallt I found a book that had the ballads of 'Chevy Chase' and 'Sir Andrew Barton' in it; these were the first real poems I remember reading. I saw how good they were. [*Goodbye to All That*, rev. ed. (1959; Harmondsworth, 1960) 22]

　前述の *The English Ballad* の序文では，生活の危機感の喪失，グループ意識の消滅，個人主義的傾向などとバラッド衰退との関わりが説得力をもって語られる。また，Graves 編纂の *English and Scottish Ballads*（London, 1957）の序文では，多くのバラッドが 'the ancient pagan witch cult' を明確に伝えていること，'folk songs'，'festival-songs'，'work-a-day songs' は民衆の生活そのものであったこと，しかし，それらが教育の普及と文明の進歩によって必然的に消滅した過程が率直に，かつ愛惜の念をもって語られる。

　一生涯のほとんどを地中海のマジョルカ島で暮らしたイギリス文壇のゴッホ的存在であった。1962 年，Auden を継いでオックスフォード大学詩学教授となる。

　本作品は $abcb$ の韻とバラッド・スタンザの変形様式に託して，素朴な言葉で白い女神への忍従をうたう，一種の恋愛詩である。語り手は突然死した自分自身を窓の外から覗き見る。死の予感に人生を回顧した彼は，冷酷な白い女神に呼

びかけ，彼女の従順な服従者たる自分に愛が長くは続かないことをなぜ予言してくれなかったのかと憤る。しかし，話は語り手の運命を甘受する姿勢で終わる。餌はすでに魚となった彼の喉に飲み込まれ，女神の鉤針は素早く彼を釣り上げる。自らの結末を客観視するというゴシック的視点の原点には，死亡記事を読んだ詩人の体験があろう。

60　Ballad of the Three Coins

Vernon Watkins (1906–67) 作，1954 年。

　Watkins はウェールズ南部マイステイグにウェールズ語を話す両親のもとに生まれ，一生をスウォンジー近辺で暮らし，銀行員として働く傍ら詩人として活動した。Dylan Thomas の長年の友人であり，二人の交流は *Dylan Thomas: Letters to Vernon Watkins* (1957) に詳しい。代表作であり最初の詩集のタイトル・ポエムでもある "The Ballad of the Mari Lwyd" (1941) は，ウェールズのフォークロアや神話を元にした長編詩である。

　Watkins の初期の作品には，1940 年代のワイルドでシュールなイメージを特徴とする 'The New Apocalypse' 運動に連なる傾向や，それ以前のシンボリスト的傾向があり，後期の作品では，20 世紀の言語の実験の世代には影響されず，叙情詩とエレジーに本領が発揮された。

　イメージやスタイルの変化はあっても，Watkins の最大の特色はバラッド韻律を現代詩に応用した技巧の妙にあることを，Friedman は "The Ballad of the Mari Lwyd" を例に次のように述べている。

> Poems in ballad measure are everywhere in modern verse, but they are often complicated in rime scheme, rhythm, and arrangement beyond folk or vulgar usage. In Vernon Watkins' magical playlet "Ballad of the Mari Lwyd" the traditional rime scheme is varied with cross-rime and even more intricate systems as a means of differentiating the dramatic voices . . . . (Friedman 342)

本作品でも形而上的なストーリーとバラッド韻律が不思議な調和をなしている。語り手は，ぼろ靴，杖，ずだ袋を持った求道者。生きているとも死んでいるとも判らぬまま，学びと愛を探して，三枚のコインが示す運命に身を委ね，現実とも煉獄とも定かでない二つの世界の間を彷徨する。夜明けに投げたコインで畑へ行き，乳搾りの女に会って「知性」の渇きを知る。昼に投げたコインで川へ行き，沐浴の女に会って「嫉妬」を知る。夜に投げた三つめのコインは海へ行けば裸の少女が待っていると男を誘うが，海辺で見たのは吹きさらされた犬と砂に埋まっ

た空きビンだけ。知るものは何もなく，辿り着いた場所は最初の場面の海辺へと循環し，男の彷徨は永遠に続く。'Mystic number'「3」や，コインが光る様を 'I see it glint and burn' と表現する繰り返し，Keats の "La Belle Dame sans Merci" (1819) にも似た場所の円環構造と男の苦悶，基本的には弱強四歩格と弱強三歩格が交互に繰り返され，*a b c b* の韻を踏んだバラッド・スタンザが刻む安定感が，この詩の不明確なトポスと心理の枠となっている。

32 **Athene:** the Greek goddess, mythically the creator of the olive-tree.
60 **the cuckoo's song:** the use of cuckoo here is evocative of 'cuckold'. Cf. the narrator's jealousy in line 66.

List of Texts

1. Lady Elizabeth Wardlaw, *Hardyknute*
   Reliques of Ancient English Poetry: Consisting of Old Heroic Ballads, Songs, and Other Pieces of Our Earlier Poets; Together with Some Few of Later Date. Vol. 2. Ed. Thomas Percy. With memoir and critical dissertation by the Rev. George Gilfillan. Edinburgh, 1858. A rpt. entire from Percy's last edition of 1794.

2. John Gay, *Sweet William's Farewell to Black-Ey'd Susan*
   The Oxford Book of Eighteenth Century Verse. Ed. David Nichol Smith. Oxford, 1926.

3. William Hamilton, *The Braes of Yarrow*
   Reliques 2.

4. David Mallet, *Margaret's Ghost*
   Reliques 3.

5. Thomas Tickell, *Lucy and Colin*
   Reliques 3.

6. Richard Glover, *Admiral Hosier's Ghost*
   Reliques 2.

7. William Shenstone, *Jemmy Dawson*
   The Poetical Works of William Shenstone. With life, critical dissertation, and explanatory notes by the Rev. George Gilfillan. Edinburgh, 1854.

8. Oliver Goldsmith, *The Hermit; or, Edwin and Angelina*
   From *The Vicar of Wakefield, The Miscellaneous Works of Oliver Goldsmith.* A new edition. Vol. 1. London, 1821.

9. Thomas Percy, *The Friar of Orders Gray*
   Reliques 1.

10. Lady Anne Lindsay, *Auld Robin Gray*
    The Oxford Book of Eighteenth Century Verse.

11. Thomas Chatterton, *Bristowe Tragedie: or the Dethe of Syr Charles Bawdin*
    The Rowley Poems of Thomas Chatterton. Ed. with an introduction by Maurice Evan Hare. Oxford, 1911. A rpt. from Tyrwhitt's third edition of 1778.

12. John Logan, *The Braes of Yarrow*

The Oxford Book of Eighteenth Century Verse.

13 William Cowper, *The Diverting History of John Gilpin*
   The Poetical Works of William Cowper. 4th ed. Ed. H. S. Milford. Oxford, 1934.

14 William Julius Mickle, *Cumnor Hall*
   Old Ballads, Historical and Narrative, with Some of Modern Date. Vol. 4. Ed. Thomas Evans. London, enl. 1784.

15 Robert Burns, *A Red, Red Rose*
   The Life and Works of Robert Burns. Vol. 4. Ed. Robert Chambers. Edinburgh, 1851–52.

16 William Blake, *Fair Elenor*
   The Poetical Works of William Blake. Ed. with an introduction and texual notes by John Sampson. Oxford, 1913.

17 Sir Walter Scott, *William and Helen*
   The Poetical Works of Sir Walter Scott, Bart. Ed. J. G. Lockhart. Edinburgh, 1841.

18 M. G. Lewis, *Alonzo the Brave and Fair Imogine*
   Tales of Wonder. Vol. 1. Written and collected by M. G. Lewis. London, 1801.

19 M. G. Lewis, *Giles Jollup the Grave, and Brown Sally Green*
   Tales of Wonder 1.

20 William Wordsworth, *Goody Blake, and Harry Gill*
   Lyrical Ballads. Ed. R. L. Brett and A. R. Jones. London, 1968.

21 Robert Southey, *Bishop Bruno*
   The Poetical Works. Vol. 6. Compiled by himself. London, 1837–38.

22 Samuel Taylor Coleridge, *Love*
   Coleridge: Poetical Works. Ed. Ernest Hartley Coleridge. Oxford, 1912.

23 William Robert Spencer, *Beth Gêlert; or, The Grave of the Greyhound*
   The Oxford Book of Narrative Verse. Ed. Iona and Peter Opie. Oxford, 1983.

24 John Leyden, *The Elfin-King*
   Tales of Wonder 1.

25 George Gordon Byron, *Oscar of Alva*

The Poetical Works of Lord Byron. London, 1846.

26 James Hogg, *Sir David Graeme*
    The Works of the Ettrick Shepherd. With a memoir of the author by the Rev. Thomas Thomson. London, 1876.

27 Thomas Campbell, *Lord Ullin's Daughter*
    The Oxford Book of English Verse of the Romantic Period 1798–1837. Ed. H. S. Milford. 1928; Oxford, 1935.

28 Percy Bysshe Shelley, *Sister Rosa: a Ballad*
    The Complete Poetical Works of Percy Bysshe Shelley. Ed. Thomas Hutchinson. Oxford, 1932.

29 John Keats, *La Belle Dame sans Merci*
    The Poetical Works of John Keats. With an introduction and texual notes by H. Buxton Forman. Oxford, 1922.

30 Thomas Hood, *Mary's Ghost*
    The Comic Poems of Thomas Hood. With preface by Thomas Hood the Younger. London, 1868.

31 Robert Browning, *Porphyria's Lover*
    The Poetical Works of Robert Browning. Vol. 1. London, 1896.

32 Alfred Tennyson, *The Lord of Burleigh*
    The Poetical Works of Alfred, Lord Tennyson. London, 1899.

33 William Edmondstoune Aytoun, *The Execution of Montrose*
    Lays of the Scottish Cavaliers and Other Poems. Edinburgh, 1887.

34 William Makepeace Thackeray, *The Knight and the Lady*
    The Works of William Makepeace Thackeray. Vol. 13 (*Ballads and Miscellanies*). London, 1899.

35 Lewis Carroll, *The Two Brothers*
    The Complete Works of Lewis Carroll. With an introduction by Alexander Woollcott. Harmondsworth, 1988.

36 Charles Kingsley, *Ballad of Earl Haldan's Daughter*
    Poems. London, 1889.

37 Sydney Thompson Dobell, *The Ballad of Keith of Ravelston*
    The Oxford Book of Victorian Verse. Ed. Arthur Quiller-Couch. Oxford, 1912.

38 Christina Georgina Rossetti, *Love from the North*
    Poems. New and enlarged ed. London, 1899.

39 William Morris, *The Sailing of the Sword*
    The Defence of Genevere and Other Poems. London, 1921.

40 George Meredith, *Margaret's Bridal Eve*
    The Works of George Meredith. With some notes by G. M. Trevelyan. New York, 1912.

41 A. C. Swinburne, *The King's Daughter*
    Ballad of the English Border. Ed. William A MacInnes. London, 1925.

42 Dante Gabriel Rossetti, *Stratton Water*
    The Collective Works of Dante Gabriel Rossetti. Ed. William Michael Rossetti. London, 1890.

43 William Allingham, *King Henry's Hunt*
    Songs, Ballads and Stories. London, 1877.

44 Henry Duff Traill, *After Dilettante Concetti*
    Recaptured Rhymes. Edinburgh, 1882.

45 Robert W. Buchanan, *The Ballad of the Wayfarer*
    The Poetical Works of Robert Buchanan. London, 1884.

46 Andrew Lang, *The Bridge of Death*
    The Poetical Works of Andrew Lang. Vol. 3. Ed. Mrs. Lang. London, 1923.

47 William Butler Yeats, *The Ballad of Moll Magee*
    The Collected Poems of W. B. Yeats. 2nd. ed. London, 1950.

48 Rudyard Kipling, *The Last Rhyme of True Thomas*
    Rudyard Kipling's Verse. Definitive edition. London, 1940.

49 John Davidson, *A Ballad of a Nun*
    The Yellow Book. Vol. 3. October, 1894.

50 A. E. Housman, *The Carpenter's Son*
    A Shropshire Lad. London, 1907.

51 Robert Bridges, *Screaming Tarn*
    Poetical Works of Robert Bridges. Oxford, 1912.

52 John Masefield, *The Yarn of the Loch Achray*

The Collected Poems of John Masefield. 1923; rpt. London, 1925.

53 Thomas Hardy, *A Sunday Morning Tragedy*
    The Collected Poems of Thomas Hardy. London, 1930.

54 Walter de la Mare, *The Ghost*
    Poems: 1901 to 1918. London, 1920.

55 William Plomer, *The Murder on the Downs*
    Visiting the Caves. 1936.

56 Edwin Muir, *The Enchanted Knight*
    Collected Poems 1921–1951. London, 1952.

57 W. H. Auden, *Miss Gee*
    New Writing. Vol. 4. 1937.

58 John Betjeman, *A Subaltern's Love-song*
    Selected Poems. Ed. John Sparrow. London, 1948.

59 Robert Graves, *The Foreboding*
    Robert Graves: Complete Poems. Vol. 2. Ed. Beryl Graves and Dunstan Ward. Manchester, 1997.

60 Vernon Watkins, *Ballad of the Three Coins*
    The Death Bell: Poems and Ballads. London, 1954.

Acknowledgements

We would like to thank the following for permission to reproduce copyright material:

Robert Graves: "The Foreboding" from *Robert Graves: Complete Poems.* Vol. 2. Ed. Beryl Graves and Dunstan Ward, 1997. Reprinted by permission of Carcanet, Manchester.
Vernon Watkins: "Ballad of the Three Coins" from *The Death Bell: Poems and Ballads*, 1954. Reprinted by permission of Mrs G. M. Watkins, Swansea, West Glamorgan.

While every effort has been made to secure permission, we may have failed in a few cases to trace the copyright holder. We apologize for any apparent negligence.

Index of Titles
(The references are to the numbers of the poems.)

No.		Page
6	*Admiral Hosier's Ghost*	21
44	*After Dilettante Concetti*	162
18	*Alonzo the Brave and Fair Imogine*	74
10	*Auld Robin Gray*	36
49	*A Ballad of a Nun*	174
36	*Ballad of Earl Haldan's Daughter*	140
37	*The Ballad of Keith of Ravelston*	141
47	*The Ballad of Moll Magee*	167
60	*Ballad of the Three Coins*	199
45	*The Ballad of the Wayfarer*	164
23	*Beth Gêlert; or, The Grave of the Greyhound*	89
21	*Bishop Bruno*	83
3	*The Braes of Yarrow* (by William Hamilton)	12
12	*The Braes of Yarrow* (by John Logan)	49
46	*The Bridge of Death*	166
11	*Bristowe Tragedie: or the Dethe of Syr Charles Bawdin*	37
50	*The Carpenter's Son*	179
14	*Cumnor Hall*	58
13	*The Diverting History of John Gilpin*	50
24	*The Elfin-King*	92
56	*The Enchanted Knight*	193
33	*The Execution of Montrose*	126
16	*Fair Elenor*	62
59	*The Foreboding*	199
9	*The Friar of Orders Gray*	32
54	*The Ghost*	190
19	*Giles Jollup the Grave, and Brown Sally Green*	77
20	*Goody Blake, and Harry Gill*	80
1	*Hardyknute*	1
8	*The Hermit; or, Edwin and Angelina*	26
7	*Jemmy Dawson*	24
43	*King Henry's Hunt*	159

41	The King's Daughter	152
34	The Knight and the Lady	133
29	La Belle Dame sans Merci	118
48	The Last Rhyme of True Thomas	169
32	The Lord of Burleigh	124
27	Lord Ullin's Daughter	113
22	Love	85
38	Love from the North	143
5	Lucy and Colin	19
40	Margaret's Bridal Eve	146
4	Margaret's Ghost	16
30	Mary's Ghost	120
57	Miss Gee	194
55	The Murder on the Downs	191
25	Oscar of Alva	98
31	Porphyria's Lover	122
15	A Red, Red Rose	62
39	The Sailing of the Sword	144
51	Screaming Tarn	180
26	Sir David Graeme	108
28	Sister Rosa: a Ballad	115
42	Stratton Water	154
58	A Subaltern's Love-song	197
53	A Sunday Morning Tragedy	186
2	Sweet William's Farewell to Black-Ey'd Susan	11
35	The Two Brothers	135
17	William and Helen	65
52	The Yarn of the Loch Achray	184

Index of First Lines

(The references are to the numbers of the poems.)

No.		Page
27	A chieftain to the Highlands bound	113
19	A Doctor so prim and a sempstress so tight	77
18	A warrior so bold and a virgin so bright	74
39	Across the empty garden-beds,	144
29	Ah, what can ail thee, wretched wight,	118
2	All in the *Downs* the fleet was moor'd,	11
22	All thoughts, all passions, all delights,	85
6	As near Porto-Bello lying	21
21	Bishop Bruno awoke in the dead midnight,	83
3	Busk ye, busk ye, my bonny bonny bride,	12
33	Come hither, Evan Cameron!	126
7	Come listen to my mournful tale,	24
47	Come round me, little childer;	167
49	From Eastertide to Eastertide	174
17	From heavy dreams fair Helen rose,	65
50	"Here the hangman stops his cart:	179
25	How sweetly shines through azure skies,	98
53	I bore a daughter flower-fair,	186
38	I had a love in soft south land,	143
60	I know this road like the back of my hand	199
32	In her ear he whispers gaily,	124
9	It was a friar of orders gray,	32
36	It was Earl Haldan's daughter,	140
13	John Gilpin was a citizen	50
43	King Henry stood in Waltham Wood,	159
57	Let me tell you a little story	194
59	Looking by chance in at the open window	199
56	Lulled by La Belle Dame Sans Merci he lies	193
58	Miss J. Hunter Dunn, Miss J. Hunter Dunn,	197
42	"O have you seen the Stratton flood	154
15	O my luve's like a red, red rose,	62
24	— "O swift, and swifter far he speeds	92

45	O'er the cheerless common,	164
5	Of Leinster, fam'd for maidens fair,	19
20	Oh! what's the matter? what's the matter?	80
55	Past a cow and past a cottage,	191
1	Stately stept he east the wa',	1
16	The bell struck one, and shook the silent tower;	62
46	'The dance is on the Bridge of Death	166
28	The death-bell beats! —	115
14	The dews of summer nighte did falle,	58
26	The dow flew east, the dow flew west,	108
11	The featherd songster chaunticleer	37
48	The King has called for priest and cup,	169
52	The *Loch Achray* was a clipper tall	184
37	The murmur of the mourning ghost	141
40	The old grey mother she thrummed on her knee:	146
31	The rain set early in to-night,	122
51	The saddest place that e'er I saw	180
23	The spearmen heard the bugle sound,	89
35	There were two brothers at Twyford school,	135
34	There's in the Vest a city pleasant	133
12	'Thy braes were bonny, Yarrow stream!	49
8	"Turn, gentle Hermit of the dale,	26
4	'Twas at the silent solemn hour,	16
30	'Twas in the middle of the night,	120
41	We were ten maidens in the green corn,	152
10	When the sheep are in the fauld, when the cows come hame,	36
54	'Who knocks?' 'I, who was beautiful,	190
44	"Why do you wear your hair like a man,	162

Index of Authors

(The references are to the numbers of the poems.)

Allingham, William, 43
Auden, W. H., 57
Aytoun, William Edmondstoune, 33

Betjeman, John, 58
Blake, William, 16
Bridges, Robert, 51
Browning, Robert, 31
Buchanan, Robert W., 45
Burns, Robert, 15
Byron, George Gordon, 25

Campbell, Thomas, 27
Carroll, Lewis, 35
Chatterton, Thomas, 11
Coleridge, Samuel Taylor, 22
Cowper, William, 13

Davidson, John, 49
de la Mare, Walter, 54
Dobell, Sydney Thompson, 37

Gay, John, 2
Glover, Richard, 6
Goldsmith, Oliver, 8
Graves, Robert, 59

Hamilton, William, 3
Hardy, Thomas, 53
Hogg, James, 26
Hood, Thomas, 30
Housman, A. E., 50

Keats, John, 29
Kingsley, Charles, 36
Kipling, Rudyard, 48

Lang, Andrew, 46
Lewis, M. G., 18, 19
Leyden, John, 24
Lindsay, Lady Anne, 10
Logan, John, 12

Mallet, David, 4
Masefield, John, 52
Meredith, George, 40
Mickle, William Julius, 14
Morris, William, 39
Muir, Edwin, 56

Percy, Thomas, 9
Plomer, William, 55

Rossetti, Christina Georgina, 38
Rossetti, Dante Gabriel, 42

Scott, Sir Walter, 17
Shelley, Percy Bysshe, 28
Shenstone, William, 7
Southey, Robert, 21
Spencer, William Robert, 23
Swinburne, A. C., 41

Tennyson, Alfred, 32
Thackeray, William Makepeace, 34
Tickell, Thomas, 5
Traill, Henry Duff, 44

Wardlaw, Lady Elizabeth, 1
Watkins, Vernon, 60
Wordsworth, William, 20

Yeats, William Butler, 47

編著者紹介

山中光義
福岡女子大学文学部教授，文学博士
著　書　The Twilight of the British Literary Ballad in the Eighteenth Century（Kyushu UP）
　　　　『バラッド鑑賞』（開文社）

中島久代
九州共立大学助教授
共編著　『英国物語詩 14 撰―伝承バラッドからオーデンまで』（松柏社）
共　訳　『バラッド―緑の森の愛の歌』（近代文藝社）

宮原牧子
福岡女子大学大学院博士後期課程在籍，佐賀大学非常勤講師
共編著　『英国物語詩 14 撰―伝承バラッドからオーデンまで』（松柏社）
論　文　「"Stratton Water"の『曖昧さ』―ロセッティは何故バラッド詩を選んだか」

鎌田明子
福岡女子大学大学院博士後期課程在籍，関東学院大学非常勤講師
論　文　「The Fall of Hyperion. A Dream の中断について」
　　　　「Endymion―女性像の合一」

David Taylor
九州大学外国人教師
共　著　Bruce Chatwin: On the Black Hill（Welsh Media Education Publications）
　　　　Travel Writing and Empire: Postcolonial Theory in Transit（Zed）

英国バラッド詩 60 撰　Sixty English Literary Ballads

2002 年 11 月 5 日　初版発行

編著者　山中光義・中島久代・宮原牧子
　　　　鎌田明子・David Taylor
発行者　福　留　久　大
発行所　(財) 九州大学出版会
　　　　〒812-0053　福岡市東区箱崎 7-1-146
　　　　　　　　　　九州大学構内
　　　　電話　092-641-0515（直　通）
　　　　振替　01710-6-3677
　　　　印刷・製本　研究社印刷株式会社

© 2002 Printed in Japan　　　ISBN4-87378-751-3

The Twilight of the British Literary Ballad in the Eighteenth Century

山中光義 著　　　　　　　　菊判 418 頁 **9,200** 円(税別)

　イギリスの口承物語歌「バラッド」は18世紀になって盛んに蒐集されるようになった。それとともに民族の遺産としてのバラッドの持つ魅力に多くの詩人たちが注目するようになり，「バラッド詩」と呼ばれる独特の模倣詩が生まれた。
　本書は，生成期の18世紀バラッド詩の模倣と逸脱をめぐるわが国最初の本格的な論考であり，Appendixに添えた 'Poets on the Ballad' は，今後のバラッド詩研究を支える重要な資料集である。

〈主要目次〉

1　Deviations from Tradition
2　The Vogue for Sentimentality
3　Roads to the High Romantic
Appendix I　　Texts of Traditional and Literary Ballads
Appendix II　 Poets on the Ballad
Appendix III　List of Literary Ballads

九州大学出版会刊